TOQUCHAR'S PRISONER

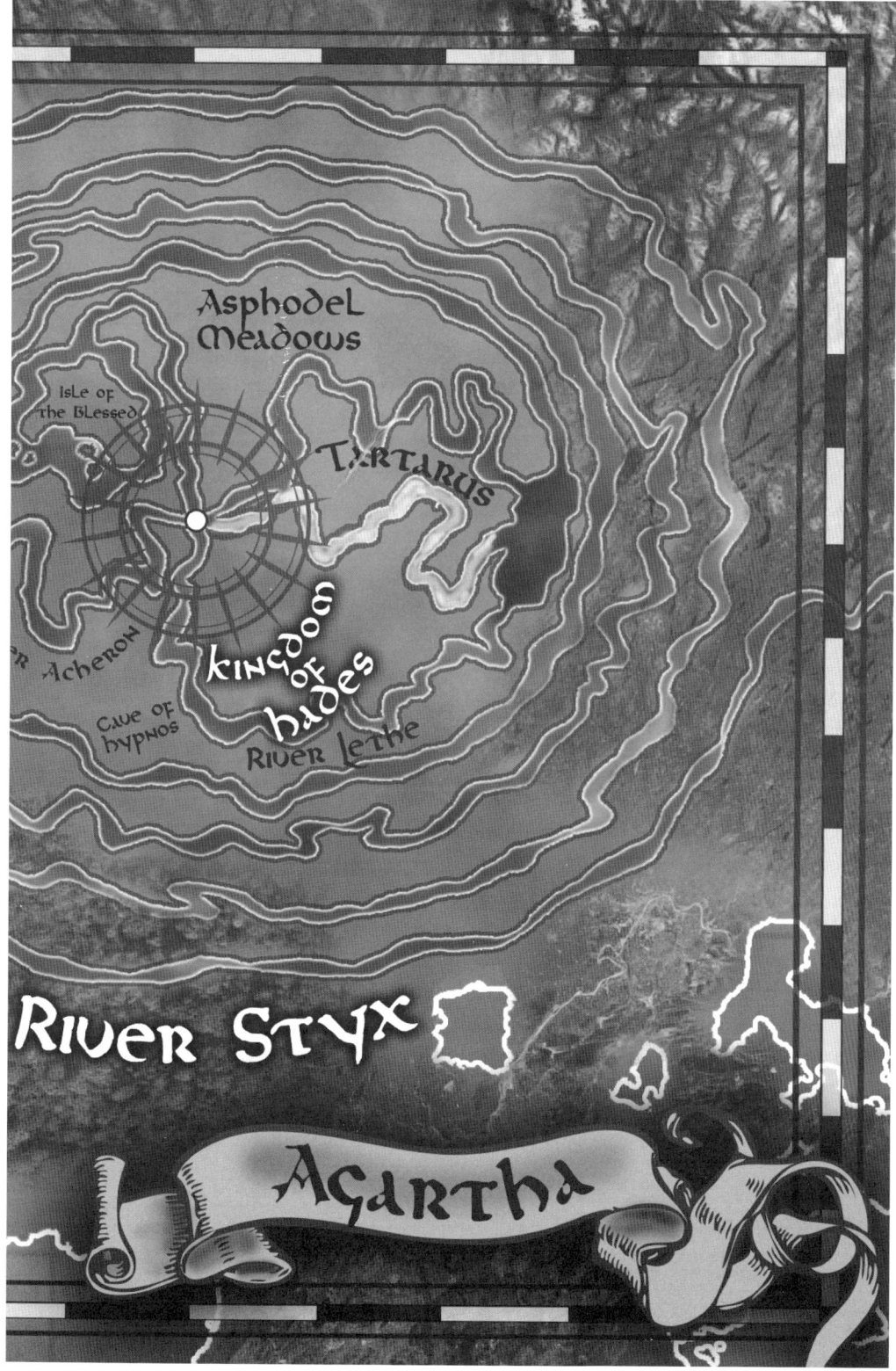

THIS BOOK IS AUGMENTED-REALITY ENABLED

TAKE THE STEPS BELOW TO GET THE MOST OUT OF YOUR READING EXPERIENCE:

1. Download Continuum.
2. Scan QR Codes.
3. Enjoy the Show!

XPERIENCE B·O·O·K·S

TOQUCHAR'S PRISONER

Enjoy the Xperience!!

Stephen Austin Thorpe

SAThorpe

CONTINUUM MULTIMEDIA / SLC

Copyright © 2019 by Stephen Austin Thorpe.

All rights reserved. No part of this publication may be reproduced, distributed or transmitted in any form or by any means, including photocopying, recording, or other electronic or mechanical methods, without the prior written permission of the publisher, except in the case of brief quotations embodied in critical reviews and certain other noncommercial uses permitted by copyright law. For permission requests, write to the publisher, addressed "Attention: Permissions Coordinator," at the address below.

Stephen Austin Thorpe/Continuum Multimedia, Inc.
PO Box 160473
Clearfield, Utah 84016

www.continuummultimedia.com

Publisher's Note: This is a work of fiction. Names, characters, places, and incidents are a product of the author's imagination. Locales and public names are sometimes used for atmospheric purposes. Any resemblance to actual people, living or dead, or to businesses, companies, events, institutions, or locales is completely coincidental.

Book design © 2013, BookDesignTemplates.com

Ordering Information: Special discounts are available on quantity purchases by corporations, associations, and others. For details, contact the publisher at the address above.

SLC / Stephen Austin Thorpe – First Edition

ISBN Hardback: 978-1-7327835-4-6

Printed in the United States of America

*For my parents who taught me to love
words -- and that I could do anything
if I set my mind to it.*

CHAPTER 1

COLLIDING WORLDS

(MARINA)

Worlds Marina knew and ones she didn't had all collided in a tragic way.

She sat on the stairway next to the Temple of Concord wondering who she really was and how she fit into her expanded understanding of the world. Her stepmother, Anastasia, had been the most prominent figure in her life but had recently died in Nero's great fire. In her hands she held the only possessions she owned—her bow and a quiver of arrows she had salvaged from the ruins of what was once her home. The death of her stepmother and the disappearance of her little sister Livia were nearly impossible to bear, and when she'd found out Anastasia was from another world and another time, it made her question everything she thought she knew. In her confusion, she'd fled from her father and new friends Andrew, Tanner, and Mick.

How could they have kept those things from me? she wondered angrily.

It had only been a few years earlier that Marina's life seemed perfect. The Empire had been a wonderful place to live. The pageantry of the city with its armor-clad legionnaires marching with precision in the shadows of spectacular marble temples and larger-than-life arenas made her proud to be Roman.

The family's newly found Christian religion had brought her new friends and an increased level of happiness and purpose.

Why did Nero have to come to power?

A hatred for the man who had forced these two worlds into opposition with one another and who had ultimately been responsible for the fire that killed her mother burned inside.

But if Andrew and his friends had never come, this wouldn't have happened.

She thought about how Tanner practically hand delivered the location of their house church to the authorities.

She wished she could return to the comfort and stability of that home, but it was nothing more than a pile of smoldering rubble now.

Where do I turn?

It started to rain, but Marina didn't care.

Decimus, she thought as the rain splashed harder and more rapidly on the marble steps.

Marina had met Decimus when Donald brought him and the other legionnaires to the house church of Sebastian. She remembered how passionate he was about removing Nero from power but turned on Donald and the others just as passionately when he felt they were trying to overthrow not just the emperor but the entire empire.

He hates the same things I do, she thought. *He wants what I want. I have to find Decimus.*

CHAPTER 2

THE STALKER

(DECIMUS)

A few days earlier

The wet stone streets reflected the moon as it emerged from behind the clouds. Decimus peered around the corner of a small apartment building, looking in every direction to make sure he wasn't being followed. He still hadn't witnessed the effects of Tanner healing him with water from the Acheron River. Darting across the street, he continued to sneak through the city until he arrived at the house church of Sebastian.

I've got to find proof. Something tangible to show they're really planning to take over the empire.

After an extensive search, he found an open upper-story window and climbed in. He tiptoed through the house until he located the girl he saw as the rallying symbol of the rebellion against Rome. After all, he had witnessed many of the mutineers risk their lives to free her from prison.

What's this? He noticed Mick's backpack on the ground next to her. *It must be where she keeps their plans.*

Stooping down, he removed Mick's journal from the bag. He strained in the darkness as he quickly flipped through the sketches of her journey through the underworld.

Always heard Christians had strange magic, he thought as he looked at drawings of unusual buildings and spectacular transportation devices.

He placed the book back in the backpack.

Now, to kill the girl and get out of here.

He pulled his sword from its sheath and raised it high above his head.

Bam!

Someone knocked him off his feet. His sword clanked on the ground. Quickly, he grabbed the backpack and fled up the stairs.

"Stop that man!" someone yelled. Decimus jumped out the open window and fled down the Via Appia.

"Decimus!" He turned to see the Praetorian Guard Titus himself giving chase.

Seconds later he was tackled and the two were locked in a fierce struggle. Titus had a reputation for being a skilled fighter, but one brutal uppercut by Decimus and the Praetorian collapsed to the ground.

I didn't realize I was so strong. He looked at his fists as he stood hovering proudly over Titus, who was bloodied and unmoving.

Is he dead? Decimus bent over and gave him a gentle shake. No response.

Clank!

Decimus snapped his head in the direction of the noise but couldn't see anyone. Murdering a Praetorian would be a sure death sentence, so he sprinted for home.

They're planning to take over the city, he thought as he looked down at Mick's backpack in his hand.

This should give me all the information I need to stop them.

Back on the Vaticanus Hill, he opened the large wooden door to his home and grabbed an oil lamp. He carried it to the dining room and excitedly pulled the journal out of the bag. As he struggled to see the pages, the light of the full moon began to stream through the window, almost magically illuminating the book.

"What's going on?" His wife entered the room in her sleeping gown.

"The Christians are planning to overthrow the empire."

"You're not serious."

"Of course I am." Decimus thumbed through the journal. "Do you recognize any of these words?"

"Looks similar to Latin, but I can't make any sense out of it. Where did you get this?" she grabbed the book from her husband and examined it more thoroughly.

"I stole it from the Christian girl I was telling you about. After looking through it, I'm more convinced than ever she's their leader."

"Didn't you say she's friends with the boys who saved your life? Why would you feel threatened by them? They seemed nice enough."

"They may have saved me, but that doesn't affect their plan to destroy the empire. Christians have infiltrated every part of Roman life, including the emperor's own guards. I actually listened to Titus tell the mutinous legionnaires he wanted to overthrow the emperor."

"Overthrowing Nero would actually be a good thing," Decimus's wife replied.

"True, if it ended there, but their evil designs go much deeper than that. They worship a God who speaks of fathers being divided from sons and mothers from daughters. It's chaos. We've already witnessed it on a small scale, but on a large scale it will destroy the unity of Rome."

"But it'll be a long time before there are enough of them to take over. They'd be no match for the legions."

"I'm not so sure."

"What makes you say that?" Decimus's wife seemed stunned by his dismissal of the legions.

"They claim this God returned to life after spending three days as a dead man in the underworld. And look at this."

Decimus grabbed the book, flipped through the pages, and then thrust his finger onto a drawing of the passageway through the Umbilicus Urbis into the Cathedral of Time.

"This must be their planned point of entry," he said, pointing at the map. "The Mundus has always been considered a portal to the underworld. It all makes sense. This supposed God of theirs is going to lead His followers through this entrance and into the city. That's why she has this drawing."

"Let me see that." Decimus's wife grabbed the book and, holding it up in the moonlight, inspected Mick's sketch more closely. "I don't believe it. You think they'd really have the courage to launch an attack in the heart of Rome?" she continued without waiting for an answer. "You're right. They've got to be stopped."

"But I can't stop them by myself."

"First you've got to confirm the things in this drawing actually exist," she said, pointing to the Cathedral on the map. "If this place really is there and not just some fantasy sketch of a deranged girl, we may be able to convince others of the threat. Until then, we shouldn't mention this to anyone."

"Agreed," Decimus said. "I'll volunteer for guard duty at the Umbilicus. I'm sure I can figure out a way to sneak through the Mundus and find out for myself if this is all real."

Decimus's wife straightened, a grin forming on her typically stoic face. "Decimus, you realize if you help stop this coup, you could end up emperor."

"Not possible," he replied. "I'm just a legionnaire."

"No matter. The revolts against Nero are growing, and if you save the city from a Christian invasion, you'll be proclaimed a god."

Decimus stared off into the distance, thinking about what the future might bring.

❖ ❖ ❖

A few days later, Decimus got his opportunity and anxiously made his way to the Umbilicus for guard duty.

"Antinuous asked me to go down into the Umbilicus and make sure the handles are secure on the stone covering to the Mundus," he said as he approached his fellow guard. "The harvest is coming, and he wants to be sure it can be easily opened."

"I'll come with you," the other guard replied. Decimus panicked but quickly said, "No, no, you need to protect the outer entrance. We can't afford to have anyone entering the Umbilicus. They might remove the stone and let evil spirits from the underworld escape and wreak havoc on the city."

"Good point."

Decimus slowly unlocked the Umbilicus door, then climbed down the wooden ladder and slid the stone covering as quietly as possible, exposing the entrance into the Mundus. Carefully he descended into the cave.

Don't want to let any evil spirits out myself, he thought as he quickly slid the stone back into place, hiding the entrance.

Decimus strained to look around the dark cave and was disappointed he couldn't see anything that resembled Mick's drawing.

Maybe she is deranged.

As he was about to turn and leave, the darkness of the cave was replaced with a bright light, and Demeter, the guardian goddess of underworld portals, appeared in the midst of the light. Decimus fell backward and shaded his eyes with his forearm. She waved her arms, and the rocks moved, exposing the entrance to the Cathedral.

It's true, he thought. *But why would this spirit reveal the doorway to me? I'm the furthest thing from a Christian.*

Dumbfounded by what had just happened, Decimus tried to form a question, but before the first word emerged, the goddess faded from view as quickly as she had appeared. Decimus approached the entrance. Gingerly he wrapped his fingers around the door latch and pulled. He gasped as he looked into the building.

Even the gods of Rome can't compete with this.

He stepped onto the platform and climbed down the metal stairs, nearly falling as he continued to gaze in wonder at the building's interior.

Drawn by the magical-looking machinery, he walked over to the command center and began to examine the mysterious equipment.

By Jupiter, I've got to get back to my post.

He had been gone much longer than it would have taken just to check the handles on the stone.

Valerius is probably already looking for me.

He sprinted out of the Cathedral and through the cave to the stone covering. Carefully, he slid the stone out of the way and slipped through the opening.

Quiet, he thought as he slid the stone back into place. *Can't afford to have him hear me moving this.*

Decimus climbed the ladder and covered his eyes as he exited the Umbilicus into the bright sunlight of the Forum.

"What took so long?"

"Nothing," Decimus replied. "I was just marveling at all the places the dirt on the floor must have come from. Did you throw a handful of dirt in from your hometown when you first moved to Rome? Where did you move from, anyway?"

The guard began to talk about his native land and his move to Rome.

Decimus continued to ask questions to keep his fellow guard distracted.

Whew. Decimus thought. He had successfully deflected the question.

Guess I would make a pretty good emperor.

When his shift ended, Decimus quickly made his way home. His wife was waiting anxiously for his return.

"So?" she asked.

"It's real. Every bit of it."

He grabbed Mick's journal.

"They're far more advanced than we are," he said as he fumbled through the pages. "I actually made it all the way here." He pointed at Mick's drawing of the Cathedral's interior. "We don't stand a chance against the magical equipment their God has in this building."

"We've got to try," she replied. "The Umbilicus will be opened November 8. You've got to follow the trail from this book. Learn as much as you can about their plans."

Just then there was a knock at the door.

Decimus opened it to see a frightened but resolute young girl standing in front of him.

"Aren't you a friend of Titus?" he asked.

CHAPTER 3

"YOU'RE UNDER ARREST"
(TANNER)

The sound of police sirens grew louder and more penetrating. Tanner struggled to open his eyes and could barely see his mom unzipping his backpack, revealing the linen cloth bundle. She carefully unwrapped it, exposing sections of a partially burned skeleton. She let out a gasp.

"It's not Mick's, is it?" she asked. Tanner was groggily trying to get his bearings and shake off the coma-like effects the water from the River Lethe were having on him. While they were in the underworld, Tanner, Mick, and Andrew had thought they were drinking from the Mnemosyne River, which heightened awareness, but instead they had guzzled from its evil "step-river," with its mind-numbing and memory-erasing effects.

"I don't know where it's from," he muttered. He banged the side of his head a couple times with the palm of his hand, trying to shake the cobwebs loose.

Ding-dong.

"That's the police. What do I do?" Mrs. Hunter moved toward the door, then back toward Tanner. She grabbed the backpack and scrambled to wrap up the skeleton.

Ding-dong.

Backpack in one hand, linen bundle in the other, she scurried out of his bedroom, slamming the door behind her.

Tanner could hear a loud commotion in the hallway.

"Why are the police here?" Tanner yelled through the doorway.

"I had to call 911 when you weren't waking up."

Knocking and banging sounded on the door.

"I'm coming! I'm coming!" Mrs. Hunter shouted over the clanking noises she was making just outside Tanner's room. He could hear her footsteps as she scurried down the stairs toward the front door.

Out of the corner of his eye, the TV in his bedroom caught his attention.

Mom must have been watching, during her bedside vigil, while waiting for me to wake up.

He grabbed the remote. Just as he was just about to change the channel, the cooking show was interrupted with a special report.

"Brownsville police were violently confronted this afternoon by a man dressed in Roman military attire."

"The man escaped into the woods," Sheriff Gardiner said as the cameras switched to a live shot. "My officers opened fire but were unable to stop the stranger. If you have any information on the whereabouts of this individual, whom we consider to be armed and dangerous, please contact the Brownsville Police Department."

Tanner looked down at the Roman tunic he wore.

There has to be some kind of connection. A shudder ran down his spine. *But what is it?*

He thought back to how hard he and his friends had laughed when they found themselves sitting in the River Lethe, back in Mammoth Cave, dressed in Roman apparel.

The bedroom door burst open. Tanner jumped as he heard the deep voice of Officer Clark blurt out, "Everything okay?"

"Yep," Tanner replied.

"Strange how he'd just suddenly showed up," his mother replied uncomfortably, "after having been missing without a trace for weeks."

The EMTs quickly moved to Tanner's bedside.

"I couldn't wake him at all when I first found him," Mrs. Hunter continued. "It was like he was in a coma. Completely unresponsive."

"Just relax, Mrs. Hunter." Officer Clark softly placed his hand on her arm, trying to settle her down. "Everything's going to be just fine."

"We're going to need you to lie down while we take your vitals," an EMT said as he gently pushed Tanner onto his back.

"What's going on?" Tanner asked.

"Just relax," a technician replied.

"Where have I been? Why are you all here?" Tanner tried to sit up.

"Vitals seem fine," one of the paramedics said as he firmly pushed Tanner back down on the bed.

"Oh, good. What do you think happened?" Mrs. Hunter asked. "Just a few minutes ago he was barely even breathing."

"Well, whatever it was, he seems completely fine now."

"So everything's okay?" Officer Clark asked.

"Seems perfectly normal," the technician said.

"Well, then . . ." Officer Clark said. He paused for a moment, and the room fell silent. "Tanner Hunter, you're under arrest for breaking and entering, police evasion, and the disappearance of Makayla Brown. You have the right to remain silent. Anything you say or do can and will be used against you in a court of law." Officer Clark continued to read Tanner his Miranda rights.

"You've got to be kidding me!" Mrs. Hunter shouted. "A kid barely snaps out of a coma after having been missing for weeks and the first thing you have to say is that he's under arrest?"

"Sorry, Mrs. Hunter. Just doing my duty."

"Well, you're not doing it very well," she retorted angrily.

"We need to take him in for questioning," Officer Clark explained as he cuffed Tanner. "Come with me."

"Don't you think you're jumping the gun?" Mrs. Hunter asked. "He just woke up, and you're ready to haul him off?"

Tanner looked helplessly at his mother, who stood with her mouth open in disbelief as Officer Clark escorted him down the stairs and into the police car.

After a short ride, Tanner found himself reunited with Andrew at the police station, both of them in handcuffs.

"What the heck is going on?" Andrew whispered as they sat on a bench, awaiting their fate.

"No idea," Tanner replied.

"I guess they're busting us for stealing those files and for Mick's disappearance."

"That's crazy, though. We were just with Mick walking home from Mammoth Cave. She's been found."

"I sort of remember that," Andrew said. "What exactly happened?"

"I remember climbing out of the Styx and then stealing Mick's papers. The police chased us, and we jumped back into the river. The next thing I knew, we were in Mammoth Cave with Mick, in the River Lethe and wearing these tunics. We had a good laugh and walked home."

"Yeah, I remember you tripped and disappeared into the river." Andrew lowered his voice to a barely discernable whisper. "I remember thinking you had gone into Inner Earth. I was trying to decide if I should follow you."

"Mom said something about us being gone for weeks," Tanner said.

"No way!"

"No, really. She was shouting at Officer Clark for arresting me."

"Why don't we remember anything?" Andrew asked. "Do you think we actually spent weeks in Inner Earth and just don't remember any of it?"

"No idea. But I do know this much—Mom was furious with Officer Clark," Tanner said.

"Yeah, my mom was pretty upset with Davenport. He was treating me like a hardened criminal."

"Finally, someone sees you for what you really are!" Tanner said with a big grin on his face. He had lost weeks of memories but not his sense of humor.

CHAPTER 4

THE ROYAL TREATMENT
(MICK)

When Mick finally began to stir, she saw paramedics, her mom, and a police officer surrounding her bed. She was connected to an IV.

"What the heck is going on?" Mick asked.

"Are you all right?" a chorus of voices asked.

"Fine. I'm fine," Mick replied.

"Please. Give her some space," Mrs. Brown said as she tried to clear away the crowd in Mick's bedroom. "She's been through a lot. She's going to need some time."

Mick watched her mother herd the emergency personnel into the hallway. She could faintly hear the front door open and shouting coming from outside the house.

"Is she all right?"

"Did she say who kidnapped her?"

"Was it the Wheelwright and Hunter boys?"

Her mother closed the door, and the noise subsided. Mick was trying to sit up when she felt something uncomfortable underneath her. She moved to the side to find a few gold Roman coins and an object consisting of two small pieces of wood held together by leather straps, like a book. Mick opened the book and read what was scratched on the inlaid wax.

Might not be enough to convince anyone else that Donald Carlton was innocent of the Brownsville Bank robbery and murders, but it's enough for me.

"What's going on?" Mick asked when her mother returned to the room.

"Everything's fine, Makayla," her mother said as she patted her shoulder. "Are you all right?"

"Pretty tired, but yeah, I'm okay."

"What happened? We've been so worried."

"Why?" Mick asked.

"You've been missing for a couple months! Any parent would be worried."

"What!" Mick practically shouted. "Okay. What's the joke? Are Tanner and Andrew trying to prank me? Am I on some kind of hidden-camera show?"

"Are you saying you didn't know you've been missing that long?" Mrs. Brown said.

"Let's start out a little more basic," Makayla replied. "I've been missing?"

"Of course you've been missing. You really didn't know that? Don't you remember anything?"

"No. I really don't," Mick replied. This wasn't completely true. She did remember following Mr. Carlton's instructions about entering the underworld, but she didn't remember anything after she'd jumped into the River Styx.

"I remember going to Mammoth Cave alone and then walking back home with Tanner and Andrew. That's it."

"Wait. You walked home with Tanner and Andrew?" her mother asked, voice rising in intensity.

"Yeah. What's wrong?"

"I *knew* it was them. I *knew* they were the ones."

"What are you talking about?" Mick was baffled by her mother's behavior.

"Tanner and Andrew are responsible for your disappearance. They must have drugged you or something."

"Those are some pretty powerful drugs if you're saying I was gone for a couple months and I don't remember any of it."

"You'd be surprised what they can do with drugs these days." Mick's mother replied. "I'm calling the police."

"No need, ma'am. I'm right here," Sheriff Gardiner said.

"Oh, right . . ." she replied. "You've got to arrest Tanner and Andrew."

"Let's not get ahead of ourselves," the sheriff said. "We'll take care of it."

"What happened to Tanner and Andrew?" Mick asked.

"They're probably up to no good somewhere," her mother replied.

"Mom, they would never do anything to hurt me. In fact, they're always looking out for me."

"We'll see," Mrs. Brown said with a tone of finality.

"Whatever happened with dad?" Mick asked.

"He's in prison," her mother replied.

Mick didn't know what to say. In fact, she wasn't sure what to think. Everything that had occurred before she jumped into the River Styx had pointed to her father being mixed up in something dodgy related to Mammoth Cave. And if this much time had passed without his name being cleared, he probably was guilty of something. Mick wanted to know more, but she wasn't sure she could pretend she didn't know about the money and the shots in the barn, if that came up. Finally, she decided to go for shutting down the topic as quickly as she could.

"Well, I'm sure they'll get it all sorted out. How are things at church?"

CHAPTER 5

HOKOLESQUA

(HOKOLESQUA—METHOATASKE'S BROTHER)

Early 1800s

Hokolesqua looked longingly at his father's headband with its striking eagle feather hanging in the family wigwam. His father, Lalawethika, had just fallen asleep. Hokolesqua rubbed his hand over his head as he looked at his father's Mohawk haircut.

I could never do it, he thought as the requirements for becoming a Shawnee warrior, etched in his brain for as long as he could remember, reappeared on the stage of his mind. Self-doubt didn't stop the young boy from dreaming. He watched inside his head as his hair was shaved and the village elders approached with a headband he could proudly call his own.

The scene was whisked away as if stirred with a large wooden spoon and replaced by the vivid events of two moons earlier, events that had turned his world upside down. He pictured the largest warrior he had ever seen bursting through the door of his family's wigwam. His mother, Mayata, fighting valiantly as the man tied her up, slamming her fists over and over against the many plates of his golden armor with no effect.

The same feeling of paralysis Hokolesqua felt that night swept over him again. Desperately he wanted to be brave and lunge at the man and fight, but he was completely petrified.

Even Father wouldn't stand chance, he thought.

Hokolesqua felt an evil, searing sensation as the warrior made eye contact and held his index finger to his mouth. It was clear Hokolesqua wasn't to tell anyone what he had just witnessed.

After the man left, Hokolesqua looked at Methoataske, who ran for the door. He knew she was going to tell someone, and even more terror swept over him as he sat alone in the wigwam with his two younger siblings.

Hokolesqua shook his head, forcing the memory to collapse in his mind.

I will never become a Shawnee warrior.

He began to think about the events that happened later that night.

Was Father right? he wondered as he reflected on how his father described his chase after the giant. *Had Mother and her captor really been dragged into the cave river and eaten by the horned serpent Kinepikwa?*

The legend of the man-eating serpent had been common conversation with the other boys his age as they tried to scare one another around the fire.

Or was Methoataske right?

Methoataske and her father had argued night and day about the serpent. Methoataske was convinced something else had happened to their mother.

But his father said he had seen Mother disappear in the river.

Then he thought of Methoataske's counterpoint.

He didn't see the serpent. He only saw Mother disappear.

He thought about the clues his sister had dropped that she was going to go find answers for herself, but he hadn't recognized them until she was gone.

Both my mother and sister are gone because I wasn't brave.

He reflected about how many times he and Methoataske had pretended to be Indian chiefs and mighty warriors as they ran around the village shouting war cries and wore the replica headdresses they'd made. Hokolesqua felt so powerful when he put them on.

Maybe Chief Tecumseh could help me, he thought.

Stories about the mighty Tecumseh were spreading. Just one moon earlier he'd promised that those unwilling to join his rebellion against the white man would feel the angry stomping of his feet from the Great Lakes to the Delta Basin. As prophesied, a powerful earthquake had rocked Hokolesqua's village, and braves up and down the Mississippi River felt the shaking of the earth and claimed the river had even flowed upstream.

Someone as powerful as Tecumseh will have answers. I must find Tecumseh.

CHAPTER 6

IT'S GONE

(MICK)

Mick picked up the wax tablet that had somehow come into her possession and read it again.

If this is real, Donald definitely wasn't guilty, but what's going on with Dad?

"I have to go to work, Mick," Mrs. Brown yelled from the kitchen. "Nathan and Addie are at school. You'll be all right here at home. Just rest. You've been through a lot."

"I'm fine, "Mick replied. "I really should be at school."

"You'll get caught up. Don't worry about school right now."

Mick wasn't happy about missing school, even though they usually didn't do much on the first day.

"Give me a call if you need anything," her mom said. The kitchen door slammed shut, and a couple minutes later, Mick heard her mom pulling out of the driveway.

Everyone's gone. Now's my chance to do some snooping around.

Her first thought was to see what she could find out about her dad's arrest. She ran into the kitchen, plopped herself down in front of the family computer, and began a search.

Here's one. She clicked on a link that read "Brownsville Man Arrested in Harvey Wilkins's Disappearance."

Come on, load. She tapped her foot, anxiously waiting for the article to display.

Here we go. The article finally appeared on screen.

Patrick Brown, of Brownsville, was arrested Friday in conjunction with the disappearance of reality TV star Harvey Wilkins. Sources say that Mr. Wilkins, who was filming the second season of Treasure in Mammoth Cave, had actually found a satchel of money from the infamous Brownsville Bank robbery of 1810 shortly before his disappearance. A few days after Wilkins's disappearance, Brown showed up at a coin shop with money dating from the same period. Wilkins's mother, Selma Wilkins, of Nashville, said, "Obviously Brown must have wanted the treasure for himself. We're just begging him to tell us where Harvey is." Police confirmed Brown had become obsessed with the show and had been skipping work to search for the treasure himself. The studio, in an apparent attempt to keep the discovery of the money a secret until the final episode is released, denied the money had ever been found.

Oh, my gosh, Mick thought. *It has to be Dad. Maybe he stole the satchel from Wilkins, and when Harvey tried to get it back out in the barn, Dad shot him.* A chill ran down Mick's spine. As much as she wanted it all to not be true, she couldn't deny how the pieces seemed to fit together.

I've got to go out to the barn.

The last time she was there she'd found the money from the robbery hidden underneath one of the planks, but after hearing strange noises, she'd fled the scene. She'd bumped into her father, who was headed to the barn, and a few minutes later heard a couple gunshots and watched him emerge with a rifle. She knew if she searched the barn, there was a chance she might find Wilkins's body.

Surely they've already searched the barn, she thought, trying to reassure herself that her worst fears weren't about to be realized.

After confirming she really was alone, she made her way to the barn. Quietly she climbed the ladder and moved to where she had discovered the loose plank concealing the leather briefcase. The shallow layer of hay was scattered haphazardly around the plank. She reached down and removed the wood.

It's gone! She gasped as she looked at the empty space where she had previously seen the satchel of money.

Dad has to be the one who took it. But why wouldn't he have said anything about it to us?

CHAPTER 7

THE DANGLING PARTICIPANT

(TANNER)

"Hey, Andrew," Tanner said as he opened the front door. "Come on in."

Tanner's mom had decided to throw a welcome-back party for her son, knowing his impending court date might send him packing to the juvenile detention center. It had been a few weeks since she'd found him asleep in his bed. She told Tanner when the dust settled he would be hailed as a hero for rescuing Mick, though there were still a lot of unanswered questions.

Several of Tanner's friends were assembled in the kitchen, where Mrs. Hunter had set out a huge spread of snacks. Andrew and Tanner had just joined in the feeding frenzy—not atypical for fourteen-year-old boys within striking distance of a table full of food—when the doorbell rang.

Tanner looked excitedly to see which of his friends his mother was letting in. To his dismay, it was Jim Sanford.

"Why did she invite him?" Tanner whispered to Andrew.

"No kidding. I'm not sure what she was thinking."

Jim had not only had jumped on the bandwagon of those accusing Tanner and Andrew when Mick went missing, he was practically driving it.

"He's nothing but trouble," Tanner said. "I guarantee this is going to come back to bite us."

"Matt told me he's been trying to put the moves on Mick."

"You're kidding," Tanner replied, his voice anxious.

"I'm not kidding. You know how he is. He's probably trying to latch on to her new celebrity status. He wants a trophy girlfriend."

Tanner's phone began to vibrate.

I wonder who that is. Pretty much all my friends are here.

There was, of course, one notable exception. Mick, Tanner's best friend since elementary school, was off-limits—part of the court order for the two boys. Tanner pulled out his phone to see who it was. Bekah. He raised his head and scanned the room.

There she is.

He looked down at his phone. It indicated she was currently typing, but he could clearly see she wasn't. She was busy talking with some of his other friends. Her phone wasn't even in her hands. He looked back at his phone. The first message simply said, "Hey, Tanner!" The "currently typing" icon was still displayed. Then the next message appeared. "Meet me outside."

That's weird.

He approached her. "Hey, Bekah, what's up?"

"Nothing. Why?"

"I just got a text from you." He showed her the screen.

"Follow me." She grabbed his arm and pulled him down the hall, away from the kitchen and living room, where everyone was hanging out.

"What's going on?" Tanner asked.

"It's Mick," Bekah whispered.

"What do you mean?"

"She's the one texting you."

"Why is she texting from your phone?"

"She's pretty sure her messages are being monitored—at least by her mom. And yours probably are as well. She borrowed my phone because she wanted to get together with you, and she thought if she could text from my phone, no one would suspect anything."

"Tanner, we're going to need some more drinks!" Mrs. Hunter shouted across the party to her son. "Can you get that water cooler for me?"

"Not right now, Mom," Tanner replied. He had to get outside and see Makayla. He hadn't seen her since they'd emerged from Mammoth Cave.

"Tanner David Hunter!"

Mrs. Hunter didn't need to say anything more. Tanner knew that whenever she invoked his full name, he'd better do what she asked. Though he knew she would do anything for him, she also had the ability to make him feel worse than anyone else whenever she was disappointed with his actions.

"Okay, Mom. What cooler?" Tanner was going crazy. He had to get this done right away. He couldn't miss this opportunity to meet with Mick.

"You know, the orange-and-white one. I think it's in the attic."

"Okay."

Tanner rushed to the upstairs hallway, where he pulled the small rope to the attic ladder.

"T, what are you doing?"

Tanner looked down to see Andrew and his other friends through the railing.

"Just grabbing something for Mom."

He climbed up into the opening. Next to the entrance, in front of the cooler, was an unusual linen bundle. As he moved it to the side, the entire arm of a skeleton fell out and began to plummet toward the hallway floor below. Luckily, Tanner didn't have time to process what was going on because he would have been in too much shock to catch it before it fell to the ground. But everything happened so fast he instinctively grabbed the bones. He took a look at what was in his hand, and then it registered.

"Oh, my gosh! What is this?"

He stared at the blackened bones in disbelief.

Probably not in my best interest to be seen holding a charred skeleton.

He quickly put the loose arm back into the attic, took a look around to see if anyone had noticed, and then continued with the task at hand. When he returned to the kitchen with the cooler, he took a breath to calm himself.

"Everything all right?" his mother asked.

"Yeah, sure," he replied with a "not in front of all my friends" look.

Tanner had two things on his mind. He needed to ask his mother about the skeleton, and he had to try to catch Mick before he lost the opportunity.

"Tanner, can you . . ."

He quickly ducked out of view.

"Whoa, were did he go?" he heard his mother say.

Tanner darted into the yard and was scouring the shadows and gingerly whispering, "Mick, Mick, are you still out here?"

"Tanner!" came a hushed reply from behind one of the bushes.

"Mick!" Tanner glanced around, and feeling fairly certain that no one was watching–particularly Jim–he darted behind the bush and gave Mick a big hug, nearly knocking her over. He pulled away.

"What are you doing here?" he asked.

"I just had to come and see you. How is everything?"

"Other than being accused of kidnapping my best friend? Couldn't be better."

"I'm sorry about that. Don't worry, I'll do everything I can to clear your name."

"I know," Tanner replied.

"What happened to us?" Mick asked. It was obvious from the expression on her face that she was in deep thought.

"No clue."

"All I can think is we must have made it into Inner Earth, and somehow our memories were erased. That has to be why there's so little information about Inner Earth. People either stay there, or if they come back, they forget everything about the place."

"Maybe so."

"We've got to figure out a way to get back there," Mick said.

"I'm not sure I'll be going anywhere for a while. I'm just hoping I won't be spending the next few years getting better acquainted with the inside of the juvenile detention center."

"Tanner! Tanner! Where are you?" his mother yelled out into the yard.

"Gotta go. Text me again. It was good seeing you."

Off he went, discreetly navigating through the yard so his mother wouldn't be able to tell where he had been.

"Tanner, where were you?" she asked. "You're the guest of honor. You can't just go ducking out."

"I know, Mom. It was just getting a bit claustrophobic with everybody wanting to ask me questions and stuff. I had to get some fresh air."

"All right, well, don't leave again."

About an hour into the party, Jim abruptly walked past Tanner and Andrew, intentionally bumping into them.

"I guess we'll see you later," he said, his voice dripping with intrigue. He quickly walked to the front door and left.

"What was that all about?" Andrew asked.

"No idea," Tanner replied. But he did have an idea. Jim's voice sounded like he had something on the boys.

Did he see me with Mick? He must know I violated the court order.

Tanner wanted to talk to Andrew about it but didn't dare. The fewer people who knew he'd met with Mick, the better, but it was eating him up on the inside.

"What's wrong?" Andrew asked.

"Nothing."

Tanner could see Andrew wasn't buying it. He gave him a stern look, and Andrew dropped it.

A few hours later, after all the guests had left, Tanner approached his mother. He wanted to talk to her about the clandestine encounter with Mick but again thought it was better to lay low on that. If Jim had seen him, he didn't want anyone else to confirm it. But he did have another issue to address.

"Mom, I think you've got some skeletons in the closet you need to talk about. Actually, in the attic." It was not something to joke about, but somehow trying to lighten the moment a bit gave Tanner some relief from the potential gravity of the conversation.

"Oh yes. Don't you remember me asking you about that?"

"Asking *me*?"

"Yeah, when you returned from wherever you were, you left your backpack on the floor of your room. I checked to see if there was anything in it that would give me a clue about where you had been. To my horror, I found that charred skeleton. I was terrified it was Mick's. When the police came, I hid it in attic, and I guess I was so relieved when I found out Mick was alive, I forgot all about it."

Tanner vaguely remembered seeing his mom discovering the skeleton as he was coming out of his coma.

"Where *did* it come from, Tanner?"

"I honestly have no idea."

"Well, until we figure it out, don't say anything about it."

"Don't worry, I won't," Tanner said. "I almost dropped it out of the attic during the party when I was getting the cooler. Can you imagine if it would have fallen? All the accusations that have been going around and then I drop a skeleton from the attic?"

"I'm just glad you've got good reflexes," Mrs. Hunter said. "That dangling party participant would have sent you to juvenile detention for sure."

CHAPTER 8

TECUMSEH

(HOKOLESQUA)

Early 1800s

"Thank you, most noble chief, for allowing me to address you." Methoataske's younger brother fidgeted as he sat down in the wigwam of the great Shawnee leader Tecumseh. "I have traveled many days to have an audience with you."

"Yes," Tecumseh said. "You are welcome."

Hokolesqua felt the piercing eye of the commanding chief look deep into his soul.

"I've been told you seek advice on the disappearance of your mother and sister."

"That is correct."

Hokolesqua squirmed as Tecumseh looked him over from head to toe. He felt extremely inferior to the tall warrior with the chiseled physique.

"Hokolesqua." Tecumseh paused.

"Yes?"

"It is time for you to go on a vision quest."

"But I'm not sure I'm ready to become a man. What if I fail? What if I don't even receive a vision or I do but I don't understand the meaning?"

"Many do not understand the meaning until the end of their life," Tecumseh replied.

"If I don't understand until the end of my life," the young Indian asked, "how will I know the vision is real—that it's sent from Kokumthena?" the boy asked, referring to the female creator goddess of the Shawnee.

"Your personal guardian spirit will help you to know the vision is true," Tecumseh replied. "You'll feel it here." The great chief thumped his fist against his glistening bronze chest.

"How do I begin my quest?"

"You begin tonight," Tecumseh said. "You must not eat this night and continue fasting all day tomorrow. Before the sun rises on the following day, you will be taught things that will guide you through the most important parts of your life. Pay close attention."

"But what if I forget them?"

"If you stay focused, you will never forget. These things must be burned into your mind. Your life and the lives of those around you depend on your ability to determine your life's course from the vision you'll receive."

"I hope I can do this," he said, unable to look Tecumseh in the eye due to his fear of failure.

"Go," Tecumseh replied. "Find a place where you can meditate. Ponder and reflect on the past and future. You must free yourself of present worries and focus on the meaning of life. I will speak with you again only after your spirit animal teaches you."

Hokolesqua left Tecumseh's wigwam and departed into the woods, apprehensive about what the next two days would bring.

CHAPTER 9

A Surprise in the Courtroom

(Tanner)

"As our first witness, the prosecution calls Sheriff Gardiner."

The big day had arrived. Tanner and Andrew were in the courtroom, along with half of Brownsville. Journalists from all over the country were anxious to report to a nation obsessed with the disappearance of Makayla Brown. Were Mick's two best friends really up to something nefarious? Would they spend years in juvenile detention, have to do community service, or be exonerated?

"Sheriff Gardiner, do you swear to tell the truth, the whole truth, and nothing but the truth, so help you God?"

"I do."

The prosecutor began to ask about the break-in at the police station.

"What time did you arrive at the station?"

"Around 6:00 a.m."

"And what did you find?"

"I saw Tanner and Andrew looking through files in the file cabinet."

"And that cabinet—it's usually locked, isn't that correct?"

"Yes, it's *always* locked."

"So Tanner Hunter and Andrew Wheelwright not only broke into the police station, they broke into a police file cabinet where sensitive information is stored. Is that correct?"

"Yes."

"And what did the boys do when they saw you?"

"They ran into the woods."

"Did they take anything?"

"Yes."

"And what did they take?"

"A folder with Makayla Brown's files."

"And why would they want Makayla Brown's files?"

"Objection! Speculation!"

"Sustained."

"Did the boys ever return the files?"

"No."

"And have you asked them for the files since they've returned?"

"Yes. They said they had no idea where the files were."

"Isn't that convenient," Mrs. Brown said in a whisper that was loud enough for everyone in the courtroom to hear.

"Could the files have been destroyed by the boys?"

"Objection!"

"Sustained."

The prosecution called a couple of additional witnesses who confirmed Makayla's files were indeed missing and who testified about Sheriff Gardiner's character, assuring the judge he would not have fabricated the story.

"The prosecution calls Jim Sanford to the stand."

Tanner let out a small gasp.

"Why are they calling him?" Andrew said, leaning toward Tanner.

"No idea," Tanner replied. "But it can't be good. You know the guy hates us."

He wasn't going to say anything, but Tanner was sure at least part of Jim's testimony was going to be about spotting him with Mick at the party, which was a violation of the court order.

"Mr. Sanford, will you please tell the judge where you were on the night of August 29?"

Oh boy, here we go, Tanner thought.

"Sure. Well, I was at a party at the Hunters'."

"And will you tell him what you saw?"

"Sure. A few minutes after I got there, I saw Tanner walk up the stairs, where he pulled down the ladder into the attic."

Tanner cringed. He knew what was coming. He had no idea Jim had seen him in the upstairs hallway.

"And you thought this was unusual, correct?"

"Yes."

"And so what did you do?"

"Well, I walked into the foyer to get a better look."

"And what did you see?"

"I saw Tanner climb into the attic."

"Please tell us what you saw next."

"Well, I saw part of a skeleton falling out of the attic." There was an audible gasp. Jim continued on. "Tanner quickly grabbed it and put it back in the attic."

"Did Tanner know you had seen him?"

"No, I'm sure he didn't see me."

"We would like to enter the skeleton into evidence as exhibit A."

"Mr. Sanford, is this the same skeleton you described?"

"It looks like the same one. I remember seeing burn marks on the bones, just like those."

"And, Mr. Sanford, burning a skeleton would be a way someone might try to destroy evidence, isn't that correct?"

"Objection," the defense attorney shouted. "Speculation."

"Sustained," the judge replied.

Tanner was furious. The objection had been sustained, but he was sure the prosecutor had influenced the judge. He had done the same thing when he questioned Sheriff Gardiner. He was carefully trying to convince the judge there was a pattern of Tanner destroying evidence.

"From what you saw, Mr. Sanford, would you say Tanner didn't want anyone to see what he had stored up there?"

"Yes."

"Thank you, Mr. Sanford. That will be all."

The hearing continued throughout the rest of the morning, and it was just before noon when the lawyers made their final arguments before the judge.

❖ ❖ ❖

Early in the evening, the judge brought everyone back into the courtroom to read his verdict.

"Will the defendants please rise?"

Tanner and Andrew stood up. Tanner turned around to look at his mom for moral support. Out of the corner of his eye, he saw the door at the back of the courtroom open and his dad walk through.

Tanner made a move for his dad, who he hadn't seen in nearly four years.

"Tanner Hunter, please remain where you are as I read my ruling," the judge said.

Reluctantly, Tanner stopped.

All eyes were on the judge as he began to read the verdict. "Members of the court, on the first count of breaking and entering, I find the defendants—"

Crash!

Everyone's focus snapped to the multi-paned window on the right side of the courtroom, which exploded, sending glass everywhere. A man wearing a red bandana across his face swung into the room on a rope. Rifles were slung over both shoulders, and he was waving a pistol in his hand, like something straight out of a Western.

"Don't move!" the man yelled. "There are explosives surrounding the entire building and in my satchel." He gently patted the bag with his hand. "Anyone sneezes and we all go up in smoke!" The man approached the table where Tanner and Andrew sat.

"You'll come with me!" he snarled as he roughly grabbed the shirts of the two boys.

"What the . . ." Tanner said as he scanned the courtroom with a panicked look while being dragged out of the building. He spotted his dad again. There was so much he wanted to say, his emotions zinging about in his head like marbles in a blender. He made eye contact and tried to express a million thoughts from the past four years in a single glance before being shoved out the door.

CHAPTER 10

SOMETHING FISHY

(MICK)

"What was that all about?" someone in the courtroom shouted once the door closed behind the man and his captives.

"Can we get out of here?" another asked.

"No one move!" Sheriff Gardiner yelled. "If the building really is rigged with explosives, none of us knows what will trigger them. Sit tight while I make some calls and we get a bomb expert down here."

Mick looked over at Tanner's mom and Andrew's parents. They were distraught.

After making some calls, Sheriff Gardiner carefully made his way over to comfort the family members. In an attempt to give them some privacy, he escorted them to an adjoining room.

The air in the courtroom was thick. Everyone was fearful that at any moment they might be blown sky high.

"Who was that?" someone asked.

"The two boys had the whole thing planned," another replied.

"But they looked terrified."

"It was all an act."

"No way! Those boys aren't that good at acting."

"I'm sure they've had this in the works for a while," someone said. "They've been coached on how to act."

"That Andrew is so smart, and with his dad's money, I'm sure they probably paid an assassin to get him out of here. I heard his father is connected to the mob. Haven't you ever wondered where he got all his money?"

"Yeah, and why did they even move to Brownsville in the first place? If I had that kind of money, I would never pick Brownsville."

"Probably trying to get away from someone or something."

"I knew there was something fishy about that family."

"Stop," Mick said forcefully. "Those two families are some of the best citizens in Brownsville. Andrew's parents have made huge donations to the school, the library, and the church. And, personally, I'm convinced Tanner and Andrew were responsible for rescuing me."

CHAPTER 11

THE VISION QUEST

(HOKOLESQUA)

Early 1800s

I have no idea what I'm doing down here, the young Indian thought as he looked heavenward. *In fact, I have no idea where "here" is.* He looked around at his unfamiliar surroundings, deep in the wilderness.

There had been no revelation or visit by a spirit animal of any kind on the first night of his vision quest.

As the afternoon of the next day came to an end, he found he was exhausted, having spent nearly an entire day meditating, fasting, and pondering. He sat quietly on a tree stump, pleading with the goddess Kokumthena to grant his vision quest. The Shawnee could see the sun beginning to set through the trees. A squirrel scampered near where he sat.

A squirrel is my spirit animal? It figures. Hokolesqua was hoping for something more exotic, like a jaguar or grizzly, but at this point he would settle for anything.

I guess there's nothing wrong with a squirrel. Prepared, aware, social, resourceful.

"Is it you?" he asked out loud, hoping for an answer. The squirrel cocked his head with a confounded look and ran into the trees.

Guess not.

Hokolesqua thought about how excited Methoataske had been when she learned her spirit animal was an eagle. Intelligent, courageous, risk-taking.

That was Methoataske.

He pictured in his mind's eye the eagle totem she'd whittled and always wore around her neck. He thought about the time they were playing and had sat down next to a tree stump to rest and an eagle swooped down and lit on the stump right next to Methoataske. The connection had always been so strong. Eagles of one form or another never seemed to be far away from her.

I can't return to Tecumseh a failure. What am I doing wrong?

It was in this state of fear that Hokolesqua passed out from exhaustion, his body collapsing onto a bed of pine needles and leaves.

A gentle nudge against his face caused him to stir, but he couldn't fully rouse himself. Exerting great mental energy, he pried one eye open. Lying next to him was a large black panther staring directly into his eyes. Normally he would have been terrified, but for some inexplicable reason he felt as calm as if his missing mother were cradling him as a baby. He climbed onto the great animal's back and hugged the panther tightly around the neck. It got up and ran deeper into the wilderness. When they came to a large river, the cat paused and bent its neck to lap up some water. After a quick drink, the panther plunged headfirst into the river. Hokolesqua closed his eyes and held his breath as the cat swam deeper and deeper.

I can't hold my breath any longer. He desperately needed air.

I'm going to die in the middle of my vision quest. He exhaled and gulped for air, fully expecting his lungs to fill with water. But they didn't. He opened his eyes. Tall buildings and beautiful palaces filled his underwater view. He passed two thunderbirds that stood as sentinels at a large, glimmering gate. The panther leapt toward the gate, and Hokolesqua braced for impact, but they passed through as if the gate weren't even there. Seated on a golden throne in front of him, he saw a being more powerful and majestic than Chief Tecumseh himself and then a series of glowing symbols he didn't recognize but which seared themselves into his mind's eye. The symbols appeared so tangible he reached out to touch them and, as he did, they vanished, though somehow he could picture them as clearly as if they were still there.

Animals of various shapes and sizes began to swim toward Hokolesqua and the panther, when Hokolesqua noticed a torch attached to the cat's tail that soon engulfed the animal in flames. The mighty cat roared in pain. Hokolesqua felt the sting of the scorching blaze and wondered how the intense fire could be burning underwater.

The panther curled into a fetal position and was sinking into the depths. The water became darker and murkier. Hokolesqua was about to give in to the darkness that surrounded him when the other animals emerged from the blackness and worked to nurse the cat back to health.

The panther surged for the surface, gasping for air. It slapped a dripping paw onto the shore and, extending its claws, dragged itself and Hokolesqua out of the water and onto the shore, where they both fell asleep. When Hokolesqua began to stir after his deep, long sleep, strange and ferocious creatures the likes of which he had never seen climbed out of the river. Circling like vultures hungry for their next meal, the beasts growled and snarled. Hokolesqua grabbed the nap of the great cat and shook its head, desperately trying to wake it as the innumerable hosts began to close in. Hokolesqua turned to look for an escape route, but there was none.

"Wake up," Hokolesqua cried as he continued to shake the panther. He looked up just in time to see a massive beast with claws as long as Hokolesqua's forearms take a swipe at him.

The young Indian awakened with a start. He looked around and found himself alone in the woods and heaved a sigh of relief. Lying near him was a small pyramid-shaped object with beautiful markings. As he gazed at the aqua-colored glow that emanated from the horizontal line at the center of the object, out of the corner of his eye he noticed a red stain spreading rapidly across the front of his shredded shirt. He lifted his shirt and could see a large gash across his chest.

Where did that come from? I've got to get back to Tecumseh.

He gathered his few belongings, scooped up the pyramid, and ran for Tecumseh's wigwam, blood continuing to stream from his unusual wound.

CHAPTER 12

HOW'D I DO?

(TANNER)

Outside the courtroom, the mysterious bandit forced Tanner and Andrew down the sidewalk with a rifle at their backs. As they got farther from the building and found themselves alone, the kidnapper broke the silence.

"How'd I do?"

"What are you talking about?" Tanner asked.

"How'd I do? How was my rescue?"

"Rescue? What do you mean rescue? You just kidnapped us!" Tanner said angrily. "You've got a gun at our backs."

"Oh yeah. Sorry about that," the man said, lowering his guns. "Get on these horses."

Three horses were parked neatly down the street from the courthouse. The three of them got on, and off they went. Within a few minutes they arrived at an abandoned barn, where they dismounted and the stranger forced them inside.

"So, what'd you think?"

"Why are you so worried what we think about how you did?" Tanner asked. "You successfully kidnapped us, all right? There. Do you feel better?"

"Tone it down," Andrew whispered. "The guy's got a couple of guns and explosives."

"So, what have the two of you been up to?"

Tanner and Andrew stared at each other with bewildered expressions.

"Wait. You don't remember me?" the man said, looking almost as confused as the boys.

"Why would we remember you?" Andrew asked. "I've never seen you before in my life."

"Oh, I see," the man said. "Luckily I came prepared. Here, drink this."

He handed them a vial filled with what appeared to be water.

"What is it?" Andrew asked.

"Just water."

"Why do you want us to drink it?" Tanner said.

"It will give you your memories back. Your memories about Inner Earth."

"How do you know about that?" Tanner asked.

"Just trust me."

"Yeah, trust the guy that just threatened to blow up the Brownsville Courthouse and everyone in it?" Tanner said.

"Come on, Tanner!" the man shouted. "Just do it!"

Hearing the man call him by name struck a chord somewhere deep inside Tanner. It sounded familiar.

"I'm not sure why I trust you, but I'll do it."

"Tanner! Don't!" Andrew yelled, but it was too late. Tanner took a swig from the vial. He paused and shook his head as if he were shaking off shackles that had been constricting his brain.

"Donald!" he shouted. "Oh, my gosh! How are you?"

Tanner gave the strong Praetorian a big hug, and then staggered backward as a wave of memories flooded through him.

"How are things in Rome? Did you ever find little Livia?"

A sinking feeling swept over his body as he thought about the little girl who had brought him so much joy. He wanted to collapse to the ground as he relived the moment he'd discovered her mother, Anastasia, burned to death by Nero's men, and then as he felt the memory of his panicked search for Livia. The desperation he felt then engulfed his entire being as if it were all happening again, right that moment.

"Tell me you found her," he said in desperation. "Tell me you found Livia."

"No, we haven't. We need your help. That's why I'm here."

"How about Marina and Marcus?" Tanner continued. "And their friend Cornelius, the ex-centurion? Is the city safe for Christians again? It's so good to see you!"

There was so much emotion running high speed through Tanner's body he didn't quite know how to deal with it all.

Tanner looked over at Andrew, who looked as perplexed as Tanner typically felt during math class.

"Come on, take a drink," Tanner said as he handed the vial to Andrew. "It's amazing."

"Did you just drug him?" Andrew asked. "Tanner, you're rambling on about people and places you've never seen or been. No way." Andrew shook his head vehemently. "I'm just fine living in reality." Tanner understood his friend well enough to know logic wasn't going to allow him to take a drink.

"T, this psychopath kidnapper is duping you. We've got to get out of here." Andrew started to make a run for it.

"Hold it!" Donald said, grabbing his gun and lowering it at Andrew. "You're not going anywhere."

Andrew stopped, turned around, and respectfully sat down on a bale of hay.

"Why are you *here*?" Tanner asked.

"First things first," Donald said. "Andrew, you've got to drink this."

"No way! And how do you know our names?"

"Grab him," Donald said, looking at Tanner. "We're going to have to force it down his throat. We don't have time to waste."

Tanner and Donald grabbed Andrew. He struggled to keep the vial away from his lips, but he was no match for the two of them. They forced the water into his mouth. Andrew was trying to spit it out, but he must have finally swallowed at least a small amount because, like Tanner, he instantly recognized Donald.

"Wow. Donald! To answer your question, that was amazing. Best rescue ever. Sorry I didn't recognize you."

"No problem."

"Wait," Tanner said. "What about everyone in the courtroom? Our families and friends are in danger. We've got to get them out of there."

"They're fine," Donald replied. "There aren't really any explosives. I made that all up."

"Convincing," Andrew replied.

"Hey, we don't have time for chitchat, then. They'll be in hot pursuit as soon as they figure that out," Tanner jumped in. "We've got to get out of town."

"My mom's car is just down the street." Tanner continued. "She always leaves the keys in it. It's our only shot. We'll never make it out of here on horseback."

The three of them jumped on the horses and cautiously rode back toward town.

"Where'd you get these, anyway?" Tanner slapped his horse on the neck a few times.

"Old stable near the center of town."

"Must be Riley's," Tanner said.

"We probably should return them," Andrew said. "Last thing we need are more charges against us."

Once they got near the town center, they returned the horses and snuck through town on high alert.

The streets were crammed with cars parked every which way, and the three of them were able to remain hidden as they crouch-ran to Tanner's mother's station wagon.

"Hang on," Tanner said as he revved the engine and screeched onto the street. "Here we go."

Tanner had very little driving experience, and it showed as they began to navigate their way out of the small town.

"So, Donald, why *are* you here?"

CHAPTER 13

I Deserve Better

(Marina)

"Marina, you must be reasonable," Marcus said as he looked at his young daughter, her dark hair braided like a crown around her head.

"I am!" she barked in reply. "You're the one who isn't. How could you keep me in the dark for so long? I'm your daughter. I'm not sure you were *ever* going to tell me my stepmother was from the underworld. If someone else hadn't brought it up, I would still be in the dark to this day. And now that she's dead, it's too late."

"You have to believe me. We planned to tell you. It just never was the right time." Marcus approached Marina and tried to put his arm around her. She angrily grabbed it and thrust it away from her.

"Don't touch me."

"We were just trying to do what was best for you."

"Don't give me that excuse. Parents have been saying that since the early days of the Egyptian dynasties."

"But it's true!"

"Well, I'm glad you believe that, but I don't. And what about the plans to take over the city?"

"What?"

"Don't pretend you don't know. Decimus told me all about the entrance into Rome from the underworld where the Christians will begin the invasion. You brainwashed me. You taught me we were supposed to love one another."

"We do," Marcus said. "I truly have no idea what you're talking about."

"Well, I'm out of here." Marina started to make her way toward the door of Lucius's carpentry shop.

"Wait. Where are you going?"

"Why would I stick around? My stepmother is dead, my sister is missing, my home has been burned to the ground, and all I have left is a father I can't trust. I deserve better than that. Decimus said I could stay with him, or maybe I'll find a husband or something, but I'm done here!" Marina shouted as she stormed out.

Marcus began to chase after her. "Marina! Marina! Come back. You're all I've got left in the world. We've got to stick together."

"Don't follow me," Marina turned and yelled. "I don't ever want to see you again."

Marina could hear her father's voice growing more and more distant as he tried to chase after her. She didn't want to admit it, but she was scared.

Where do I go?

When she could no longer hear her father's voice, she looked apprehensively around, thinking of everything Anastasia and her father had taught her about the dangers of the Roman night.

CHAPTER 14

THE DIRECTOR

(HOKOLESQUA)

I'm going to die if I don't find Tecumseh soon.

His shirt was becoming more soaked with blood as he sprinted through the woods.

I'm lost.

He looked around for anything that seemed familiar.

I should have arrived at Tecumseh's wigwam by now.

He felt weak from the lack of food and loss of blood.

It must be in that direction.

Hokolesqua stumbled over a fallen tree, and the top of the pyramid in his hand flipped open.

A small pointer was silhouetted against the glowing, aqua-colored background inside the pyramid. It began to move, then came to an abrupt halt.

Am I supposed to follow the pointer?

Holding the pyramid in front of him and close to his chest, he walked in the direction of the arrow. He was surprised at how quickly he was back to Tecumseh's wigwam.

"Tecumseh," he said as he knocked on the entrance to the wigwam. "I need your help. I was slashed by some kind of beast. I'm going to bleed to death."

"I'm coming," Tecumseh responded as he quickly made his way to the door. "Yes, this is a very bad wound. Dark spirit. Come," he motioned for Hokolesqua to enter. "Lie down."

Tecumseh mixed some herbs into a paste and applied it to the wound. Hokolesqua cried out in pain, but the pain was only a small distraction from what he was really focused on.

Dark spirit? What does that mean? Did my vision quest not really come from Kokumthena? Hokolesqua had tried so hard to understand, to approach the vision quest properly, and now he was completely befuddled. He didn't want to ask Tecumseh, afraid that by so doing the mighty chief would lose any respect he might have for him.

As Tecumseh applied a fabric wrap to the wound to stop the bleeding, he noticed the pyramid.

"Where did you get this?" Tecumseh examined the item so respectfully Hokolesqua assumed it must be sacred.

"In the woods."

"Good spirit," Tecumseh said. "This pyramid will help you."

So maybe just the wound was a bad spirit. Maybe the whole vision quest wasn't a waste after all.

Hokolesqua looked at Tecumseh.

Should I tell him about the vision quest?

His father had taught him that vision quests were a very private matter, but the great chief had been so involved in his quest, and Hokolesqua desperately wanted to know what it all meant. He scoured Tecumseh's face for any indication as to whether or not he should say anything, but there was nothing there that encouraged him to talk.

Better not say anything.

"Can I ask Tecumseh one question?"

"Yes."

"Will I ever be brave enough to become a Shawnee warrior?"

Holding the points of the pyramid between his fingers, Tecumseh tumbled it around, analyzing its surface.

"According to the writing on the pyramid," Tecumseh said, stopping the object in his hand, "you have the opportunity to become a mighty warrior. It all depends on your choices."

It wasn't the absolute assurance Hokolesqua wanted, but it did give him hope. He reached for the pyramid. "Can I see?"

Tecumseh handed the pyramid to him.

He carefully examined each side but couldn't see any writing. Hokolesqua looked at the chief, a bit confounded.

"Patience," Tecumseh said.

Hokolesqua did a double take to confirm the ever-so-small smile breaking at the corners of the great leader's mouth.

CHAPTER 15

ESCAPE FROM BROWNSVILLE

(TANNER)

"Like I said," Donald answered, "I need your help. Livia is still missing, Nero is continuing to terrorize the city, and Marina has turned on everyone. It's a disaster."

"What do you mean Marina's turned on everyone?" Andrew asked.

"You remember how angry she was when she learned about Anastasia's true identity as Methoataske?"

"I'd never seen her so mad," Andrew replied.

"She's let that destroy her. You wouldn't recognize her. She stormed out on her father, and Lucius claims he saw her with a group of Christian persecutors. You've got to talk some sense into her."

Tanner was doing his best to drive his mother's station wagon farther and farther out of town.

"Drop me off," Andrew said. "I'm not going back."

"What are you talking about?" Tanner responded. "You've got to. You're the only one who can get through to Marina."

"I guess the water Donald gave you didn't fully restore your memory," Andrew said. "Did you forget about the three-headed dog? And Phlegyas? How about the Great Hall of Judgment and the River Acheron? Personally I wish my memory about those things *hadn't* been restored."

"But think about what's at stake," Tanner said.

"We're desperate," Donald added.

"But . . ." Andrew started.

"We've got to go back and get Mick." Tanner interrupted. "She'll never forgive us if we go without her."

"There's no way *we* can go *or* get Mick!" Andrew retorted. "You saw how many reporters were covering the trial. The whole country is looking for us now."

"We need her!" Tanner shouted.

"But . . ." Tanner didn't allow Andrew to finish. He had made up his mind.

"We're going back. Hang on!" He slammed on the brakes and spun the car around. "Just like you see on TV," he added, proud of his fishtail U-turn.

"Where'd you learn to drive like that?" Andrew asked in shock.

"Just like driving a go-cart, only bigger," Tanner replied.

Andrew shook his head and smiled.

"There's only one road in and out of town," Andrew said. "The police will be stopping every car."

"They won't be stopping the cars going *into* town," Tanner replied.

Andrew opened his mouth to reply and then paused.

"True, but we stole your mom's car. The police will be looking for it."

"No, they won't."

"Come on, T, of course they will," Andrew said. "We get kidnapped from the courtroom and your mom's car is missing? They aren't stupid, you know."

"Trust me. She wouldn't tell the police it's gone. She'll think we got away. And she doesn't want us doing time in juvenile detention."

"Hmm. Maybe. But how are we going to smuggle Mick out of Brownsville?"

"We'll figure it out," Tanner said.

"She probably has police protection. I mean, everyone suspects us, and now that we've been sprung, don't you think she'll be guarded 24/7?"

"Maybe, but we've got to try. We promised Marcus we'd return to help him find Livia. We need all the help we can get."

"Where are the lights on this thing?" Tanner asked out loud as he fumbled around for the lights. The sun had gone down, and it was quickly getting dark.

"Ah, here they are," he said, sighing in relief.

"How are we even going to find Mick?" Andrew asked.

"She'll probably be at work."

"Oh, yeah. I forgot she was working over at Bertie's."

Andrew continued. "Why does she have to work on the busiest street in town?"

"I know, but I think we might be in luck," Tanner said.

"What do you mean?"

"Well, everyone should be at the game."

The entire town of Brownsville ground to a halt on Friday nights when the Edmonson Wildcats played football.

"If we can get to the drive-through before the game is over, we should be able to get Mick and get out of town."

"Donald, you're going to have to drive," Andrew said. "No one knows you. Tanner and I will duck down in the seats. If anyone sees either one of us, it's over."

"You forget I've never driven one of these contraptions," Donald replied. "In fact, I've only even seen them on the few occasions I tried to come back."

"It's not that hard," Andrew said. "You're going to have to learn between here and town. Tanner, pull over and let Donald drive."

Tanner and Andrew gave Mr. Carlton a crash driver's-education course. His driving was a bit rocky at first, and he kept complaining about how much harder it was than riding a horse.

"We're getting close to town," Andrew said. "We need to get down."

Tanner and Andrew ducked down onto the seats.

"You need to slow down," Andrew said. "Take your foot off the accelerator."

Tanner raised his head slightly above the dashboard just in time to see Donald about to run a stop sign and broadside another car.

"Look out!" he yelled as he reached over the seat and yanked at the steering wheel, allowing them to miss the car and go careening into the ditch.

"Everyone okay?" Tanner asked.

"I'm good," Andrew replied.

"I'm fine," Donald added.

"I guess we never told you what those red signs mean, did we?" Tanner asked.

"So much for a subtle entrance," Andrew said angrily.

"Luckily we're not far from Bertie's," Tanner said. He climbed over Donald and out the driver's-side door since the passenger door was wedged against the ditch bank. "Let's go."

Donald and Andrew quickly got out of the car and crouched as they ran from the scene of the crash.

"I think you're right," Andrew said as they crossed the normally busy street in front of the ice cream shop. "Everyone must be at the game."

"You go ahead," Tanner said, giving Donald a push in the back. "We'll watch from under here." He pointed at the ground below one of the picnic tables in front of the shop.

Tanner watched as Mr. Carlton approached the window. It opened, and there was Mick.

"Hi, Mi–" Donald started to enthusiastically greet Mick but caught himself. "–ster Titus here. I'd like three ice cream cones." Mick gave him a puzzled look. "One for me and one for each of my friends. He turned and pointed to one of the wooden picnic tables in front of the shop. Hidden underneath were Tanner and Andrew. Mick let out a gasp.

"Lindsey!" she shouted to her coworker in the back. "Call the police."

Tanner waved his hands from side to side hoping Mick could seem him as he tried emphatically to wave her off. He could see Donald trying to calm her down as well.

"What did you say?" Lindsey yelled back.

Mr. Carlton handed Mick a note Tanner had written.

Mick stood frozen.

> *Drink the water he has, and everything will make sense. Come with us. It's a life-and-death situation.*

"Is there a problem?" Lindsey yelled.

"No, nothing," Mick yelled back. "Everything's good."

Tanner's heart leapt when he realized she might actually take a drink and restore her memory.

She stared at the note and then up at the boys and back at the note. Tanner could see the wheels in Mick's brain going a hundred miles an hour. His were going just as fast. He was trying to imagine what it must look like to Mick with their "captor" pointing at the two of them hidden under the table.

Maybe we need to just go to the window too, he thought. *No, we can't risk being seen.*

Mick looked over at the two of them again, shrugging her shoulders and looking for a prompt. Tanner stretched his neck forward, got very wide-eyed, and aggressively shook his head up and down; trying to signal that it was all okay. He could see Andrew doing the same.

Mr. Carlton slowly raised the vial of Mnemosyne River water to window level, and Mick took it. She pulled out the cork, examined the contents while swirling it around, and gave the boys one more questioning look. They vigorously nodded in approving fashion. She tipped her head back, took a drink, and put the vial in her purse. Looking at Mr. Carlton, she immediately said with a big grin, "Donald! I didn't recognize you."

Their muted celebration was short-lived, however. No sooner had they exchanged greetings than they heard sirens wailing. The sound was coming from the direction of the high school.

"Did you get those ice creams finished?" Mick turned and asked Lindsey.

"Just about done."

"I'll bring them out in a second," Mick told Mr. Carlton. The sound of the sirens was getting closer.

"Thank you," Donald replied as he moved away from the window to the side of the building opposite where the sirens were coming from.

"Do you think someone saw us?" Andrew asked Tanner above the noise that was becoming deafening.

"I guess we're about to find out."

The boys could see the police cars rounding the corner at breakneck speed and heading toward the ice cream shop. They braced themselves for the worst, but the cars raced past and continued down the street.

"Whew! That was close," Tanner said.

"I don't think we're off the hook," Andrew replied. "Remember, we just abandoned your mom's car in the ditch. If they don't know we're in town now, they'll figure it out in about thirty seconds."

"Donald!" Tanner yelled. "Let's get going."

Mr. Carlton returned to the window. Leaning in, he said, "Excuse me, we have to get going. Are those ice creams done?"

"I'm on my way out with them right now!" Mick replied. It was obvious she sensed the panic Donald was trying to disguise in his voice.

Mick sprinted out the door.

"To the woods!" Tanner yelled.

Tanner quickly scanned his surroundings, trying to work out a plan for their escape, but to his horror, he saw Jim Sanford turn into Bertie's parking lot and look directly at him.

CHAPTER 16

JIM SANFORD

(TANNER)

"It's Jim!" Tanner yelled.

"We're dead!" Andrew replied as he turned around and confirmed what Tanner had seen. "The game must be over."

Sure enough, there was a steady stream of cars heading down KY-259.

"Run for your lives!"

The three fugitives and Mick fled down Center Street.

"We've got to get back to Riley's stables! We'll never get out of here on foot!"

Jim sped down Center Street, restored Mustang roaring. He fishtailed off the side of the road and jumped out of his car. In a flash he was in hot pursuit of the escapees. Tanner looked back. Jim was less than twenty yards behind and gaining rapidly.

"Go get the horses! I'll catch up!" Tanner yelled. "I've got Jim."

"You're not getting away with this again," Jim shouted. "I knew you kidnapped Mick, and this proves it."

"You don't know what you're talking about," Tanner replied.

"You're going to get what's coming to you. I'm not going to let you mistreat her!"

Tanner was fuming. Not only had Jim just testified against him, he was now lofting all kinds of false accusations. On any normal day, if Tanner and Jim were in a fight, no one would have put money on Tanner. Jim was the toughest kid in school. But the rage

Tanner felt leveled the playing field. Tanner turned around, lowered his shoulders, and ran full speed at Jim. The hit could have made a highlight reel on a national sports program. Jim found himself sprawled out on his back before he even knew what hit him.

"This is what's coming to *you*," Tanner said as he put his hand on Jim's chest, reared back, and punched him as hard as he could in the jaw. Tanner hadn't thought through what he would do if Jim got up, and luckily, he didn't have to deal with that. With the impact of the fall and the uppercut to the jaw, Jim was out cold.

Got to get out of here.

Tanner hadn't bought them much time. Jim would come back around, and the police had surely found his mother's car in the ditch. The place would soon be crawling with cops. He sprinted to Riley's stables, where his friends had a horse ready for him.

"Hope ol' Mr. Riley doesn't mind if we borrow these for a few days," Tanner said as he hopped on.

Donald signaled for the others to follow. He had lots of experience riding horses in the area, and although they came across a cell phone tower and the occasional house that hadn't been there when Mr. Carlton rode in the early 1800s, he was able to discreetly guide them out of town in the darkness.

"I think we made it!" Tanner said as he exhaled loudly.

"Just one small problem," Andrew said. "How are we going to get back to the underworld? We'll never be able to go near Mammoth Cave again."

A deafening silence enveloped the group.

CHAPTER 17

PECULIAR WATERS

(HOKOLESQUA)

"Now that you received guidance from your spirit animal . . ." The Indian chief paused before continuing. "You did receive guidance, correct?"

"Yes."

"Good. Now, tell Tecumseh about the disappearance of your mother and sister. I'll do what I can to help."

Hokolesqua described how his younger brother had disturbed a sacred burial site and how, not many days after, his mother was abducted. He explained how his father was convinced the human-eating horned serpent Kinepikwa had dragged his mother and her abductor into the depths of a river in a massive cave.

"And where is your father?"

"I left my homeland without telling my father."

"Why wouldn't you tell your father you were coming? The path from your land to my wigwam is not easy one. Why would you risk traveling it alone?"

"My father is a stubborn man. I don't believe Kinepikwa killed my mother. But my father will not listen. Now my sister is gone too. She told my father many times she would learn the truth for herself."

"Did your father actually see Kinepikwa?" Tecumseh asked.

"No."

"And why was your father so sure Mayata was killed by Kinepikwa if he never saw this beast?"

"My father said he witnessed the captor carry Mayata into the stream and then they disappeared. He went to the water's edge to kill the monster, but there was nothing."

A small smile began to form on the great chief's lips.

"Why would you smile?" Hokolesqua said, obviously angered. "My mother and sister may have been killed."

"Your grandparents must have been moved by the Great Spirit when they named your mother." Tecumseh replied. "Did you know that her name, Mayataakamhsi, means 'one who reclines in peculiar waters'?"

"No. But I still don't understand why you would smile."

"The reason I smile is because I don't believe your mother *has* been killed . . . *or* your sister. I shall teach you about peculiar waters. Did anyone ever tell you the legend of the Water Panther?"

Hokolesqua's heart stood still as he thought about his spirit animal. He paid extra attention as Tecumseh recounted the legend.

"For now, return to your wigwam," Tecumseh said. "I will contact the goddess of sunrise. She will help you fulfill your destiny."

CHAPTER 18

AN ALTERNATE ENTRANCE

(TANNER)

"We need to find an internet café or something," Tanner said, "so we can find another entrance to Inner Earth."

"There are other entrances?" Mick asked.

"According to the map of Agartha I found on the internet," Tanner replied, "there are lots of entrances. Only trouble is, I think the closest one is in the Grand Canyon."

"That's the closest?" Andrew asked. "That's clear across the country. How are you thinking we're going to get there? 'Cause I'm not riding a horse from Kentucky to Arizona."

"Sheesh," Tanner replied. "Give me a chance to think about it. We've been running for our lives for hours now. I haven't had a chance to think about anything other than survival."

"This is the worst," Mick said.

"Don't worry," Tanner replied, trying to calm his every-*i*-dotted, every-*t*-crossed friend. "We'll figure it out. Just give me a minute."

"We're going to need some cash," Andrew said. "We can use my debit card, but I think the max I can get is $800 per day."

"As soon as we use your card, they'll be able to track us to whatever ATM we use," Mick said.

"True," Andrew replied. "We'll need to quickly distance ourselves from the ATM. If we can get all the way to Arizona on $800, we might be able to get to Inner Earth before anyone can find us."

"So where do we make this strategic ATM withdrawal?" Mick asked.

"Based on where Jim saw us, everyone will think we're going either north or west," Andrew said. "So let's use an ATM east of town, then head south to Bowling Green. We'll catch a bus from there to Phoenix."

"That'd be great if we had faster transportation," Tanner replied. "I say we ride all night to Bowling Green, use an ATM as far from the bus station as we can, then head for the station."

"Let's go back to my house," Mick said. "We can grab some supplies, look up the bus schedule, and buy our tickets in advance."

Tanner looked at Mick, then shook his head and rolled his eyes.

"You think we can buy four tickets for under $800?" Andrew asked.

"We'll just go as far as the $800 will take us," Tanner replied.

Everyone agreed, and they set off for Bowling Green.

❖ ❖ ❖

"Its $175 each," Donald said when he returned from the counter holding up four tickets. "And the bus leaves in five minutes."

"Did you get a receipt?" Mick asked.

"Stop sweating all the details," Tanner replied.

"You might want to start sweating them," Mick said. "You are a fugitive, you know."

"But why do we need a stupid receipt?"

"You never know," Mick replied.

"That leaves us with $100," Andrew said, looking at the five twenty-dollar bills Donald handed him.

"I hope we don't get hungry," Tanner said.

"And what about a place to stay once we get to Phoenix?" Andrew asked.

"It's gonna have to be a pretty seedy hotel for under $100 in a big city like that."

"We might be sleeping on the street," Andrew said.

"Well, it is what it is," Tanner said as they boarded the bus. "We'll just have to make it work."

The four of them walked down the aisle and sat about three-quarters of the way back.

Andrew sat next to a window and was looking out when he began to jab Tanner in the ribs with his elbow without breaking his gaze.

"Someone just snuck into the luggage hold underneath the bus."

"That's cool," Tanner replied.

"Cool? What are you talking about?" Andrew aggressively whispered. "What if someone's following us?"

"It's just a stowaway," Tanner replied. "Anyone following us is going to put us in handcuffs. You think the police are going to hide in the cargo hold so they can follow us to Arizona and then arrest us?"

"Still, I don't like it."

"You're just paranoid."

"Someone should know about this." Andrew stood up and tried to step past Tanner.

Tanner grabbed his arm and yanked him back into his seat.

"What are you doing?" Tanner whispered angrily. "We can't be drawing attention to ourselves. Just stop worrying. I'm sure people stowaway on these things all the time."

Andrew continued to stare out the window until the bus pulled out of the station.

It wasn't long before Tanner's friends were fast asleep, and he wasn't far behind.

❖ ❖ ❖

They arrived in Phoenix a few days later, exhausted and hungry. The morning sun was creating spectacular colors along the desert landscape.

Donald, being the least likely to be recognized, asked the man at the ticket counter for directions to the nearest library, which was only about a mile away. They stopped for a cheap fast-food breakfast to share on the way. Once they entered, Tanner and his two friends parked themselves in front of the computers and began researching the Grand Canyon entrance to the underworld while Donald kept an eye out for anyone who might discover their identity.

"What are you doing?" Tanner asked Mick when he saw her about to log in to the Edmonson County Middle School website.

"Just checking to see if I have any assignments due," she replied matter-of-factly.

"What are you thinking? We can't sit around and wait for you to make sure your homework is complete. The rest of us are trying to save a bunch of lives here."

Tanner was able to get Mick on task, and a few minutes later she had something.

"Is this the story you were talking about?"

Tanner scanned the web page. "Yep. That's the one."

"I don't see anything that would help us figure out exactly where the entrance is, though," Mick said.

"We've got to find something precise," Andrew said adamantly as he rolled his chair up next to Mick. "We could wander the Grand Canyon for decades and never find the entrance."

"I agree," Tanner replied. "We've got to see if we can pinpoint the entrance."

"All this website says is that some Hopi kid and his friend rode for a long time before they got to the entrance," Mick said.

"We could find some Hopis and see if they'll give us more details about the story," Andrew said.

"I'd rather not talk to anyone if we can help it," Tanner replied.

"I'm not sure we *can* do this by ourselves," Andrew said. "It would be worth a try to talk to them, and I doubt they'll turn us over to the authorities."

"Let's see what else we can find first," Tanner said, leaning over Mick's shoulder and pointing to a name on the screen. "Andrew, see what you can find about the Hopi kid's friend Hank Krastman."

"Mick," he continued, pointing farther down the page, "search this secret cave, Pupovi. I'll look for stuff about Kopavi, the Hopi kid."

The three went to work on their respective assignments.

"Look at this." Tanner had found a possible lead.

"What is it?" Andrew asked.

"Kopavi's ancestor Jacob Waltz, a Dutchman, was shown an entrance by the Pima Indians so he could exchange salt, which was supposedly rare in the interior, for gold. That's how the legend of the Lost Dutchman's Mine started."

"Okay, but does it say where the entrance is?"

"No, but I think we might be able to find it."

"Why do you say that?" Mick asked.

"Some old guy named Adolph Ruth got his hands on a map to the mine and went looking for it."

"Did he find it?" Mick asked.

"Well, he never returned," Tanner said.

"He must have found it, then," Andrew said.

"Actually, no one knows. They found his skull with a couple of bullet holes in it somewhere in the Superstition Mountains."

"Whoa," Andrew said. "Why was he murdered?"

"For the map," Tanner replied. "When they found his skull, a bunch of his belongings were close by, but the map was missing."

"You really think someone killed him for a map?" Mick asked.

"A lot of people would kill for a map to a bunch of gold," Tanner said.

"I don't like where this is heading," Andrew exclaimed.

"What are you talking about?" Tanner replied.

"I know when you're selling us on something. And let me make one thing perfectly clear. I don't want to go looking for a map a guy already took a couple bullets to the head for."

"Come on. Where's your sense of adventure?" Tanner said grinning while jabbing Andrew in the gut. He continued. "The old man must have known someone was after him, because they found key details from the map on a folded note hidden in his checkbook. If we can get our hands on that note, we'll be on our way back to the underworld."

"What part of what I said wasn't clear?" Andrew asked. "I'm not interested in taking a couple bullets to the head."

"Get real, Andrew. That was back in the 1930s."

Tanner wasn't telling Andrew that according to what he was reading, disappearances and strange things related to those who went in search of the mine had continued even up to the present day.

"We don't even know the map was accurate," Andrew responded. "It may have been bogus, a decoy."

"You think someone would go as far as shooting Mr. Ruth for a bogus map?"

"Sure. If the murderer didn't know it was bogus. He might have shot Mr. Ruth and found out later it was a fraud."

"Maybe you're right, but listen," Tanner said, not ready to give up. "In the 1940s, the headless remains of another explorer were found in the Superstition Mountains. He had also gone in search of the Lost Dutchman's Mine."

"I hope you're not thinking that additional story is going to give me extra incentive to go there," Andrew said. "Do you really think you're going to get us to go into a remote mountain area looking for something that got one guy shot and another decapitated?"

"Look, I read some other version of the story that said Ruth wasn't shot. He was an old man. He probably just died of natural causes."

"Now you're saying he wasn't killed because he knew how to get to the underworld?"

Andrew had Tanner trapped. Tanner could continue his argument that the men were killed because they knew how to get to the gold, in which case neither he nor Mick would want to take that kind of risk, or he could downplay the reason for their deaths and by so doing downplay the idea that there was anything worth going in search of. He decided to try to convince them the entrance did exist and they would have to overcome their fears to find it.

"I'm sure the entrance exists!" Tanner said, refraining from talking about the excerpt from the book *Thunder God's Gold* he read, about another explorer who narrowly escaped a mysterious sniper nicknamed Mr. X.

"There are others who went looking for the mine and were never found." Tanner continued. "They must have made it."

"Unless they were killed too," Andrew replied.

"Guys, come on," Tanner said. "We promised we would help Marcus find Livia. We've got to find her and talk some sense into Marina!"

"That's the best argument you've come up with yet," Andrew said. "But we need something more definite about where the entrance is."

"The note from Ruth's checkbook was found," Tanner said. "We just have to get our hands on it."

"Sorry to change the subject," Mick said. "But while we're here, we should see if we can find anything that might help us find Livia once we get to Rome."

"What do you mean?" Andrew asked

"Well, we've got the advantage of having access to the history of the Roman Empire," Mick said.

"And you think that will help us find Livia?" Tanner asked.

"It might. We need to search for anything connected to the name Livia, or anyone associated with her—like Marcus, Anastasia, and Marina—from roughly the same time period."

"Makes sense," Tanner said. "I'll see if I can figure out where we can get our hands on Ruth's note, and the two of you see if you can find anything that will help us find Livia."

The three Brownsvillians continued to work on their searches.

"Hey, I found something," Andrew said. "North of the Circus Maximus is the church of Saint Anastasia. Apparently it was named after a martyr named Anastasia."

"That's exactly the type of stuff we're looking for," Mick replied. "The church could have been named after our friend."

"Methoataske was deserving of a church being named after her," Donald said referring to Anastasia by the Indian name she had when he first met her.

"The original building on the site was destroyed in the Great Fire during Nero's reign."

"Hmmm," Mick said. "It was built after her death. Maybe it *was* named after her."

"Here's another interesting tidbit," Andrew said as he continued to scan the page. "Many believe that the cave where Romulus and Remus were raised by the she-wolf is under the church."

"You don't think maybe . . ." Andrew started, but Tanner excitedly interrupted.

"That's got to be where Livia is. Marcus and Anastasia taught her a lot about the history of Rome. I bet Livia figured if Romulus and Remus were protected in that cave, she would be too."

CHAPTER 19

A Normal Life

(Mick)

"We've got to get to the Superstition Mountain Museum," Tanner said. "According to what I just found, they have a copy of Adolph Ruth's note."

After reviewing his discovery, Andrew and Mick concurred.

Donald asked the librarian for directions, and the four began the three-mile walk to the museum.

"If they really do have the note, we're in," Tanner said excitedly as they walked in the hot Arizona sun.

"If we can make it that far," Andrew replied as he wiped the sweat off his brow. "I think we should just hitchhike. I mean, a couple of miles in the hottest part of the day?"

"We can't hitchhike," Tanner said. "We're fugitives."

"No one would recognize us this far away," Andrew replied.

"We can't risk it."

❖ ❖ ❖

"Apache Junction," Tanner said as they trudged past a sign at the city limits. "Finally."

The sun was getting low in the sky. "Let's stop at the first hotel we see and get some sleep. We've got a big day ahead."

"I'm all for that," Andrew replied. "I haven't had a decent night's sleep in days."

"How much money do we have left?" Mick asked.

"About ninety-five dollars," Andrew replied.

"Enough for a cheap hotel, a shared breakfast, and some food to take with us into the mountains," Mick said. "If we don't find the entrance soon, we're going to need to stop and get more money."

"We better hope we can find it then, 'cause the second we use that card again, the whole country will know where we are," Andrew replied.

"We're going to find it. Don't worry," Tanner said. "I've got a good feeling about this whole thing."

"Adolph Ruth probably did too, before he took the bullets to the head," Andrew replied.

They found a small hotel, checked in, and moments later Donald was strewn across the bed snoring.

"Psst. Mick. You awake?" Andrew asked.

"Yeah," Mick said. "Pretty hard to sleep with that racket. What's up?"

"This is so stupid to go through all of this," Andrew said, looking up from the floor to where Mick was lying on top of the covers. "It was one thing when you were missing. You're our best friend, but we're about to risk our lives for Marcus and his kids. We barely even know them."

"Does that make their lives worth less than mine?" Mick asked.

"No, I know. But, seriously, we could die in the process."

"Don't forget about helping overthrow Nero as well. All of Christianity might be at stake. I really don't think he's going to have a change of heart and stop the persecutions."

"I guess you're right."

"Plus, for whatever reason, I think we're destined to do this."

"What does that really mean? What if we're destined to do it and we decide not to?"

"I don't know, maybe someone else is destined to be our back-up if we fail, or maybe the history of the world will change if we don't fulfill our mission. I haven't really figured out how it all fits together."

"Do you think we'll ever have a normal life again?"

"Not a chance," Mick replied. "Especially for you and Tanner. You're fugitives, and the tough thing is, none of us can ever come clean with the truth."

"That's true. I hope we survive tomorrow."

"I hear you," Mick said. "But I don't think all this information has just fallen into our laps by chance. I think it really *is* our destiny." She thought about how the gods of Olympus had told her she had an important mission to fulfill.

"I hope you're right," Andrew continued. "Do you think we'll ever see our families again?"

"Maybe eventually," Mick replied. "But it'll be a long time before you'll be able to go near Brownsville. Plus, what would we tell people if we did go back?"

"Maybe our families can come to us. What if we were able to get a message to them and they could meet us somewhere?"

"Someone's probably tracking them, knowing they'll make contact with us."

"We're prisoners," Andrew replied. "Completely trapped. And the frustrating thing is we've done nothing wrong."

"Think of all the good we've done, though." Tanner inserted himself into the conversation.

"I didn't know you were awake," Mick said.

"Yeah, too much to think about. Anyway, think about what we've done."

"Like what?" Andrew asked.

"Like rescuing Mick, for starters."

"But we also created Decimus," Andrew added.

"Yeah, but obviously he didn't have any effect on history. Everything was normal when we returned to the present."

"Wait, who's Decimus?" Mick asked.

"No one," Tanner replied quickly.

"All right, out with it. I'm not stupid. Who is Decimus?"

"No one," Tanner said again.

"Andrew?" Mick swiveled and said glaringly. She knew Andrew couldn't hold up under her evil eye.

"Just someone we met in Rome."

"So what did you mean when you said 'We created Decimus'? There's something you aren't telling me."

"All right, all right. I'll tell you," Andrew said. "But it's nothing to worry about, all right?"

"I'll be the judge of that," Mick answered, confident it would be something to worry about.

"When we first arrived in Rome, we crashed for the night near the Tiber River. We woke up to some commotion on the bridge. Nero and one of his men stabbed a guy and threw him into the river."

"You actually saw Nero stab someone?"

"Yeah, it was a pretty scary introduction to the city," Tanner said.

"So then what happened?" Mick asked.

"Well, we jumped in and dragged him to shore," Tanner said.

"Weren't you afraid Nero would do the same to you?"

"Are you kidding?" Andrew said. "I was scared spitless. Tanner literally had to drag me into the water. Anyway, when we got Decimus to shore, we couldn't get the bleeding to stop. So

Brilliant over there decided to pour water from the Acheron into his wound to try to heal him."

"He was dying," Tanner inserted. "We had no choice."

"But the Acheron, isn't that water poisonous?" Mick asked. "Doesn't it dissolve things?"

"Yeah, but the River Styx flows into Acheron," Andrew replied. "And water from the Styx has the power to make things invincible."

"We had to try something," Tanner said.

"Not only did the water completely heal the wound, it formed some kind of magical shell around the man before it disappeared," Andrew said.

"So you're saying you think you made him invincible?"

"We're not sure," Tanner said.

"Well, at least if you did, he owes you something for saving his life."

"I don't think he feels that way," Andrew said. "He was super anti-Christian, so when he found out about our cause, he turned on us."

"What ever happened to him?" Mick asked.

"We lost track. He was one of the legionnaires who was supposed to lead you and Andrew from prison to your deaths."

"Didn't Donald convince all of them to join our cause?" Mick asked.

"Originally they all joined with us, but then Decimus defected," Tanner replied.

"I'm 95 percent sure it was Decimus who tried to kill you that night in the house church of Sebastian," Andrew said.

"But why would he want to kill me?" Mick asked.

"That was the same night he nearly killed Donald," Tanner added. "Remember how he told us he chased Decimus down when he saw him fleeing Sebastian's?"

"Wait, did you say he was a legionnaire?" Mick asked Andrew.

"Yeah, why do you say it like that?" Andrew said.

"Oh, nothing."

"Hey, we told you who Decimus was. You can't go all secretive on us now," Tanner said.

"Well, my mom told me the day we returned to Brownsville that the police had a confrontation with someone dressed in Roman armor. Since I was wearing a tunic, they assumed there was a connection between the two of us. They asked me a lot of questions about him, but I had no idea who he was."

"Yeah, I actually saw something on TV about that," Tanner added.

"You don't think Decimus followed us, do you?" Andrew said, looking fearfully at Tanner.

"No," Tanner replied. Mick could sense the lack of conviction in his voice.

"I'm the one who should be worried here," Mick said. "It was me he tried to kill, after all."

"It couldn't have been him that followed us," Andrew said. "He wasn't in the golden orb when we flew from Olympus to the River Lethe."

"Hmmm," Mick said.

"I don't like the sound of that," Tanner said. "What are you thinking, Mick?"

"I kept a journal with all the details about my trip through Inner Earth. It was stolen the night I was nearly killed at Sebastian's."

"You don't think Decimus stole it, do you?" Tanner asked.

"Maybe you just misplaced it," Andrew said.

"No, after I was rescued from prison, I went to Priscilla's, where I had been staying, and retrieved that journal and Donald Carlton's. After that, I kept them in my backpack. It went missing that night for sure."

"It had to be Decimus," Andrew said.

"Why didn't you say anything?" Tanner asked.

"I knew you guys would be worried. That kind of information in the wrong hands would not be a good thing."

"Yeah, especially in the hands of an invincible enemy," Tanner said angrily.

"I just kept hoping it would turn up."

"This is not good," Tanner said.

"Well, I guess we've got one more item for our to-do list—find Decimus and stop him," Mick said.

Andrew agreed. "If an invincible man has full access to the Cathedral of Time, the potential impact to world history is mind boggling."

"Maybe it was just Donald they saw the day we returned," Andrew said. "After all, we know *he* came back to Brownsville."

"We'll ask in the morning," Mick said. "For now let's try to get some sleep. We've got a lot of hiking to do tomorrow."

Though Mick hoped it was just Donald who'd followed them from Rome, the pit in her stomach was telling her something different.

CHAPTER 20

INVINCIBLE?

(DECIMUS)

"Invincible?" Decimus said quietly as a grin spread across his face. He had stowed away in the cargo hold of the bus, followed the Brownsvillians to the hotel, and had been listening to the three teenagers through a cup he'd placed against the wall of the hotel room. "I'm invincible?"

Decimus had been surprised at his own strength ever since the confrontation with Donald, when he'd defected from the mutinous group in Rome. But hearing he was invincible started a whole new series of thoughts in his head.

"I could rule the world. Be more powerful than Alexander the Great or Caesar himself."

He continued to listen as the trio from Brownsville discussed the situation.

". . . find Decimus and stop him," he heard Tanner say.

Good luck stopping me, Decimus thought. *You seem to be forgetting I'm invincible. No need to worry about those kids anymore. I've got bigger fish to fry,* Decimus thought. *I just need to get back to Rome, where before long it will be Emperor Decimus.*

He opened the door of the hotel room and savored the fresh air. He inhaled like he never had before. His chest inflated as he looked out over everything he saw with a whole new perspective. Anxious to begin this new life, he quickly ran down the stairs to the parking lot. *Wait,* he thought. *I have no idea how to get back to the underworld. I guess I'll need to follow those kids a bit longer. Until they lead me to the entrance. Then ...*

He stood up straighter as he imagined himself in royal robes with a scepter in hand.

CHAPTER 21

WATER PANTHER

(HOKOLESQUA)

"Hokolesqua!" Nemhsi yelled as she ran to hug him when he entered their family wigwam.

"Where have you been?"

"No time to explain, little sister. I'm going to search for Methoataske and Mother."

"What?" Nemhsi replied. "But Father said they were eaten by the horned serpent Kinepikwa!"

"Hold on while I explain," he said as he sat down. "Listen well."

Nemhsi sat, looking attentively at her brother.

"When Mother disappeared, Methoataske and Father argued many nights about where she went. Methoataske never believed Kinepikwa ate Mother and the evil giant who kidnapped her."

"Yes, I remember how angry they were at each other," Nemhsi said.

"When Methoataske disappeared, I knew she had gone to find Mother. I decided to find answers for myself."

"And did you?"

"Yes. Two moons ago, I decided to travel to the northern lands. I didn't tell anyone because I was afraid Father would try to stop me."

"Why did you leave?" Nemhsi asked.

"I went in search of Tecumseh."

"Tecumseh? Did you actually meet the great chief?" Nemhsi asked enthusiastically.

"Yes."

"Wow! What was it like?"

"Tecumseh is a great warrior, but he's a better man. At first I was worried that the great leader would not take the time to meet with me, but Tecumseh is very generous."

"So you were able to speak with the chief?"

"Yes."

"Why did you want to meet with him?"

"I wanted to ask him about Kinepikwa and to tell him about Mother and Methoataske. I was hoping Tecumseh would share his great wisdom."

"And?" Nemhsi asked. "Does he think Methoataske and Mother were killed by Kinepikwa?"

"No."

"Then he thinks they're still alive?" Nemhsi asked enthusiastically.

"Yes. But he believes they're in grave danger. I must hurry."

"Where does he think they are?"

"That's the interesting part. You must take an oath to never tell anyone as long as you live."

"Tell me, tell me!" Nemhsi said. "I promise."

"Tecumseh's name means–"

Nemhsi interrupted. "It means 'panther passing across' or 'shooting star.'"

"Yes, but do you know how he got his name?"

"No."

"Tecumseh explained it to me as we sat by the fire."

"Please tell me." Nemhsi was obsessed with the great warrior.

"When Tecumseh was a young brave, he participated in raids near here. One night he awoke late. He gazed at the stars and thought about the wonders of heaven and earth. Tecumseh saw a shooting star. He took it as sign from the Great Spirit that there was an important work for him to do. While Tecumseh thought about the star, he saw Water Panther."

"He really saw Water Panther?"

"Yes."

"Did he say what he looked like?"

"Just like the legends say. A mix of a cougar and a dragon. Tail of copper, able to grab things with his tail. Horns and a saw-toothed back."

"What did Tecumseh do? Was he scared?"

"No. He saw the Water Panther as another sign. The panther stared at Tecumseh, and then turned its head a few times as if it were asking him to follow. Tecumseh grabbed a spear and followed the panther."

"What happened?" Nemhsi asked, moving to the edge of the stump she sat on, eyes as big as the full moon.

"The panther went into a great cave, and Tecumseh followed. After a long walk, the panther jumped into a stream. Tecumseh thought this was strange since cats hate water. When Tecumseh looked where the Panther had entered, the great cat was gone. Tecumseh couldn't see the animal anywhere. He was convinced the Great Spirit was responsible because the animal completely disappeared."

"So what happened?"

"The cat suddenly reappeared in the water, and Tecumseh felt like the Great Spirit wanted him to follow the cat into the water."

"Did he go?"

"When the great cat disappeared again, Tecumseh followed."

"And what happened?" Nemhsi asked, listening with great anticipation.

"Tecumseh said when he emerged from the water, he was in a beautiful meadow. He was no longer in the cave. The panther continued to lead Tecumseh around the mysterious land and finally back into the cave."

"So his name became Shooting Star, Panther Passing Across because he saw the shooting star and then the Water Panther helped him pass across from the cave into the meadow underneath," Nemhsi surmised.

"Yes."

"Did he ever go back to this mysterious land?" Nemhsi asked but interrupted herself before Hokolesqua could answer. "Wait. Do you think it's the same cave where Mother disappeared?" Nemhsi looked at Hokolesqua, questioning.

"Yes."

"Then you think Mother might be alive in the mysterious meadow?"

"Yes, and Methoataske too."

"So is that where you're going?"

"Yes!"

"Then I'm coming too," Nemhsi said enthusiastically.

"Tecumseh said we must wait for the goddess of sunrise to take us there. We must be ready when she comes."

CHAPTER 22

THE TABLOID

(MICK)

The group left the hotel the next morning and made their way into the diner.

"Four?" the hostess asked as she approached.

"Yes," Mick replied. "And can we have a booth?" She wanted to keep the number of people who could get a good look at them to a minimum.

"Where's Tanner?" Mick asked as they sat down.

"Distracted by something, I'm sure," Andrew replied.

"Hey, look at this!" Tanner whispered as he slid onto the bench a few minutes later. He had a tabloid in his hands. "We made the cover."

"Shhhh." Andrew looked around to see if anyone had overheard.

"Let me see that." Mick grabbed the tabloid.

She read the headline. *Donald Carlton Tablet Complete Fraud.* "What?" The anger was thick in her voice. "How can they say that?"

"No idea," Tanner replied. "If you wouldn't have ripped it away from me, I might have been able to answer."

Mick wasn't listening. She was rifling through the pages trying to find the article.

> *Forensic work on the mysterious tablet found with Makayla Brown when she reappeared*

after having been missing for over a month proved it to be a fraud. After scientific analysis, it turns out the wax was etched less than a month ago, obviously debunking the idea it could have been written by Donald Carlton, as claimed.

Authorities are still searching for Makayla, who police believe was kidnapped by the same man who kidnapped Tanner Hunter and Andrew Wheelwright from the Brownsville courthouse.

Investigators have learned Makayla is a descendant of Mr. Carlton, and speculation is running rampant in Brownsville that the prominent Brown family, anxious to disavow its connection with the infamous murderer, concocted the whole scheme in an attempt to clear Mr. Carlton's name.

"You have got to be kidding me!" Mick said as Andrew scowled and motioned for her to be quiet.

"I went through all that, and they still think you were the murderer?" Mick said, looking at Mr. Carlton.

"It's fine," he replied. "I know who I am. People can say whatever they want."

"And now not only Brownsville but the whole country thinks I'm the descendant of a murderer," Mick replied. "And that I made up the whole tablet thing to clear you. I should have just left well enough alone."

"It doesn't matter," Tanner replied. "You know the truth, and that's all that matters. You'll always be the one in control of your own destiny."

"Still, it's kind of embarrassing," Mick replied

"Maybe we can find the actual murderers," Donald said, "and the weapon."

"But the murders happened over two hundred years ago. They'd be dead," Andrew responded

"You're forgetting something. *I* disappeared over two hundred years ago, and I'm still around."

"You're not saying you think they used the Cathedral of Time, are you?" Andrew asked. "'Cause having a couple of murderers popping in and out of history could be . . . well, catastrophic."

Mick grimaced thinking about the impact both Decimus and the Brownsville Bank robbers could have on the space-time continuum.

"I hope not," Donald replied. "But I don't think so. I think they're probably just running loose somewhere in Inner Earth. People live to be hundreds of years old there."

"How is that possible?" Tanner asked.

"There aren't any ultraviolet rays," Andrew said matter-of-factly.

"The murderers probably just returned to the Surface," Tanner said. "They had no reason to stay in Inner Earth."

"Other than the fact they committed three murders on the Surface?" Andrew said snidely.

"Yeah, I guess there's that," Tanner said.

"If the Rule of the Fates is a real thing," Donald said, "then they're going to be stuck in the underworld forever, because Methoataske and I intentionally led them far enough in that they would have needed food from the underworld to survive."

"Smart move," Mick said, proud of her ancestor.

"Finish your bacon and let's go find them," Tanner said, looking at Andrew.

Once Andrew finished, the four of them left for the Superstition Mountain Museum.

When they arrived, Tanner rushed to the counter.

"We understand you have a copy of the note found in Adolph Ruth's checkbook when they discovered his body."

"That's correct," the woman behind the counter replied.

"Any chance we could take a look at it?" Tanner asked.

"If you buy a ticket to the museum."

"How much is it?" Tanner said after a brief pause.

"Eight dollars per person."

Tanner turned around and looked at his friends. "What do we do?"

"We just spent the last of the $800 on breakfast," Andrew replied.

"Then we've got to use your debit card again," Tanner said.

"Everyone will know where we are as soon as we use it," Andrew said, Tanner motioning anxiously at him to lower his voice. "And it's not like we're going to be able to get lost in a sea of humanity out here. We're talking about letting everyone in the world know we're in a small gift shop several miles outside of Phoenix with nothing but miles of wilderness in every direction."

"We've got to do it," Tanner said. "We've come this far."

"Tanner, we might as well just hand ourselves over to the authorities."

"We'll have a huge head start into the mountains," Tanner said. "We'll just have to watch out for choppers overhead. It's not like we haven't done that before."

"We'll probably have a bunch of bloodhounds trailing us too," Andrew said.

"We really don't have a choice," Tanner replied. "We're out of money. We're going to have to use your card today one way or another. Might as well be at the entrance to a massive wilderness."

"I think we're going to regret this," Andrew said.

"We better make it worthwhile," Mick said. "Grab some snacks and water bottles we can take on the trail with us."

Andrew handed Tanner his card, and they all braced themselves as Tanner swiped it.

"Okay," Tanner said as the woman handed him the receipt. "If you can just show us that note as quickly as possible. We're kind of in a hurry."

"I'd be happy to show it to you. Right this way."

The woman slowly walked toward the gated entrance to the museum and, after fiddling for some time to find the right key, unlocked it.

Mick wanted to give the woman a push. She looked like she had been retired for at least a couple decades and was humming as she sauntered toward the back of the museum. The four of them were all squirming anxiously as she seemed to stop at every display and dust it with the feather duster she had in her back pocket.

"Um, we're kind of in a hurry," Tanner reiterated.

"Yes, dear, I know," she replied sweetly. "I'm going just as fast as my little legs will carry me."

Tanner rolled his eyes.

Mick could imagine half a dozen police cars waiting for them when they exited the museum.

The woman pulled a small key out of her pocket as she neared a door in the back.

"Just one second," she said. "You wait right here. I'll be back in a jiffy."

Mick strained to see where the woman was going. There was a small staircase leading down.

"Oh, great. This could take forever," she said, looking desperately at Tanner.

"Andrew, you and Donald go stand watch by the front door. Someone needs to give us a heads-up if we need to slip out the back or something."

The two of them went back to the front entrance.

"Here it is," the woman said as she emerged from the doorway what seemed like an eternity later.

"Fantastic," Tanner said. "Can I just take a picture of it with my phone?"

"Sure," the elderly woman said as she reached for her duster to give the paper a swipe.

"Its fine," Tanner said as he attempted to take the picture between swipes but came up with picture after picture of the feather duster.

"I want you to be able to get a nice picture. Don't worry, my dear. And you shouldn't be in such a hurry. You young people need to slow down and enjoy life more. Always in a hurry, always in a hurry," she continued to mutter.

"All right, all right," Tanner said reaching for the note.

"Oh no, you mustn't touch it. This is delicate."

"Please just hold it steady."

The woman tried to hold it steady in her right hand, which she couldn't seem to stop from shaking. She grabbed her wrist with her left hand and slowed it down but apologized profusely as her hand still shook.

"That's going to have to be good enough," Tanner said as he took the picture.

"Thanks," Mick said as they turned to run for the entrance.

Just then they heard sirens.

"We're doomed."

Mick surveyed the room.

"Through that window over there," she said, pointing to a window behind the woman.

"Donald, Andrew! Over here!" she yelled.

The woman looked in astonishment as the four of them sprinted past her.

"Oh my," she said as they opened the window and started to climb out. "You can't do that," she said. There was a certain urgency in her voice even though it sounded like her blood pressure hadn't changed at all.

The sirens were growing louder as Donald finally made it through the window.

They sprinted through the desert.

"Maybe we should just stay and face the consequences," Andrew said breathlessly.

"What are you talking about?"

"While Donald and I were waiting out front, I was looking at one of the books in the gift shop, and it said something about the Superstition Mountains being home to the largest population of Mojave green rattlesnakes in the world, the most potent rattlers in existence."

CHAPTER 23

THE SUPERSTITION MOUNTAINS

(TANNER)

"I really think we should find a different entrance," Andrew said once more as they neared a trailhead into the Superstition Mountains. "This place is creepy. In fact, juvenile detention is actually sounding pretty good right now."

"It's all in your head," Tanner replied.

"That's exactly what I'm afraid of—a couple bullets in my head."

"Stop with the bullets already," Mick replied.

"Did you happen to notice the name of the saloon back in town?" Tanner asked.

"No. What was it?" Andrew asked.

"Mammoth Saloon."

"You're not thinking . . ." Andrew said.

Tanner interrupted. "Of course. It's obvious. Mammoth Cave was named for the mammoths living in the underworld beneath it. There's no way Mammoth Saloon just happened to be named that. What are the odds?"

"I've got to hand it to you, Tanner," Mick said.

"Come on, guys," Andrew replied. "It's just because it was such a big saloon. You're reading too much into it."

"Is that a chopper?" Tanner asked as he froze. "Find cover."

"Over there," Andrew said, pointing to a small rock outcropping about fifteen feet away.

They scrambled for the shadows of the outcropping as the sound of the chopper blades cutting through the dry Arizona air grew louder and louder.

"Don't move," Andrew shouted above the noise. The chopper flew almost directly overhead and then disappeared into the distance.

"Let's stay here and rest for a bit," Andrew said.

"We can't," Tanner replied. "This is the most critical time. The farther away we get from the museum, the better chance we have of not being found."

Reluctantly, Andrew agreed, and they continued their flight into the mountains.

It was late in the afternoon when Tanner finally agreed to a short rest in the shade of a cluster of cacti.

"Let's take a look at Ruth's note," Mick said.

Tanner pulled out his phone, and Andrew and Mick huddled around it.

"I'm not very good at reading old handwriting," Andrew said as Tanner swiped through photo after photo of the museum guide's feather duster until he found the note. "Especially as blurry as this is. Couldn't you take a better picture than that?

"The lady couldn't keep her hands still."

"I can read it," Mick said.

"Tell us what it says," Tanner said.

"Okay," Mick replied.

> *It lies within _____ square _____ else where the diameter is _____ about five miles and whose center is marked by weaver's needle*

about 2500 feet high—among a confusion of lesser peaks and mountain masses of basaltic rock. The first gorge on the south side from the west end of the range.

They found a monumental trail which led them northward over a lofty ridge, thence downward past Sombre Butte into a long canyon running north and finally to a tributary canyon wooded with a continuous thicket of scrub oak.

Veni, Vidi

"Let me see that," Donald's previous lack of interest changed in an instant.

"Veni, Vidi?" he asked.

"What's that?" Tanner asked.

"It's part of a phrase Julius Caesar made famous," Donald replied. "The full phrase is actually '*Veni, vidi, vici.*' It means 'I came, I saw, I conquered.'"

"So Ruth was saying he came, he saw?" Andrew said.

"Sounds like it," Donald replied.

"He must have found the mine," Mick said.

"Why do you think he used a Roman phrase?" Tanner asked. "Do you think he went to Ancient Rome like we did?"

"Interesting thought," Andrew said. "Regardless, we need to figure out what the heck the rest of the note means."

"It sounds like the entrance is near Weaver's Needle and Sombre Butte—wherever that is," Mick said.

"We should have grabbed a map of this place before we left the museum," Tanner said.

"There wasn't time," Mick replied.

Slowly, with a big grin on his face, Andrew reached for his back pocket and pulled out a map.

"Where did you get that?" Tanner asked.

"I grabbed it while Donald and I were waiting for you in the gift shop—thought it might come in handy."

Tanner shoved Andrew a couple of times in the chest.

"You know, sometimes you really surprise me," he said, shaking his head while smiling broadly. "Let's see that thing. Is Weaver's Needle on it?"

Andrew was quickly scanning the landmarks on the map.

"There it is, right there," he replied.

"Looks like about ten miles," Mick said after measuring the distance with her finger. "Almost straight east."

They got their bearings and charted a course for Weaver's Needle.

Several hours later, they arrived.

"Now we just need to find this canyon of scrub oak Ruth was talking about," Tanner said.

"The note says it's over a lofty ridge," Andrew said. "Maybe that one over there."

The small group was restless, famished, and scorched from the desert sun. They found a canyon of scrub oak almost an hour from Weaver's Needle and explored it until the sun was about to go down, but found nothing. There had been a few choppers flying overhead, but each time, the group was able to hide in the dense scrub oak.

"Let's camp over there tonight," Donald said, pointing to the clearing between the scrub-oak canyon and Weaver's Needle. "Tomorrow we'll work our way back to town."

"I can't believe we haven't found the entrance," Tanner said. "Everything the note said was exactly where it was supposed to be, but no entrance."

"Ruth's map was a hoax," Andrew said. "This whole thing has been a giant waste of time." He threw the map of the Superstition Mountains on the ground and stomped on it a few times. Mick picked it up, dusted it off, and began reviewing it.

"Actually, we never found the Sombre Butte place he mentioned," Mick said.

"I couldn't find anything about it on the map," Andrew said.

"This is interesting," Mick said. "On the back of the map it says another name for Weaver's Needle is El Sombrero. It was called that because it resembled a sombrero, which provides protection to the wearer from the hot desert sun. Do you think that's a reference to Weaver's Needle providing protection to those who live underneath it?"

"It all adds up to me," Tanner said.

"You never were very good at math, though," Andrew razzed.

Tanner stuck out his tongue slightly and wagged his head in a mocking fashion.

I think we've been looking in the wrong place," Tanner said. "The beginning of the note said it was within a five-mile diameter of Weaver's Needle. We got distracted by the scrub-oak stuff at the end of the note. Let's spend the morning tomorrow searching right around Weaver's Needle. If we don't find the entrance in the morning, we're going to have to head back to Apache Junction. We're out of water."

The four trekked back to Weaver's Needle.

"Let's build a fire and get settled for the night," Andrew said as they neared the base of the formation. "Tomorrow we'll scour the area for an entrance."

The group busied themselves preparing a place to sleep, and then Donald went to work getting a fire started.

"So, where did you and Methoataske lead the bank robbers?" Mick asked.

"The mountains west of Delfi," Donald replied. "Really remote area. They would have been lucky to survive."

"You hid the money you wrestled away from the bank robbers in the loft of your old barn, right?"

"That's correct."

"Was that all of the money?"

"No, I only brought one bag on that trip."

"What happened to the other bag? There were two bags, right?"

"Yes. Well, after we lost the bank robbers, I decided we should hide the money in the underworld, but I thought it would be best to hide each bag in a different place. When I went back to Brownsville, I passed the bag I hid near the River Styx, so I grabbed it and took it back with me. I'm guessing the other bag is still where I hid it."

"Which is . . . ?"

"In Persephone's Garden."

"Andrew, isn't that close to where we ran into Harvey Wilkins?"

"What?"

"Didn't we run into Harvey Wilkins near the Garden of Persephone?"

"Yeah, I think it was around there somewhere."

"My dad and Wilkins must have found different bags," Mick mumbled. Tanner could tell she was in deep thought.

"What are you talking about?" Tanner asked.

"Nothing," Mick replied dismissively.

"Well, I'm going to call it a day," Andrew said. "We probably should all get some sleep–another long day ahead of us."

Everyone climbed under the small lean-tos they had created, and before long Tanner could hear Donald snoring loudly.

❖ ❖ ❖

"Get off me!" Andrew shouted, waking Tanner in the middle of the night. Tanner could see his friend wildly flailing his arms in all directions.

"Wh-What is it?" Tanner asked.

He grabbed his flashlight and shone it on his friend.

"Tarantulas. Thousands of Tarantulas." Mick winced as she sprang to her feet. A sea of spiders was headed their way.

Blanketed with hairy tarantulas scrambling across the terrain, the ground looked as if it were actually moving.

"Grab your stuff and let's get out of here," Tanner said.

"Where do we go?" Andrew said with a whimper as he shone his flashlight in every direction, long enough to see the ground was moving everywhere.

"Where did they come from?" Mick asked.

"Wherever it was, I'm going the opposite way," Andrew replied.

"We've got to go toward wherever they're coming from," Tanner said.

"What are you thinking?" Andrew replied. "Did you read the underworld is a breeding ground for tarantulas or something?"

"Zip it, Andrew," Tanner replied. "I think they're protecting something."

"Well, whatever it is, I don't want it."

"It's got to be the entrance."

"Like I said, I don't want it," Andrew replied. "Get away," he said as he violently shook his leg, trying to get one of the tarantulas off.

"The passageway in Mammoth Cave was so well hidden," Tanner said. "Maybe this one isn't as well hidden, so spiders have been put here to keep people away. If we push forward, we're going to find it."

"I guess it doesn't really matter which way we go," Andrew said as he spun around again, looking at the blanket of spiders.

"Looks like they're coming from over there," Mick said, pointing her flashlight toward the mountain wall.

"Let's head that way, then."

"Why are we doing this again?" Andrew asked.

"Come on, don't make me run through it," Tanner responded.

The group began to quickly tiptoe through the spiders as they made their way toward Weaver's Needle.

"Shhh," Mick said. "Do you hear that?"

"I was hoping I didn't," Andrew replied.

Everyone went silent, and Tanner's heart froze as he realized the sound Mick and Andrew heard was a very distinctive rattling.

"You've got to be kidding," Tanner said. "Really? Rattlesnakes?"

"It's worse than that," Andrew said.

"What's that supposed to mean?"

"Don't you remember the article I was telling you about? These are Mojave green rattlesnakes—the most deadly rattlesnake in the world. And we're a full day away from civilization."

"Just our luck," Tanner said.

"Any ideas?" Mick asked. "'Cause I respect your idea that the spiders and snakes might be protecting the entrance, but I'm not going to go walking through a field of poisonous rattlesnakes to get there."

They all looked around for another path toward the mountain face.

"Is that a campfire over there?" Donald asked.

"Someone's following us," Tanner replied.

"Great, we can go west and take a bullet to the head from whoever's following us, south into a sea of tarantulas, or north into a bed of rattlers. East and then home is sounding like a really good option about now."

"You don't think we could beat off those snakes if we had a couple of sticks?" Tanner asked.

"Maybe, but it would just take one to slip past and we'll be digging one of our graves," Andrew said.

"You're right."

Tanner was panning his phone's flashlight back and forth in an attempt to keep himself away from the snakes when he saw one strike at Mick's leg.

"Ahhhhhhh!" Mick cried out in pain.

"Oh, my gosh!" Tanner yelled. "Mick's been bitten."

Mick was kicking her leg back and forth trying to free herself.

"Don't move," Tanner said as he took a swing at the large serpent.

The snake slithered away, but the sound of hissing and rattling seemed to be swelling as fast as Mick's leg.

"Stay still. Don't move," Tanner said as he quickly swept Mick into his arms. "We've got to get her to a hospital."

"We're a full day's hike from civilization," Donald replied. "We'll never get there in time."

"Does anyone have service on their phone?" Andrew asked.

"Grab mine out of my pocket," Tanner replied.

Andrew pulled both Tanner's and Mick's phones out of their pockets. Tanner was devastated to see that both had large letters that clearly read "No Service."

"What about that campfire? Maybe they can get help for us," Tanner said.

"You said it was someone following us." Andrew quickly replied. "I don't want to get shot."

"We've got to take that chance," Tanner replied.

"How are you feeling?" Tanner asked Mick as they walked carefully toward the campfire.

"She's bleeding like crazy," Andrew interrupted as he tried to shoo away the spiders to create some space to set Mick down. "We've got to stop and get that under control."

"Put her down," Andrew said. "We need something to wrap the wound with."

Tanner ripped his T-shirt off and bent down, lifting Mick's leg so he could examine it more closely. He couldn't help but let out a small gasp as he looked at the bloody, swollen mess.

"Too bad we don't have any water from Acheron," Andrew said.

"Yeah," Tanner replied. "Have you got *any* water?"

"I think there's still a little left in my bottle."

Andrew detached his water bottle from his belt and gave it a quick shake.

"Yeah, there's still a little in here."

Tanner snatched it away and poured it over the bite, then started to scrub it.

"Oww!" Mick cried out.

"Sorry. Sorry," Tanner replied. "Just have to get this clean."

"He quickly wrapped the wound but could see the blood starting to soak through the T-shirt."

"Try to stay calm," he said, looking Mick in the eye.

"My body is starting to feel numb."

"That can't be good," Andrew said.

Tanner glared at him.

"You're going to be all right," he said as he turned back toward Mick. He could see the muscles in her face and neck beginning to twitch and her breathing becoming more difficult.

"Keep the spiders away," Tanner said "I'm going for help."

He quickly stood up and made a mad dash for the campfire in the distance.

He could hear Andrew's voice fading away behind him.

"But what if . . ."

CHAPTER 24

THE CAMPFIRE

(TANNER)

Tanner quickly approached the campfire, desperate to get help. He could see the dancing flame illuminating half the face of a man sitting a few feet from the fire. Tanner struggled to make out the man's features as he quietly continued to move forward. He thought about all the stories he read—Adolf Ruth and the bullets to the head, and the sniper Mr. X. He thought about the stories of others who had gone in search of the mine and never returned. Maybe they really hadn't found it. Maybe they had all been killed.

He stared at the man's face, wondering what to do. Now just a couple dozen feet away in the shadows, he noticed the man was sharpening a knife.

I've got to take a chance. Mick might be dying.

"Excuse me," Tanner said as he threw caution to the wind in an attempt to save his friend.

The man looked up, and Tanner could clearly see his face for the first time.

Decimus, Tanner thought as a chill ran down his spine. *What do I do?*

Even though Mick had told the boys she was convinced Decimus had stolen her journal, Tanner had completely disregarded the idea that he had been able to follow them to Brownsville, let alone to the Superstition Mountains, but here he was. The invincible man, less than five feet away.

I saved his life. He owes me. But if Andrew's right about what he saw, he's also the guy who tried to kill Mick and almost killed Donald.

"I need your help," Tanner pled. "I'm begging you. My friend— she may be dying."

"You're asking the wrong man," Decimus replied.

"But I saved your life," Tanner continued.

"Christians destroyed my life," Decimus said. "And I'm about to make sure they don't destroy anyone else's. I've seen your plans. I know you're trying to take over the empire."

"But we're . . ."

That was all Tanner was able to get out. Decimus sprang to his feet, dagger in hand, and then lunged at Tanner.

Tanner torqued his body to the right just in time to avoid what would have otherwise been a fatal blow.

Decimus tumbled to the ground when the forward motion of his dagger wasn't slowed by Tanner's body.

Tanner looked down and saw Decimus scrambling to get up. He stood in stunned silence, until his body caught up with his mind and he took off into the desert night.

I've got to lead him away from the others, but I've also got to get back to Mick.

CHAPTER 25

ADRENALINE WANING

(TANNER)

As Tanner sprinted into the dark night, he was terrified. He had to somehow draw Decimus away from the area he was convinced was an entrance to the Underworld. This man he had endowed with power really was invincible.

If Decimus gets back to Rome, the history of the world is going to be turned upside down. I've got to get him as far from the entrance as I can. But the farther I get from my friends, the less chance I have one-on-one against Decimus. What am I thinking? Decimus is invincible. I don't have a chance. And Mick. I've got to get back to her.

All it would take was a simple twist of an ankle and Decimus would terminate his life.

I can't do this.

He panicked as he continued to run, his mind racing. He thought of the tarantulas and snakes they had faced earlier.

Was that an isolated situation, or am I going to stumble into another patch of deadly venom?

Tanner bobbed and weaved over tumbleweeds and between cacti. He glanced over his shoulder and could see Decimus in hot pursuit, dagger poised to strike. This wasn't anything like a race with Andrew. This was a well-trained physical specimen in the prime of his indestructible life chasing him, bent on revenge for some reason Tanner knew nothing about.

How could anyone be that bitter, he wondered, *to turn so completely on someone who saved their life? Someone who gave them incredible powers and capabilities.*

He looked back again. Decimus seemed to be gaining on him.

The adrenaline that had sustained Tanner from the moment the tarantula attack began until this point seemed to be waning. Tanner could feel his legs starting to wobble.

Do I turn back toward the others?

CHAPTER 26

USE YOUR PYRAMID

(HOKOLESQUA)

"Hello? Anyone here?"

Hokolesqua strained to make out the features of the dark silhouette in the doorway of their wigwam.

"I'm Anatolia, goddess of the sunrise."

"Come in," Hokolesqua said. "Tecumseh told me you would be coming."

When the goddess stepped inside, Hokolesqua could see she had flaming red hair and a countenance that glowed. She was carrying a beautifully etched golden disc about the size of a large drum.

"I'm here to escort you to your destiny."

"What does that mean? I am just trying to find my sister and mother."

"Yes, that's part of your destiny. But just part."

"Are you taking me to the meadow where Methoataske and Mayata disappeared?"

"Yes, but we must make a short detour."

"Detour?"

"Yes, we have to go somewhere else first, and then I'll return you to Mammoth Meadow."

"Can Nemhsi come?" Hokolesqua asked.

"The path will be one filled with danger," Anatolia replied. "If Nemhsi is willing to risk everything to go along, we can take her with us."

"I'm ready," Hokolesqua's sister replied as she sprang to her feet. "Let's go."

"Follow me." Anatolia exited the wigwam, and the three walked to the River Styx entrance to Inner Earth inside Mammoth Cave.

"Jump into the water after me," Anatolia said.

Nemhsi leaned forward and opened her mouth as if she were about to ask a question, but she was too late. Anatolia had already disappeared.

The two Shawnees looked at each other, and then Hokolesqua jumped in. He emerged in Mammoth Meadow and watched the small stream where seconds later his sister emerged as well.

"This is the place where both your sister and mother disappeared," Anatolia said. "It's *where* you'll start your destiny, but not *when*. I must take you to Mount Olympus to fix that."

Holding a semicircular-shaped tube attached to the disc she had been carrying, she gave a flick of her wrists, and the disc extended out along a beam of light until it was about four feet from the handle. Seams in the disc opened as it spun and quickly grew to at least twice its original size.

"Hop on," she said.

Anatolia was holding the tube like the reins on a horse and standing on the enlarged disc. Hokolesqua and Nemhsi climbed onto the platform and away they went.

Both grabbed Anatolia around the waist when a quick takeoff nearly threw them off. Quickly they were zooming along about a foot above the meadow grass.

"Hang on," the goddess said. "We're going up."

Almost instantly, the device changed direction from traveling horizontally to a direct vertical ascent.

"Hope you're not afraid of heights," Anatolia said as the objects below became smaller and smaller.

"I didn't think I was," Nemhsi replied.

"It helps if you don't look down the first time," Anatolia replied.

Hokolesqua thought he was going to lose his breakfast. He decided to take Anatolia's advice and looked up instead.

"I don't like this," he said as the personal craft was heading toward the sun-like object in the sky.

"Hold on, it's going to get pretty hot," Anatolia said just as the device was about to make impact.

Just as fast as it got hot, it cooled back down, and the three were inside the scorching orb.

"Are we actually inside the—" Nemhsi started to say when Anatolia interrupted with the answer.

"Yes. Welcome to Mount Olympus."

Anatolia landed the craft next to the Cathedral of Time and stepped off.

"Follow me."

She waved away the translucent dome over the Cathedral, and then escorted the two Shawnees into the building and to the central platform.

"Stay right there," Anatolia said as she walked over to the control room.

Before they knew what was happening, Anatolia had joined them again on the platform just before a spectacular light show erupted. Then everything went dark.

"What was that all about?" Nemhsi asked.

"Just part of getting you where—actually *when*—you need to be in order to fulfill your mission."

"What is this mission and destiny you talk about?" Hokolesqua asked.

"Didn't you go on a vision quest? Didn't your spirit animal show you anything?"

"Yes, but—"

"You have everything you need to know, then."

"But I didn't understand the meaning."

"You will."

"Now, back to Mammoth Meadow."

Anatolia led Hokolesqua and Nemhsi back to the personal flying craft, and they quickly made their descent.

"Good luck," Anatolia said as they landed and the two Shawnees stepped off the craft. "Whatever you do, don't give up."

"We won't," Hokolesqua said, still perplexed by everything that was happening.

"Thank you," Nemhsi said.

"Oh, and when in doubt," Anatolia's voice was fading away as her craft sped away, "use your pyramid."

It took a few seconds for what Anatolia had said to register. Once it did, Hokolesqua took out his pyramid and looked at the needle.

"Let's cross this meadow."

CHAPTER 27

THE VENOM

(ANDREW)

Mick was fading fast.

"What are we going to do?" Andrew asked.

"My purse," Mick said. "Get my purse. Quick."

"What's in—"

"Just get it," Mick feebly insisted.

"Watch her." Andrew beckoned for Donald to come over and keep her propped up so her heart was above the bite. "You've got to keep her up like this. The venom will work less quickly if she's propped up."

Donald came over and put his arm around Mick as Andrew darted for Mick's purse. In seconds he returned. Mick was mumbling now, and it was hard to understand what she wanted. Andrew dumped the whole thing out onto the ground and was frantically waving his flashlight above the contents.

"The vial," Donald said. "The water from the Mnemosyne River. Pour it on the wound."

"That's not water from the Styx, though. It's not going to make her invincible," Andrew said, working out the logic in his head.

"Just do it," Donald replied.

Andrew grabbed the vial and was fumbling to open it as he looked at Mick, who was struggling to keep her eyes open.

"She's losing consciousness," Andrew said.

"Just concentrate on getting that water on the wound," Donald said angrily.

Andrew got the vial open and poured some of the water across the two bite marks. He watched anxiously to see if the water would behave like the water from the Acheron had when Tanner poured it on Decimus. But nothing happened. No water pushing back out of the wound. No instant healing. No protective shell.

"It's not doing anything," Andrew said. "We're going to lose her. Maybe she wanted something else." Andrew set Mick gently back down and again shone his flashlight back and forth across the contents of Mick's purse.

He paused. "We can't lose you, Mick. You've got to stay with us. Fight this."

A small smile formed across Micks lips before she twitched and shut her eyes. There was a sense of finality in the way they closed this time, and Andrew knew something was different. He looked heavenward.

"Nooooo!" he cried out in agony and continued to look to the skies, wondering how this could have happened.

As he moved his head to look back at Mick, he saw Tanner running toward them.

CHAPTER 28

VISITORS

(TANNER)

"Bad news," Tanner said huffing and wheezing. "It *is* Decimus following us, but I think I lost . . ."

Tanner noticed Andrew cradling Mick.

"How is she?" he asked anxiously.

"I think she's dead, T," Andrew said.

"What!" Tanner replied. "She can't be."

He pushed Andrew aside and gently shook Mick.

"Mick! You can't die." He hugged her limp body. He put his ear to her chest and his hand around her wrist. "She's still alive. I can feel a heartbeat. It's faint but definitely still there."

"But we have no way to help her," Andrew replied.

"Persephone!" Tanner cried out to the goddess who had helped them in the Great Hall of Judgment. "We need you!"

Almost instantly, two lights began to form next to Tanner. The small group jumped back in astonishment. The lights became larger and brighter until two glowing beings were clearly visible in the dark desert night.

"Who are you?" Tanner asked.

"Zeus sent us," the male figure replied. "I'm Hermes, and this is Panacea."

Hermes was wearing a golden winged helmet and winged shoes. Panacea had a white dress decorated with pearls of all sizes that formed exquisite shapes across its surface. She held a vial of liquid in one hand and a staff around which a snake was coiled in the other.

"We're here to assist your friend."

Tanner looked back and forth between his friends and the visitors in shock.

"You called for help, didn't you?" Panacea said. She obviously had noticed Tanner's expression.

"Yes, yes," Tanner replied. "It's just that . . ."

"Don't tell me," Panacea replied. "You've never had someone from the Underworld appear before to answer your pleading."

"We try to let you Surfacers do as much as you can on your own. That's how you grow. But once in a while, extreme measures are required to keep things on course—especially when the stakes are this high."

"So can you save her?" Andrew asked.

"Of course," Panacea replied as she stooped down at Mick's side.

"Hold her mouth open for me," she said to Andrew, whose jaw still appeared to be unhinged from the rest of his skull.

"Uh, yeah, sure," he stammered.

Andrew knelt down across from Panacea, pried Mick's mouth open, and went back to staring in shock at the goddess.

Panacea bit the cork with her teeth, pulled it out, and spit it to the side of her. She poured some of the liquid into Mick's mouth, and then set the vial on the ground next to her. Standing erect, she gently waved the staff in sweeping motions above Mick. Instantly, Mick began to cough, then propped herself up on her arms.

"What happened?" she asked as she grabbed her leg and looked for the snake bite, which had completely disappeared.

"I guess you'd call it a miracle," Panacea responded. "We'd just call it science."

"Wow," Mick replied. "I feel great. Never better."

"Thanks," Tanner said, bowing slightly in respect for the two visitors.

"Of course," Hermes replied. "Now, you must get back to your quest. There are forces at work trying to stop what you're doing. You must not be deterred. Before long you'll understand just how important the mission you've been called on to fulfill really is."

And with that, the visitors began to fade from view.

"What did you mean when you said the stakes are this high?" Andrew asked, but he was too late.

"No need to worry about Decimus anymore," Tanner said. "We're invincible too."

"What are you talking about?" Andrew replied.

"We were in trouble, we called on the gods, and they bailed us out," Tanner said. "We never have to worry about anything again."

"You obviously didn't pay much attention when we studied mythology," Mick replied.

"Why do you say that?"

"The gods were completely unpredictable. We must have just caught them on a good day."

"Plus, they never agreed on stuff," Andrew added. "I guarantee that if Zeus really did send Hermes and Panacea, half of the other gods were trying to stop it. Zeus turns his back for a second, and whoever is opposing us will destroy us. We're just pawns."

"Still," Tanner said less confidently, "it's nice to know we have gods helping us."

"I think it's worse," Andrew replied. "I was content back in Brownsville when I had no fear that *any* gods were potentially plotting against me. Somehow we've moved off neutral ground."

"You really think we might have gods working against us?" Mick asked.

"Of course," Andrew replied. "Hermes just said there are forces trying to stop what we're doing."

"And you think he meant gods?"

"Well, Hades nearly swatted Tanner and me out of the sky when he found out we had taken the golden orb."

"And based on what I've heard, he's the type who holds a grudge," Tanner added.

"So, what do we do now?" Mick asked.

"You heard Hermes," Tanner said. "We've got to get back to finding that entrance."

"And we better do it fast," Andrew replied, pointing at the silhouette of a man climbing over a small rock formation less than fifty yards from where they were.

CHAPTER 29

THREE MOONS?
(HOKOLESQUA)

"I don't think we should go straight across the meadow," Nemhsi said. "We don't know what we're going to encounter down here. We'll be sitting buffalo if we cross through the middle."

Hokolesqua wasn't sure what to think. The needle definitely was pointing to the other side of the meadow, but Nemhsi's point was valid. Was he supposed to follow the needle with precision or generally? He looked at the needle again, which was fluctuating back and forth slightly.

"Smart thinking." Hokolesqua closed the lid of the pyramid.

The two young Indians followed the river upstream until they arrived at the edge of the woods. They climbed up the riverbank and into the trees. All day and into the night they hiked through the woods. When both were physically exhausted, they found a spot where they made a bed of leaves and slept for the night.

When morning came, they continued deeper into the woods.

"Shhh," Hokolesqua said as he heard voices not far from where they were walking.

"It's only a matter of time now," a deep voice said.

"He's been trying unsuccessfully for a few years, though. I think Spider Woman is preventing him from finding it."

"It was because of the wickedness of Anatok that they were led away in the first place. And Anatok is even more wicked now than it was then."

"Which is why he'll never find the passage."

"But he has such incredible technology. How can Spider Woman possibly stop him?"

"She's a goddess. That's how."

"I don't know."

Hokolesqua, who had been holding his breath in his attempt to not make a noise, quietly inhaled deeply through his nose and immediately felt a strange tickle. Try as he might, he couldn't control it and let out a sneeze he felt all the way to his feet.

"We're being followed," the voice in the woods said. "It's the king's spies. We can't let them get away."

"Run," Hokolesqua whispered to Nemhsi.

Hokolesqua looked back as they ran through the forest and could see two men quickly gaining on them. It wasn't long before the two young Indians were tackled and being held tightly.

"What are you doing here?" the smaller of the two men asked as Hokolesqua and his sister thrashed around trying to free themselves.

"Let us go," Hokolesqua said angrily.

"Why are you here?" the larger man demanded.

"We came in search of our mother, who was captured from our land and brought here three moons ago."

There was a long pause.

"Did you say three *moons*?"

"Yes."

The two men looked at each other and then said in unison, "They're Surfacers."

"We're so sorry," the smaller man said, bowing reverently to Hokolesqua and then to Nemhsi. "We thought you were the king's spies."

"Yes, yes, please accept our apologies," the larger man said. "You're free to go. But I must ask, you do realize how dangerous this place is for you right now, don't you?"

Hokolesqua and Nemhsi looked at each other with puzzled expressions.

"The king would give anything to capture you, dead or alive."

Nemhsi's eyes got as big as two moons.

"Why is that?" Hokolesqua asked.

"He's desperate to find a passageway to the surface of the earth. You would be his ticket to expanding his treacheries."

"I'm sorry, we should introduce ourselves. I'm Kwatoko," the larger man said. "And this is Lapu."

"Stay with us," Lapu said. "We can't guarantee anything, but we'll protect you the best we can."

CHAPTER 30

THE LOST DUTCHMAN'S MINE

(ANDREW)

"Mick, can you run?" Andrew asked as he glanced back at the rock formation where he had spotted Decimus. When he looked back at Mick for a response, all he saw was her dark outline running for the back side of Weaver's Needle.

"I'll take that as a yes," he said.

Andrew, Tanner, and Donald sprinted to catch up.

Dawn was just beginning to break across the desert landscape.

"Let's hope there aren't spiders and snakes on the other side, too," Tanner said.

"I'd rather not have to choose between Decimus and a sea of Mojave rattlers," Andrew huffed, looking over his shoulder and seeing Decimus not far behind.

When the four Brownsvillians arrived on the back side of the mountain, they scampered up its face.

"The spiders and snakes were protecting the other side," Tanner said. "If we can get back to the front side and climb down the face, we're sure to find the entrance."

PaZing!

"What was that?"

PaZing!

"Someone's shooting at us," Mick said in a panic. "Find cover."

"There is no cover," Andrew said, looking around.

"We've got to get around to the front as fast as possible," Tanner said.

Chunks of Weaver's Needle were exploding around them as bullets continued to impact the mountain face.

"I told you this was a bad idea," Andrew said angrily. "We're going to end up like Adolph Ruth."

"Just shut it and keep moving," Tanner replied.

"What's that?" Andrew asked, excitedly pointing at an anomaly along the mountain face. "Over there. Looks like a small cave."

"That'll give us some protection!" Donald shouted. "Everybody to the cave."

Garnering what little energy they had left, they scrambled across the face of Weaver's Needle until they reached the small opening. Donald entered first.

He grabbed Mick's hand and carefully pulled her through the opening.

PaZing!

"Hurry! Get in here," Mick exclaimed as Andrew and Tanner struggled to enter.

"That was close," Mick said.

"Trouble is," Andrew replied as he looked around the space, which wasn't even as big as his bedroom, "now we're sitting ducks."

"When do you think Decimus learned how to shoot?" Mick asked.

"Couldn't have been Decimus. He wouldn't even know what a gun is," Donald replied.

"I did read about someone searching for the mine who claimed to have been fired on by a sniper they called Mr. X," Tanner said.

"And when were you planning on sharing that little nugget with us?" Andrew said, clearly furious.

"I thought it was just an urban myth," Tanner replied.

"It would have been nice to be able to make that decision myself. I can't believe you. Do our lives mean nothing to you?"

"They do. It's just that . . ."

"It's just that nothing." Andrew ran at Tanner and started shoving him.

"Boys, come on," Donald said. "We don't have time for that. We've got to figure out a way to get out of here. We can't just stay in this little cave and wait for whoever that was to come and kill us all."

Andrew gave Tanner one last shove and turned away. When he looked back in disgust, Tanner was gone.

"Where'd he go?" Andrew asked.

"Through the wall," Mick replied.

"Huh?"

"Looks like we found our entrance."

Andrew walked to where he had last seen his *former* friend. He put his hand against the wall of the cave where Tanner should have made impact, and, sure enough, his hand went right through.

"We found it!" Mick exclaimed. "The Lost Dutchman's Mine."

Andrew stepped through the wall. Mick and Donald followed. The space reminded Andrew of a subway station. There was a tunnel to their right and another to their left, and running between the tunnels in the center of the space was a moving sidewalk. But that's where the similarities ended. Andrew's gum fell out of his mouth as he stood mesmerized by the beauty and cleanliness of the cave. He stooped over and without hesitation put the gum back in his mouth—something he never would have considered doing at any subway station he'd been to on the Surface.

"This doesn't fix everything, you know that, right?" Andrew said to Tanner.

"Yeah, I get it."

"Is that a bed?" Andrew asked as an object attached to the moving sidewalk emerged from the tunnel where the sidewalk was entering the space. About thirty seconds later, another of these unusual devices that looked like futuristic hospital beds entered the space. They continued to emerge at regular intervals. The beds had intricately sculpted metal rails with beautiful engravings. Monitors attached to the beds in several locations displayed a variety of readings. One display had what looked like a topographical map that was continuously updating itself. The beds were propped up at an angle that would allow someone sitting in the device to be comfortably upright.

The four approached the moving sidewalk to get a better look.

"Ladies before gentlemen," Tanner said, motioning for Mick to board.

"Very funny," Mick replied. "I love how you're so chivalrous when it's convenient."

"All right, all right," Tanner replied. "Follow me!"

Tanner approached one of the moving beds. The conveyor stopped, and the side railing lowered, allowing Tanner to climb on. He positioned his arms on the rails, and metal clamps wrapped themselves tightly around his wrists. A seat belt emerged and encircled his waist. Tanner panicked and tried to wriggle free, but the restraints moved with him. He wasn't being held captive. It was only a security measure. A transparent bubble formed over the bed.

"Good luck!" Mick started to say as the bubble finished enclosing Tanner.

Tanner looked over and mouthed "Thanks."

Four shafts of light appeared parallel with the moving sidewalk, then there was a flash of light and Tanner was gone.

"Andrew, you go next, then Mick," Donald said. "I'll bring up the rear."

"You think this thing is safe?" Andrew asked, his voice oozing with reservation.

"Probably safer than anything we have on the Surface," Mick replied.

"You're probably right," Andrew had to agree. "It's just going into the unknown that I don't like."

"You can do it. Tanner will be waiting. Don't miss this one, though, or he might get too far ahead of us."

"All right."

Andrew climbed in, and in a flash he'd disappeared into the tunnel on the other side of the cave.

"What a ride!" Andrew exclaimed as the device came to a stop and the bubble around him dissolved. Tanner was waiting on a platform.

"Hey, I'm stuck," Andrew said as he tried to pull his arm free.

"It's that bracelet thing you wear," Tanner replied.

Andrew's magnetic bracelet was anchored to the armrest.

"Help me," he said as he struggled to free his arm.

"Why do you wear that thing, anyway?" Tanner asked as he helped Andrew pry his wrist free from the device.

"My parents say it's supposed to get rid of pain."

"So if I bought one, you'd go away?" Tanner said, laughing.

"It must not work. You're still here," Andrew shot back. "What'd you think of that ride?"

"Better than any ride I've ever been on."

"It was so smooth but so fast."

"Everything around me was a blur," Tanner said. "Couldn't make out a thing."

The boys could hear a gentle whooshing sound.

"This must be Mick!" Tanner said.

A bubble-domed bed emerged into the space, slowing down as it approached.

"What?" Tanner shouted.

"There's no one in there," Andrew added.

"Do you think Mick and Donald are all right?"

"They should have been right behind us. Why do you think no one's in there?" Andrew asked. "We shouldn't have done this. I told you this was a bad idea. The sniper probably got to them."

"He couldn't have scaled the mountain that fast," Tanner replied.

"Maybe it was Decimus, then," Andrew said. "We've got to go back and help them."

"I don't see an option to go back."

"And I don't have any idea where we are."

The story of Adolph Ruth taking a couple bullets to the head was looping in Andrew's mind.

"Donald can handle anyone. He's one of the toughest men I know," Tanner said.

"Not tougher than Decimus, or a sniper."

"This must be Mick," Tanner said as they heard the whooshing noise again.

CHAPTER 31

THAT'S FLATTERING

(MICK)

Back at the entrance to the cave, Mick was about to sit down when she heard a voice call her name.

"Mick! You all right?"

She just about got whiplash as she turned to see Jim Sanford, who had just entered through the holographic entrance.

"What are you doing here?" she asked in complete shock.

"I wasn't going to let Tanner and Andrew kidnap you again. I've been trailing you guys for a while now."

"You followed us across the country?"

"Yep. I followed you to Bowling Green and was able to get on the same bus. I just hid in the back. I've been trailing you ever since."

"Well, that's flattering Jim, but I'm fine. They didn't kidnap me. I volunteered to go. Now just go back to Brownsville. Everything's fine."

"Are you kidding?"

"No, really. Everything's fine."

"I'm not talking about the 'everything's fine' part, I'm talking about the 'going back to Brownsville' and missing out on whatever you're up to. This place is sick!"

Mick realized that now that Jim had discovered the cave, there was no way he wasn't on board for the entire adventure. If he had been able to follow them this far, it was going to be pretty hard to shake him at this point.

"All right. Climb in and go next." Mick didn't want to be around Jim any more than she had to without Andrew and Tanner around.

"Okay. What do I do?"

"Just climb on that bed thing. I'm not sure what happens after that, but Tanner and Andrew already went, so they'll be waiting at the bottom."

Jim climbed in and was on his way.

Mick wished she could be on the other side to see the expressions on Tanner's and Andrew's faces when Jim Sanford showed up.

CHAPTER 32

WE DIDN'T CHOOSE

(ANDREW)

Tanner and Andrew waited anxiously at the bottom of the tunnel.

"This has got to be Mick!" Andrew said as he heard the next vehicle whooshing through the tunnel.

The boys could see there was someone in this device, but it didn't look like either Mick or Donald.

The bubble disappeared, and the person inside turned and looked at Tanner and Andrew.

"Boys," Jim said as he looked smugly at Tanner and Andrew.

"Jim?" Tanner said in shock.

"Looks like you've got a new partner," Jim said.

"But . . . how?" Tanner added, unable to form a complete sentence.

"I caught the same bus and followed you all the way here."

"What are we going to do?" he whispered to Andrew.

"You're taking me along," Jim said. "I'm not missing out on this."

A few seconds later, Mick appeared, then Donald.

"All right. Let's get moving," Tanner said.

Off to their left was an exquisitely tiled tunnel. They entered, and after a short but winding fifty yards, it opened into another cavern.

Sitting in front of the five explorers was a beautiful white flying machine that looked like a winged shark. It was hovering a few feet from an access platform. As they entered the room, a glass cockpit-like entrance into the craft opened, and an access ramp extended down to the platform.

"Looks like we're supposed to board," Tanner said.

"Yep," Andrew chimed in.

The five boarded and were quickly being flown through a labyrinth of tunnels and caverns.

When they finally landed, they emerged onto a platform in a circular cavern. The craft they had flown in departed, leaving the five travelers alone in the room.

"Welcome, Surfacers," a deep voice announced. "You are now in the center of the earth. Choose your destination."

"I was abducted on my last trip to Inner Earth because I was a Surfacer," Mick said. "I still don't understand why we're such a novelty worth fighting over,"

"A city we were in came under attack because they were harboring Surfacers," Andrew added.

"Why do you think Surfacers are so important?" Tanner asked.

"No idea," Mick replied.

"We're going to have to be on high alert," Tanner said.

"I really don't like this entrance," Andrew said. "At least at Mammoth Cave I always felt like I could go back anytime I wanted. Hopefully, wherever we're heading isn't hostile toward Surfacers, because I don't see any way for us to go back where we came from."

"Did you just say there's an entrance to the underworld in Mammoth Cave?" Jim asked.

Andrew had forgotten Jim was there.

"I didn't hear that," Tanner said. "Did you hear that?" he said, looking around at the others.

"Don't try to cover it up. I know what I heard," Jim replied. "So this is what you've been up to."

"Nice going," Tanner said, jabbing Andrew in the gut with his elbow.

"I have to agree with Andrew," Mick said. "I really don't like the fact there's no way to get back to the entrance from here."

"Looks like we're committed," Tanner said.

"Are you saying you guys have no idea what you're doing or where we're going?" Jim chirped.

"Look, no one invited you," Tanner replied. "You decided to crash the party on your own. So either get lost or don't criticize."

Jim rushed Tanner, ready to tackle him.

Mr. Carlton jumped in and grabbed Jim. Jim was no match for a member of the Praetorian Guard.

"Listen boys. I can see the two of you have some hard feelings toward one another. But we've got to get along," Mr. Carlton said. "We have to stay united. If we can't stick together, the underworld is going to rip us apart, and I'm not going to let that happen. Is that clear?"

"Got it," Jim said. Mr. Carlton had instantly gained Jim's respect. The way he completely took command of the situation told Jim that Donald was not to be messed with.

"We need to keep moving," Andrew said. "We can't just sit around and talk. Decimus or the sniper are going to be right on our tail."

Spaced at regular intervals around the cavern walls was a series of doors. Each was uniquely designed with intricately carved cityscapes on the panels. In the center of every door at eye level was a circular medallion with a raised symbol. Between each of the doors, waterfall features playfully danced off the rock walls. They fed into a channel that ran around the entire room. A small bridge allowed access to each of the doors.

"Any of you recognize these symbols?" Tanner asked.

"Oh yeah," Mick said. "The one over there says 'Tanner is an idiot.'"

"Well played," Tanner replied.

There were twelve doors to choose from. "Anyone feeling lucky?" Tanner asked. "Someone's going to have to pick one."

Andrew walked up to one of the doors and was examining it. Fascinated by the silky-smooth metal medallion in the middle of the door, he was gently reaching up to rub his hand across the raised symbol when a white vapor filled the room.

"Whoa! Whoa, what's going on?" Tanner yelled. "We didn't choose a door yet!"

The mist began to swirl in a circular pattern. Then the center of the room cleared, and before long the whole room was clear again and looked the same as it had before—with one small difference. Andrew was standing in front of an open door—the only door that remained in the room.

"What did you do?" Tanner said, glaring at Andrew.

"I just wanted to see what the medallion felt like."

"This is on you if this turns out badly," Tanner grumbled.

The Surfacers moved through the doorway onto a dirt path. It took a minute for their eyes to adjust to the darkness of the place where they found themselves.

"Anyone have a flashlight?" Tanner asked. Mick pulled out her cell phone. They couldn't see very far in front of them due to the undulating terrain, but what they did see wasn't encouraging.

"Must have been some kind of fire that ripped through here," Andrew said.

The landscape looked like it had once been a beautiful forest. All that remained were scorched tree trunks.

"I'm not likin' Andrew's choice," Jim added. "I'm trying a different door."

Everyone turned to look at their point of entry, but there was no sign of the door they had entered through.

"Looks like we're stuck," Tanner said. "Thanks a lot, Andrew."

After wandering for about an hour, the lights of a massive city began to come into view in the valley below. The charred forest began to clear, and they could see sophisticated aircraft buzzing around at various altitudes. Many of them were firing at one another. The sky was lit with lasers and exploding spacecraft.

"Look out!" Mick yelled. The others turned just in time to see a spacecraft corkscrew out of the sky and explode as it crashed about fifty feet from where they stood.

"Yeah, for once I agree with Jim," Tanner said as he scowled at Andrew. "Not liking your choice."

"So what's the plan?" Mick asked looking at Tanner.

"I'm still sorting that out."

CHAPTER 33

THE THIRD WORLD

(MICK)

"This must be the Third World of Hopi legends," Tanner said.

"The Third World?" Mick asked.

"Yeah, the Hopis believe their ancestors lived in another land. Many became wicked and rebelled against the plan of Spider Woman, their creator."

"Spider who?" Andrew asked.

"Spider Woman."

"Like the one from the comics?" Jim said.

"You're thinking of Spiderman," Andrew replied.

"No, there's a Spiderwoman too," Jim said. "Kind of like how there's a Batgirl."

"Okay. Well, different Spider Woman," Tanner said impatiently.

"Continue on, Tanner," Mick said.

"Eventually, Spider Woman led the righteous away from the wicked land. From what I read, she created a pathway for them to travel from the Third World up into the Fourth World at a place called sipapu, in the Grand Canyon."

"So you think *this* is the wicked Hopi civilization of the Third World?" Donald asked.

"Bingo!"

"This could get interesting," Mick said.

"Doesn't sound very safe," Jim added.

"Based on the small sampling we've seen, I'd say that's a pretty accurate assessment," Andrew said.

"Well, let's get moving," Tanner said. "The sooner we get through here, the sooner we'll get to Rome."

"If we survive," Andrew added.

The outskirts of the city were filled with makeshift lean-tos, tent-like shelters, and temporary shacks made from leftover construction materials.

"Can you believe the stench?" Mick asked.

"It's horrible," Tanner said. "And the haphazard construction."

"Looks like the trash collectors must be on strike," Mick said.

"Maybe we can find someone who can give us directions to Olympus," Tanner said.

Before they could even make it to the city center, a small personal spacecraft buzzed closely overhead, nearly hitting the small group.

"What was that all about?" Tanner yelled, gesturing toward the small craft.

It circled back around and began to hover directly overhead.

"What do you want?" Jim yelled, looking up. "Stop pestering us!"

A cylinder of light projected from the craft and encircled the small group. Jim tried to walk through the translucent "wall" and was instantly repelled. Somehow this light had actual substance. They were trapped—captive to a beam of light. The spacecraft began to move, the cylinder with it. They were being herded forward by the back edge of the cylinder. Donald lowered his shoulder and rammed it against the shaft—with no effect. Mick noticed him grit his teeth and wince ever so slightly.

"What is this?" Tanner shouted. "Andrew, what's going on?"

"No idea. Never seen anything like this before."

"What do you want with us?" Tanner yelled.

There was no reply from the spacecraft.

"Where are you taking us?" Mick screamed.

Again no reply.

The Surfacers were forced to follow below the hovering craft as it entered the narrow alleys of what was just a small step above the lean-to shacks of the ghetto they had just passed through. They were now in a dark labyrinth of stairways and crooked paths. Mick was amazed that the hovering aircraft was able to navigate through narrow passageways not wide enough for a car. The buildings were an entangled hodgepodge that twisted up and down, sideways and slantways.

"Didn't anyone have a level when they built this place?" Mick asked. The lack of orderliness was grating on her like fingernails on a chalkboard.

"No kidding," Tanner replied.

Finally, the spacecraft came to a stop, and the entrapping light shaft parked itself in front of a doorway.

A tall, roughed-up man jumped out of the craft above and moved to the entrance, where he swiped a security panel on the exterior door and then again on a secondary inner door.

"Why have you taken us here?" Tanner asked.

There was no reply.

Mick stared at the lush furnishings inside. "Not quite what I expected. How about you?"

"I'll say," Tanner replied. "Based on the exterior, I would have expected it to look more like Andrew's bedroom." Tanner shoved Andrew slightly with his forearm, and the three of them laughed.

The cylindrical light shaft pushed them into the residence. Realizing that the flying craft was no longer overhead, Mick looked around to see what was controlling the beam now. The man had a joystick-like device in his hands. He navigated their "prison cell" until it was in a room just to the left of the entryway.

"What are you doing?" Mick asked. "Why did you bring us here?"

"You," their captor paused dramatically, "are about to make me a very rich man."

The look on his face made it clear he was extremely proud of himself.

He was wearing a beat-up black leather jacket with an unusually high number of buckles and latches across its surface. His skin was a beautiful bronze tone and looked extremely tough—but only slightly wrinkled. He was magnificently sculpted, and his jet-black hair was parted in the middle and pulled back in a ponytail.

"Who are you?" Mick asked.

"Cheveyo—Hopi Spirit Warrior of the people of Anatok."

"And what do you want with us?" Mick said.

"I'm a bounty hunter."

"But we're not fugitives," Andrew said.

"At least not from your law," Tanner mumbled, thinking back to their most recent flight from the police.

"Yeah, we haven't done anything wrong," Jim added angrily.

"Other than being in the wrong place at the wrong time," the Hopi replied.

"What's that supposed to mean?" Tanner asked.

"King Tohopka, also known as Wild Beast, has been looking for your kind for years. There are legends about a group that departed into the same woods you came from hundreds of years ago. They bragged that Spider Woman was taking them to a promised land rich in natural resources—a Fourth World. These prudes asserted that their adherence to the Creator's plan and laws made them worthy of attaining this sacred inheritance. They were never heard from again."

"So, you're saying because we came from the same woods, we must know the whereabouts of this 'promised land'?" Donald asked.

"That's right. I'm sure you noticed the charred remains of the forest on the outskirts of the city."

"Pretty hard to miss," Tanner replied.

"Earlier this year, Tohopka ordered every last tree burned in an attempt to find any sign of where these people might have gone. He's obsessed with adding this resource-rich land to his conquests and has vowed to spare no expense to find and conquer it. By this time tomorrow, he'll be paying my heavy price tag for leading him to it."

"Someone will stop him," Donald said.

"Believe me, many have tried," Cheveyo replied. "In fact, rumor is that a group of Spider Woman's followers are secretly assembling in hopes of overthrowing the king, but now that we have you, it's too late."

He let out a grim chuckle.

"So how did you get involved?" Mick asked.

"Legendary bounty hunter that I am, Tohopka enlisted me to find this land or any travelers who might have come from there. He was growing weary at my lack of success, but now . . ."

"And what makes you think we come from this Fourth World?" Mick asked, knowing full well they did.

"The traditions say the inheritors of the Fourth World would be overrun by a fair-skinned people. I've never seen anyone with fairer skin than you." He reached through the light beam and grabbed Mick by the jaw, pulling her to the edge of the beam so he could examine her more closely. Mick jerked free of his grasp.

Mick looked down at her arms. She prided herself in what she thought was a nice tan, but compared to this man, she *did* look pale.

"King Tohopka will reward me handsomely."

"You won't succeed," Donald said firmly.

The Hopi left the entryway of the home and walked to another room.

"We have to keep him talking," Tanner said.

"Why?" Mick asked.

"I've watched enough superhero shows to know you have to keep the villain talking as long as you can. Somehow it always leads to an opening for escape."

"Come on, Tanner!" Mick replied. "This is real life."

"What are we going to do?" Andrew asked. "Tomorrow morning we're going to face this brutal king who is bent on finding the Surface. With these kinds of technologies," Andrew ran his left hand up and down the beam, "he'd have no problem taking over our world."

"At all costs, we can't tell him where we're from and how we got here," Mick said.

"He's going to torture us for the information," Andrew replied.

Cheveyo reentered the room.

CHAPTER 34

THE GRAVEYARD
(HOKOLESQUA)

"Just a day and a half's journey," Lapu told Hokolesqua and Nemhsi as they resumed their trek through the woods in the morning.

"Still that far?" Nemhsi asked. "What were the two of you doing so far from your homes?"

"Hunting," Kwatoko replied.

As the four of them continued deeper into the woods, Hokolesqua checked his pyramid. The needle was definitely pointing the direction they were going, which put his mind at ease. He thought back to his vision quest. *Is this the Water Panther leading me farther and farther into the underworld? Is that what the vision meant? But what was the fire that nearly destroyed us?*

When they arrived in Anatok, it was almost morning. The central sun of Inner Earth was obscured but was equally as bright as a full moon on the Surface. Hokolesqua was in shock over the strange mixture of incredible technology and the utter disarray that existed in the city before them. It was somehow spectacular and disgusting at the same time, and there was an overall feeling in the air he didn't like.

"Let's turn around," Hokolesqua said, grabbing Nemhsi by the arm and turning away from the city.

"You can't," Kwatoko said. "It's not safe. The king's men are everywhere."

"But this place—I don't like how I feel."

"Anatok *is* very wicked," Lapu said. "That's what you feel. To anyone with a connection to the Great Spirit, it's offensive. But you'll feel differently when we arrive at the Place of Gathering."

They continued through the outskirts until they arrived at the gates of a large and gloomy graveyard. A cold wind was howling, and threatening clouds hung so low Hokolesqua felt as though he could reach out and touch them.

"We need to split up," Kwatoko said. "We can't enter with this big of a group. We'll raise suspicions."

"I can't do it," Hokolesqua said.

"Can't do what?" Lapu asked.

"Go in the graveyard. First you asked me to enter a city where I didn't feel safe. Now you ask me to enter the graveyard."

"But that's where the others are assembled," Kwatoko said. "It's the safest place in Anatok.

"There's no reason to be afraid of the graveyard, Hoko," Nemhsi said. "Be brave."

Hokolesqua bristled and wanted to lash out. There was nothing he wanted more than to be brave. He bit his tongue and looked inside himself.

Am I afraid? He thought back to how his little brother had unknowingly dug up a sacred burial site and, just like the elders of his village had warned, his family had been punished. It was that one small incident that had set in motion this entire chain of events.

He looked at Nemhsi. "Don't you remember? Mother was kidnapped because Mingan disturbed a burial site. I'm not afraid. I'm trying to be smart. I won't enter."

"But, Hoko, we'll be respectful. We won't disturb anything. We're not going to be digging like Mingan."

"I don't know what the dead might think is disrespectful," Hokolesqua said. "Just walking around the graveyard might be enough to curse our family forever. I can't take that chance."

"We have to go," Nemhsi replied. "If what these men say is true, we're in much greater danger by not following."

"These men say the graveyard is a safe place of gathering," Hokolesqua replied, "but maybe whole reason they're being threatened by the king is because they're cursed for disturbing these sacred burial grounds. And we're about to add to the curse? I will take my chances on the outside."

Hokolesqua noticed a small group of young men strutting smugly down the street. The black leather clothes they wore were futuristic but tattered and tight fitting enough that their muscular definition was easily visible even in the low light.

"Quick. Hide," Kwatoko whispered emphatically, grabbing Hokolesqua by the shirt and pulling him behind a large trash receptacle outside the graveyard. Lapu dove behind the receptacle, and Nemhsi followed.

Hokolesqua strained to get a better look.

From the expressions Hokolesqua saw on the war-painted faces of the young men, he was grateful the man had grabbed him.

CHAPTER 35

THE VISUALIZER

(ANDREW)

Andrew spotted a pair of tusks mounted on the wall of Cheveyo's home and thought about his entry into Inner Earth from Mammoth Cave.

"Where did you get those?" he asked.

"From a mammoth I slew on a hunting expedition. Gigantic beast."

"But *where* did you get them?" Andrew inquired more insistently, hoping it might help him figure out how far they were from the meadow near Mammoth Cave.

"In the forests of Delfi, far from Anatok." Cheveyo replied. "A nice addition to my sabretooth tiger collection, don't you think?"

"Yes. Your collection is amazing," Andrew said, playing on Cheveyo's ego.

"How were you able to kill such a massive beast?" Donald asked.

"Ah, let me show you!"

Andrew figured Cheveyo was about to show them some pictures or maybe a video of his expedition, but he was in for a big surprise.

Cheveyo picked up a small metallic ball from the credenza. A tablet-like device emerged from the ball, and Cheveyo made some hand gestures above its surface. When done, he gave a quick flick of the hand and the tablet disappeared. He walked over to the tusks and held the ball against one of them. A mercury-looking substance poured out and molded into the shape of the tusk. Pulsating green lights began to flow in geometric patterns across the surface.

"Whoa! What is that?" Andrew asked, thinking he might have to switch out his plan for the next science fair.

"It's a visualizer," Cheveyo replied.

"Visualizer?" Andrew queried. "What's a visualizer?"

"It allows you to visualize things from the past," Cheveyo answered.

The green lights abruptly shut off, and a holographic image appeared above the tusks.

"You wanted to know how I was able to kill the massive beast? Hang on. Here you go."

The Surfacers' eyes were fixed on the image as it began to display the hunt from the elephant's perspective. The mammoth emerged from the forest with its family and was grazing at the edge of a beautiful meadow. Suddenly the animal looked back into the woods, and there was Cheveyo, headed straight for it on his hovercraft. The mammoth turned as if it were alerting its family to the attack, and they bolted across the meadow.

"Here," Cheveyo said, handing the ball to Andrew through the cylinder of light. "Go ahead and control the image."

Andrew could barely contain his excitement.

"Just roll it around to see different angles of the action."

Cheveyo demonstrated by rolling the ball until they could see what was happening behind the mammoth. Cheveyo's hovercraft was flying low in the grass and gaining on the creature. There was a burst of light from Cheveyo's vehicle and a jolt in the image. It was clear the mammoth had been struck. It continued to lumber through the grasslands, but its pace slowed, and the image wobbled as it veered to its right. Andrew rolled the ball to change the perspective. He could now see what was in front of the mammoth. The image showed him and Tanner running from the mammoths into the woods.

It's a video of when we first entered Inner Earth.

Andrew let out a gasp.

Their backs were toward the creature, so Andrew was pretty sure no one else knew what was going on, but the two boys looked at each other in shock.

"Roll it the other way!" Tanner barked at Andrew. "I want to see Cheveyo."

Andrew rolled the ball, and they saw Cheveyo. There were a few quick changes in the angle of the image, drastically changing what was displaying. Andrew recognized it was caused by the mammoth tilting its head to scoop him up and carry him to the edge of the forest.

"What a magnificent animal!" Andrew said, his voice full of emotion.

"I'll say!" Tanner replied.

The mammoth stopped when it reached the edge of the forest. Andrew knew this was the point where the mammoth had gently laid him down. He had no idea the mammoth was wounded when it had gone out of its way to carry him to safety.

The hologram displayed the River Styx as the mammoth made its way to the clearing. Tanner and Andrew were visible but, in the shadows of the forest, they were undiscernible by the others. No sooner had the mammoth entered the forest than it collapsed.

They watched as Cheveyo navigated his vehicle behind the great mammal. With pride, Cheveyo grabbed the ball from Andrew and rolled the view until the group could clearly see him rear back with his spear and thrust it into the great beast. Both boys let out another gasp. Andrew remembered how whatever had been chasing the mammoths had turned around and headed in the opposite direction. He'd thought the mammoths had escaped.

"After you shot the mammoth, I lost sight of you in the image," Andrew said. "What happened?"

"I knew I hit the male, but I was out of ammunition and didn't want to be stampeded by the whole family. I went to the other side of the meadow and watched from a distance. Once I saw the male collapse and didn't see the rest of his family, I returned and finished him off."

Andrew was saddened and even more furious with Cheveyo than before. Not only was he holding them hostage, he'd killed the animal that had saved his life. He looked respectfully at the giant tusks that had saved him that first day in the underworld.

"How does the visualizer work?" Mick asked.

"Ah yes. It's quite simple, actually."

"Pretend for a minute that it's really not that simple for us," Tanner said.

"Well, you're familiar, I'm sure, with how sound waves work, is that correct?"

"What aspect of sound waves?" Andrew asked.

"Well, sound waves move out from a source, expanding until they make contact with a receiver, like your ear. The same thing happens with light waves."

"Yeah, we understand that," Andrew said.

Donald, looking a bit bewildered, said to Andrew, "Speak for yourself."

Jim added, "Yeah—what he said."

Cheveyo continued. "I'm sure you've seen how light can affect objects. For example, objects fade from exposure to light. Well, when light waves bump into the molecules of an object, they leave a mark, albeit an incredibly small impression. One of our top scientists discovered a way to re-create the light waves from the impression they make on the molecules."

"You're kidding," Andrew said.

"No. The visualizer allows a user to view all the light waves bouncing off a molecule at particular point in time. That way an entire 360-degree image is available."

"That's a staggering amount of data!" Andrew said.

"You're right," Cheveyo replied. "When the early versions became available, they functioned very slowly. After a few iterations, they finally got it right."

"Cheveyo, we're prepared to make you a better offer," Tanner blurted out.

Andrew looked at him in amazement, wondering what he was talking about. Tanner's comment was completely unrelated to anything they had been talking about.

"A better offer than what?" Cheveyo asked.

"Better than what King Tohopka is offering."

"Ha, ha," Cheveyo said. "That's impossible. King Tohopka is one of the wealthiest men on the earth."

Again Cheveyo left the room, laughing as he did so.

"Wow," Andrew said. "How about that visualizer?"

"Pretty amazing, huh?" Tanner replied.

"I just thought of a small problem," Mick added.

"What's that?"

"We said we weren't going to tell the king how we got here and where we came from. Looks like that won't matter."

"What do you mean?" Jim asked.

"He'll just hook a visualizer to us and show the king."

"Good point," Andrew replied.

"You know what that means, don't you?" Tanner said.

"No, what?"

"If we want to save the planet, we have to make sure tomorrow's meeting with the king never happens."

CHAPTER 36

A Devastating Turn of Events

(Tanner)

"Pretty scary thought," Andrew said as he adjusted his glasses and scanned the surface of the light-beam cell they were trapped in, "especially since I've got no idea how to get out of this thing."

Tanner could hear Cheveyo begin to snore in another room.

"Well, we've got until sunrise to figure it out," Tanner said. "Don't fail me now." He began massaging Andrew's shoulders like a boxer's trainer trying to loosen him up before entering the ring.

"No, really. I've got nothing," Andrew replied. "I've never seen technology like this."

"I don't care if you've never seen it," Tanner said. "No excuses. There is no plan B. We've got to get out."

"We're completely surrounded by this light," Donald said. "There are no openings."

"We're doomed," Jim said.

"Wait," Andrew said. "How was Cheveyo able to pass the visualizer through? Did you notice? Was there something he used to make an opening in the light?"

"I didn't see anything," Tanner replied. "He just reached in."

"He had an unusual arm bracelet," Mick said. "Did anyone else notice that?"

"Yeah, I saw it," Jim added, "but it's not going to do us any good. There's no way we can get our hands on it."

"But it might give us some clues," Mick said.

"Maybe his bracelet was magnetic," Andrew said. "You know how magnets can repel one another. Maybe it was repelling the beam."

"Sounds feasible," Mick said.

"Problem is, I don't have any magnets," Tanner said. "Plus, we'd need to get more than just our hands through. Anyone happen to bring a magnetic suit of clothes?"

"Tanner! This isn't the time for sarcasm," Mick said.

"What about your bracelet?" Tanner said, pointing to Andrew's health bracelet. "That thing's magnetic, isn't it?"

"Hey, you're right. I never thought about that."

"Try it!" Tanner shouted.

Andrew moved his right wrist up against the beam of light, and, sure enough, a small hole opened.

"That's it," Tanner said. "We're out of here."

Andrew thrust his arm through the small opening. Everyone watched anxiously.

"Yes!" Tanner said when as Andrew's entire forearm was on the other side of the light.

Their enthusiasm was short-lived, however, when the opening collapsed around his arm and he couldn't move it.

"I'm stuck! My arm won't move!"

"You've just got to get the magnet back against the light beam," Tanner said.

"I can't move my arm at all. There's no way for me to get the magnet near the light."

"Well, that was brilliant," Tanner said. "Whose idea was that, anyway?"

"I think it was yours," Mick replied.

"Oh. Well, I'm sure we'll figure some way of getting you out."

"I feel *much* better," Andrew said.

"Maybe we're thinking too hard," Tanner said. "Maybe there's a simple solution. I remember hearing about a semi-truck that was about an inch too tall to go under an overpass. A bunch of engineers were trying to figure out how they were going to solve the problem when a little kid walked up and told them to just let some air out of the tires."

"Come on," Jim said. "That's just an urban legend."

"Legend or not, sometimes there's a simple solution."

"Anybody seen the movie *The Great Escape*?" Mick asked. "Maybe we can dig our way out."

"That took them months, didn't it?" Tanner asked.

"Yeah, but they had a lot farther to dig," Mick replied.

"I know, but you think we can dig a tunnel to the street in a few hours?"

"We don't have to dig it to the street. We just have to go from one side of the beam to the other. I'm sure we could pull that off."

"What are we going to use for a shovel?" Jim asked.

"First we've got to figure out how to break through this flooring surface," Mick said.

"Without waking Cheveyo," Andrew added.

"What are we going to do about Andrew?" Mick asked. "Just leave him here?"

"Yeah, he just gets in the way," Tanner said. Andrew tried to lunge for him but couldn't move.

"Once we're out, we can take off his bracelet and move it next to the beam," Mick said. "That should create an opening big enough that he can get his arm out. It'll be easy."

"Oh, well," Tanner said. "It would have been kind of nice to leave him behind."

"Tanner, get serious," Mick said angrily.

It didn't take long to search their assets for something to dig with. They'd only brought the few things they had on them, having abandoned everything else on the last night they camped on the Surface. The best they could come up with was a nail file Mick had in her pocket.

"That's not going to do any good," Andrew said. "It would take you guys a year to even dig a small hole."

"Well, it's our only option, so let's make the best of it," Tanner said.

Tanner stuck the nail file into one of the corner seams in the rubberized floor. He was able to pry it up just enough to get a finger under the edge. He pulled the rubber tile up, exposing a wooden subfloor.

"Tell me you're going to use a nail file to saw your way through that board," Jim said.

"Just shut up unless you have a better idea," Tanner replied.

"I wish we could get that torch over here," Donald said, pointing at a torch resting in a stand just outside the beam that held them captive.

"Wait a second. How does your purse close?" Andrew said, looking over his shoulder at Mick's small purse.

"It's a magnet," Mick said excitedly.

"Maybe we can open a hole large enough to get that torch over here and burn our way through the floor."

"How would we put the fire out?" Jim asked. "It might burn the whole house down."

"Who cares?" Tanner said. "I'm not worried about burning down this psychopath's house. I just want to get out of here."

Mick held her purse near Andrew's arm, allowing him to pull it free. The two of them held their magnets along the bottom edge of the beam near the torch stand. A small opening appeared, and Tanner reached through, grabbing the torch. After a bit of a struggle, Tanner was able to get the torch through the opening and into their light-beam cell.

"Let's set that floor on fire and get out of here," Mick said.

Before long they had burned an opening into the dwelling below that was large enough for Mick to lower herself through. She used pieces of the rubber flooring to prevent herself from burning her hands. The smoke was thickening, the smell of burning rubber quickly spreading.

Suddenly, as Jim was about to lower himself through the hole, he heard "No one move!"

It was Cheveyo. With a gun.

"Where do you think you're going?" he said.

"You didn't seriously think we were going to stay around to meet your king, did you?" Tanner angrily replied.

"The nice thing is I don't need you to come. I only need your molecules. You saw how the visualizer works. I don't care if you meet the king alive or dead," Cheveyo responded callously.

"You're plan's not going to work," Tanner said.

"Nothing can stop us," Cheveyo said with a big grin. "The Surface is all but ours now."

"Mick will stop you," Andrew replied.

"The girl?" Cheveyo said, sneering.

"Don't underestimate her," Tanner said passionately.

"She won't survive the night in this city," Cheveyo replied. "A woman alone on those streets?" he added, shaking his head.

The flames and smoke continued to engulf the room as Cheveyo lowered the sights of his gun at the Surfacers.

There was the sound of gunfire and several flashes of light. Tanner watched as, one-by-one, Andrew, Jim, and Donald slumped onto the burning floor.

Tanner fell to his knees and attempted to attend to the others.

"No!" he cried out as he realized they were unresponsive.

Angrily, he looked up at Cheveyo, who grinned evilly, then raised the weapon to his shoulder and squinted through the sight. Tanner sprang to his feet and lunged for the man. Then there was a brief flash of light, and everything went dark.

CHAPTER 37

A WOMAN ALONE

(MICK)

As Mick had fallen to the floor of the dwelling below, she'd glanced around to see if anyone had witnessed her arrival, but when she heard Cheveyo's voice in the room above, she bolted for the door. She had to get as far away from Cheveyo's place as she could.

Why couldn't it have been one of the guys who jumped through first? Why did it have to be me?

When she opened the door, it was an instant awakening to the dangers of Anatok. The sounds, the smells, and the very feeling in the air itself made her sense she had no chance of surviving the night.

Should we have just waited and tried to flee when he took us to the palace?

There was no turning back. With her friends held captive, she was all that stood between this technologically superior race and her fellow Surfacers. If her world was going to survive, she had to thwart Cheveyo's plans.

She climbed the few steps that brought her to street level and then secreted herself in a shadowy corner adjacent to the entrance of Cheveyo's home. Streaks of lightning illuminated a street Mick would have rather not seen.

The water! Mick thought. *I've got to drink some of the Mnemosyne water. I need the heightened awareness.* She reached for her purse where she kept the vial Mr. Carlton had given her at Bertie's ice cream shop.

It's on the floor at Cheveyo's. I could have really used that.

Frustrated and emotionally drained, Mick wanted to just give up.

Four shots rang out, and she stiffened, her heart sinking as she realized where the gunshots had come from.

"Noooo!" she quietly cried.

Maybe it didn't come from Cheveyo's, she failed to convince herself.

Mick felt numb. Her best friends had just been gunned down in cold blood, and here she sat, facing an unknown world of evil.

How could he have? she wondered as she sat in the corner and sobbed. *It's not possible! He needed them. He needed to use the visualizer on them.* Her hope was short-lived when she remembered how the visualizer worked on the tusks of a dead mammoth. *He never needed us alive—just our molecules.* She thought about how King Tohopka was planning to take over the entire surface world and how he had the technology to pull it off. Unless she could somehow stop Cheveyo, the rest of her world and everyone else's on the Surface would crumble. She had to make sure the king never witnessed what the visualizer would show him.

I've made everything so much worse. If I just would have left well enough alone. So what if I took some persecution for the Brownsville Bank robbery. My obsession with that has led me to being single-handedly responsible for the downfall of the whole planet.

I can't let it happen. Like Tanner would say, I've got to go down swinging. But where do I go?

A thought came to Mick's mind. It wasn't one she wanted, but it was load and clear. Tanner had told her a story his mother shared about when the two of them faced difficulties. The way Mick remembered it, when lions eyed a herd of deer, the slow, older lions would position themselves on the opposite side of the deer from the younger lions. The older lions would roar with all their might. Scared, the deer would run away from the roaring and into the younger lions. If the deer would run toward the roaring, they would be safe. There were many times when the friends had been adventuring that Tanner would say "We've got to run toward the roar." As hard as she tried, Mick couldn't get the phrase out of her head, and she knew exactly what it meant.

I've got to get to the king's palace before Cheveyo.

It was the opposite of what she wanted to do, but it was running toward the roar, and she felt strongly that she had to do it.

A sketchy character emerged from the dark haze. He had a strange weapon in his hand that was shooting electrical charges like lightning and destroying everything he fired at as he staggered down the street.

Looks like he's drunk.

Mick tried to keep even her rapidly beating heart from making a noise. A load clap of thunder caused that heart to nearly explode. She looked around for a weapon. All she had was the piece of rubber flooring she'd used to protect her hands as she'd jumped through the floor. With what hung in the balance, she needed to hit this stranger with everything she had. It was the element of surprise and her little piece of rubber against his lightning blaster.

I've only got one shot. If I don't take him down, I'll end up like my friends.

As he walked unknowingly past her, Mick leapt out, and with as big a swing as she could muster, she smashed him across the back of the head. Down he went. Mick grabbed his weapon and dragged him into the shadows. Quickly, she changed into his rubberized suit and stared in awe at the collection of flexible screens that began to illuminate across its surface.

No time to figure all this out. Just got to get out of here.

Mick looked over at Cheveyo's spacecraft. *I wonder...*

No way I'll make it out of here on foot, but I might have a chance if I fly out.

The spacecraft was parked on a small platform about a half story above her. She jumped and was barely able to latch onto an exposed piece of rebar dangling from the edge of the platform. After a struggle, she pulled herself up, then jumped into the hovercraft's seat and scanned the controls.

Mick noticed a button positioned prominently on the dashboard. *This must be how you start this thing.* There was a joystick-like device situated near her left hand. *And that must be how you steer.* She clicked the button, and a goggle-like apparatus extended from the control panel and positioned itself near her eyes. A blue line of light scanned her left eye. The goggles returned to the control panel and—nothing. Mick realized it was a security device. She wasn't the owner, so there was no way to get it started. But going on foot was out of the question.

As risky as it was, Mick decided to sneak back into Cheveyo's dwelling to see what resources she could commandeer. She lowered herself from the platform down to the entrance. The doorway had a display screen attached on the front. Groups of glowing blue symbols, some two digits in length and some three, flashed across the panel. These symbols were of various sizes and were randomly floating in different directions across the screen. Mick reached out and realized she could control the movement of a grouping of symbols with her finger. After playing with the numbers for a few minutes, she became frustrated.

I'm never going to figure this out.

She pulled her finger away from the panel and noticed something she hadn't before. On the underside of her right forearm on the rubberized suit was a diagram displaying an arrangement of the same symbols she saw on the screen in front of her.

There's no way, she thought. She began arranging the symbols in the pattern she saw on her arm, and, sure enough, the door opened.

Did I just steal the suit of a professional thief? Wouldn't surprise me. Everyone around here looks like a thug.

Mick entered, and then closed the door behind her. She listened as a series of locks secured it. She felt safe in this space between the street and Cheveyo and relished the moment. But she had to keep moving.

There was a similar security panel on the second door, but in this case, the image was a lifelike 3-D picture of Cheveyo and what looked to be a bunch of hunting buddies. Confidently, Mick looked at the underside of her right arm. Nothing. She shook it, hoping something would display. Still nothing. She looked at the underside of her left arm. Again, nothing.

Hmmm. Cheveyo's security system is sophisticated enough to stump even a pro. Mick stood in front of the image, wondering where to begin.

She tried to think back to when Cheveyo first brought them to his residence.

He ran his hand across the screen in a pattern that looked familiar. What was it? Think!

With the fate of the world resting on her shoulders, she was so beside herself she couldn't remember the shape.

The number four. Yeah, that was it. But what if I'm wrong? Do I only get one shot? Will an alarm go off if I'm wrong? Panic seized her. *Stop second-guessing yourself. That was it.* Mick braced herself for the worst as she placed her finger at the center of the lower part of the screen and ran it up to the top, then across to the middle left on a diagonal, and then straight across to the middle right. She felt slightly more confident when she realized each change in direction fell upon the face of a hunter. But she knew it might have been a coincidence, because there were around fifteen hunters in the picture.

As soon as Mick removed her finger after the final line, she heard a small whirring noise as a series of locks around the perimeter of the door unlatched themselves.

"Yes!" she whispered, pumping her fist. "Now to get what I need and get out of here."

Mick stepped into the room where her friends had been murdered. Smoke filled the air, and the four bodies were heaped on the rubberized black floor. Tears rolled down her cheeks as she stared through the beam. She wanted to just stay and mourn, but there wasn't time. Quietly, Mick tiptoed from room to room. A loud snore startled her. It was coming from the back of the house. She approached the room and peered around the doorway. Sure enough, Cheveyo was sprawled out, asleep on his bed.

Don't swear, she thought, looking at the man who had destroyed her life.

She glanced around the room through her tear-filled eyes and saw a golden vase filled with huge, fresh-cut flowers. Everything in Anatok was so dark and lifeless the brightly colored bouquet seemed wildly out of place.

"Stay focused," she whispered as she grabbed the vase, removed the flowers, and gingerly approached the bed. *He just killed my friends. He wants to help Tohopka rule the world. Just go through with it.*

"Smash!" Mick hit Cheveyo over the head, knocking him out cold. She reached for her camera and pried open Cheveyo's left eye.

Flash.

Got it. Now to the spacecraft!

Mick was back to the platform in no time. She hopped in the hovercraft and clicked the button. The goggles moved into position.

This better work.

Mick held her phone with the photo of Cheveyo's left eye in front of the goggles and held her breath. The blue light scanned across her phone and, sure enough, the spacecraft started up.

Now, where's the owner's manual? She started to look around the craft. *What are you thinking? You don't have time for that.*

She grabbed the joystick and gave it a slight pull back and to the left. The craft dislodged from the platform, and she was airborne.

Too bad I didn't spend more time playing video games. The few times she had played, she'd failed miserably, her lack of skill now showing as she attempted to fly. Luckily the craft was moving slowly. She found acceleration buttons along the side of the joystick and gradually began to pick up speed. She navigated left and right, up and down, underneath overhead walkways and over bridges, and around balconies and platforms where other spacecraft were perched. She was beginning to feel comfortable.

I can do this!

Seconds later she heard several explosions in quick-fire succession all around her.

Whoa. She jerked her head around and saw a small craft in pursuit. *I've got no chance. I'm barely able to fly this thing. Got to get to the king's palace.*

Mick pulled back on the joystick and accelerated in an attempt to get herself above the tall buildings and create distance between herself and her pursuer. The explosions continued. She yanked the controls hard to the right as she saw a spectacular palace in the distance.

I should be able to fly a straight line at full acceleration. She held down the throttle and rapidly outdistanced her enemy.

Should have known Cheveyo would have the best spacecraft available.

As she began to relax, several explosions again rocked the small craft. This time they were coming from an unknown location on the ground.

A straight line makes me an easy target. She began to fly in a more random pattern. Another explosion came, and a large chunk of the right side of her craft was destroyed. A trail of black smoke began to stream from behind her. Mick grabbed the joystick with both hands as her craft wobbled toward the palace. She was quickly losing control.

I'm going down! She scoured the city for the inevitable crash site.

There's a clearing. She eyed the target. Another explosion. More of the right side was destroyed. The craft began to spiral downward. Mick pulled back as hard as she could on the controller only to have it break off in her hand.

She braced herself as she plummeted toward the clearing.

Is that an eject button?

She gave it a push, and her seat shot out of the craft, then gradually began to descend toward the clearing. A set of balancing jets slowly lowered her toward the ground. Mick could see the clearing below was a murky, trash-filled swamp. With a loud thud, her former craft splashed into it and exploded. Mick let out a gasp as she watched the flames.

"That could have been me."

When she landed, Mick removed herself and sloshed in the direction of the palace. Again, explosions were going off all around her, and bursts of gunfire were descending from the city buildings behind her. She moved as fast as she could through the muddy swamp in an unpredictable zigzag pattern.

She cried out and nearly collapsed into the marsh as an excruciating pain shot up her right calf. Something had penetrated the rubber suit.

Just a few hundred more yards!

Every time she planted her right foot, the pain shot up her leg. Almost there. She reached the edge of the swamp and hobbled to the palace gate, where she was met by a massive guard.

"Who are you? What is your purpose here?" the mighty guard asked.

"I am here to make you one of the most powerful men in all of Anatok," Mick said, trying to sound as confident as she could through the pain.

"You?" the guard inquired, looking her over from head to toe. "What do you mean?"

"I have something in my possession that will make the king far wealthier than he already is. I am offering you the opportunity to be the one to share it with him. Sound interesting?" Mick asked with an air of intrigue. She was trying to do her best impression of Tanner. He was always good at enticing people to do what he wanted them to do.

"So how do *I* become powerful?" the guard asked.

"The king rewards those who help him add to his wealth. What I am willing to share will make him more money than anything anyone has ever done before."

"Then why don't you share it directly with him—why do you need me?"

"You are the one who can get me access to the king. I would never be able to get an audience without you."

"That makes sense. Go ahead, I'm listening."

"You won't be disappointed," Mick replied. "I know where the passage to the Fourth World is."

"You lie!" the guard replied, pounding his spear forcefully on the pavement. "No one knows where that passageway is."

CHAPTER 38

THE GATHERING PLACE

(MICK)

"No, I swear," Mick said when she saw him shake his head in disbelief. She crossed her heart with her hand. "I came from the Fourth World."

"If you speak the truth, then, yes, the king will reward me handsomely."

"Then you're in?"

"I'm in."

"Great. Now, there's one small thing that might be a problem," Mick said.

"What's that?" the guard asked.

"There are four men, enemies of mine, who also came from the Fourth World in hopes of being richly rewarded by the king for this information. They were captured and killed by Cheveyo, who plans on using the visualizer in the morning to show King Tohopka the path to the Surface. You and I, however, will provide the king with an irresistible second offer to assure he will work with us."

"What's this second offer? Your hand in marriage?"

"Very funny," Mick said angrily.

"No, I'm not joking. The king is a sucker for beautiful women."

"Well, let me make one thing perfectly clear—that is not on the table!"

"Fine, I get it."

"In all seriousness, the king is concerned there's a group of Spider Woman followers who plan to warn those in the Fourth World and help prepare them for battle against the king's forces. Since its obvious—based on my fair skin—that I come from the Fourth World, I can infiltrate their organization."

The man leaned closer, scraped some mud off Mick's face, and then nodded in agreement.

"I was told these 'believers' have been recruiting forces and are gathering at some hidden location. Once I find out where it is, the king will want to work with us, and you will be promoted to captain of the guard, or maybe even second in command."

"What do you need from me?"

"I need you to take me to a 'believer.' From there I'll work on finding this hidden location."

"I'll need to find someone to take my shift. Can't leave my post, you know."

"Yes, but be quick. We must arrive at the palace before Cheveyo."

"I'll be quick."

A few minutes later, the guard returned.

"All set. Let's get going."

"We never did introductions. I'm Mick."

"And I'm Ayawamat," came the reply. "Follow me to my vehicle."

Ayawamat flew Mick through the city to a platform in a section of town that looked even worse than the area where Cheveyo lived.

"The family who lives here are believers."

"Wait here," Mick said. "They'll never give me the information about their gathering place if they see you."

"That's certainly true."

"See you shortly."

Mick scurried down the stairs from the platform and knocked on the door. When no one answered, she knocked again. She knew it was far too early for anyone to be awake, but she was desperate.

"Who is it?" a sleepy voice eventually called out.

"I'm from the Fourth World. I need your help," Mick said.

A light beam scanned Mick from head to toe in the darkness. When the light turned off, she could hear a series of locks being unbolted.

The door opened slightly, and a short woman peered apprehensively from around the door.

"How can I be sure you're from the Fourth World?"

"Look at me. Have you ever seen someone from the Third World with skin this fair?"

"You're either from the Surface or maybe Delfi. They have all skin colors in Delfi. Or perhaps you're from some distant land of Kuskurza."

"Well, my skin is the only tangible proof I have. But I can tell you about the fulfillment of the prophecies that a fair-skinned people would overtake those who fled to the Fourth World. I can assure you it all came true. Hundreds of years before I was born, many of your people died of diseases and in battle, when my ancestors first came to their lands of inheritance."

"Please, won't you tell us more?" the woman said, her fears concerning Mick seeming to wane.

"I understand you're believers," Mick said. "Is that correct?"

"Yes, we are," the woman said, looking nervously around to see if anyone was watching them. "Come in." She gently pulled Mick into the dwelling.

"I would love to tell all about your people and the Fourth World right now, but what I really need to tell you, and the reason I'm here, is that King Tohopka is about to discover the passageway to my world. He has to be stopped."

"I couldn't agree with you more. What makes you say he's about to discover the passageway?"

"Several of my friends from the Surface and I were captured by Cheveyo the bounty hunter. He said his plan was to use a visualizer on us so the king could see how we arrived. I escaped just moments before Cheveyo killed my friends. He's planning to bring their dead bodies to the palace first thing in the morning. My whole civilization is at risk unless I can stop him."

"Ours is too. What do you want from us?" the woman asked.

"Cheveyo said the believers were assembling somewhere. I need you to take me there. I need their help to stop the king from taking over the world."

"Have a seat. Let me get my husband," the woman said.

"Please hurry. We don't have long before the visualizer will show the king the passageway."

"Yes, yes, I understand. I'll be right back."

Mick sat nervously fidgeting on the sofa. She could faintly hear the woman talking with a man in the other room.

A few moments later, a tall man entered the room with the woman. "My wife says you want us to lead you to the Place of Gathering. Is that correct?"

"Yes."

The man looked Mick over from head to toe. She felt him trying to assess her character.

"We're just as desperate to stop him as you are." The man paused. "Two nights ago, one of the king's guards abducted our daughter. I'm sure he plans to offer her to the king to wife because of her exceptional beauty." Mick thought about how Ayawamat had talked about offering her hand to the king and panicked. The man continued. "We'd gladly help you with anything that might thwart whatever he has planned."

Was Ayawamat the abductor? Mick thought. *Is that how he knew where this family of believers lived?*

"Oh, thank you," Mick said, clearly distracted. She was even more concerned about Ayawamat and her own personal safety, but at least this man and his wife were willing to help her with a key element of her plan to stop the king. "I don't know how I– that is, we, citizens of the Surface, can ever repay you."

"We haven't done anything yet," the man said. "Save your thanks until we stop the king. Believe me, it won't be easy.

"I have no way to take you to the Place of Gathering. Our hovercraft was stolen last week. But I can tell you where they're located."

"Even better," Mick said with great excitement. She knew things would get complicated if they found out a palace guard, perhaps the one who had kidnapped their daughter, had brought her to them. The man gave her a quick look as if to question her motives.

Mick noticed the questioning glance. "Just don't want to burden you any more than necessary."

"Let me try to explain how to reach the Place of Gathering. The city is circular in shape." The man drew a circle on the table with his finger.

"At the top of the circle is the king's palace. At the bottom, just to the right of center, is a sacred burial ground. It's huge. After entering the main gate, if you turn left and walk along the wall, in the far corner of the site you'll find a simple tomb in a small garden area. There are a few gnarly old olive trees near it. When you enter the tomb, it will appear empty. Explore it very carefully. You'll find that the better acquainted you become with this tomb, the more its secrets will unlock themselves to you, and you'll be able to solve whatever difficulties you're facing—regardless of how hopeless it may seem. I wish I could tell you more, but if you're sincere, I've told you enough to be successful."

"You really can't tell me more? How will I know if I've found what I need if I don't even know what I'm looking for?"

"I've told you all I can. Good luck!"

Mick had to get going. The gentleman wasn't going to give her any additional information, and she was running out of time.

"Thank you so much. If I really can solve the difficulties I face, like you said, I thank you on behalf of the entire population of the Surface."

Mick hustled to the door and was gone. She ran for Ayawamat's hovercraft.

When she jumped in, she gave him a long stare, trying to ascertain whether he was the kidnapper. "Take me to the ancient burial grounds!" she shouted, putting aside her concerns for her personal safety in order to save the planet.

"We'll have to be fast. Dawn is about to break," Ayawamat replied.

Ayawamat was full speed ahead, and it wasn't long before his craft descended in front of the cemetery.

"Wait here," Mick said. "And don't try anything. Remember, you need me and my molecules." Mick was a bit nervous that Ayawamat would betray her now that he knew the general whereabouts of the rebel forces. "I'll be right back."

Mick dashed to the corner of the burial ground, looking for the gnarled trees and simple tomb.

That's got to be it.

She approached the doorway of the tomb and was surprised by the instant feeling of hope, something that had been sucked out of her from the moment she saw the scorched trees entering Anatok. She straightened up.

This is going to work out.

The whole world was collapsing around her. Her best friends were dead, and yet, as she entered this mysterious tomb, her attitude began to change. She tried to think why. Was it merely the power of suggestion working wonders on her mind? Or was there really something about this tomb—some magical power already taking hold of her?

Mick began to scour the place for clues. There really was nothing there. She had expected to find petroglyphs or markings, symbols she needed to study, or buttons needing to be pressed in a certain order. But it was just plain and bare. She took a step up and back out of the tomb to reexamine the outside, hoping that maybe she had missed a clue. She walked all the way around the tomb. The old, weathered trees were alive—she hadn't noticed that before. They were only living plants she had seen since arriving in this horrible land. Was that what had made her feel hope?

Mick ran her hands across every surface outside the tomb. But still nothing unusual. She reentered the tomb. She took out her phone and was using the flashlight to examine everything more closely when a loud grinding noise startled her. Before Mick knew what was happening, the large stone that stood outside the tomb was closing. Instinctively Mick darted to the opening and reached out to stop the massive stone, but realizing she'd never be able to do so, yanked her hand back just before it slammed shut.

Whew, she thought. *What was I thinking! I would have been pinned. The only way I would have been able to free myself would have been to cut my arm loose, and I would have bled to death.* She shuttered thinking about it. *And without anything to cut myself loose, I would have died, trapped in here. Wow. Too close.*

Thinking about it a little more as she stood in the darkness, she realized she was going to die in the tomb either way. There was no way to get the stone away from the entrance, so she was trapped. Destined to suffocate in the small chamber. Had she been set up? Had the man sent her into a death trap? Did he know she was with the king's guard and decided to send her to her mortal end?

Mick began feeling around the tomb, trying to find the stone bed where the dead would have been laid to rest. She wanted to sit down and think. Tapping along the walls, she finally reached the bed and put her hand down, breathing a sigh of relief. Then something moved. Mick about jumped out of her skin. It was the bed itself. She listened to the sound of the heavy slab as it slid along the stone it rested upon. She began to see slivers of light streaking out of a small gap that was gradually growing as the slab slid farther away from the base. Mick's heart leapt. A fully illuminated stone stairway began to come into view. It had been hidden by the bed of the tomb. The fear melted away and was replaced with a welcome sensation of peace. The light emanating from the stairway was warm, bright, and inviting. Once the lid had moved completely out of the way, Mick climbed onto the base, then began her descent into whatever it was that awaited her below.

How did that happen? she wondered. She wasn't sure what she had done to trigger either the closing of the outer door or the opening of the stairway's entrance. *It's brilliant, I guess. I'll never know how to tell anyone else how to get in because, even after doing it myself, I still don't know how to do it.*

Carefully she descended.

CHAPTER 39

THE TOMB

(HOKOLESQUA)

From his view behind the dumpster, Hokolesqua watched the thugs climb into an open-topped space vehicle that had been hovering at the side of the street. After playing with the controls for a few minutes, they began to slowly move away.

"Hey! That's my XG!" someone yelled. Hokolesqua turned to see a middle-aged man lumbering toward the boys with his arm extended in their direction.

Two of the boys in the craft turned, and pressing their wrists, sent multiple streaks of lightning hurtling toward the man, who ducked behind a metal crate. The boys fired again, and the crate exploded in a ball of fire. The man fled down a side alley, and the boys sped away.

"I changed my mind. I will go to the graveyard."

"It really isn't safe on the streets," Kwatoko said quietly. Then, lowering his voice even more, he added, "especially for Surfacers."

From his crouched position, he scanned in every direction.

"It looks clear. Follow me."

They entered through the main gate of the graveyard.

"We can't all go to the tomb together," Kwatoko said as he started to walk along the fence line. Looking back, he whispered, "We'll draw too much attention to the Place of Gathering."

Lapu added, "Follow the fence all the way to the corner. You'll find a few weathered olive trees obscuring the front of a tomb.

They might be the only living things in the entire cemetery. We'll meet you there."

"I do not like this place," Hokolesqua whispered to Nemhsi.

"These are good men," she replied. "They're trying to help us."

"We should have stayed in the forest," Hokolesqua said, shaking his head. "You go first." He gave Nemhsi a gentle push in the back. "I will watch to make sure you're safe."

Hokolesqua waited for his turn.

Boom!

An explosion sounded behind him. He turned and saw a fireball roar out of a second-story window across the walkway from where he was.

I go now.

He quickly made his way to the tomb.

When he entered, the tomb was completely dark and empty. Hokolesqua panicked. He stepped back out and looked around again, but seeing no other structure that matched the description the men had given him, he stepped inside again. A sliver of light appeared from an opening in a small bench inside, growing larger until he could see a stairway leading down.

CHAPTER 40

THE FOLLOWERS OF SPIDER WOMAN

(MICK)

"Welcome."

"We're so glad you're here!"

Mick was greeted by an array of well-groomed Indians of all shapes and sizes shaking her hands and hugging her—a stark contrast from her arrival in Anatok.

"Where am I?" she asked.

"You're in the Place of Gathering—meeting place of the followers of Spider Woman," a tall man with a commanding presence replied. "Your determination, perseverance, and sincerity have led you here. Tell us about yourself." He motioned toward the large group assembled in the room before them. "What is your purpose for coming?"

"I don't have much time," Mick said, looking around in surprise at how the acoustics of the room seemed to be amplifying her voice without a microphone. "I'll be brief. King Tohopka is determined to conquer the surface of the earth—where I come from." An audible gasp filled the room, and Mick could hear "She's a Surfacer" being whispered throughout the hall. She continued. "Soon, the dead bodies of my friends who were captured and killed by his bounty hunter Cheveyo will be transported to the palace." Mick looked around. The massive cavern was filled with warriors and common folk as far as the eye could see. There were stacks of weapons stored around the perimeter.

Mick continued. "Using a visualizer, he plans to show the king the passageway to the Surface. Once he knows how to get there, I fear the end of my civilization. I need your help!"

"We'll gladly help," came the reply from an older gentleman toward the front. "What can we do?"

"Let me explain," Mick said. "I was brought here by one of the palace guards. I told him I could help him rise to fame and fortune by allowing the king to use the visualizer on me instead of on my dead friends. He wouldn't accept my plan because there was no advantage over what Cheveyo would already be offering. To sweeten our deal, I told the guard we would also divulge the location of the rebel followers of Spider Woman."

"You betrayed us!" one of the women shouted and rushed at Mick. The leader stepped between them. The chatter in the room ramped up. Mick felt as much anger and hostility as she had warmth and hospitality moments earlier.

"Please, quiet. Quiet," the leader said. "Hear her out."

"I have no intention of actually sharing your location with the king," Mick said. "What I'm here to ask is that you storm the palace before I get that far. Tohopka will be so giddy he's about to find the path to the Surface that he'll let his guard down, and you'll be able to overthrow his government."

"If the Palace Guard brought you here," the woman who had rushed Mick said, "he already knows the Place of Gathering is here. He's probably on his way to tell the king right now."

"No," Mick said. "He needs the visualizer to be used on me in order for the plan to work. He won't leave."

"Since he knows our location now anyway, why don't you lure him down into the tomb?" the tall leader said. "That would make it easier to guarantee he doesn't flee without you and will give us a chance to persuade him to join us. If he doesn't go along, we keep him as a prisoner."

"That sounds like a great idea," Mick replied. "But I need him to bring me to the palace so I can get an audience with the king."

"You're right," the leader said. "If we can't persuade him . . ." he grabbed a weapon and looked it over from top to bottom, ". . . we'll *persuade* him." He looked Mick in the eye and smiled. "Look, I'll get everyone to hide until the two of you are deep into the hall. It will be easier to block any attempted escape that way. Oh, and don't say anything about our plans to storm the palace. We'll have no way of knowing what he's truly persuaded by."

"Don't worry. I won't say anything," Mick said.

Mick raced up the stone stairs. She saw the outer stone sliding open to reveal Ayawamat.

"Ayawamat, come quickly. You've got to see this. I found the Place of Gathering."

"But someone will recognize me."

"No one's there. When you see what these rebels have amassed, you'll understand how happy the king is going to be that we've uncovered the place."

Ayawamat followed Mick as she sprinted toward the tomb, and then led him down the stairs. The followers of Spider Woman were hidden in the passageways and various rooms of the cavern.

"Look at all these weapons," Mick exclaimed.

"It's incredible," the guard replied as he reached for one of the guns.

"Be careful," Mick said. "We can't do anything that might tip them off that we've been here. If they figure out we're on to them, they'll change locations."

"Good point," Ayawamat replied.

"Look at these weapons over here," Mick said as she drew Ayawamat into the center of the space and away from the weapons so he wouldn't be able to arm himself when the followers appeared. As they neared the center of the room, Spider Woman's followers emerged. A couple of the largest men ran to Ayawamat and held him tight.

"You set me up!" Ayawamat shouted as he angrily tried to wrestle himself free, lurching in Mick's direction.

"Actually, she saved your life." The leader of the followers stepped between Ayawamat and Mick. "Tohopka's wickedness will be his downfall. Eventually we'll overthrow Wild Beast, and you would have ended up dead. Instead, you have a chance to rise to a position of stature in a new regime—one that will restore Anatok to its former greatness. But we need your help. You must get an audience with the king."

Looking around at the forces that surrounded him, Ayawamat agreed.

"I'll help," Ayawamat said. "I've seen the corruption of Tohopka up close, and you're right. The kingdom is ripe for destruction."

Mick had no way of knowing if the guard was sincere, but she needed him to play his role whether he was doing it out of fear or truly believed in their cause.

"Will you still follow our original plan, then?" Mick asked.

"I'll play my part," Ayawamat said.

"Let's get moving, then," Mick replied. "No time to waste."

"To the palace!" Ayawamat replied.

Mick, Ayawamat, and two men from the Place of Gathering fled up the stairs.

CHAPTER 41

HOKO'S NEW FRIENDS

(HOKOLESQUA)

"Come on, Hoko," Nemhsi's voice whispered from below. "It's safe down here."

"Excuse us!" a reddish-brown-haired girl said, looking Hokolesqua straight in the eye as she ran up the stairs and past him. Three large warrior-types followed close behind her.

Hokolesqua watched as the four strangers fled the tomb and headed toward the gate leading out of the cemetery. Turning back, he carefully descended the narrow staircase toward his sister's voice. When he got to the bottom, the space opened into a large cavernous room filled with people. Kwatoko grabbed Hokolesqua and Nemhsi by the arms, pulling them close to him.

"Attention, everyone, attention," he said.

The noisy room began to grow steadily quieter. Once the noise stopped completely, the man continued.

"Meet Hokolesqua and Nemhsi. They are here to join with us." A small buzz began to go around the room.

"Silence," Kwatoko said, waving his hand above his head. "I need your full attention."

The room fell silent again.

"They're Surfacers." A collective gasp echoed through the cavern.

"More Surfacers?" someone asked. "Why so many all of a sudden?"

"Are they actual descendants of those Spider Woman led away from Anatok?" another asked with reverence in her voice.

Kwatoko waved his arms to quiet the crowd again.

"They arrived a couple days ago. We must protect them with our lives."

"Those willing to defend Hokolesqua and Nemhsi?" He paused. Everyone in the room made a fist with their left hand, raised their left arm to a square, and then thumped it against the center of their chest twice.

"Those unwilling?" Kwatoko scanned the room. Hokolesqua and Nemhsi watched intently. No one made any sign that would have indicated an unwillingness to protect them.

Kwatoko and Lapu took Hokolesqua and Nemhsi down off the speaking platform and into the crowd.

A tall man heading toward the platform grabbed Lapu.

"We must enlist the Delfians," the man said. "Tohopka's men have made even the woods outside Delfi completely unsafe. I'm sure they'll join with us. My personal craft is just outside the graveyard." He handed a card to Lapu.

"Done," Lapu said and fled up the stairway.

The tall man stepped up on the platform and urged everyone to arm themselves.

Watching the mass of humanity preparing for battle, Hokolesqua leaned over to Kwatoko and asked, "What's going on? This isn't all to protect us, is it?"

"No." Kwatoko chuckled. "Although, I guess in part it is. For years we've been persecuted by the king and his followers, and now he's making preparations to attack the Surface. This morning we plan to overthrow his government."

"I've never seen weapons like those before," Hokolesqua said.

"Don't worry." Kwatoko continued. "They aren't designed to kill. They render their victims immobile, long enough for us to capture and imprison them. Then our missionaries teach the prisoners the ways of Spider Woman. Many of them have been blinded by the hatred of their families. They've been taught lies and half-truths, poisoning them against us. Often these prisoners become true followers themselves. Those who don't remain our prisoners. We put them to work on various projects around the Place of Gathering."

"Let me show you around," Kwatoko said as he began to walk away. Hokolesqua and Nemhsi followed.

Hokolesqua was shocked at how extensive the cavern was as their guide led them from room to room.

"Looks like the prisoners are kept busy," Hokolesqua said.

"Yes, most of this was built using their labor," Kwatoko replied.

"Excuse me." A man tapped Hokolesqua on the shoulder.

"I'm Matcito, and this is Tocho," he said, pointing to a man standing next to him. "So excited to actually meet a Surfacer."

"Nice to meet you," Nemhsi replied.

"We've heard so much about the Fourth World. But, you know, it becomes kind of hard to continue to believe without evidence."

Matcito added, "My grandmother told me stories about how some of her ancestors went to the Fourth World, but my parents weren't believers."

"So how did you end up here?" Nemhsi asked.

"I was torturing a follower when someone stunned me. I spent the next three years as a prisoner. In fact, I installed a lot of the lighting," he said, motioning around the room. "I was taught by many missionaries. Then one of them reminded me of the things my grandmother taught me, and I converted. It's taken a long time for me to forgive myself for the way I behaved before my mighty change."

"And you?" Nemhsi asked Tocho. "Have you always been a believer?"

"No, but I wasn't as stubborn as Matcito. I converted right away."

Hokolesqua could sense their guide wanting to continue with his tour.

"Nice to meet you. We'll speak again," Nemhsi said to the two men as she and her brother were whisked away by Kwatoko to the next introduction.

Hokolesqua was thinking about how welcoming everyone was. He had never experienced anything like this from adults–other than his parents. His thoughts turned to them.

Father must be so worried. I should have told him what I was doing. Now his wife, two daughters, and son are all missing.

Will I ever find Mother and Methoataske?

"Hoko?" Nemhsi elbowed him in the ribs, bringing him back to the present. He noticed a hand extended in front of him, and he was reaching out to shake it when the atmosphere around them was suddenly turned upside down, a massive explosion overhead rocking the entire cavern.

"What was that?" someone yelled.

There was no time for anyone to answer. Gunfire erupted from the stairway. Everyone's heads snapped in that direction. One of the king's troops stood in the entryway. The entire stairway appeared to be teaming with additional troops following behind.

"We're under attack!" someone screamed from near the entrance.

"It was the girl!" someone shouted. "She betrayed us!"

CHAPTER 42

AN AUDIENCE WITH THE KING

(MICK)

Ayawamat and Mick arrived at the king's palace as the sun began to illuminate the golden building. As they sprinted down the corridor, they caught a glimpse of Cheveyo a split second before a guard closed the door of the throne room.

"He's already here," Mick said in panic. "We've got to get to the king before he uses the visualizer!"

Ayawamat approached his fellow guard. After what seemed to Mick like an eternity of back-and-forth discussion, the guard reluctantly opened the door and a short, middle-aged man inside escorted them toward the throne. Mick gasped at the sight of her four friends lying in a heap in front of a large, well-fed man whose headdress was nearly as tall as he was.

The king's attendant announced the arrival of Ayawamat. Cheveyo turned and made eye contact with Mick, who could see the anger sweep across his entire body. He scowled at Ayawamat.

"Great King, Controller of Earth and Sky, God of Light and Darkness, Master of All . . ." the middle-aged escort declared.

All right, come on. Get on with it!

Mick took a peek at Cheveyo, who began to pace rapidly back and forth and looked as though he was trying to adjust his plan.

The attendant reeled off a few more elaborate titles before finally getting to the matter at hand.

"Ayawamat, who recognizes himself unworthy to approach your noble throne, has requested the privilege of being able to interrupt the important matters you face in protecting and preserving this great people."

Oh, brother! Mick thought. *Is this guy full of himself or what?*

Finally, after another lengthy speech by the attendant, the king himself spoke in third person. "The Great and Powerful King Tohopka will grant his request. But if the thing he has interrupted Tohopka for is not deemed worthy of the king's precious time . . ." The king looked over at the attendant and asked, "Has he been made aware of the consequences?"

"Yes, my lord," the attendant replied.

"Then state your purpose for approaching the king's omnipotent throne," King Tohopka said.

"All Wise and Knowing King," Ayawamat began. "I know of your desire to find the passageway to the Fourth World, where the traitorous followers of Spider Woman fled so many years ago. I found this Surfacer last night and bring her before you so you can utilize the visualizer and witness how she arrived in Anatok. This will allow the mighty Tohopka to lead his troops to the Surface and become the supreme ruler of both the interior and exterior of the planet." Ayawamat paused. "It looks as though Cheveyo has also brought Surfacers before you, All Powerful King. I know it doesn't matter to the visualizer if the Surfacers are dead, like the ones Cheveyo brought, or alive, like the one I brought. But you must know that having a live Surfacer would most certainly come in handy if any of the things the visualizer shows need explanation or clarification."

"But—" Cheveyo tried to insert himself into the dialog.

"Silence," King Tohopka bellowed.

Cheveyo thrust both arms downward in frustration.

"The floor has been given to Ayawamat," Tohopka said, angrily dismissing Cheveyo with a wave of his hand.

"Yes, I can see the advantage of using the visualizer on the young woman," the king said.

"Great Ruler of Sea and Land, I also offer another advantage that this man doesn't," Ayawamat said, gesturing at Cheveyo.

"Her hand in marriage?" Tohopka asked.

"No," Ayawamat said. "Although she *would* be the luckiest girl in earth."

Mick cringed. Ayawamat continued. "I did think about offering her to you, but soon you'll have the choice of any woman in or on the earth, and with those kinds of choices, I assumed you'd choose someone else."

Mick was both relieved and at the same time slightly incensed.

"So, if you're not offering her hand in marriage as an additional benefit, what are you offering?"

"I can lead you to the Place of Gathering, where the followers of Spider Woman are assembling at this very moment in preparation to overthrow your kingdom."

Ayawamat paused again, and he and Mick looked on in excited anticipation to see the king's reaction. Mick was sure this was going to be the clincher.

"Off with them!" the king yelled. Mick smiled and waited for the king to motion or point toward Cheveyo, but the gesture never came. Fear began to pulse through her body. "Bind Ayawamat and this woman and throw them in the dungeons. We'll behead them tomorrow!"

Mick and Ayawamat looked at each other in horror and complete disbelief.

"You're not interested?" Ayawamat said.

"Of course I'm interested," Tohopka replied. "Cheveyo and I will use the visualizer on these Surfacers," he pointed to the bodies of Mick's friends on the ground in front of him, "and soon I'll rule the planet. What I'm *not* interested in is working with traitors. You see, I embedded a live body visualizer into the molecular structure of everyone who works for me. It allows me to watch for treachery and treason. And you, Ayawamat, are guilty of both! I watched every step of your trip to the burial grounds, and my troops have already surrounded the site. The good news for you is that soon you'll have lots of companionship in the dungeons!"

The two guards flanking Tohopka had made their way to Mick and Ayawamat and were shackling their hands and feet.

Mick stood in stunned silence. She had been so proud of her improvised plan, but it had completely backfired. Every noise in the room faded as she turned completely inside herself. Her entire soul felt ripped out. A few feet away were the bodies of her four dead friends, she was about to be beheaded, and this wicked king was about to overtake the planet.

Tohopka stood, the flash of moving color from his headdress snapping Mick out of her numb state.

"Cheveyo, let's get the visualizer attached to your bounty and find that entrance."

"Follow us," one of the guards growled as he forcefully grabbed Mick by the arm. Mick looked back over her shoulder, and her heart sank as she watched the king step down from his throne and hand Cheveyo a visualizer. The weathered warrior grinned in satisfaction as he manhandled the lifeless bodies of her friends in an effort to find the best location to secure the visualizer. The guard shoved Mick in the back.

"Get moving. Nothing to see here."

Mick and Ayawamat were being shoved toward a large door on the right side of the throne.

CHAPTER 43

MOST WANTED

(HOKOLESQUA)

Hokolesqua froze as he stood looking at warriors of Tohopka battling for control of the entrance to the Place of Gathering.

"I'll protect you," someone said, grabbing him by the arm.

It was Tocho, the convert he and his sister had just been introduced to.

"Stay with me."

He grabbed weapons for both Hokolesqua and Nemhsi, and they ran toward the entrance. The strongest warriors had assembled themselves there and were battling the ferocious Anatokian fighters trying to force their way in.

The followers of Spider Woman were smart. Even though the intruders were better equipped and stronger than his new friends, the entrance was so narrow only one warrior was able to enter at a time. As each entered, he was met by three or four combatants opposing him. It didn't take long before the forces of Tohopka recognized they didn't stand a chance. Many fled, and those who didn't either surrendered themselves and their weapons or were captured as prisoners.

As three followers of Spider Woman made their way past him with an especially ferocious prisoner, the man snarled, spit flying everywhere, and looked Hokolesqua directly in the eye.

"Tohopka will conquer the Fourth World . . ."

Hokolesqua gulped.

"... and destroy every last follower of Spider Woman."

Hokolesqua cowered. He was on the most-wanted list for two different reasons.

"We've got to get back to the Surface," he whispered to Nemhsi as the prisoner was dragged away kicking and growling.

"But, Mother and Methoataske."

"What about Father? You don't want four family members never to return to Father, do you?"

"It's going to work out," Nemhsi replied.

"I'm not so sure."

CHAPTER 44

"TO THE PALACE"
(HOKOLESQUA)

When Lapu returned from Delfi, the cave quickly fell silent.

"The Delfians have agreed to help us."

A collective cheer filled the space. The man motioned for the crowd to quiet down. "They followed me here. To the palace! We've got a kingdom to overthrow."

Before Hokolesqua and Nemhsi could process what was happening, Tocho was at their side.

"Stick with me. I'll make sure you're safe. Many will meet their Maker today. I'm very familiar with the palace, having worked there before my conversion. I can assure your safety."

"Thanks," Hokolesqua said.

Hokolesqua was both excited and fearful about this chance to prove himself worthy as a warrior. Tocho's offer helped dispel the emotion he was afraid would win the day–his fear.

Tocho gave Hokolesqua and Nemhsi a quick lesson on how to use their weapons. Even though Hokolesqua destroyed a few overhead lights when he accidently pulled the trigger, Tocho assured him he'd be fine.

Hokolesqua wasn't so sure.

"Let's do this," Tocho turned and said as he entered the narrow staircase that ascended into the city of Anatok.

Hokolesqua nodded and followed.

When they exited into the graveyard, Hokolesqua found himself staring at a large and beautiful spacecraft hovering above them in the air.

"The warriors of Delfi," Tocho said. "The fate of the planet may very well be decided today."

Hokolesqua was growing more confident by the minute. He had seen some small personal flying crafts when he and his sister had first entered Anatok, but they were piles of graffiti-ridden junk in comparison to these pristine vehicles hovering above him and carrying hundreds of warriors each.

"I'm ready," he said to Tocho. "To the palace."

The clean-cut followers of Spider Woman ran unopposed through the trash-filled streets of Anatok toward the palace. The immaculate Delfian aircraft provided cover overhead.

"Nemhsi, are you all right?" Hokolesqua asked.

"I'm fine."

As the palace of Tohopka came into view, Hokolesqua thought about Tecumseh, the greatest military leader he had ever known. He lived very modestly. As Hokolesqua gazed at the intricately sculpted doors of the palace while the troops assembled at the entrance, he thought about how it was as far from modest as you could possibly get.

CHAPTER 45

MICK'S DOUBLE TAKE

(MICK)

A thunderous noise startled everyone in the throne room, and all eyes turned to the back entrance, where the doors had been broken down and hundreds of troops were storming in. This time it was King Tohopka whose jaw dropped in terrified surprise.

"Get me out of here!" the king yelled as he ran for the guards who had been escorting Mick and Ayawamat. The two men began firing their weapons in every direction as they tried to get Tohopka safely out of the throne room. The troops entering the room fired relentlessly back.

"Hit the deck!" Ayawamat yelled. He and Mick were stuck in the crossfire.

As Mick lay on the ground, she did a double take. Her four "dead" friends were slithering across the floor in an attempt to escape the crossfire.

Mick's heart leapt. Unable to contain her excitement, she started to stand up and run to them.

"You're alive!" she yelled at Tanner through the din.

"Mick! Get down!" he yelled as he looked back at her.

The fighting became exceptionally fierce as scores of Anatokian troops entered the palace.

"Grab the visualizer and let's get out of here!" Mick said as she spotted the powerful tool on the floor behind Tanner.

"Great thinking," Tanner replied.

Tanner turned back, grabbed the visualizer, and the five of them bolted for the exit.

"What happened?" Mick asked. "I thought you were dead."

"Me too," Tanner replied.

"I heard the shots," Mick said as they exited onto the open plaza, where more rebel forces were heading for the palace.

"He must have shot us with tranquilizer darts," Andrew said. "He had to know we'd be more valuable alive."

"When he lowered his sights on me, I thought it was over," Tanner said. "I started to wake up when I heard all the gunfire in the palace."

Mick gave Tanner a big hug.

"Hey, what about us?" Jim asked. Mick gave each of them a hug.

CHAPTER 46

TOHOPKA'S FLIGHT
(HOKOLESQUA)

"There's Tohopka!" Tocho said, pointing to a pompous-looking man flanked by a couple guards. "He's getting away. We've got to stop him." Tocho grabbed Hokolesqua by the arm. "Follow me!"

Tocho sprinted toward the king. Hokolesqua was hesitant to follow, but he could see that the king wasn't armed and that his guards only had spears. They did look far more advanced than the spears his father owned, but, nonetheless, they didn't look like a match for the weapons he and Nemhsi carried.

Tohopka ran out a side door and into the gardens behind the palace. Tocho and the two Shawnees weren't far behind and opened the door to the garden just in time to see Tohopka disappear behind two large tombstones.

Hokolesqua envisioned the headband and feather his father wore.

This is my chance to become a true Shawnee warrior. Today I'll prove my courage.

This was the day he had dreamt about his whole life.

He sprinted for the spot where Tohopka had disappeared.

"Hoko, stop!" Nemhsi yelled. "Check your pyramid first."

Nothing's going to get in the way of me fulfilling my destiny, Hoko thought. *Tecumseh said I had the chance to become a great warrior. I'm not about to change direction.*

Nemhsi ran to catch up with her brother. As he neared the tombstone, he carefully moved around to the back side.

"He's gone," Hokolesqua said.

"Maybe there's a secret passage," Tocho replied.

Hokolesqua gently tapped a couple of times to see if the tombstone sounded hollow, and a section of its back disappeared, revealing a staircase.

"Why do the people of Anatok always hide under the dead?" Hokolesqua asked, shaking his head.

Hokolesqua stepped into the tombstone.

"Don't," Nemhsi said. "It's a trap."

"It can't be a trap," Hokolesqua replied. "The warriors of Tohopka are all fighting Delfians—except those who escaped into the woods."

"And we can easily defeat the king and his guards with these," Tocho said, pointing to their weapons.

"Let's go," Hokolesqua said.

"I don't like this," Nemhsi said.

"The king's reign is over," Tocho said.

"That doesn't mean he can't kill us in one final act," Nemhsi replied.

"Come," Hokolesqua said.

Nemhsi gave him an odd look. Hokolesqua was sure the look was because he had never been that forceful before.

Hokolesqua descended into the tomb. Tocho and Nemhsi followed. When he arrived at the bottom of the stairs, it was dark except for the remnants of light coming from someplace far in the distance.

"We follow the light," Hokolesqua said as he began running down the long corridor.

CHAPTER 47

"LET'S TAKE A VOTE"

(TANNER)

As they were crossing the plaza, Mick stopped one of the followers of Spider Woman heading for the palace entrance.

"What happened?" Mick asked. "The king said his troops had the Place of Gathering surrounded."

"He did," she replied. "We were severely outnumbered, but they couldn't force themselves into the space any faster than one warrior at a time. They could see there was no chance to defeat us, so his soldiers fled into the wilderness. A few of them surrendered."

"Why would they surrender?" Mick replied.

"He threatened to kill every last one of them if they returned with even one of us still alive. They had two choices—flee or join us."

"But once you left the tomb, you no longer had that strategic advantage," Andrew said.

"You're right," the woman responded. "We knew his forces might just be waiting for us to emerge from the Place of Gathering. So we contacted the Delfians and asked for reinforcements. Having been victims of Anatokian brutality themselves, they sent thousands of troops."

"Is Delfi the city next to the River Styx?" Andrew asked. "The one with the pavement of round stones surrounding it?"

"Yes, that's the one."

"That's where we need to go," Mick said.

"Once this is over, I'll see if I can arrange for the five of you to be taken there."

It didn't take long for the rebel forces, with the assistance of the Delfians, to secure the palace and take control of the seat of government.

Mick approached the woman who had agreed to help them. "Were you able to find anyone who could take us to Delfi?"

"Follow me."

"Thank you so much," Mick said.

The woman approached a warrior who agreed to take the five Surfacers with him. They boarded a beautiful steampunk-style aircraft and were comfortably seated with about forty warriors.

"Did we hear correctly that you are Surfacers?" one of the warriors asked.

"Yes, that's correct," Tanner replied.

"What brings you to Inner Earth?"

"We need to get to Mount Olympus," Mick said. "There's a Cathedral there that . . ." She stopped herself. "Let's just say we have some unfinished business there."

"Ah yes. Well, would you like us to take you directly to Olympus?"

"Wait," Tanner said. "Is that possible?"

"Of course," the men replied as Mick nodded in agreement.

"You mean we won't have to go down the Styx and Acheron Rivers?" Andrew asked.

"Or scale the cliffs of hell and the ice stairway of the Hall of Judgment?" Tanner added.

"Or face Cerberus, the three-headed dog?"

"That's right."

"So, Mick, how did you know they could take us directly to Mount Olympus?" Andrew asked.

"That's how I got there last time. When I arrived at Delfi, they asked me where I wanted to go. I told them Olympus, and they took me there."

"Wait, so if we would have told that guy in the spaceship we wanted to go to Olympus instead of the River Styx, we could have missed out on all that drama in the kingdom of Hades?"

"You idiot!" Tanner said, punching Andrew. "Why didn't you ask him to take us to Olympus?"

"I never thought it would be an option. Why didn't you ask?"

"You're supposed to be the brains of the group," Tanner replied.

"So," Andrew said to Mick, "you missed out on all the excitement."

"I guess so."

"But your papers," Tanner said. "We were following them to the letter. They talked in great detail about each of those places. How did you know so much about each of them if you hadn't been there?"

Mick looked over at Donald. "I used his writings as the source material for all that stuff."

"Really?"

"Yep."

"I can't believe how stupid we are!" Andrew said. "We didn't have to go through any of that stuff?"

"I guess the good news is we don't have to go through any of it again," Tanner said.

"That's definitely good," Andrew replied.

"So, the two of you actually went through all of that when you were looking for me?" Mick asked. "I'm flattered."

Jim scowled at Tanner and Andrew.

"Yeah, you owe us big-time," Tanner replied. "And don't think we're going to forget it."

"So how is it you can take people directly to Olympus without them being judged?" Andrew asked. "I thought everyone had to be judged."

"Oh, you'll be judged," came the reply.

"The only place we're permitted to land is on the Judgment Platform. We're required to wait there until the worthiness of the passenger is assessed. If found worthy, you're allowed to remain on Olympus, otherwise it's back to Delfi with us."

"Wait, so you're saying . . ." Tanner didn't finish. He began to think about past transgressions that would offend the gods. Particularly sneaking into the Cathedral of Time.

"There's really no other way?" Tanner asked.

"Nope. You either have to be found worthy in the Great Hall of Judgment or on the Judgment Platform."

"Maybe we should go to the Great Hall," Tanner replied.

"No way!" Andrew replied. "Are you kidding? Don't you remember the lightning and hailstorm and how we almost fell into the jaws of hell?"

"Yeah, but judged by the gods? Mick might be the only one who makes it."

"Come on, Tanner. You haven't done anything *that* bad," Mick said.

"Um, Andrew and I basically broke into the Great Hall of Judgment without Hades knowing. The way Hades responded would make me think the gods considered that bad. And we snuck into the Cathedral of Time."

"How *did* Hades respond?" Jim asked. Tanner could see the fearful expression on his face.

"Well, he nearly destroyed us as we flew from the Great Hall to Olympus," Andrew answered. "I think we were only saved because the orb entered the realm of Olympus."

"Let's see if we can find Persephone," Tanner said. "She'll get us to Olympus without being judged. Of all the gods, she's probably the most partial toward Surfacers."

"Still not very comforting," Andrew said.

"I've been thinking about it," Tanner put his hand over his mouth and whispered to Andrew, "and I think if we can get back to Hades's throne in the Great Hall, I can steal his helmet."

"Why would you want to do that?" Andrew asked.

"Shh," Tanner said.

"He's already mad enough at us," Andrew replied. "And having one of the three most powerful gods in the universe mad at you isn't a good thing. Now you want to make it worse by stealing something of his?"

"It makes you invisible," Tanner whispered. "You don't understand. We've got an invincible man out there who's bent on our destruction—Hades, who wants us dead, and the vilest Roman emperor of all time, who wants to torture and then kill us. We need all the help we can get."

"Take us to the kingdom of Hades," Tanner said to the pilot. He looked over at his friends. "We'll find Persephone. She'll help."

"Let's take a vote," Andrew replied.

"We're not taking a vote," Tanner said.

Andrew leaned over to Tanner and whispered, "You're not planning to ask Persephone to help us steal her husband's helmet, are you?"

"Of course not."

"T, are you forgetting how treacherous it was to get to Hades's throne? We'll never survive it."

"I remember. But don't worry. I've been thinking about it, and I don't think we'll have to climb the cliffs and ice stairs."

"Unless you're sure, I don't think we should take a chance." Andrew looked over at the pilot. "Bring us to Olympus."

"Don't listen to him," Tanner said emphatically. "We want to go to the Garden of Persephone."

"I don't like this," Andrew mumbled under his breath.

CHAPTER 48

THE WATER MOCCASIN
(HOKOLESQUA)

"How far does this passage go?" Hokolesqua asked after they had been walking for nearly an hour.

"I have no idea," Tocho replied. "My guess is that it's an escape route into the woods—could be another hour. Let's stop and rest."

Hokolesqua wanted to say no. He wanted to confront the king. He wanted to feel like he had finally proven himself, but he was exhausted. The adrenaline that had been pumping through his system since they'd arrived in Anatok had run out, and he agreed to stop for a short rest.

Sitting against the wall of the corridor, he quickly fell into a deep sleep.

He found himself on the back of the black panther, his spirit animal. He recognized the scene. He was descending into the water and afraid he was going to drown. Then an unfamiliar scene began to play. Even though he was in a dream, Hokolesqua wondered why this deviated from his original vision.

Did I do something wrong, something that is going to cause a different destiny than what was originally intended for me? Or are these just more details?

A long, slithering water moccasin swam up alongside them. It's forked tongue extending and contracting; it turned its head and looked Hokolesqua directly in the eye. Then the great snake began to circle them. As if it were a large boa constrictor, it wrapped itself around and around Hokolesqua and the panther, its grip tightening with each pass.

"Stop," Hokolesqua gasped as he fought for freedom.

He awoke in a pool of sweat.

"There they are," Tocho said. "Exactly what you've been looking for—Surfacers."

Hokolesqua gazed up from his shackles in horror. Tocho, King Tohopka, and his guards had surrounded him and his sister. He looked for his weapon, and then noticed it in the hands of one of the guards. It was leveled at him.

CHAPTER 49

PERSEPHONE

(TANNER)

"Can you show us where you hid the second bag of money from the robbery?" Mick asked Donald once they disembarked the Delfian craft just outside the Garden of Persephone.

"Sure," Donald replied.

"We don't have time for this," Tanner said. "People's lives are at stake in Rome. This has taken way too long already."

"T, just relax," Andrew said. "We have access to a time machine. We could stay here for a year and it wouldn't matter."

"Yeah, I guess that's true, but still, I want to get going."

"This won't take long," Mick replied.

Donald led them to a remote area of the garden that looked far less manicured than the other areas they'd been in.

A stone pathway led to an old statue mostly covered in ivy. Donald paused as they got close to the stone goddess. He counted five stepping stones back.

"It should be under that stone right there."

"Looks like someone beat us here," Andrew said.

There was fresh dirt around the stone.

"Help me move this," Mick said as she ran to the stone and tried in vain to lift it.

Tanner walked over, and together they lifted the stone.

"Looks like we're out of luck," Tanner said, looking at the barren hiding place under the stone.

"Au contraire," Mick replied, a big grin on her face. "Dad's innocent," she muttered.

"The bag's gone?" Donald asked.

"Yep," Mick said enthusiastically. "And Harvey Wilkins took it."

"What river have you been drinking from this time?" Tanner asked. "You're not making any sense."

"Long story," Mick said. "But, basically, my dad's in jail because he's been accused in Harvey Wilkins's disappearance. Harvey claimed to have found the money from the Brownsville Bank robbery and then disappeared. My dad showed up at a coin shop shortly after with money from the early 1800s."

"Huh?" Tanner said.

"Don't you get it?" Mick asked. "We saw Harvey in the underworld. The bag that was under this stone is the one he found. My dad found the one in our barn."

"You're weird," Tanner said, shaking his head in confusion as they let the stone drop back into place.

They made their way back to the central area of the garden. Tanner noticed a skip in Mick's step that hadn't been there for some time.

"Persephone!" Tanner said as he approached the goddess, who was gathering flowers in her garden.

"Remember us? You helped us get to the golden orb?"

"Of course I remember you," the goddess replied.

Tanner nudged Andrew in the ribs. "Told you so."

"You have no idea how angry Hades was that I helped you," Persephone said, looking down at the ground and shaking her head.

"He banished me from my gardens and kept me locked up like a prisoner in my own palace for days."

"I'm so sorry," Tanner said, losing confidence that she would help them again.

"How's Zagreus?" he asked, referring to Persephone's son, realizing he might need to take her mind off her banishment before asking for additional aid.

"He's fine," Persephone replied.

"And your mother, Demeter?"

"She's well."

Not getting very far with this line of questioning, Tanner thought.

"Demeter was very helpful to us in getting in and out of Rome," Tanner said.

"She fulfills her duties as guardian of the portals to the underworld very faithfully."

Wow. She just really isn't biting on any of my ice-breaker conversation, Tanner thought. *I'm just going to have to jump straight to asking for help, I guess.*

"I don't suppose you would be willing to help us again, would you?"

"You know," Persephone paused, "I'm so angry with Hades right now I'll help you just to spite him."

"You're kidding," Andrew replied.

"No, I am not. He had no right treating me the way he did. The two of you earned your way to the golden orb. That's how it's always been. If one chooses not to be judged in the Great Hall, it is acceptable procedure to allow the individual to pass the tests of the hall to obtain access to Olympus on their own. It is incredibly rare for someone to succeed, but he should not have been upset that the two of you did. I asked him to explain, but he could barely speak he was so angry."

Tanner was feeling guilty about their plan to steal Hades's helmet, realizing how much trouble he was about to get Persephone in. She had been so nice and helpful to them, after all.

But if she knew the whole situation, she'd want to help, even if it meant banishment for a time. Stopping Decimus and Nero will preserve the history of the world.

"What is it you need?" Persephone asked.

"We need you to take us to the golden orb."

"Tanner, you know you must earn access to the golden orb."

"But we've already proven ourselves worthy," Tanner said. "Surely you don't require someone to scale the cliffs of hell and that ice staircase twice."

"I hadn't really thought about it," Persephone responded. It was apparent from the look on her face that she was in deep thought. "I guess that is true. I mean, I have never had someone come back around for a second judgment. You have proven yourselves worthy already."

Tanner clenched his fist and let a small "Yes!" leak out of his mouth.

"All of you except for him." Persephone pointed at Jim. "He's never been judged."

Tanner looked over at Jim. He couldn't help but smile, knowing what Jim was going to have to endure.

Jim glared at Tanner.

"But," Persephone paused, "I guess if he's one of your friends, I can assume he's worthy as well. I'll trust him."

"What!" Tanner said curtly. "I mean, yes, I guess that makes sense." Tanner looked at Persephone incredulously.

Jim raised his eyebrows and shot a satisfied grin at Tanner, who was fuming on the inside.

"Then you'll take us all to Hades's throne in the Great Hall?"

"I will."

Persephone waved her arms, and a small hovering transportation device appeared. It was similar to the one the boys had seen her use when she'd offered them words of encouragement on their first trip. She pushed a button on the handle, and the platform expanded so it was large enough for the six of them to fit comfortably.

Tanner and the others grabbed the intricately carved railing, and the craft sped through the garden. A flock of large griffins seemed bent on disrupting their access to the Great Hall as they swooped back and forth in all directions around the travelers, squawking and cawing.

"Get away from me." Mick swung her arms as a griffin flew by and pecked at her shoulder.

After repeated commands from the goddess for them to depart, they eventually flew away.

"I'm so sorry," Persephone told her passengers. "They usually don't behave like that. I'm not sure what has gotten into them."

When they arrived at the entrance to the Great Hall, Persephone pushed a few buttons on her hovercraft, the doors of the hall opened, and the vehicle zoomed inside. When Tanner caught a glimpse of the interior, his mind flashed back to his experience scaling the cliffs and stairs with Andrew.

"You don't deserve this. You know that," he whispered angrily at Jim, who just smiled coyly.

The five of them thanked Persephone profusely and stepped off her hovercraft when it arrived next to Hades's throne.

Tanner watched anxiously as Persephone left.

"There it is," Tanner whispered to Andrew, discreetly pointing to the helmet on the armrest of Hades's throne.

"I've been thinking . . ." Andrew started.

"Stop, just stop. You shouldn't be thinking," Tanner replied.

"Seriously," Andrew whispered, shaking his head. "Look, we can't do this. You're talking about stealing one of the most valuable items in the universe from one of its most powerful beings."

"What are you two mumbling about over there?" Mick asked.

"Nothing," Tanner replied.

"Look, Andrew, I'm not sure you understand what's at stake," Tanner quietly replied. "We barely escaped from that Tohopka guy who's bent on taking over the entire planet." Tanner pulled the visualizer out of his pocket. "And he's got the technology to do it. Plus, the guys who robbed the Brownsville Bank are roaming around down here, and they'd be more than happy to team up with him. They proved that by what they did to Brownsville in exchange for a couple satchels of cash. Honestly, I wouldn't be surprised to see Tohopka try to team up with Hades himself. You know Hades would love nothing more than to take over the domains of Zeus and Poseidon."

Andrew stood in dumbfounded silence.

"I guess you're right," he finally whispered back.

"Whoa. Hold on," Tanner replied. "Let me record that." He pulled out his phone. "Say that again."

"Shut it," Andrew replied.

"Are we going, or do the two of you plan on continuing your little chitchat until Hades shows up?" Mick asked.

"You're right. Let's get moving," Tanner said. "Everyone get in the judgment chair. I know it's going to be crowded, but we've only got one chance at this. I'll push the button and jump on before the chair shoots up."

Tanner grabbed Andrew by the shirt and whirled him around.

"You've got to distract the others so they don't see what I've stolen," he whispered.

"Places, everyone," he said, letting Andrew go.

Tanner looked at Hades's helmet with its ram's horns.

Wish that thing was a little smaller.

The helmet was sitting on a piece of green satin fabric.

I've got to be fast. There must be some kind of security on it.

Andrew pointed up at the golden orb, and everyone's eyes went there.

Here goes.

Tanner grabbed the helmet, threw the fabric over it, and reached for the button, but his finger disappeared before he could get it there. He hadn't thought about that. He fumbled around trying to figure out exactly where his hand was and what he was touching.

"Tanner, hurry!" Andrew yelled.

He connected with the button and sprinted for the chair.

Whoosh!

The judgment chair shot up into the golden orb, and the five were on their way to Mount Olympus.

Tanner wrapped the helmet securely in the fabric and tied a big knot at the top.

"Tanner," Mick whispered angrily. "Did you just steal—"

"Shh," Tanner replied with a small grin. "Wouldn't want him to hear you, would we?"

"This is not going to end well," Mick muttered, shaking her head.

"You worry too much," Tanner said, knowing full well there was a good chance she was right.

"Knock on wood, but Hades hasn't batted us around yet," Andrew said after they had been airborne for a few seconds.

"Well, last time he actually saw us in the chair," Tanner replied.

"He's going to figure it out sooner or later," Andrew said.

"Let's just hope it's later," Mick said. "Much later."

It wasn't long before they felt the burst of heat and heard the overhead announcement that they would soon be landing on Mount Olympus.

"I feel much better now that we're actually on Olympus," Andrew said as they touched down.

"Me too," Tanner replied.

"So this is *the* Mount Olympus?" Jim asked, looking around in awe as he stepped out of the golden orb. The ground below became transparent where he stepped, allowing him to see down to the underworld.

"This is it," Mick said.

"I can't believe it's actually a real place," Jim said.

"Wouldn't have believed it either until I came here," Mick replied.

"Aren't we supposed to be judged or something?" Jim asked.

"If the Delfians would have brought us here directly, yes, but since Persephone let us use the golden orb, we were able to avoid the Judgment Platform," Andrew answered.

"Let's get over to the Cathedral," Tanner said. "We've got a lot to do in Rome."

The group made its way down the slope and over to the Cathedral, with Jim asking lots of questions along the way.

"Were we like that when we first came?" Andrew asked.

"You were worse," Tanner said.

"How are we going to get through the dome?"

"Oh yeah," Tanner replied. "I almost forgot about that. I guess we'll just wait until one of the gods enters. They use this thing pretty regularly, I would think."

It was the middle of the night when one of the gods finally approached.

"Hey, it's Demeter," Tanner said.

"She'll let us through for sure," Mick replied.

When they explained their current situation, Demeter let them through the transparent dome, and they walked the short sidewalk to the entrance.

"What's this place again?" Jim asked.

"It allows you to travel anywhere in time," Mick replied as she opened the door and the group descended down to the control room.

"Wait," Donald Carlton interrupted, his voice full of hope as he quickly restrained Tanner with the palm of one hand against Tanner's chest. "Are you saying you figured out how to adjust the settings so you can go to *any* time period you'd like?"

"Yes," Mick replied.

"Then I can go back to my Hannah? And my children?"

"Yes," Mick answered.

"Maybe I could go back early enough to stop the bank robbery."

"I don't think we're supposed to stop things that already happened," Tanner said.

"Just getting back to my family would be incredible," Donald said. "Show me how."

"Right now we need you to come with us to Rome," Mick said. "Once we've solved everything there, we'll all go back to our respective places and times."

"I'm not sure I can wait that long."

"You have to," Tanner said. "Think about little Livia."

"And Marina," Andrew added.

"Don't forget Nero," Mick said.

"I guess you're right," Donald said. "But it's going to be hard, knowing that after so many years I can finally rejoin my family."

"We'll get you back there. Just help us complete our unfinished business in Rome," Mick said as she began to survey the glass surface in the control room and change the settings on the screen.

"Let's see. If I just adjust the settings to right after we left Rome the first time . . ." She continued to tap the screen.

"We're really going back in time?" Jim asked.

"Why would that be such a surprise after all you've seen so far?"

"I don't know," Jim continued. "It's just easier to wrap my head around visiting some place I've never been than time travel. It's something people have talked about forever, but it just never made sense how it could be possible. Just mind-boggling, that's all."

"I've seen that look before," Tanner said. "Um, let me think. English class?"

"Zip it, Hunter," Jim replied. "Or I'll wrap *your* head around that pole over there."

"I hope we're not too late to fix everything in Rome," Mick said.

"Of course we won't be," Andrew replied. "We could just adjust the settings. Hey, actually, we could go back before the fire and even save Anastasia."

"It's the whole changing-history thing again," Tanner said. "Plus, I think it's too risky. The possibility of running into ourselves seems like it could somehow blow up the history of the world, and if we tinker too much with the past, we'll end up creating an alternate present for ourselves. I don't want to do that, either."

"That didn't happen with our first trip into Rome," Andrew said.

"That's true," Mick said. "But I think Tanner's right."

"Did you hear that?" Tanner said. "She said I'm right."

"Cut the drama," Mick continued. "I've been thinking about everything I studied about Roman history, and it matches up with what happened while we were there. It's like we didn't alter history but were a part of it all along. I think if we try to force certain events, we might create an alternate future. In other words, we can't try to change the past, but we can live in it."

"Hmmm. Interesting concept," Andrew replied. "Sounds reasonable, and I'd rather be safe than sorry."

They adjusted the settings on the control panel in the Time Room to the evening of November 8, 64 AD, so they would just miss running into themselves.

"Let's hurry and get this done," Tanner said. "Everything set?"

Mick nodded affirmatively.

"To the platform!" Tanner yelled as Mick pushed the button on the control panel and the lighting on the floor activated.

Everyone sprinted for the platform.

The lights began to flash, and everything went dark.

"We're here," Tanner said as the lights came back on.

"This isn't Ancient Rome," Jim quickly responded, looking around the unchanged room. "I know I wasn't the best student in school, but even I recognize this isn't Ancient Rome."

"Once we exit the Cathedral, we'll be in Rome," Mick said. "Don't worry."

After leaving the Cathedral, they climbed up the cave walls of the Mundus, and Donald, Tanner, and Andrew removed the stone covering. Everyone climbed through the opening, and they began to discuss ways they could get out of the Umbilicus Urbis and enter the city.

CHAPTER 50

MEET DECIMUS

(MARCUS)

"Decimus," the prison warden said, "this is Marcus—one of the Christian rebels."

The warden turned his head and addressed Marcus. "Decimus has been given responsibility for the ninth legion. Tomorrow you'll be joining his labor force. Hope you know how to work, because if you don't, I'm sure you'll make a nice torch for Nero's garden."

Marcus gave a simple nod of acknowledgment, which was more than he wanted to do.

"Show a little more respect!" Decimus said as he grabbed Marcus by the throat. "I hold your life in the palm of my hand."

You can't do anything worse to me than what has already been done, Marcus thought as he reflected on the devastation he had just endured.

Anastasia dead. Livia missing. Marina never wants to see me again. Death couldn't be any worse than this.

"Don't glare at me." Decimus said as he pulled a dagger from its sheath and held it to Marcus's throat. "I could do it, you know."

"Death doesn't scare me," Marcus replied.

Decimus's brow furrowed, and he shoved Marcus to the ground in frustration.

"Why do you hate Christians?" Marcus asked. "Why do all of you hate us?"

Decimus growled under his breath and gave Marcus an evil glare.

After an awkward silence, Decimus blurted, "What's not to hate? You don't worship the gods of Rome. You burned down half the city. Do I need to go on?"

"We didn't burn down the city—that was Nero's men," Marcus replied. "But I want to hear the real reason you hate Christians. Because, based on the tone of your voice, it sounds more personal."

Decimus kicked over a chair.

"Can I ask what happened?" Marcus asked gently.

"No!" Decimus shouted as he backhanded Marcus across the face, shoved him into a cell, and stormed up the stairs.

CHAPTER 51

THE SEARCH FOR LIVIA

(TANNER)

"I've got an idea," Andrew said. "See that ledge up there?" He pointed to a small ledge that went around the Umbilicus at the same height as the base of the door. If we can get up there, a couple of us can either tie the door open or hold it open so when the guard tries to close it, he won't be able to. He'll be forced to come down into the Umbilicus to see why the door won't close, and we can overpower, bind, and gag him. When his partner comes down to see what happened, we'll do the same thing to him. We'll steal their clothes and just walk out of here."

"I like it," Tanner said.

The group quietly moved the ladder away from the door and over to the ledge.

"We need the two strongest guys to go up and hold the door," Mick said.

"No, we've got to leave the strongest down here to overpower the guard," Donald replied. "Mick, Tanner, Andrew, you go up on the ledge. Jim, you and I will stay here."

Jim straightened up and puffed out his chest slightly.

Everyone positioned themselves, and the plan unfolded exactly like Andrew had designed it.

They entered the city, which was illuminated only by the full moon and a few torches burning here and there.

"We've got to find Priscilla and Julia and see if they have any news about Livia," Tanner said.

"I know where they live," Mick replied.

"How?" Tanner was surprised.

"Don't you remember? I stayed with Priscilla and Aquila when I lived here in Rome."

Tanner thought back to how, when he first met Priscilla, she had mentioned a Christian refugee had lived with their family for a time and how surprised he was when Mick had confirmed it was her.

"I guess I had forgotten. Lead the way, Mick."

"Don't forget we're still fugitives," Andrew said as they quietly traversed the dark city.

"Nero would make it well worth someone's time to capture and turn you over to the authorities," Donald added.

"Hopefully we don't run into him on one of his evening 'kill for sport' strolls," Tanner replied.

"Good point," Andrew replied.

Tanner looked over at Jim, whose eyes were as big as the moon overhead.

He wanted to laugh, but thinking back to how he and Andrew watched as Nero stabbed Decimus and threw him off the bridge, he realized Jim's eyes should have been even bigger than they were.

"That's it over there," Mick said in a hushed tone as she pointed to a door down the street.

The group quickly made their way to Priscilla's home. The flickering light of a candle was visible through the window. Mick knocked on the door.

The door opened just wide enough for the person inside to assess those standing outside, then flung wide open.

"Mick, you're safe! We've been so worried."

Mick embraced Aquila.

"Priscilla!" he yelled into one of the adjacent rooms. "It's Mick. She's alive!"

A middle-aged woman appeared in the doorway. A big grin spread across her face, and she ran to Mick and gave her a hug.

"It's so good to see you. We were sure you were de—" She stopped herself as she visibly shuddered.

"Hey, and aren't you the boy who sent us to search for Livia?" she asked, looking at Tanner.

"Yes," he replied. "Any luck? Were you able to find her?"

"No. Still no clues," Priscilla replied. "Not even any sightings. Come on in." Priscilla motioned with her hands for them to quickly enter her home.

A boy and girl about their age stepped out of the shadows of one of the corridors in the home and into the atrium.

"Did you say Mick's back?" the girl said as she scanned the visitors. When her eyes locked on Mick, she ran and embraced her, then pulled her head back slightly, looking Mick in the eye with a big grin. She started asking a million questions rapid-fire.

The other teenager was hanging back slightly.

Priscilla looked over at him and made a small jolt.

"I'm so sorry," she said. "I forgot to make introductions. This is Appius," she said, pointing to the boy who had been hanging back in the shadows. When he stepped into the light, Tanner could see he wasn't much older than they were, but he looked like the statue of a Greek god. Describing him as tall, dark, and handsome was an insult. Tanner looked over at Mick, whom he could tell was instantly smitten.

Priscilla continued. "Appius came to stay with us just a few days ago. His family disowned him about a year ago when he joined the faith, and he's pretty much been a vagabond ever since. Some friends of ours told him about Livia, and he agreed to help in the search. That's how we met him."

"Nice to meet you," Mick struggled to say.

"Pleasure," Appius replied.

Tanner made eye contact with Mick and rolled his eyes. Once everyone had been introduced, they mingled in Pricilla's atrium. Mick was standing across the room talking to Appius.

"Well, it's getting late," Priscilla said. "Let's coordinate sleeping arrangements and get back to the search in the morning."

"Sounds great," Mick replied. "We're exhausted."

Priscilla made assignments, and everyone filed off to their respective rooms.

"Where do you plan to keep Hades's helmet?" Andrew whispered.

"I'm not sure," Tanner replied. "I don't feel safe carrying it around with me everywhere."

"A little bulky to do that. Maybe you could store it at Lucius's shop."

"Too many people coming and going from there. Maybe Donald would keep it at his house. He seems to have stayed pretty private."

"And, most importantly, we can trust him."

"We'll talk to him in the morning."

❖ ❖ ❖

After a good night's sleep, Tanner woke up early and was ready to get moving.

"Come on, Andrew," he said, shaking his friend, who was struggling to detach himself from his bed. "We've got to get over to the cave of Romulus and Remus and see if Livia's been there.

"Can't you let a guy get a little sleep?" Andrew asked as Tanner continued to shake him.

"We've had plenty of sleep. Livia might still be in danger. Do you remember exactly where the Lupercal's supposed to be?"

"Not exactly, but I can get us close enough that I think we can find it. Aren't we going to wait for the others?"

"I'm not waiting," Tanner replied. "Who knows how long it will take to get everyone up. Then they'll all want breakfast, and we'll all sit around talking. We'll be here forever."

When they exited their room into the atrium, to their surprise, Donald, Mick, and Jim were already awake and ready to go.

"What are you guys doing up so early?" Tanner asked in shock

"Jim was anxious to walk around and see the city in the daylight," Mick said.

"Oh, and where's your Greek-god friend, Appius?" Tanner added while raising his eyebrows and winking at Mick.

"Shut it," she replied.

"Hey, we're going over to the Lupercal to see if Livia's been hiding out there," Andrew said. "Want to join us?"

"Sure," Mick said.

Tanner stayed back and spoke with Donald about hiding the green satin bundle in his home, which he agreed to do.

"What is it?" Donald asked.

"Just a little souvenir I brought with me from the underworld. You have to promise not to open it, though."

"Fine," Donald replied.

"Swear it," Tanner said.

"All right, I swear."

"And you've got to be willing to protect it with your life,"

"Why would I be willing to protect it with my life when I don't even know what it is?" Donald asked.

"You've just got to trust me. I've trusted you on a lot of things. This time you've got to trust me. The fate of the entire planet may rest on your ability to keep it safe."

"I trust you," Donald said.

"You'll protect it with your life?"

"Yes," he said impatiently.

Donald immediately left with the sack and agreed to meet up with them at the Lupercal.

"What's this?" Andrew jumped back as he opened the front door. Everyone looked at each other. There was nearly a foot of snow on the ground. It was a complete whiteout.

"Is this normal?" Tanner asked Priscilla.

"Not at all," she replied. "I've never seen weather like this."

"We're going to have to brave it," Tanner said. "Livia's even more at risk in these kinds of conditions."

The group trudged through the snow toward the Circus Maximus. Jim's head swiveled back and forth as he strained for a glimpse of the majestic city through the blizzard.

"I think the Lupercal's on the opposite side of the circus," Mick said as they walked along the south side. "Near the Tiber."

"Is this where you were the whole time you were missing?" Jim asked Mick.

"This is the place."

"What was it like to actually live here?"

"I missed Brownsville, but for someone who loves history, it was paradise."

"I bet," Jim replied, obviously awestruck by what he was seeing.

"The cave should be near this building," Mick said as they approached a shop across from the circus. The city was eerily quiet. From the way it looked, the Brownsvillians were the only ones willing to brave the elements.

"Where did you go?" Mick asked as Donald approached.

Tanner gave him a glare.

"Had to run a quick errand. Nothing, really."

"You two go around that side, and we'll go this way," Tanner said, pointing to the side of the building.

"No way," Jim said. "You're not sending me off with the Praetorian. I'm coming with the three of you. I'm not risking you guys ditching me."

"Come on, Jim! We're just going around this building. How do you think we're going to ditch you?"

"In this blizzard? You guys get more than ten feet away and I might never see you again," he replied. "Maybe there's some secret passageway, and before I know it the three of you will be gone and I'll freeze to death in Ancient Rome."

"Hmm. I hadn't really thought about it before, but it's not a bad idea," Tanner replied.

Jim shoved him. "Don't mess with me, Hunter, or you'll pay for it."

"Look! Over here!" Donald said. "I think I found something."

Donald was brushing snow away from a small wooden door angled along the ground. He pulled it open, revealing a set of primitive stone stairs leading down.

"Lead the way!" Tanner said, patting Jim on the back. He was toying with tough-guy Jim's newly demonstrated fear and apprehension.

"No way. You go first," he replied.

"Okay. I've got it," Tanner said as he descended into the darkness.

"Ahhhhh!" Tanner yelled.

Everyone still at ground level jumped.

"Just messing with you," he shouted from below.

"You're so stupid," Mick replied.

"This is it! This has got to be the cave of Romulus and Remus. Come on down."

One by one, the rest descended into the pit. It was pitch-black, with only a small amount of light entering from the open doorway above.

"Livia! Livia!" Tanner called out.

No response. He tried again. "Livia?!"

Still nothing. "It's me—Musclosus!"

"What the heck is he talking about?" Jim asked.

"It's a nickname Livia gave him."

"We've got to get some light. She's probably afraid to come out. She has to be traumatized by the fire and losing her entire family."

"I'll find a torch," Donald said. "Wait here."

Donald returned a few minutes later with a torch.

"Much better," Mick said as Donald descended the stairs and the light began to make its way into the room.

The cave wasn't very large, and as they moved the light around, they could see there was no little girl.

"I'm sorry T.," Andrew said.

"Looks like someone's been here, though," Tanner replied. "Shine the light over here."

Tanner was right. There were scraps of food and a blanket on the ground in a niche on the right side of the cave. He kicked a few of the items around with his foot.

"Oh, my gosh!" Tanner said.

"We're not falling for it," Mick replied.

"No. I'm serious this time. It's Livia's toy chariot! The one she and I used to play with."

Tanner stooped down and picked up the small toy. She may still be alive."

"She's going to freeze to death if she's outside in that weather," Andrew said.

"There weren't any footprints in the snow around the door, so she must have left before the storm started," Tanner said.

"Are any of the food scraps fresh?" Mick asked.

"Good question. Come closer with that torch."

Tanner studied the food. "I think some of this stuff is pretty fresh."

"She must be alive, then," Mick replied.

"Unless someone else has been using this cave as well," Andrew chimed in.

"She must be going out at night to find food," Donald said. "Smart little kid."

"That's why no one found her," Tanner said.

"You're right," Andrew replied. "Priscilla said they had been searching from dawn to dusk."

"You need to put that light out," Tanner said. "If she opens that door and sees a light, she'll be afraid to come down."

"Good point," Donald replied as he extinguished the torch.

"Man, if I were a five-year-old, I'd be terrified sleeping down here at night," Andrew said.

"You're terrified when your nightlight burns out," Tanner said.

Andrew shook his head.

"We need to be quiet," Mick said.

After about an hour in the dark silence, they heard the creaking hinge of the doorway entrance.

"It's her! It's Livia!" Tanner whispered excitedly.

"Shhhh," Mick replied, giving Tanner a shove.

They could hear footsteps coming down the stairs.

Unable to take it any longer, Tanner quietly said, "Livia, it's Musclosus. Is that you?"

"Musclosus!" Livia replied. "Where have you been? Where is everyone? I'm so scared."

Tanner could barely make out her little silhouette but rushed over to pick her up and hug her.

"Have you been hiding here the whole time?"

"Yep."

"You smart little girl. And you've been going out at night to find food?"

"Yep."

"I'm so glad we found you. We've been so worried.

"My mommy died," Livia said as she began to cry on Tanner's shoulder. "You saved me, Musclosus."

"I'm so sorry about your mommy, Livia. We all loved her so much. I'm sure she's in heaven watching out for you."

"Really?" Livia replied excitedly.

"I'm sure of it, Livia."

"If there is anyone who deserved to go to heaven, it was Anastasia," Donald said. "Now let's go find your dad and Marina"

"Are they okay?" Livia asked with concern in her voice.

"I'm sure they are," Tanner replied, knowing Marcus might not be.

"So can we go back home now?" Jim asked.

"I wish you would," Tanner replied.

"We still have to track down Marina and talk some sense into her," Andrew said.

"And find their dad," Mick said.

"And overthrow Nero," Donald added.

"Did you say Nero?" Jim replied. "Even I know how bad Nero was. Count me out."

"You know where the exit is," Tanner said, pointing in the direction of the Umbilicus.

"Shut up."

The group climbed the stairs, and Donald pushed open the large wooden door into the drifting snow.

"Let's head over to Lucius's," Tanner said.

They made their way to the shop that had been the headquarters for their activities when they were previously in Rome. Tanner figured it would be the best place to find out what they could about the whereabouts of Marcus and Marina.

"I figured out why it's snowing," Andrew whispered to Tanner as the snow crunched underfoot.

"Since when did you become a weatherman?" Tanner replied.

"Stop it," Andrew said. "It has nothing to do with barometric pressure or cold fronts. It's Persephone. Hades knows we stole the helmet."

"How would that affect the weather?" Tanner asked.

"Don't you remember? Demeter causes it to be winter during the months Persephone is forced to be in the kingdom of Hades. Demeter has caused this storm. Persephone must be in trouble."

"What happened to my friend Mr. Logic?" Tanner asked.

"It *is* logical," Andrew replied.

"Wow, you've come a long way," Tanner said, shaking his head.

"I know how we can be sure," Mick said. "Let's go ask Demeter."

"We can't," Tanner replied. "The Umbilicus will be locked up."

"No one's going to be guarding it in this kind of weather," Andrew said. "We should be able to break in easily."

"We could try," Tanner said. "Plus, once we get in, we can send Jim home."

The five of them went to Lucius's and grabbed some tools to help them break into the Umbilicus.

"We don't all need to go," Tanner said. "Donald, stay here with Jim. Don't want him to have to be out in this weather."

Jim glared at Tanner.

"It's fine," Mick said. "Jim can come with us."

They slogged through the almost knee-deep snow until they arrived at the Umbilicus.

"Got it," Andrew said after picking the lock.

The four entered, slid away the stone, and slipped inside the Mundus.

"T, slide the stone back in place, or Demeter won't appear," Andrew said.

No sooner had Tanner moved the stone back into place than the Mundus began to fill with light.

"Demeter," Andrew said. "What's going on with this weather? Is Persephone in trouble?"

"In trouble? That's putting it mildly," Demeter replied. "I guess you haven't heard—someone stole Hades's helmet."

Tanner looked at Andrew and then Mick.

"He's on a rampage. He's locked her up and threatened Zeus that if the helmet isn't returned soon, there'll be trouble."

"Can we do anything to help her?" Tanner asked, not sure he was ready to fess up but hoping they could do something for Persephone.

"Not unless you feel like braving the depths of Tartarus's prisons to rescue her and face the wrath of Hades yourselves."

"Maybe if one of us had the key to set her free we'd do it," Andrew said, glaring at Tanner.

"Well," Tanner said. "We'll try to think of something to help her. She's been so kind."

"What does Zeus think about all of this?" Mick asked.

"I have never seen him like this. He is almost as livid as Hades. When Zeus, Poseidon, and Hades finally agreed upon how to divide up the realms, they were able to coexist peacefully. The fact that the helmet is missing has rocked the delicate balance between the three. Now that the fuse has been lit, we'll just have to wait and see how long it is. I would recommend that you stay away from the underworld entirely until this all gets straightened out. Even the perception you're taking sides would put you at great risk."

Tanner gulped.

A somber mood enveloped the four as they left the Mundus and returned to Lucius's carpentry shop. Tanner could periodically feel Andrew's searing gaze.

CHAPTER 52

THE BRAVE
(HOKOLESQUA)

"You betrayed us. How could you? We trusted you."

"I never converted," Tocho said. "I was just waiting for an opportunity like the one that presented itself. You have no idea what the two of you have done for my future."

"Now we just need to find the boy who took the visualizer," one of the guards said. "We need to inform the troops to be on the lookout.

"Once we secure a visualizer, we'll be on our way to the Fourth World and," Tocho said, pointing to the king, "our very own King Tohopka will be the almighty ruler of the entire planet."

"I told you it was a trap," Nemhsi said as the guards wrestled the two of them to their feet and began shoving them forward down the corridor.

One of the guards was spinning Hokolesqua's pyramid in his hands.

"Hey! That belongs to me."

"Not anymore," the guard replied with a smirk.

Hokolesqua fought his shackles in an attempt to attack the man and get the sacred object back, but it didn't take long for him to realize it was no use.

"Move along." The guard pushed them in the back again. Hokolesqua torqued his body in a show of resistance but then did as the man asked.

The two Shawnees continued down the long corridor with their captors for almost an entire day, when they finally reached a staircase that led them out into the woods.

It was dark, and Hokolesqua heard strange and unusual sounds coming from every direction. He thought about his vision quest and how he and his spirit animal were surrounded by vicious creatures he had never seen before.

Is this the scene from my quest? He rubbed the scar on his chest.

Hokolesqua and Nemhsi were bound to a couple of trees by the guards while Tocho and King Tohopka made camp.

Hokolesqua's mind was racing. He had to figure a way to free the two of them. About twenty feet in front of him, the dancing flames periodically reflected off his pyramid as the guard continued to spin the object in his hands. Hokolesqua bristled in anger. The object held such significance for Hokolesqua. A few minutes later, the other guard returned to the fire, dragging an unfamiliar, large animal. The larger guard put the pyramid on the ground next to him, and the men went to work preparing the animal to be cooked over the fire.

Hokolesqua was starving. He hadn't eaten a good meal in a few days. The wind was blowing the smell of the meat his direction, and he could hardly stand it. However, the idea that the man had killed a beast that large so quickly was concerning. It meant such animals were close by and he and Nemhsi could be easy prey during the night. It also meant if they did escape, significant dangers awaited. The slashing he experienced as part of his vision quest leapt onto the stage of his mind.

We have to get out of here!

Hokolesqua continued to observe as the men cooked and devoured the large beast. The guard who had been playing with his pyramid ate nearly half the beast himself, which wasn't surprising since he was half as wide as he was tall. After a long evening of talk about how King Tohopka would regroup his forces and make an assault on the Surface, the men played a game to determine who would watch the prisoners. The smaller guard lost and made his way to where Hokolesqua and Nemhsi were tied while the others went to sleep.

All night long Hokolesqua discreetly tried everything he could think of to unlock the shackles. He looked over at his sister, who slept quietly a few feet away.

Should I have told her about the vision quest?

Her only worry was her captors, and all she knew was that they wanted to learn where the entrance to the Fourth World was—not too threatening. She had no reason to be concerned about the idea they might be slashed and devoured by wild beasts at any moment.

Halfway through the night, the guards switched.

"What would it take for King Tohopka to set the two of us free?" Hokolesqua asked the large man.

"Once King Tohopka has learned where the entrance to Fourth World is, he'll have no use for you. There's a chance he'll set you free then, but I doubt it."

"That is the only way?"

"Yes. He will keep you as prisoners until then."

"I don't remember where I entered Inner Earth."

"Tocho told us you were lost in the woods and wouldn't remember. That's why we need to find the boy with the visualizer. The visualizer will show us where you entered."

"I will help you find the boy."

"How?"

"Do you know how the magic pyramid works?" Hokolesqua asked.

"What do you mean works?" he replied angrily.

"That pyramid is a sacred object and works only for me. Have you been able to open it?"

"No."

"Give the object to me."

The guard returned to what was left of their fire and came back with the pyramid, which he handed to the young Shawnee. A light began to glow along the seam where the pyramid opened, and Hokolesqua flipped the lid, displaying the compass.

"This magic object points me to wherever I need to go. Since my only chance for freedom is to find the boy who has the visualizer, the pyramid will point the way to the boy." He pointed to the compass as it moved around and then jolted to a stop.

"Let me see that." The man took the pyramid from Hokolesqua, and the pointer began to spin randomly.

"We will guide you to the boy now. You can get the visualizer and return to the camp a hero. Tohopka will reward you mightily."

"Hokolesqua, don't do it," Nemhsi said.

"How long have you been awake?"

"Not long. You can't guide them to the visualizer. They'll find the entrance to Inner Earth and take over the Surface."

"But it's the only way we can be set free."

"It's not worth it," Nemhsi replied. "We can't let them take over the Surface."

"It's the only way," Hokolesqua replied sharply.

Nemhsi shook her head adamantly. "Even if it means we die, we can't let the king get to the Surface. The whole planet is at stake."

"Show me how that thing works again," the guard said, handing the object to Hokolesqua.

Nemhsi continued to protest.

The guard watched as the needle jolted to a stop again.

"Let her try." He took the compass from Hokolesqua and handed it to Nemhsi.

The needle began to spin wildly again.

The guard grabbed the pyramid from Nemhsi and handed it to Hokolesqua.

"Take me to the boy," he said.

"Yes," Hokolesqua said. The guard untied him from the tree.

"Let's go," he said.

"I won't go if Nemhsi stays here."

"But we don't need her."

"I'm not sure Nemhsi will be safe if she stays here. Wild beasts, the king, the man who betrayed us? No. I won't go unless Nemhsi comes."

"All right," the man said, and he untied Nemhsi.

"The chains stay," the guard said, pointing at the shackles on their feet and hands.

"Fine. It will just make the trip slower," Hokolesqua said.

Hokolesqua looked down at the pyramid, and then pointed into the woods.

"Let me see that," the guard said. "I don't trust you." He looked closely at the needle, verified that Hokolesqua was telling the truth, and the three were on their way. Hokolesqua continued to watch the needle as they walked, and he adjusted their course each time the needle changed direction.

"Hoko, we can't lead them to the visualizer," Nemhsi whispered as they walked.

"Trust me," he replied.

"Father and the rest of our tribe will be in danger," Nemhsi said.

"Father is not in danger. Remember, Anatolia brought us into the future. Many moons have passed."

"Still," Nemhsi replied. "We shouldn't sacrifice the safety of the planet just to save ourselves."

"Shhh," Hokolesqua said. "Trust."

The sky began to lighten, and Hokolesqua knew they had been walking nearly half the night.

"I'm tired. Can we take a short break?"

"Fine," the guard replied, and they found a place to sit down. "Does the pyramid say anything about how far we must go before we find the visualizer?"

"No. Only the direction," Hokolesqua replied.

Hokolesqua eyed the weapon the guard had placed on the ground next to him. Even though Hokolesqua was still in shackles, he had been able to pick the lock on his wrists while they were walking. He quietly removed the shackles, and then looked down at his feet.

Can't do anything about those.

Fear swept over him.

I can't do this.

A feather slowly drifted down from the sky and landed near where the guard had placed his weapon.

Just like Father's, he thought. *Must be brave.*

He looked at the distance between himself and his captor, trying to assess whether or not he could make it to the weapon with one quick lunge. Before he could decide, he heard a hissing like that of a large cat when cornered. His captor jerked his head in the direction of the sound. Instinctively, Hokolesqua dove for the weapon.

CHAPTER 53

AN UNFORTUNATE ENCOUNTER

(MARINA)

Marina approached Lucius's carpentry shop in the center of Rome.

The door slowly opened, spreading light across the snow-covered street. "I've got to get some fresh air. I'll be just outside," someone said.

She crouched behind a wooden barrel as she watched a boy about her age emerge.

Must be a new recruit, Marina thought. *Perfect. He won't recognize me. I'll be able to get some information about what's going on with everyone.*

Marina stood and walked toward the shop door.

"Salve," she said as she approached the boy.

"Hello," came a stunned reply.

"Are you a friend of Lucius?"

"No, I just met him."

"Oh, are you new here?" she asked, even though it was obvious from his accent.

"I am. Came here with my friend Mick. Name's Jim."

"You're friends with Mick?" Marina was stunned. "She's back?"

"Yeah, she's inside. You know her?"

"Yeah." The young woman looked at the ground, avoiding eye contact.

"What's wrong?"

"Nothing. Did Andrew and Tanner come with her?" she asked, looking a bit sheepish.

"Unfortunately."

"What do you mean?"

"Well, I've hated Tanner and Andrew for a long time. I thought they actually kidnapped Mick, so I chased them trying to save her, and got myself pulled into this whole mess."

"You're not really here to help them?"

"No. Now that I know Mick went willingly, I've just been hanging around 'cause I don't know how to get back home."

"Why did they come back?"

"To find some little girl who got lost during a big fire."

"Have they had any luck?"

"Yeah. They found her."

"They did?" Marina asked excitedly. "So are you going back home, then?"

"Not yet. I guess the girl's father was captured. So now they're trying to figure out how to rescue him."

"What did you just say?" Marina asked.

"The girl's father was captured."

"When did all this happen?" Marina's mind traveled back to when she'd turned and looked at her father, yelling, "I don't ever want to see you again."

"Well, from what I was told, his older daughter ran away, and he chased after her. Lucius went looking for them and saw the man get captured by a couple of legionnaires," Jim replied. "Why all the questions? Who are you anyway?"

"Doesn't matter," Marina mumbled, devastated by the new developments. "How would you like to get back at Tanner and Andrew for whatever they've done to you?"

"Where do I sign up?"

"What?"

"Just an expression where I come from. Anyway, yeah, I'd love to get back at them."

"I'd like to talk with you more," Marina said. "Swear you won't tell your friends you saw me."

"Why would you care if they know?"

"I'll explain later. I really need your help."

"Don't worry. I won't say anything."

"Meet me on the Scalae Gemoniae by the Temple of Concord once the others are asleep."

"The what?" Jim replied.

"The stairway across from the Umbilicus Urbis over there." Marina pointed in the direction of the staircase. "It's the one that leads up to the Temple of Jupiter."

"Okay," Jim said.

"I'll be waiting for you!" Marina grabbed his hand and gave it a little squeeze.

"Okay," Jim replied with a big grin as he opened the door and reentered the shop.

❖ ❖ ❖

"Finally," Marina said as Jim approached her on the stairs a few hours later. "What took so long?"

"No one was going to sleep. By the way, what's up with the bow and arrow?"

"Rome's not a very safe place at night."

"Do you even know how to use that thing?"

"If you'd call being able to draw blood out of a blood orange from fifty paces knowing how to use it, then yes."

After a stunned silence, Jim asked, "Why didn't you want me to tell the others you wanted to meet?"

"It's their fault my stepmother is dead, right?"

"Wait. Who's your stepmother?"

"I'm the daughter of Marcus, and Livia's sister."

"You are?"

"Yes, and it's Tanner's fault all this happened."

"I'm not surprised," Jim replied.

"We were hiding from Nero," Marina said. "He's been torturing and killing Christians in unspeakable ways. Tanner practically led the authorities to our home. Nero's men set fire to the place, and my stepmom died in the blaze. I had a perfect life until Tanner and Andrew showed up."

"Yeah, me too," Jim replied.

"Why did they come here in the first place?" Marina asked. "I know Tanner and Andrew came to rescue Mick, but why did she come?"

"How much time do you have?" Jim asked, knowing that the full story, as he'd heard it, might take a while.

"Just give me the main details."

"Well, Mick was trying to find some ancestor who disappeared from the town we live in. It turned out he was Titus, or Donald."

"And why was he here?"

"He came with a woman named Methoataske. They were trying to find her mother, who was kidnapped and taken to the underworld."

"Methoataske was my stepmother, who died in the fire."

"This is all pretty confusing," Jim said. "You must be the one they claimed is screwed up in the head."

"What?" Marina said, totally bewildered.

"Just another expression. It means they think you're not thinking straight."

"Sounds like something they'd say. They're the ones who are not thinking clearly. Did you know Mick is trying to overthrow the empire?"

"What? Mick's trying to . . ."

"I've seen the plans."

"No way."

"Sometime I'll take you to Decimus's house and show you. You said Methoataske came here from the underworld to find her kidnapped mother. Did anyone ever find her?"

"No."

Marina was in deep thought. "Then it was the kidnapper of my step-grandmother who started this whole thing?"

"That's how I understand it," Jim replied.

"Then we've got to find him. I want revenge. He's the one who truly destroyed my life. Any ideas where he is?"

"Well, Donald seems to think he and Methoataske picked the wrong location in the Cathedral of Time."

"Cathedral of What?"

"The Cathedral of Time. It's the room we used to go back in time and arrive here in Ancient Rome."

"What do you mean 'Ancient Rome'? This is modern Rome," Marina said. "Now Romulus and Remus–*that* would be Ancient Rome."

"I get it. Anyway, the Cathedral of Time allows you to travel to different periods in time. For example, you and I could go to the

Time Room, change the settings, and actually go back and meet Romulus and Remus."

"You're not serious, right?"

"Of course I'm serious. In fact, your stepmother coming from the underworld is only half the story. She was actually born in the future. She was born nearly 1800 years after you."

"Wait. That's impossible."

"Nope. It's the stuff of the gods. The Cathedral is on Mount Olympus."

"You mean you've actually been to *the* Mount Olympus?"

"That's right."

"Would you take me there?" Marina asked anxiously.

"Sure," Jim replied.

"So tell me more about Donald and Methoataske picking the wrong location."

"Well, when they entered the Cathedral of Time, they assumed the last people to use the Time Room were your step-grandmother and her captor. So they just used the machine without changing the settings."

"So, if we went there, we could try a different point in time?"

"Sure."

"Let's do it. I can get revenge on the man who kidnapped my step-grandmother, and we can be free of the pain he caused us!"

"The pain he caused you, you mean."

"No, the pain he caused *us*! Mick wouldn't have disappeared if he hadn't done what he did, and Tanner and Andrew wouldn't have gone to her rescue and become her heroes. Hasn't that caused you pain?"

"You're right. Let's rid ourselves of the pain he caused us."

We've got to get Livia away from them, though," Marina said angrily.

"Why?" Jim replied.

"She's my sister. They act like she's theirs. They'll brainwash her if she stays with them. They may even take her to your land. We've got to get her. With my father captured, she's the only family I have left."

"So are you thinking about kidnapping her?"

"It's not kidnapping. She's my own sister! I should be the one who had her to start with. Your friends have no right to her. They're the kidnappers. Will you help?" Marina asked.

"Uh . . ." Jim hesitated. "Sure. So what's your plan?"

"I'm still working that out," Marina replied. "Money always comes in handy, though. Do you think you could get your hands on some of the gold from Lucius's shop?"

The two spent most of the night discussing ideas for how they would steal Livia away from Tanner, Andrew, and Mick. It was early morning when Jim returned to the shop.

CHAPTER 54

YOU CAN'T DO THIS
(MICK)

Tanner and Andrew had gone to the open market to get some food, and Mick sat in Lucius's shop watching Livia play with some of her toys.

Bam.

The door swung open. It was Jim and Marina.

"Jim," Mick said in a shocked and disappointed tone when she saw Marina.

"We're here for Livia," Marina said. "Don't try anything."

Mick grabbed Livia and pulled her to her side. "Don't worry. I'll protect you," she told the young girl.

"From what?" Livia asked. No one had told Livia that Marina had turned her father over to the authorities.

"Let go of me!" Livia said as she attempted to break free of Mick's grasp. "Let me go to my sister!"

"Livia!" Mick cried out in vain as the young girl broke free.

"That's right," Marina said, stooping down to welcome Livia into her arms while looking at Mick with an evil smile.

Oh no, Mick thought. *This can't be good.*

She didn't know what to do. It would seem strange for her to try to prevent what was going on. Livia loved her big sister, and yet Mick knew she was in danger.

"Livia, why don't you stay here and show me your toy chariot? You know, the one you use when you play with Musclosus." It was Mick's best attempt to compete.

"No, I want to go with Mare."

"Marina, you can't do this." Mick looked sternly at Marina, discreetly trying to communicate her anger.

"Why don't you want me to take her?" Marina replied. "She is my sister, after all. Jim, you take care of Mick while I get Livia situated outside."

Marina walked outside with Livia and shut the door behind her.

"Jim, what are you doing? You can't do this. This is kidnapping."

"No, it's not. Livia is her sister, and now that her father's been captured, Livia should be with family."

"Come on, Jim. Be reasonable. She's duped you."

"No, she hasn't. I've made this decision on my own. She has every right to her sister. The rest of you have no business with her. Now shut up."

He grabbed Mick and wrestled her onto the bench, then began tying her up. Mick wasn't going down without a fight. She was scratching and clawing and trying unsuccessfully to reason with Jim, but he was so much stronger. After an epic struggle, he had Mick tied tightly to the bench.

"Goodbye, Mick," Jim shouted triumphantly as he fled through the front door.

Mick struggled to talk through the gag Jim had tied around her mouth. "You know you're never going to get back to Brownsville without us."

❖ ❖ ❖

About an hour later, Tanner and Andrew returned with the breads and cheeses they'd purchased for breakfast.

"What happened?" Tanner exclaimed. "Are you all right?"

Mick was struggling to communicate.

Tanner quickly worked to get her untied.

"It's Marina—and Jim," Mick blurted as soon as the gag was off. "They've kidnapped Livia!"

"I knew having Jim along was going to come back to bite us," Tanner said.

"I think we all did," Mick replied.

"Where were they heading?" Tanner asked.

"I don't know. They could be anywhere by now."

"When did Jim and Marina even meet?" Mick asked.

"No idea," Tanner said.

"We've got to think through everything Jim said or did in the last few days," Mick said. "There have to be clues about what they were planning."

"The only thing I remember was he was asking a lot of questions about the Christians here in Rome—where they meet, why they're so secretive, how you know if you've met another Christian, stuff like that. Egad!" Tanner paused. "You don't think they're planning to hand the whole Christian population over to the authorities, do you?"

"I don't think Jim would do something that horrible."

"Come on, Mick. Quit looking at Jim through rose-colored glasses. He's a thug—and officially a kidnapper. So why not a Judas?"

"I don't know. I don't think he could really do that."

"Jim's a follower, Mick. When he was hanging around you, he followed you in good ways." Tanner continued. "When he was with a bad crowd, he followed them in bad ways. Now he's hanging around Marina. He doesn't have enough courage to be his own man. He's Marina's puppet, and there's no telling where she's headed."

"Well, we've got to figure out a way to warn the other Christians," Mick said, "or find a way to track down Marina and Jim and stop them."

"Hey," Andrew said. "I just thought of something else Jim was asking about."

"What?"

"He asked a lot of questions about Anastasia and the capture of her Indian mother."

"What?"

"Yeah, he was really persistent and kept prying for information about the disappearance."

"You don't think they're going to try to find Anastasia's mother, do you?" Mick asked.

"Maybe," Andrew replied.

"But Marina's so furious about everything related to Anastasia right now," Tanner said. "Why would she want to go looking for Anastasia's mother, of all things?"

"No idea. I just thought it was odd that Jim was asking me all those questions. He's not the inquisitive type, you know."

"Definitely not his style," Mick said. "Marina put him up to it, for sure."

"They're headed for the Cathedral of Time," Tanner shouted.

"What?"

"Donald told me he and Anastasia had decided her mother must have been taken to a different place and time when she was kidnapped."

"We've got to get down to the Umbilicus now."

CHAPTER 55

STRANGE SYMBOLS
(HOKOLESQUA)

"Got it!" Hokolesqua said as he grabbed the weapon.

"We'll be leaving now," he said, boldly leveling the weapon at the guard, who sat in stunned silence.

"How did you . . ." Nemhsi started to ask.

"Not now."

Weapon still trained on the man, Hokolesqua unshackled Nemhsi.

"Bind him," he said as he handed his sister the shackles. Hokolesqua then unbound his own ankles.

"You were planning that the whole time, weren't you?" Nemhsi said once the guard was shackled and tied to a tree. "Where to now?"

"Follow the pointer," Hokolesqua said. He picked up the golden pyramid and opened the lid.

"I hope that thing's right, 'cause I'm sure this forest is full of Tohopka's warriors."

"Has it let me down yet?" he asked.

"I guess not."

"Then you must trust it."

After nearly a full day's journey, they arrived at the plaza surrounding the city of Delfi.

Hokolesqua bent down to take a closer look at the small, round stones that filled the plaza.

"What are these?" he asked. He reached down to pick one up, but he couldn't get the stone to budge from its current location.

He stood back up and, looking apprehensively at the pavement, stepped onto the stones, which immediately began to pull him toward the center of the plaza. He flailed his arms wildly as he tried to compensate for the unexpected motion. Hokolesqua had never been on anything with wheels, so he continued to struggle. He finally began to steady his arms like a tight-rope walker, and after a few seconds began to trust the stones and stood upright as they escorted him toward three circular designs in the pavement between the forest and main gate.

When they arrived at the center of the symbol, a light shaft matching the shape of the central triangle encompassed them.

A voice from above startled Hokolesqua.

"State your purpose."

"We're trying to find our mother, who was captured and taken to this land, and our sister, who went looking for her," Nemhsi replied.

"What are their names?"

"Mayata and Methoataske."

"Ah yes. We've been expecting you," the voice said.

Hokolesqua felt the words sink into the foundations of his soul.

"Don't move."

Hokolesqua wasn't sure that last phrase was necessary as he felt his body lift off the ground and gradually ascend. The light above them was too bright for them to discern where they were heading, and Hokolesqua was too afraid to move. After a few seconds, both he and Nemhsi found themselves in a strange hovering craft.

"We've been instructed to take you to Mount Olympus the moment you showed up. Brace yourselves."

"How did they know we'd be coming?" Nemhsi whispered to her brother.

Hokolesqua shrugged his shoulders.

The craft sped forward in a rapid ascent. Hokolesqua pulled out the golden pyramid, flipped open the lid, and felt a rush of peace sweep over him when he saw the needle pointing steadily in the exact direction they were heading.

In an instant, a blinding light shot through the windows of the craft, and the temperature soared. Sweat poured off Hokolesqua's face, but almost as quickly as it rose, the temperature dropped again.

"What was that?" Nemhsi asked.

"We just entered Olympus."

"Hold on to something. We're about to land," the man said as the craft made impact.

"Next time it would be helpful if you warned us before we landed," Nemhsi said after nearly falling over.

She and her brother disembarked, and the craft sped away. Hokolesqua marveled at how he could see Inner Earth below him with every step he took. When the novelty of the transparent ground wore off, he finally looked up.

That's the gate, he thought. *The one from my vision quest. I'd recognize it anywhere.*

He sprinted toward it.

"Hoko, wait!" Nemhsi yelled as she set off after him. "Stop, Hoko! Don't you see the—"

Clank!

He ran straight into the gate and fell clumsily backward.

Nemhsi was quickly at his side.

"Didn't you see that gate? What happened? Are you all right?"

"I'm fine," he said as he brushed himself off and got back on his feet.

I guess vision quest isn't exact.

"You made it back," a beautiful voice seemed to almost sing from behind them.

They turned to see Anatolia.

"I was beginning to wonder if you would find us. Come with me. We must be quick."

She escorted Hokolesqua and Nemhsi from the Judgment Platform to the Cathedral of Time, dissolved the protective dome, and left them at the door.

Hokolesqua and Nemhsi entered the large structure in awe. Their father, Lalawethika, had taught them to show great respect for places and things of a spiritual nature, and a profound feeling of reverence enveloped Hokolesqua to know that he was in one of these places. He'd felt the same way the first time he had entered, but this time the sensation was more profound. After standing on the entry landing and absorbing the aura he felt, he and Nemhsi made their way to the control room.

Hokolesqua had never been in the control room. When they were in the Cathedral before, Anatolia had made them wait on the central platform. He looked at the great glass display in front of the window overlooking the platform, and his heart skipped a beat.

The symbols from my vision quest.

He carefully examined the glowing markings.

Not the same. Very close, but not the same.

Confused and in a stupor, the young brave wondered what to do.

The glow, the color, the material are all the same, but the markings are different, not right.

He reached out and cautiously touched the glass. Nothing changed.

He swept his hand across the surface, never having felt an object so smooth. When his hand reached the right-hand side of the glass, the symbols changed. He placed his hand there again. Another change. And then a third change.

"That's it," he said out loud.

"That's what?" Nemhsi replied.

"Nothing. Just thinking out loud."

"Thinking about what?"

"Nothing."

The symbols on the glass were exactly as they had been seared into his mind the night of his vision quest. The pulsating green button seemed to call out to Hokolesqua. He reached out to touch it. Illuminated arrows began to flash across the floor.

"Come on." He grabbed Nemhsi by the hand and dragged her along, following the arrows. They arrived at the central platform, and after a series of strobing lights, everything went dark. Then another series of flashing arrows illuminated the path to one of the doorways.

"Follow the lights," Hokolesqua said.

They ran across the room, up the stairs, and Hokolesqua opened the door at the top.

"Where are we?" Nemhsi asked.

CHAPTER 56

THE FUGITIVES

(MARINA)

"Livia, do you remember Mom saying anything about any of the places we've mentioned?" Marina asked as she stood with Jim in front of the control-room display in the Cathedral of Time.

"I think I heard her say Nishapur."

"Nishapur?" Jim said. What the heck is Nishapur?"

"If this magical glass is correct," Marina said, "the population of Nishapur was 1,747,000. That's huge."

"Wow," Jim said. "I guess I should have paid more attention in history."

"You're sure you heard Mom talk about Nishapur?" Marina asked Livia.

"I'm not sure, Mare, but I think so," Livia said.

"I wonder why she never went there herself," Marina wondered out loud.

"Let's give it a try," Jim said. "Everyone stay here while I start this thing up."

"We're ready," Marina said, grabbing Livia by the hand. "Let's go find your grandma."

"Whoa," Jim said as he was about to press the green pulsating button on the display. "That was close."

"What?" Marina asked.

"Good thing I was paying attention when I came through here earlier. Tanner and Andrew said the settings continue to count time from when the last person used that setting until the current time."

"What do you mean?"

"Well, if Anastasia's mother was kidnapped two hundred years ago and we used the settings the way they are right now, we'd arrive wherever she went two hundred years too late."

"That would have been bad."

"Yeah."

"So do we know when she was kidnapped?" Marina asked.

"If I remember right, she was kidnapped about the same time the Brownsville Bank robbery happened, in 1810. It's 2019 where I come from, which means we'll have to subtract 209 years from whatever the settings for Nishapur say—unless someone else went there between then and now."

"That sounds like a big 'unless'!"

"Yeah, but if he did take her to Nishapur, how many people would want to go there?" Jim said.

"I guess we'll find out soon enough."

"Yep. Let's see. The screen for Nishapur is set for March 1430. If I subtract the 209 years, it should get us there about the same time Mayata and her kidnapper arrived—March of 1221. Okay. All set. Here we go."

Jim touched his finger to the start button, and the lights in the Cathedral began to flash.

"Follow the lights," he shouted.

They quickly positioned themselves on the platform. There was a bright burst of light, everything went dark, and then lights began to flash, directing them to the door just to the right of the command-center chapel.

"Here we go," Jim said as he opened the door and proceeded through the doorway into the darkness.

"Where are we?" Livia asked.

"Nishapur, I guess," Marina replied.

"I can't see anything," Livia complained.

"We'll have some light before long," Jim said, trying to reassure Livia. "Just stay close."

The trio had wandered in the pitch-black darkness for about thirty minutes when they finally began to see a light flickering in the distance.

"Looks like a fire up ahead," Marina said.

After a few more minutes, they came upon a torch mounted against a wall. Jim grabbed the torch and waved it in front of him in an attempt to better acquaint himself with their surroundings.

"We're in some kind of mine," Jim said as he noticed a collection of tools propped up against the wall of the cave. The light reflected off veins of bright blue along the walls.

"It's a turquoise mine," Jim said as he examined the stones more closely.

"Let's get out of here," Marina said. "This seems dangerous."

After another fifteen minutes, they saw a small campfire. As they approached the fire, they could make out two kids about their age who appeared to have made the mine a temporary lodging.

"How far until we reach the surface?" Marina asked when they reached the two strangers.

"It's not far from here," the boy replied. "But if you're going there, I wouldn't stay out after dark. It's dangerous to be out at night."

"Thank you."

"You're welcome," came the reply.

They continued to walk through the passages of the mine for a few more minutes, when they finally began to see light from the outside.

"This must be Nishapur, huh?" Jim asked as they emerged from the mine. "Let's take a look around."

The shadows were long in the city in front of them. The sun was just setting, meaning before long they'd be trying to get their bearings in the dark.

"I'm freezing," Livia said.

"It is pretty cold," Marina replied.

"We've got to find someplace to spend the night," Jim said. "Let's try to get to the city center and see what we can find."

"I think it would be safer to try to set up camp here," Marina said. "You heard what the boy in the cave said about it being dangerous at night. If this place is anything like Rome, I don't want to be wandering the city streets after dark."

"Good point," Jim said.

"Mare, are you sure we'll be safe?" Livia asked.

"Don't worry, Livia, I've got my bow if we need it." Marina grabbed at the leather strap that held her quiver of arrows.

"Jim, why don't you gather some firewood, and let's set up camp over there," Marina said.

"Okay," Jim replied.

Jim returned a few minutes later with some wood, and before long they had a crackling fire.

"You really think my step-grandmother is here somewhere?" Marina asked.

"I guess we'll see, right?"

"It's so hard for me to believe I have traveled into the future," Marina said.

"I can relate. I still am having a hard time believing I've traveled into the past."

"Yeah, but traveling into the future just seems so much stranger. I'm seeing things that haven't happened yet, based on where I come from."

"I guess you're right. It does seem stranger than traveling into the past."

"Well, I think I'm done for the day," Marina said as she lay down near the fire. "It's been an eventful day."

"I'll say," Jim replied.

"Let's get some sleep. We've got a busy day ahead."

CHAPTER 57

FOLLOWING THE TRAIL
(TANNER)

"Where do you think they took Livia?" Andrew asked.

"You mean WHEN?" Tanner said.

"You know what I mean."

"I've never been able to understand the way Jim thinks," Tanner replied. "So I really don't know."

"Jim's not calling the shots," Andrew replied. "Marina is."

"We can't just sit around talking about this," Mick interjected. "We've got to get to the Umbilicus."

"Let's go, then," Tanner said.

"Should we take Hades's helmet with us?" Andrew whispered to Tanner. "Might come in handy."

"Trouble is, I don't know where Donald lives, and I don't think we can afford to wait until he shows up."

"You're right."

Tanner, Mick, and Andrew sprinted for the Umbilicus. They were shocked to see the door wide open and no one guarding it.

"Marina and Jim must have already taken care of the guard problem," Mick said.

The three friends descended the ladder, pushed the stone out of the way, and climbed through the opening in the floor into the Mundus. Demeter appeared and cleared the stones away from the Cathedral entrance.

"Did a little girl come through here earlier with a boy and a girl about our age?" Tanner asked the goddess.

"Yes."

"Can you tell us where they went?"

"It's forbidden."

"They went somewhere forbidden?" Tanner asked, "Or it's forbidden for you to tell us?"

"The latter."

"Okay. Thanks anyway."

They entered the Cathedral and scampered down to the control room.

"Whoever was here last went to Nishapur," Tanner said as he looked at the great glass display.

"Nishapur? What the heck is Nishapur?" Andrew replied.

"I think it was a city in Persia," Mick replied.

"Do you really think that's where they went?" Andrew asked. "There's no reason for them to go there."

"Maybe they just wanted to be anywhere but here. Marina had really grown to hate this place."

"You're right. Well, I doubt anyone has used the Time Room since they came through," Tanner replied. "We've just got to try Nisha-whatever."

"Let's do it," Mick said.

Tanner touched the green button, and before they knew it, they were exiting the Cathedral into a dark and mysterious cave.

"Whaddya think this Nishapur place is going to be like?" Tanner asked.

"Well, if it's Persia," Andrew replied, "it's probably a bunch of sand dunes with an oasis surrounded by a few palm trees. Some adobe homes clustered around it. Probably a small open market."

"You've got a better imagination than I thought," Tanner replied. "I hope you're right. Wouldn't be too hard to find Marina and Jim in a place like that."

"It's probably not that small," Mick replied. "There were some pretty big cities in Persia, but at least it's not Babylon or Baghdad. I remember reading something about Nishapur, but if it was a big city, I'm sure I would have heard more about it."

"I guess we'll find out soon enough," Tanner said.

After walking through the cave for some time with only the light of a cell phone, they could see light from a small fire dancing on the cave walls and two figures silhouetted against the orange flames.

Carefully they approached.

"Looks like a couple kids about our age," Andrew whispered.

"It's not Marina and Jim, is it?"

"I don't think so."

"Hello," Tanner said as he got a little nearer.

The two strangers jumped.

"Sorry to startle you," he continued. "We're looking for a couple of friends who might have come through here recently. Two about my age and a little girl about five." He motioned with his hand to demonstrate the approximate height of Livia. "You haven't seen them, have you?"

"Yes, they came through not long ago," the girl replied.

"Oh, great! Which way did they go?"

"That way—toward the entrance. Wouldn't follow them now, though," the girl said.

"Why not?"

"It's nighttime. This area is full of Mongols who'll torment anyone they find. The people of Nishapur say this has been going on for many moons. It won't be long before Genghis Khan himself destroys the entire city."

"Did you say Genghis Khan?" Mick asked.

"Yes. Everyone knows an attack is coming," the boy said.

"I think we'll just stay in the cave tonight," Andrew said. "I'm mean, Livia's probably fine. Marina is her sister, after all."

"You're not chickening out on me, are you?" Tanner asked Andrew in disbelief. "Remember, Marina turned Marcus over to anti-Christian factions in the city. He may have been crucified by now. You don't really think she's the best one to raise Livia, do you?"

"No, but I'd like to give my parents a chance to raise me," Andrew replied. "Which might not happen if we meet the Mr. Khan I've read about."

"We'll be fine," Tanner replied.

"Do you mind if we stay here with you for the night?" Andrew asked.

"Come on, guys," Tanner said. "We need to go find them."

"T, the kid said Genghis Khan," Andrew replied. "And, personally, if I'm going to meet him, I'd prefer to see him coming—not meet him in a dark alley somewhere. Let's let Marina and Jim do that."

"You really think Genghis Khan might be out there?" Mick asked the stranger.

"His warriors are all over the countryside," the boy replied. "It's very dangerous at night."

"You can stay with us," the young girl said. "We come to the cave every night for protection. You'd be smart to stay out of the Mongols' way."

"We never did introductions," Mick said. "I'm Mick, and these are my friends, Tanner and Andrew."

"I'm Nemhsi, and this is my brother, Hokolesqua."

"Wait, do I know you?" Mick asked. "You look so familiar."

"I don't think so," Hokolesqua replied.

"What are the two of you doing here?" Mick said.

"We came in search of our mother, Mayata" the girl replied. "She was captured and taken to this land three moons ago. Our oldest sister went in search of her, and we have no idea where either one of them are."

"Well, maybe we can help each other out," Mick replied. "You can help us find our friends, and we'll help you find your mother and sister."

"That would be helpful. We haven't made much progress," Hokolesqua said.

"There must be a million people in Nishapur," Nemhsi added. "Trying to find someone in a city so big hasn't been an easy task."

Tanner could see by the expression on Andrew's face that he was trying to expand the image in his mind from a handful of adobe homes to a sprawling metropolis.

"Your mother was captured three moons ago, and when did your sister disappear?" Mick asked.

"Methoataske disappeared about two moons ago," Hokolesqua said.

Tanner did a double take. "Did you just say Methoataske?"

"Yes, Methoataske. Why?"

"I knew a woman named Methoa . . ." Tanner paused. "Wait, did you say that your mother went missing and Methoataske went searching for her?"

"Yes."

"Did you come here through Mammoth Cave?"

"Yes, very large cave."

"It's not possible! We knew Methoataske." Tanner pointed back and forth between himself and Andrew.

"You know Methoataske?"

"She was a great woman."

"How do you know Methoataske?"

"She invited us to stay in her home for a while when we were strangers in Rome," Tanner said.

"So where is Methoataske?" Hokolesqua asked excitedly. "Take us there now."

Tanner hung his head. "I'm so sorry. I don't know how to say this, but there was a terrible fire—and she died in the blaze."

Tanner felt a pang of guilt as he thought back to the situation. Why hadn't he noticed Anastasia and Livia weren't with the others when he watched them be escorted out of their home by the guards? "It was devastating." Tanner continued. "She was such an amazing woman." He walked over and put his arm on the shoulder of Hokolesqua, who had wrapped his arms around his knees with his head down.

"I'm sure your mother is somewhere in Nishapur, though," Tanner said, trying to soften the blow. "And we're going to help you find her."

Hokolesqua was quietly sobbing now. It was easy to see how the news would crush him. Tanner thought back to how his own heart sank when he found Anastasia dead in her home, and he had only known her for a short time. He tried but failed to comprehend how her brother must be feeling.

They continued to discuss the search for Mayata until late at night. Eventually they all lay down.

"Psst, Andrew," Tanner said once he was confident the others were asleep.

"What?"

"Remember when we went into the Mundus to talk with Demeter about the blizzard?"

"Yeah."

"Did we close the Mundus after we left?"

"Huh?"

"You know, did we slide the rock that covers the opening into the Mundus back over the hole?"

"I don't remember," Andrew paused. "Actually, I think we might have left it open. Why?"

"Think about all the bad stuff that's happened since then," Tanner said. "Marina handed her father over to anti-Christians and then lured Jim into kidnapping Livia. Plus, Lucius told me Decimus has been given command of a legion."

"And what does that have to do with the covering to the Mundus?"

"Come on, Andrew. You mean I actually know something you don't? So this is how it must feel for you all the time. This is awesome!"

"Shh," Andrew said. "You're going to wake everyone up."

"Sorry. It's just that . . ."

"All right. You know something I don't. Out with it."

"Well, Mick's paper said the Romans only open the Mundus three times a year because when it's open, evil spirits enter the city. With all the bad stuff that's been happening . . . you don't think it's because we left that open, do you?"

"Come on, T. That's ridiculous."

"Yeah, well, you thought Inner Earth was ridiculous, too, don't forget, and the fact that the Greek myths were true."

"Yeah, but evil spirits influencing everyone because we forgot to move some stupid rock? No way."

"I'm not so sure," Tanner replied.

CHAPTER 58

THE MINE'S EXIT

(HOKOLESQUA)

Hokolesqua's world had been ripped out from under him. As he tried to sleep, he kept thinking about his sister dying in a fire, the flames filling his head. It was as if there was no room for any other thoughts. The death of his sister seemed more than he could bear, and he convulsed over and over as the realization that he would never see her again sank deeper into his soul. It was the middle of the night when he finally let his body relax. He could no longer fight the flames searing his mind. As he stopped his internal wrestle, he thought about what had brought him to the mines in the first place.

Maybe Mother is still alive, he thought. *Maybe I'm not too late to save her.*

Andrew had been very convincing that it was too dangerous for them to go searching for anyone at night with Genghis Khan and his men in the area.

It's dangerous for Mayata too, Hokolesqua thought.

I cannot risk my mother dying too. I would never be able to forgive myself if something happened to Mayata tonight and I waited too long to find her.

Hokolesqua looked at his sister sleeping peacefully a few feet away.

Do I leave her and go alone?

He was putting his own life at risk by going in search of his mother and didn't want to put Nemhsi at risk too, but he also wasn't sure how she would fare if he left her behind. Tanner, Andrew, and Mick seemed nice enough, and they were taking precautions that would keep his sister safe, but he'd only met them a few hours earlier.

The pyramid, he thought. *I must check the pyramid.*

In the dim light from the embers that remained, he fumbled in his sack and pulled out the treasured object. He looked over every side in the hope that something was written that would make it clear what he was to do, but unlike when Tecumseh viewed the object, there was nothing.

I need help, he thought with energy from the bottom of his soul as he flipped open the lid. He had never seen the pointer move with such precision. In the past in had moved back and forth until it eventually seemed to settle on a course. This time the needle flung to a position and screeched to a halt. He followed the pointer with his eyes to its edge and looked up. It was pointing directly at the mine's exit.

I must leave now to search for Mayata.

CHAPTER 59

WELCOME TO NISHAPUR

(MICK)

Mick was first to wake up. She relit the torches and noticed right away that Hokolesqua was missing.

"Nemhsi, Nemhsi." She gently shook Hokolesqua's sister, trying to wake her.

"What? Huh?" Nemhsi replied with a jolt.

"It's Hokolesqua. He's gone," Mick said.

Nemhsi moved her head side to side as if she were trying to wake up and look for her brother simultaneously.

"What are you doing, Hoko?" She shook her head in a defeated manner that sent a clear signal to Mick that Hokolesqua had done this type of thing before.

"He'll be back," Nemhsi said.

"I hope you're right," Mick replied. "But he can't just go running off. Genghis Khan is one of the most dangerous men to ever live. This is not some kind of game."

"Hoko is desperate to become a brave warrior like his father," Nemhsi replied. "He'll do almost anything to prove his bravery. One day it's going to catch up with him."

"Let's just hope today's not that day," Mick added.

Tanner and Andrew woke up, and Mick and Nemhsi explained what was going on.

"We'll find him," Tanner said. "Don't worry."

"Hey." Mick could see a light bulb go off in Andrew's head. He gave Nemhsi a gentle shove on the shoulder. "You remember the little girl you said come through the cave earlier?

"Yes," Nemhsi replied.

"She's Methoataske's daughter. Your niece."

"What?" Nemhsi said in shock. "That's not possible. Methoataske hasn't been gone long enough to have a child, let alone a child as old as that girl."

"That's the craziness of time travel!" Tanner chimed in. "It makes things that seem impossible–possible."

"Okay," Mick said. "We better get moving. Now we've got three people to rescue."

"What do you mean three?" Nemhsi asked. "The little girl didn't look like she needed rescuing."

"The two kids she was with basically kidnapped her," Mick said.

"She didn't look like she was opposed to being with them," Nemhsi replied.

"It's a long story," Tanner mumbled.

"I've got time," Nemhsi said.

Mick explained the story to the young Indian.

"So who do we rescue first?" Nemhsi asked.

"I think Livia," Tanner said. "She's the most vulnerable."

Everyone agreed.

"Let's get moving before Marina and Jim get too far ahead of us," Tanner said. "We can split up. We'll cover more ground that way. We'll meet back in the mine tonight."

"Did you forget what Hokolesqua said?" Andrew said. "Genghis Khan is preparing to attack."

"Tanner doesn't know who Genghis Khan is," Mick replied.

"No, I've heard of him."

"You haven't heard much if you're thinking we're going to split up," Andrew said.

"All right," Tanner said, a bit put out. "We'll stick together."

The four of them exited the mine, shielding their eyes as they emerged from the darkness into the brilliant sunlight. Once their eyes adjusted, they began their descent into the sprawling city of Nishapur in the valley below.

When they reached the foot of the mountain, they could see nearly endless rice fields in all directions. Thousands were working the fields wearing nothing but loincloths and large hats to shade themselves from the blistering sun.

"It's so hot," Andrew said as they were nearing the city.

"I don't know how they can stand it," Mick replied.

"At least we'll be getting some shade soon," Tanner said, pointing to a narrow, winding street inside the city gate they were just about to enter. The shade from the high walls of adobe and brick created a welcome respite from the broiling sun.

"Hallelujah," Andrew said.

"What a difference," Mick said as they walked under a tunnel formed by two buildings with a connecting archway. She wiped the sweat from her brow. She was drenched.

Mick stared in awe as she moved deeper into the vibrant city.

"Let's ask those ladies if they've seen Marina and Jim," Mick said, pointing to three female musicians standing in front of a small residence. One was playing an instrument similar to a harp, and another a ukulele-like device with an extra-long neck. The third was singing.

"Excuse us," Tanner said. "Have you seen a boy and girl about our age with a small girl about five or six come through here?"

"Haven't seen them," the vocalist replied, returning immediately to her music.

As the Brownsvillians moved farther into the labyrinth of the city, the chorus of sounds became almost deafening. There was the shouting back and forth between buyers and sellers in the massive bazaar. Belly dancers with rattles made from the skulls of small animals performed to the steady beat of percussive instruments, and musicians sang and played on nearly every corner.

"Look at those gardens," Andrew said as they approached a canal lined with flowers and foliage of all shapes and sizes. "I totally expected nothing but sand dunes."

"I think this is the fourth canal we've crossed," Mick said as they walked over a narrow bridge with beautifully carved stonework railings on either side.

"There are twelve such canals that run through the city," an eavesdropper replied.

Mick looked over toward the source of the voice to see a stranger about her age with sunbaked skin and eyebrows that looked as though a couple of caterpillars had been glued to his face. Behind the boy and not far from where they stood was a churning water mill.

"Welcome to Nishapur," he said with a wink as he sped past.

He stopped at a thick wooden door directly in front of them at the end of the bridge. When he opened it, the wave of heat emanating from the building nearly knocked Mick over.

Her eyes widened as she looked directly into the opening and saw the largest tapestry she had ever seen being woven in an exquisite pattern of embroidered gold and silver and studded with precious stones. The green silk for the rug was being wiped of excess moisture after being drawn from a black cauldron the size of a small elephant, a scorching fire blazing beneath. Surrounding the cauldron were three men dumping a constant stream of beautifully colored clay into the pot. The stranger made eye contact with Mick as he was closing the door. He shook his head as if to say no. A shiver ran down Mick's spine at the strange connection she felt with the boy.

Continuing down the street, they came upon a series of shops where craftsmen spun pottery wheels, creating elaborate ceramics.

"Did you see that carpet back there?" Mick asked.

"I did," Andrew exclaimed. "This place is unbelievable."

"I've never seen anything like it," Tanner replied. "I had no idea places like this existed in the Middle Ages."

"You never studied." Mick and Andrew looked over at Tanner, shaking their heads in disgust.

"Snakes!" Tanner yelled, pointing across their bodies and causing them to snap their necks in the opposite direction.

A snake charmer was seated Indian style against the wall playing his pungi. Two cobras weaved their heads back and forth and braided their bodies as they emerged from a weathered basket.

"That wasn't funny," Mick said. "I nearly died from the last one. Do not do that again."

"You're right," Tanner said. "I apologize."

"We should have asked that boy back there if he'd seen Marina and Jim," Andrew said. "He seemed like the type who would be willing to help."

"I'm not so sure," Mick replied as she thought about the glance he'd given her before closing the door. She tried to process the strange sensation she felt as she made eye contact with him.

"Might as well try," Tanner said.

Mick was hesitant but curious.

The four returned to the shop, and Tanner rapped on the large wooden door. The voices coming from behind the door stopped instantly as Mick and her friends waited for someone to answer. But no one came. Tanner rapped even harder. Nothing.

CHAPTER 60

TALL AS TWO MEN

(MARINA)

"Yes, I have seen a woman who matches that description," a shopkeeper in the market told Marina.

"Did you hear that?" Marina said, leaning down and giving Livia a gentle shove with her forearm.

"This man has seen your grandmother." Marina straightened back up and gave Jim a confirming look.

"Where did you see her?" Marina asked.

"I was working in the turquoise mine when a Mongolian warrior emerged from the forbidden passageway.

"Forbidden passageway? Why is it forbidden?"

"It's home to the Manticore, of course. Those who enter never return."

"But you said the warrior came out of the forbidden passageway."

"That's true. On rare occasion people emerge. Usually they don't even see the Manticore in the darkest corner of the mine. It only attacks those who attempt to enter the passageway.

"What is a Manticore?" Jim asked.

"Only the most dreaded of all beasts," the man replied. "Body of a lion and wings of a bat, with three rows of flesh-tearing teeth. It's scorpion-like tail strikes with precision—fatally wounding its victims, which it devours bones and all."

"Wish I hadn't asked," Jim replied.

◆ 283 ◆

"So, was the woman we described with the warrior?" Marina asked.

"Yes, she was a small, beautiful woman with hair as black as an Arabian night, and the man was forcing her through the mine against her will."

"Why didn't you help her?" Jim asked.

"If you had seen the man, you would know why. He was nearly as tall as two men and was wearing armor from head to toe, which surely cost more than I've made in my lifetime," the shopkeeper said. "The angry scowl on his face made it look like he would just as soon have killed you as look at you.

"I've got to stop asking questions," Jim said.

"He had to be one of Genghis Khan's men."

"We need to find this man," Marina said. "Do you have any idea where he might have gone?"

"Word is that Genghis's armies attacked the city of Nisa just weeks ago. A rebel force from Nishapur is heading to Nisa to attack the men Khan left to maintain the city. The man is probably somewhere in Nisa or the surrounding area with Genghis's armies."

"How far away is Nisa?" Marina asked.

"You can't go there," the shopkeeper replied. "It wouldn't be safe."

"How far is it?" Marina asked more assertively.

"Nearly five days by horse," the man replied. "You're free to do what you want, but if it were me, I wouldn't go."

"If we're going, we need to figure out where to get some horses," Jim said, looking at Marina.

"Are we going on another horse ride?" Livia chimed in, bobbing up and down on her tiptoes.

"We'll try, Livia, but please try to be quiet," Marina said. "We're trying to find your grandmother. Let us talk."

"Okay, Mare."

"Any idea where we can get some horses?" Marina asked.

"Do you have any money?" the man asked.

"Yes, we have gold," Jim replied.

"Told you that would come in handy," Marina whispered to Jim.

"Ah, then, yes. I can find you some horses."

"Are you sure you want to do this?" Jim asked Marina. "Five days on horseback is a lot, and it doesn't sound very safe."

"To avenge everything that has happened to me and to finally find peace and rest for my soul, five days of danger is nothing!"

"All right, where do we get these horses?" Jim asked.

"The stables are just outside the city. I'll take you there."

About a half hour later, they arrived at a small ranch.

"You wait here while I speak with my friend," the shopkeeper instructed.

"Can we go and look at the horses?" Livia asked.

"Sure," Marina replied and they walked over to the wooden fence to take a closer look.

"Look at that brown one with the black legs and tail. Can I ride that one?" Livia asked. "Never mind, Mare." Livia continued as a beautiful white Arabian stallion emerged from behind a black horse. "I want that white one! And we really get to ride them for a total of ten whole days?"

"This is Imari," the shopkeeper said "He says you can use two of his horses."

"Pleasure," Imari said. "Since I don't know you, I'll need the price of two horses in gold for a deposit. When you bring them back, I'll give you 75 percent of your money back. How long do you plan on being gone?"

"Ten days."

"Let's agree to fifteen. That will give you a little extra time in case anything slows you down. What do you have for payment?"

Jim pulled out the bag of gold coins he had stolen from the treasury heist at Lucius's shop.

"That should be sufficient," the man said as he eagerly examined the coins. "Remember, fifteen days. No later. Now, let's pick out the horses."

"How about that white one?" Marina asked.

"No, I can't let you take that one. Too easy to spot at night. Lots of bandits and Mongols lurking in the Persian darkness. You'd never make it back alive with that one. For that very reason, let's have you take the bay over there," he said, pointing to the brown-and-black stallion, "and the black one."

"Perfect."

"Can you give us directions on how to get to Nisa?" Marina asked.

"Never been there," the man replied. "I wish I could help you."

"That's fine," Jim said. "We can just ask around."

"Excuse me." A boy with a long ponytail tapped Marina on the shoulder.

"Did you say you're going to Nisa?" the boy asked.

"Yes," Marina replied.

"Can I take you there?" He took a small pyramid shaped object out of his bag and flipped open the lid. He stared into the object. "I would be happy to show you the way."

"What do you think?" Marina asked Jim.

"I'd feel safer if someone joined us since we know nothing about this place," Jim replied.

"You think we can trust him?" she whispered.

"He looks trustworthy," Jim replied.

"We could use the help," Marina said. "How much would you charge us?"

"Nothing. I will take you there for free. But I don't have a horse."

"That's fine," Marina said. "You can ride with my friend Jim, and I'll ride with Livia."

"Do we get to ride the horses now?" Livia asked, tugging on Marina's tunic. "Do we? Do we?"

"Yes, yes, Livia."

"My name's Hokolesqua—Hoko for short," the boy said.

"I'm Marina, and this is Jim and my little sister, Livia," Marina said.

Jim hoisted Marina and Livia onto the brown-and-black horse, and then he and Hokolesqua climbed onto the black one. Hokolesqua flipped open the lid of the pyramid and glanced inside again.

"This way," he said, and the four rode off into the hot Persian afternoon.

"Are we there yet?" Livia began to ask after only about thirty minutes of riding.

"Liv, we have ten full days of riding. This is going to be very long. Please be patient. Try to think about how nice it will be to meet your grandmother."

"Livia has never seen her grandmother?" Hokolesqua asked.

"No, Livia's grandmother was abducted by a tall warrior we think is in Nisa."

"I am also looking for a tall warrior who took my mother, Mayata, not many moons ago.

"Your mother's name is Mayata?" Marina asked.

"Yes," Hokolesqua replied.

"Livia's grandmother's name is Mayata," Jim said.

"That is not possible," Hokolesqua said. "My mother and Livia's grandmother have same name?"

"That is unusual," Marina replied.

"And you say her grandmother was captured by a tall warrior also?"

"That's right."

"My mother didn't have any grandchildren, though, so I guess they're not the same Mayata."

"Still, it is very strange that so much is the same about them," Marina said.

Hokolesqua continued to shake his head. Marina could tell he was in deep thought about the whole thing. A few minutes later he spoke again.

"My sister did time travel, though. Maybe she had a child." Hokolesqua was getting excited. "The *mother* of Livia? What's the name of her mother?"

"Anastasia," Marina replied.

"Oh," Hokolesqua replied, sounding extremely disappointed. "I guess it is just a coincidence."

He pulled the pyramid out of his bag again and opened it.

"What is that?" Marina asked.

"A director," Hokolesqua replied. "Shows the path to Nisa."

"A compass," Jim said.

"Are we there yet?" Livia continued her questioning throughout the day. Jim and Marina tried to find creative ways to keep her engaged.

"Pretend you're the charioteer Musclosus," Marina said.

The first day was long and uneventful. They passed a few small streams where they were able to water the horses and quench their own thirst. It was a hot ride, but bearable.

"Let's call it a day," Marina said as the sun began to get low on the horizon. "Jim, why don't you and Hokolesqua gather some firewood? Livia and I will clear an area over there."

Jim nodded.

It wasn't long before they had a small fire burning.

The temperatures dropped significantly as daytime turned to night. Jim gathered some additional wood to get them through the night.

"Look at the stars, Mare," Livia said, shoving Marina's shoulder. "They look like jewels spread out on a purple carpet."

Tired from their long journey, the four travelers quickly fell asleep near the fire.

Marina was awakened in the middle of the night by the cold and moved closer to the glowing embers. She was in the process of rekindling the fire and adding a couple of logs when she spotted the silhouette of a man moving toward Jim in the darkness.

"Jim, look out!"

Jim sat up straight, but that was all he had time to do. He turned just in time to see a Mongol warrior reach down and grab him.

"Stop!" Jim yelled. He pointed toward Marina and Livia. "They're the ones you want!"

Marina grabbed Livia, and the two bolted for their horse.

"What's going on?" Hokolesqua said, sitting up and looking around.

Jim was struggling with the Mongol, but he didn't stand a chance. He was a tough kid, but this was a battle-hardened warrior equipped for a fight.

Hokolesqua ran toward the Mongol and Jim.

Marina looked back as she and Livia rode into the starry night, wondering what would become of Jim.

"What's going on, Mare?" Livia said, still trying to wake herself from a deep sleep.

"Some bad men just captured Jim."

"Are they going to capture us, too?"

"No. We're going to be safe. Just stay with me."

"Okay, Mare."

Marina and Livia fled in the direction they had been riding all day.

"It's just the two of us now, Liv. How tough are you?"

"I'm tough, Mare. Where's Hoko?"

"We had to leave him behind," Marina replied. "I don't know if we can trust him. He may have led us into a trap."

Day two was, without question, far more difficult. They were out on the plains where there wasn't much water or shade, and they didn't start off nearly as refreshed as they had the day before. It was about halfway into the day when they finally came to a small river surrounded by trees. They dismounted and led the horse to the stream. As the horse drank, Marina and Livia shoveled water into their own mouths.

"This is the best water ever!" Livia said.

"I agree," Marina replied.

"What's that, Mare?" Livia asked, pointing downstream from where they were drinking.

Marina glanced to her right to see a massive military encampment.

A man emerged from the trees, moving toward the stream.

"Quick! Hide behind that tree."

The two girls crouched behind a tree along the river's edge. The man looked their direction. Marina couldn't tell if he had seen them or not.

"Don't move!" Marina told Livia as she wrapped her arms around her.

"Who are they?" Livia asked.

"I think they're Mongols, like the warrior who captured Jim and your grandmother."

"Are they going to get us, too?"

"Not if we're careful."

"I'll be careful."

The man returned to the trees.

"Did he see us?" Livia asked.

"I don't think so, but he may have seen the horse. We need to get out of here. Someone will come for the horse."

"Get on," Marina said as she hoisted Livia onto the bay.

"We'll cross the river downstream from them and see if we can get a better look at their encampment. If it is the Mongols, we may be able to find the man I'm looking for."

"What man?" Livia said. "I thought we were looking for my grandmother."

"Yes. We're looking for her, but there's a man I'm looking for as well–the man who captured your grandmother."

"Why, Mare?"

"I want to make him pay for what he's done."

"How much are you going to make him pay?"

"I'll figure that out."

"Okay, Mare."

The two girls carefully moved closer to the encampment.

"It's your grandma!" Marina whispered. "Over there, tied to that chair! It has to be her. She looks just like you and your mother."

"Where?"

"Over there. By the big tent. We have to sneak over there and talk to her."

"But what if we get caught?"

"We can't get caught."

Marina was busy trying to figure out how to get Livia's grandmother separated from the encampment so she could rescue her when she saw a large hand part the tent door behind Mayata. The top of a man's head poked through the tent. He was bent in half in order to get through the opening. Marina's heart stood still.

It's him. The man who started everything.

"The shopkeeper was right," Marina said as she watched the mighty warrior straighten up. "He *is* as tall as two men."

"I've never seen anyone that tall," Livia replied.

CHAPTER 61

THE CHOICE

(MARINA)

Rage filled Marina as she looked on the man she considered the source of all her problems. Arrayed in spectacular armor, he strutted over to Mayata, stooped down, and whispered something in her ear. Mayata snarled and rocked the chair she was sitting in back and forth, trying to free herself. The man snapped his head back in laughter. Marina was so angry she could barely see straight.

"Mare," Livia whispered. "Is that the man you're going to make pay?"

"Yes, Livia, that's the man."

"Look at his armor, Mare. He must have lots of money," Livia said. "If you can make him pay, we'll be rich."

"Don't concern yourself, Livia. This is adult business."

Carefully hidden in the trees, Marina and Livia watched the large tent as warriors entered and exited. Marina wanted to punish this man who had caused her so much pain, but the longer she watched, the more frustrated she became that she couldn't come up with a plan. She could still see Mayata, who had given up on her attempts to free herself, sitting outside the tent. Mayata's captor and several other men made their way to the river. They began to remove their clothes.

"Don't look," Marina whispered as she reached over and covered the little girl's eyes.

"Why?" Livia replied.

"The men are going to bathe."

This is my chance. Marina looked at her bow, which was tied to several ropes hanging over the horse's back.

Can I do it? He's vulnerable.

She looked at the large encampment of tents and all the men in the river around the tall warrior.

There are too many of them. I'd never be able to make it safely back to Nishapur.

She looked over at the pile of clothing the men left on the banks out of their sight.

That's it. Marina laughed inside. *I'll steal his pompous clothing, rescue Mayata, and we'll flee for Nishapur.*

"Livia?"

"Yes?"

"Can you stay hidden right here and not move?"

"Why?"

"I told you I was going to make that man pay, right?"

"Yes."

"I'm going to steal his stuff, rescue your grandmother, and be right back. Together we'll all ride back to Nishapur. Can you do it? Can you be still?"

"What if someone captures me like they captured Jim?" Livia asked.

"No one has come over to this side of the river all day. You stay hidden right here, and don't move. You'll be safe."

"If you say so, Mare. I can do it."

Marina carefully mounted the bay and rode toward the river. She spotted a bend that had just enough foliage that she could cross without being seen. Cautiously, she approached the clearing where the men had entered the river. She could see the tall warrior's elaborate clothing lying on the ground in front of her along with a sword in a jewel encrusted sheath. She imagined it was worth a small fortune. She had to chuckle thinking about this man she was so bitter against returning to his tent without a stitch of his spectacular trappings. It didn't compare with what he had caused her, but still it seemed satisfying.

If I hop off and walk on the opposite side of the horse from the river, they won't see me. I'll grab his stuff, and then get Mayata. It's perfect.

Marina listened carefully as she approached the clothing. None of the men said anything that made her believe she had been seen. Quickly, she grabbed his stuff. Still nothing but the continued banter coming from the men in the river.

No need to jump on and create a scene. Marina thought as she continued to walk along, hidden by the horse.

As soon as she passed the clearing, she hopped on the bay and fled for the tent. When she reached the spot where her step-grandmother had sat, there was no trace of her—only the chair she was tied to, which had been tipped over and was lying a few feet from where she had been. Marina looked around in a panic. Had she been set up? Was this a trap? She didn't see any immediate danger and wanted desperately to look inside the tent to see if Mayata had been moved inside, but she also knew the chances of a warrior being in the tent were extremely high.

Livia.

She panicked.

She started to cross the river when she heard a scream.

"Mayata's gone!"

Marina kicked the horse in the ribs and raced for the spot where she'd left her little sister.

When she arrived at the site, Livia was gone.

Marina circled the horse multiple times in a small radius near where she'd left the little girl, but there was no sign of her.

What have I done? Marina felt like a hollowed-out shell of herself.

I don't ever want to see you again. The memory of her angry voice reverberated in the chambers of her head. The echo bounced back and forth, and each new time she heard it, she thought about another person she would never see again. She looked down the embankment and could see four Mongol riders crossing the river.

Though she felt like she had completely destroyed her life, with everyone she ever felt any connection to now gone, there was still enough fight left in her to wheel the horse around and flee.

CHAPTER 62

LOOKING FOR US

(MICK)

"Let me try," Mick said after Tanner knocked on the door of the tapestry shop for a third time with no answer.

"We know you're in there," she said. "Please. We need your help."

"Who is it?"

"The girl you were talking to on the street."

"You can't come in."

"We don't want to come in. We just need your help."

"One second."

Mick could hear commotion around the door, and when it finally opened, there was now a curtain behind the young boy, blocking her view into the space beyond.

Why is he being so secretive? Mick wondered. She had already gotten a good look at the tapestry and massive caldron when he'd opened the door before.

For some reason, I wasn't supposed to see all that stuff. That's why he was shaking his head at me when he realized I had seen it.

"What can I help you with?" the boy asked after stepping onto the street and shutting the door behind him.

"We're strangers from another land," Tanner said while Mick was still trying to sort out the mysterious nature of the situation. "We're looking for someone and are hoping you can help."

"Who are you looking for?"

"We're actually looking for several people," Mick said, snapping back to the present. "A woman in her thirties with straight black hair who was abducted by a very tall warrior, two kids about our age with a little black-haired girl who's about five or six, and this girl's older brother." Mick motioned toward Nemhsi.

"I haven't seen any of them," the boy replied. "I'd be happy to try to help you, though. My father is well connected with people who might be able to track these friends down for you. Wait here and I'll ask him what we can do."

"Can we just come in?" Mick asked. She knew what the answer was going to be but was hoping to get some clues about what was going on inside.

"You'll be fine outside. I'll be right back."

Nothing, Mick thought disappointedly. But based on the look she'd seen on the young boy's face, she was more convinced than ever that something of intrigue was going on inside. She tried to peek around the edge of the curtain when he opened the door but wasn't able to see anything.

A few minutes later, he returned.

"My father is good friends with the ruler of our land. He's very busy with an important project right now, but this evening after he finishes, he'd be happy to introduce you."

"I'm not sure we can wait that long," Tanner said.

"I think it's worth it," Andrew said. "In a city this size, we'll never find them unless we have help. If their leader were to spread the word, we'd have a much better chance of finding them."

"I guess you're right," Tanner replied. "But what do we do until then?"

"My father said you can stay with us until you find who you're looking for. He's pretty confident the tall warrior will come looking for *us*."

Mick looked at Tanner and Andrew. "Why would he come looking for us?"

"He said he's part of the forces they expect to invade the city soon. Finding the kids will be a lot harder. Follow me. I'll bring you to my home. By the way, I'm Farzin." The boy extended his hand toward Mick. "It means 'learned person.'"

"Nice to meet you," Mick replied. "I'm Mick."

"It means OCD teenager," Tanner added, laughing.

Farzin gave her a puzzled glance. Mick just shook her head and continued to introduce the others.

CHAPTER 63

HOKO'S BRAVERY

(HOKOLESQUA)

Hokolesqua looked around. Riding off in one direction was the Mongol warrior with Jim, and in the other, Marina and Livia. A few smoldering embers glowed softly in front of him. He grabbed the pyramid and flipped open the lid.

Don't fail me now.

He hopped on his horse and followed the director through the night and into the next day until he was outside the Mongol encampment. As he was surveying the area, he saw her.

Mother.

She was alive—tied to a chair, but other than that, she looked fantastic. It was the greatest sight he had ever seen. He had taken his mother for granted until she disappeared. It wasn't until he saw her captive outside the largest of the Mongol tents that he realized just how much he had missed her. Patiently he watched and waited for an opportunity to ride in and rescue her. As he waited, he heard a noise in the trees not far from where he was. He looked intently but wasn't able to see anyone.

Someone is spying. I must be very quiet and act quickly.

He turned his attention back to his mother, who finally appeared to be alone. He crossed the river and swept into the encampment on horseback. His mother didn't see him until he was right in front of her and hopped off his horse.

"Hoko! You found me. How did you do it? You brave boy."

"Mother, Hoko would go to ends of earth to find you."

He cut her loose and gave her a quick embrace.

"I need to get you out of here."

He helped her onto the horse and, recognizing the dangerous circumstance, checked the pyramid, which pointed across the river to the area he had heard the noises coming from in the trees.

I can't go there. It might be a Mongol warrior.

He looked at the pyramid again. The needle didn't move.

I have to follow it.

He gulped and then nudged the horse across the river and up the small embankment on the other side. They started into the trees when Hokolesqua heard the rustling noises again.

Pyramid has always been right, but—

"Mayata's gone!" The scream echoed through the trees.

Must trust the pyramid.

He continued to scan the woods intently, and then he saw the little girl huddled behind a tree.

"Livia, you must come with me. The Mongols are coming."

Mayata was looking back toward the tent where she had been held captive.

"But my sister told me . . ." Livia replied.

"Someone's coming!" Mayata yelled.

Hokolesqua jumped off, threw Livia on, and climbed back on himself. Seconds later they were racing through the countryside.

"But I wasn't supposed to move," Livia said, looking back at the spot she had been hiding.

"Trust me," Hokolesqua said. "Marina doesn't want you captured by Mongols."

Hokolesqua, his mother, and Livia had a head start, but they were in a sprint for their lives.

"Hang on," Hokolesqua said as he gave the horse another kick and she galloped into higher gear.

CHAPTER 64

Mayata is Gone

(Jim Sanford)

"Where's Mayata?" a stark-naked Toquchar bellowed as he ran into the tent where Jim was being held captive.

"What are you talking about?" one of the warriors in the tent replied. "And where are your clothes?"

"Someone stole them," he replied. "But where's Mayata? She was just outside when we left. Didn't you hear anything?"

"No," the warrior replied, looking at the other warriors in the tent. "She doesn't know this country at all. She wouldn't just take off like that."

"She's been kidnapped," Toquchar said as he shuffled through his belongings trying to find something to put on. "One of the warriors saw her beauty and took her. Search the camp. Whoever's done this will pay!"

The massive Toquchar got right in Jim's face.

"Do you know anything about this?" he demanded eyeball to eyeball.

"Nothing," Jim whimpered.

"You're lying," he barked as he pushed Jim and his chair over onto the floor.

"If I find out you're involved in any way, you're a dead man."

"We have to search beyond the camp," the warrior replied. "Whoever did this is not going to hang around."

"That's true," Toquchar said, throwing a shirt over his long torso. "She should be easy enough to track down. My father-in-law has troops crawling across this whole region. Spread the word."

"Yes, sir."

"Send some warriors to guard the entrance to the turquoise mines," Toquchar added. "That's where I found her. She may be headed there."

Jim's heart was racing. Marina had convinced him to come to this land to find Mayata. Was it Marina who had successfully rescued her? Would she be coming for him? Or was he going to be a dead man like Toquchar had threatened?

Jim could see the fire in the mighty warrior's eyes. They almost seemed to glow red. While captive, Jim had learned that Toquchar had brought his primary wife, the daughter of Genghis Khan, with him on this military expedition and had added Mayata as an additional wife after capturing her from the Surface through the turquoise mines.

"Good riddance, I say," Khan's daughter said to Toquchar. "She was never good enough for you anyway." Jim had seen the jealousy of Khan's daughter from the moment he arrived in the camp.

"Shut up!" Toquchar yelled.

"I'm sorry," she said apologetically. "It's just that I love you so deeply. I hate sharing you with other women." She walked over and hugged the massive warrior. Jim could see in Toquchar's eyes that he wasn't present. He was focused on getting his beautiful Shawnee captive back.

His wife pulled slightly away and looked him in the eye. "You'll find her," she finally said when she could see he was staring vacantly into the distance.

About twenty minutes later, a warrior returned to the tent.

"We found two sets of tracks heading toward Nishapur."

"Cut them off. It will be much more difficult to rescue her if they get to Nishapur."

"Yes, sir. Right away, sir! We'll send two of our best riders."

"Send four! We can't take chances."

"Done!" The man rushed off.

"Let's break camp. We'll follow them," Toquchar said. "Whoever has done this will pay. We need to make a public example of them."

The Mongol army under Toquchar broke camp and began the trek to Nishapur.

CHAPTER 65

TOQUCHAR

(MICK)

Farzin opened the door to his home and motioned for Mick and her friends to enter. Like the exterior, the floors had been whitewashed, which made the colorful rugs stand out even more. Deep-blue and green carpets with ornate designs woven almost perfectly in gold and silver accents left only whitewashed margins along the walls. A handful of equally elaborate rugs was tied in rolls and secured against the walls near the door as if waiting to be delivered to a fortunate buyer somewhere in the city.

"How long has your family been in the rug-making business?" Mick asked.

"I'd prefer not to talk about it," Farzin said in a way that completely shut down the line of questioning.

Mick looked over at Tanner, puzzled. What was it about their business Farzin didn't want them to know? Was it a front for the mob? She looked around at the opulent furnishings in their home and wondered even more.

I don't think you could make this kind of money just from selling rugs. And would an average rug maker be as well connected as Farzin claims his father is?

Mick began to grow uneasy.

As Farzin showed them around the house, Mick became more and more convinced something nefarious was afoot.

"Something besides carpet making is going on in their shop," Mick whispered to Tanner as they were climbing the steps to the second floor.

"You're just being paranoid," Tanner replied.

"But you've seen how secretive Farzin is about everything."

"He's just private."

"I'm not so sure," Mick replied. "Just keep your guard up."

Farzin showed them the room they would be staying in, which was spacious and had four beds.

"You look tired," he told them. "Just relax for a while. My father will be home before long, and we'll have dinner. Get some rest."

Farzin was right. They were exhausted. Sleeping on the floor of a turquoise mine wasn't exactly the best way to get a good night's rest, and with the stress of everything going on, the four were ready for a good nap. Everyone but Mick quickly fell asleep. She was too busy snooping around the room, trying to learn anything she could about this family.

About an hour and a half later, Farzin appeared in the doorway and told them it was time for dinner.

"Your son was telling us you feel like the tall warrior will come and find us," Tanner said after they had been introduced to Farzin's parents. "Why is that?"

"The tall warrior you're referring to is Toquchar," his father replied, "son-in-law of Genghis Khan. There have been many sightings of him over the past few weeks. I believe Toquchar is planning for battle with Nishapur."

"You're not the only one who thinks that," Farzin's mother added. "There were over two thousand people at the mosque this afternoon praying for the safety of the city, and more waiting to enter."

"Everyone realizes we're in a precarious situation," his father added.

"Do you think it will get bad enough that we'll have to . . ." Farzin started to say when his father looked at him sternly.

"Only as a last resort," his father replied. "Only as a last resort."

Mick glanced over at Tanner.

"Now, where do you come from again?" Farzin's mother asked.

"We come from a long way away," Mick replied. "I'm sure you've never heard of it. Small town."

"Come on, try us,"

"Rome," Tanner said. "We came from Rome."

"Hardly a small town," his father replied, looking at Mick, who in turn looked at Tanner.

"Well, in comparison to Nishapur, it's small," Andrew said.

"I guess that's true. And you came in search of the tall warrior?"

"Yes," Tanner replied.

"And a couple of friends," Mick added.

"And my mother and brother," Nemhsi said.

"You're going to be busy. Tell me a little more about them all. Tomorrow I have an important meeting with the vizier, and I'll ask for his help in locating them."

Mick just about lost it when Farzin's father mentioned he was a friend of the vizier. She didn't know a lot about Persian history, but from some of the movies she had seen, the vizier was always the evil antagonist.

"What is a vizier, exactly?" she asked.

"He's the primary adviser to the sultan. If he can't help you locate your friends, no one can."

The evening progressed, and eventually it was time for the four visitors to go to bed.

When Mick awoke the next day, her hosts had already left, and she began discreetly snooping around to see what she could learn about this mysterious family.

The carpets . . . She thought back to the rolled-up carpets by the front door. *Maybe there were notes or invoices or something. Or maybe something is hidden in them.*

She quickly ran for the front door, but the rugs were gone.

"Mick, you're too paranoid," Tanner counseled when he spotted her checking the place out. "They're not up to anything. Just a nice family that's willing to help."

Mick shook her head. "I think they're hiding something."

"You need to stop worrying. We need to be spending our time trying to find everyone," Andrew said as he joined the others.

They spent a long day looking for their friends under the hot Nishapuran sun.

❖ ❖ ❖

"I let the vizier know about your search," Farzin's father said when they met back at Farzin's home in the evening. "He's working on it and will let me know if anything turns up."

"Thank you," Tanner replied.

It was already fairly late, and the group had an uneventful dinner and went to bed.

CHAPTER 66

THE RACE TO NISHAPUR

(HOKOLESQUA)

"Are you my grandmother?" Livia asked Mayata as they fled across the plains toward Nishapur.

"No, I don't have any grandchildren yet," Mayata replied.

"But my sister said you were," Livia replied.

"She must have mistaken me for someone else," Mayata said.

"Okay."

"It looks like whoever was chasing us out of Nisa is giving up," Mayata said.

For the first time since throwing Livia onto the horse, Hokolesqua looked back.

"Wait, that looks like Marina. What's she doing out here?"

"It is," Livia said. "We've got to go help her. She doesn't know how to ride a horse very well."

"Let's go," Hokolesqua said, turning the horse and heading back.

The three quickly made their way to Marina, who jumped off her horse and sprinted toward them.

"It's so good to see all of you!" Marina yelled as she ran. "I thought I had lost you forever."

Hokolesqua, Mayata, and Livia jumped off their horse, and there was a round of embraces.

"We don't have much time," Hokolesqua reminded them. "We have to keep moving. Mother, take the bay and Marina. I will take Livia."

CHAPTER 67

Grandmother

(Marina)

"So, tell me about yourself," Mayata said to Marina as they galloped behind Hokolesqua and Livia.

"It's a long story," Marina replied.

"We have a long ride."

"Well..." She paused as she looked at Mayata's black hair flowing behind her. It reminded her of her stepmother's. A thousand thoughts of her wonderful life with Anastasia flooded her mind.

"I think you're my step-grandmother."

"What?" Mayata said. "I don't have any grandchildren. None of my children are married."

"Your daughter Anastasia married my father."

"But I don't have a daughter named Anastasia. I only have Methoataske and Nemhsi."

"Yes, that's right, Methoataske."

"What do you mean?"

"She changed her name. I knew her as Anastasia, but her original name was Methoataske."

"I'm confused."

"Believe me, I was confused too. And that little girl in front of us... is your granddaughter."

"Granddaughter? It's not possible. That's so strange. She asked me if I was her grandmother. Now I know you're not speaking the truth."

"I barely understand it myself, but I'll do my best to explain."

Marina described how Methoataske had gone in search of Mayata and used the Cathedral of Time, ending up in Rome. She explained how she'd changed her name to Anastasia, then married Marcus, and had a daughter shortly after.

"And Methoataske? Where is she now? Is she still in this place you call Rome?"

"Methoataske is dead."

Mayata turned and looked at Marina in horror, then gritted her teeth and kicked her heels into the horse until it ran at a frenzied gallop.

It was a long day riding across the plains. Marina could sense the pain Mayata was feeling. She watched her swipe at her eyes many times along the journey.

The sun was getting low in the sky when Mayata finally slowed their horse.

"I'm so sorry about Methoataske." Marina finally got the courage to break the thick silence when they came to a stop near a small stream. "I can't imagine your pain. It was devastating to me as well. I only knew her for about six years, but those years were fantastic. Unfortunately, I let the pain I felt from her death consume me." Marina hung her head as she reflected on the things she had done. An image of her telling her father she never wanted to see him again played over and over in her head.

"Why don't we stop here for the night?" Mayata said as she stopped the horse and dismounted.

"I agree. We're not far from Nishapur," Marina said. "But soon it will be too dark to continue."

Marina dismounted as well, and Hokolesqua and Livia joined them shortly after.

"I was wrong," Mayata said as she approached Livia. She crouched down to the level of the five-year-old. "You *are* my granddaughter." Mayata spread her arms wide, and Livia ran into them. Mayata rocked back and forth. This little replacement for the daughter she'd lost meant so much to her.

"I should have seen it before," Mayata said with a smile as she pushed Livia back a little and stared at her beautiful face. "You look just like your mother."

"My mother died," Livia said.

"Yes, I know," Mayata replied hugging Livia tightly again. "But at least now we have each other."

"Let's get a fire started," Marina said. "Hokolesqua, Livia, help me gather some firewood. Mayata, wait here while we make preparations."

"Mayata is so nice, isn't she?" Livia asked Marina as they walked around gathering wood for the fire.

"She is," Marina replied.

Mayata was softening Marina's heart. When her stepmother died, Marina had let the pain she felt at the loss turn to rage. With Methoataske's mother in their company, she was forced to remember her wonderful home environment, and she began to feel the same type of love again from Mayata. Sorrow began to fill her soul for not having stayed with her father. She blamed herself for his capture, and a horror set in to think that, because of her actions, she would probably never see him again.

How did I let this all happen? How did I become so bitter?

"Mare! What is that?" Livia asked, pointing to the silhouettes of four men on horseback.

"We're being followed," Marina replied in horror, dropping the firewood from her arms. She grabbed Livia's arm and ran back to the others.

"Mayata! Hokolesqua! Back on your horses," she yelled. "Over there!" She pointed in the direction of a ridge not far away. They looked just in time to see the warriors begin their descent into the valley.

CHAPTER 68

Human Shield

(Marina)

"To Nishapur!" Hokolesqua yelled as he gave his horse a swift kick.

"I'm right behind you!" Mayata replied.

The two horses were quickly at a gallop.

"Faster! Faster!" Hokolesqua yelled. He was good on a horse but wasn't sure he could outrun skilled Mongol warriors. His only hope was that the head start was enough to get them to Nishapur before they were overtaken.

"We're almost to the city gates!" Marina yelled.

"They're catching up!" Livia shouted.

Marina glanced behind her and felt something graze her shoulder. One of the warriors was in range and had fired an arrow at her.

"Lie low!" Marina shouted, and they all crouched forward, making smaller targets of themselves.

Zing! Another arrow narrowly missed them.

"Almost there!" Hokolesqua yelled as he looked over his shoulder.

Thunk!

An arrow lodged into Marina's right arm.

"Ahhhh!" she yelled out in pain.

We're so close.

They were close enough she could clearly see the blue and gold colors of the lion reliefs on the city walls adjacent to the gate.

Thunk!

She heard the sound of another arrow hitting its mark but didn't feel any pain. Had Mayata been struck?

"Are you all right?" she asked.

"I'm fine!" Mayata shouted just as Marina felt the horse begin to stumble.

"Jump!" Mayata yelled. "Don't let her fall on you!"

The horse tumbled to the ground just as Marina and Mayata jumped off. Hokolesqua had reached the gate, and he and Livia were dismounting. Marina and Mayata sprang to their feet and raced for Nishapur. The guard was opening the gate for Hokolesqua. He was going to make it.

Clank!

An arrow lodged itself in the canteen Marina had slung over her shoulder. It pierced both sides and stopped after just slightly puncturing her skin.

The ladies were close enough that they found themselves in a crossfire between the guards and the Mongol warriors.

"We've got this!" Marina yelled.

They crossed the bridge over the moat, dashed through the gate, and positioned themselves behind the brick wall.

"Mayata, are you all right?" Marina asked, breathing heavily.

"I'm fine."

Livia ran to her sister and jumped into her arms. "I'm scared, Mare."

"We're safe now. It's going to be all right."

"You were amazing!" Mayata said as she scurried around and gave each of them an embrace.

"Marina, are you all right?" Mayata asked as she saw Marina tug at the arrow lodged in her arm. "Hold still." Mayata carefully removed the arrow, and blood began to stream down her step-granddaughter's arm.

"We're safe. That's the important thing," Marina said. "They'll protect us here."

Mayata went to work creating a wrap from strips of cloth she tore from her clothes, which she then wound tightly around Marina's wound.

The guards secured the gates.

"You are lucky you're still alive," one of the guards said.

"You don't look like you're from here," another guard said.

"No, we come from a faraway land," Marina replied.

"Do you have a place to stay? Do you have friends or relatives here?"

"Nope."

"I'm sure my wife wouldn't mind having some additional help around the house," one of the guards said. "You're welcome to stay with us. Name's Rahim."

"That would be great," Mayata replied. "Are you sure she wouldn't mind?"

"I'm sure. Let me make sure the Mongols have left, and then I'll take you to my home."

The guard slid open a small window in the gate, and after re-assuring himself the city was safe, he closed the window and escorted the four of them to his home.

"What do the Mongols do with prisoners?" Marina asked as they walked through the city.

"Usually they use them as human shields," Rahim said. "When they attack a city, they put their prisoners in front. Those under siege are hesitant to fire on their own people, so it becomes much easier for the Mongols to advance. The Mongols are treacherous strategists. Why do you ask?"

"My friend was captured," Marina said.

"Then he's in grave danger," Rahim said.

"I've got to figure out how to rescue him. Any suggestions?"

"Not really. They keep the prisoners in the center of camp, so there's no way you'll be able to rescue him from an encampment. Many have tried in vain. Your only hope is to pray he doesn't get killed in the crossfire. It's all a matter of luck."

"That's unacceptable," Marina said. "My stupidity got him into this situation."

"Don't blame yourself," Rahim replied.

"But it's clearly my fault. My anger sent my father to his certain death, and now I've endangered Jim's life as well."

"It would be suicide to try anything. Your only chance of rescuing him is from the front lines. And that's a slim chance at best."

"Then that's what I'll do," Marina said. "They're encamped about a day's journey from here. They must be headed this way."

"You can't be serious," Rahim replied as he stopped and opened the door of a modest dwelling and motioned for the four of them to enter.

"I am serious. Why?"

"We're on the brink of war," he replied.

"Why would they attack Nishapur?"

"Who knows? Power? Authority? Greed?"

"But what have you done to them?"

"Nothing, other than try to defend ourselves. Look, I'm sorry, but I don't have time to explain. If you saw their encampment that close, I have to alert my superiors."

The guard introduced the group to his wife and explained what was happening. She agreed to help them but quickly pushed Rahim out the door to inform their leaders of the impending threat.

"Sounds like we've got some excitement headed our way," Marina said, trying to make it sound less threatening to Livia.

"More excitement than I'd like," Mayata said. "We need to get to the turquoise mines and back to our homeland."

"I can't go," Marina said with a determined expression. "I can't leave Jim. I got him into this, and I've got to get him out. Mayata, you'll stay, right? I'm going to need you to watch Livia. Plus, I need your strength and courage."

"Yes, Marina, I'll stay. Livia and I will be here for you."

"I'm sorry, but I'm afraid I'm too weak to see this through without your support."

❖ ❖ ❖

As dawn broke over Nishapur, Marina awoke to shouts of "Mongols at the War Gate! We're under siege!"

Marina had to see if she could find Jim, the human shield. She grabbed her bow and quiver and dashed through the streets toward the main gate. She ran to the stairway that led to the top of the city walls, but the guards at the base wouldn't let her pass.

I've got to find another way.

CHAPTER 69

A Surprise Hero

(Tanner)

"Mongols at the War Gate!"

Tanner, Mick, Andrew, and Nemhsi were awakened to the screams spreading across the city.

When they went downstairs, they saw Farzin's father, quiver slung over his back, bow in hand.

"We want to help," Tanner said.

"No, you need to stay here," he replied.

"We're not staying," Tanner said. "You were kind enough to let us stay in your home, and now we're going to help you defend it."

"It's not safe."

"We know that," Andrew replied. "But you're not going to stop us from helping."

"All right, but be prepared for the worst," he said. "The Mongols have already destroyed many cities in Persia."

"Then give us some weapons and let's get going," Tanner said.

The man equipped Tanner and Andrew with bows and arrows.

"Hope we're better than we were that night at Scouts," Andrew said.

"Speak for yourself," Tanner replied.

"Yeah, well, we're not going to be shooting at nonmoving bales of hay this time."

"What about us?" Mick asked pointing to Nemhsi and herself.

"Nishapuran women don't fight."

"Well, we're not Nishapuran." Mick grabbed for one of the bows he was holding. "And you need us."

"I wouldn't try to stop her," Tanner said.

"Yes, I can see that. Here you go." He reluctantly handed Mick and Nemhsi bows and quivers. Mick slung the quiver over her back and began to pull back on the bow, pretending to fire at the beautiful vases around the room.

"All right, follow me."

"The five made their way to the War Gate on the east side and up the stairs to the top of the city walls. Tanner was stunned when he peered over the wall and saw tens of thousands of Mongols surrounding the city.

"There's no way we're going to defeat that," Andrew said.

"They're not planning to attack yet," a man replied. "They want to cut off our supply routes and attack us in a depleted condition. But we have enough supplies to hold out longer than they can. Plus, reinforcements from nearby cities will be coming."

"I'm glad *you're* confident," Andrew replied.

"Oh, my gosh, it's Marina!" Mick shouted, pointing to the stairs leading up the wall near the south side of the gate.

Tanner looked up in time to see Marina sprinting up the stairs, bow in hand. He watched as she arrived at the top and was talking with some of the men on the wall. She moved to the front edge and quickly scanned the Mongol army.

"What's she looking for?"

"No idea."

"Who's that?" Tanner asked as a massive man emerged from the Mongol troops on horseback. He was dressed in exquisite armor and was obviously their leader.

"It's Toquchar," Farzin's father replied. "Son-in-law of Genghis Khan."

"Wow!" Mick replied.

"No kidding," Tanner added. He was stunned by the appearance of this mighty leader.

He looked back at Marina, who had just pulled an arrow out of her quiver and loaded it into her bow.

"Marina! Don't do it!!" Andrew yelled as loud as he could, but she was too far away. Someone else on the wall noticed she was ready to let her arrow fly and dashed toward her. The next few seconds seemed to unfold in slow motion as Tanner watched helplessly.

"Noooooo!" he yelled to no avail. Marina let the arrow fly a split second before the man pushed her over. Everyone watched as the arrow pierced the thick air of impending battle—and struck its intended target, sinking deeply into the neck of Toquchar. He grabbed frantically at the shaft, which broke in half in his massive hand, the other part remaining lodged in his throat. His body began to sway, and he fell to the ground. There was a chaotic scene around the fallen Mongol leader. The Mongol warriors armed their bows and fired on the city in haphazard fashion, but the Nishapurans sent a massive volley of arrows and stones raining down in organized fashion on the disheveled Mongols. In their state of disarray, it was no contest. The Mongols began to flee the onslaught. The Nishapuran who tried to stop Marina was hoisting her onto his shoulders in jubilation.

"The Mongols are gone! Driven from Nishapur!"

The chants quickly spread through the city. "Down with the Mongols!"

Tanner, Andrew, Mick, and Nemhsi fought their way through the din to Marina—along with everyone else. She was a hero. She had slain the mighty Mongol leader Toquchar. As Tanner and his friends got closer, the chants began to change to "Marina! Marina!"

After battling the crowds, the Brownsvillians reached Marina. She looked down and spotted Andrew first.

"Andrew?" She jumped off the shoulders of the Nishapuran warrior and ran to the group.

"Is that really you?" She lunged for Andrew and gave him a big hug.

Andrew remained stiff as a board and glanced side to side at his friends with a look of uncertainty.

"I'm so sorry for what I've done. Can you please forgive me? I really don't know what I was thinking."

Marina pulled back and looked back and forth between all of them.

"I was just so bitter. It nearly destroyed me."

"Where's Livia?" Tanner asked coolly.

"She's fine. She's staying at the home of one of the city guards who took us in. She's with her grandmother."

"Grandmother?" Andrew gasped. "You found Mayata?"

"We did," Marina replied.

Nemhsi nearly knocked Marina over with a hug. "You found her? You really found her?"

"Yes." Marina gave Nemhsi a strange look, obviously not recognizing her.

"How?" Nemhsi asked. "How did you do it?"

"It's a long story. Follow me, and I'll tell you all about it."

"Where's Jim?" Mick asked.

"He's been captured by the Mongols," Marina replied.

"What?" Mick said.

"I'm worried about his safety." Marina explained what she had been told about human shields and how she had seen him on the front lines before the Mongols dispersed.

"We've got to rescue him," Mick said.

"Follow me back to Rahim's house," Marina replied. "We'll work out a plan there."

The group zigzagged through the city until they arrived at the guard's house.

"Musclosus!" Livia yelled when she spotted Tanner.

"Livia! How are you?" Tanner replied as he crouched down and the young girl ran into his arms. "It's so good to see you."

"Hoko!" Nemhsi shouted as she saw her brother. What are you doing here?"

"You know each other?" Marina asked.

"He's my brother," Nemhsi replied. She gave her brother a big hug. "I thought you'd been captured. Where did you go?"

"I had to find my mother," he replied.

"He's the one who rescued Mayata from Toquchar," Marina added.

Nemhsi squeezed her brother more tightly.

"We got to ride horses," Livia said to Tanner, wide-eyed. "And people were shooting arrows at us."

Tanner looked over at Marina.

"Yeah, it was quite an adventure, wasn't it, Liv?" Marina said. "How about we tell these guys all about it?"

Marina and Livia rehearsed the whole story. Once they finished, a woman who looked strikingly similar to Anastasia walked into the room.

"Mother!" Nemhsi shouted and ran to her mother, giving her a long embrace.

The group spent the rest of the day getting caught up on their various adventures, celebrating Marina's newfound celebrity, and strategizing on how to rescue Jim.

CHAPTER 70

THE PYRAMID OF SKULLS

(MARINA)

"What? What's going on?" Marina said as Rahim tried to wake her.

"The Mongols are back! The troops want you on the city wall to inspire the people."

When her arrow had struck Toquchar and the Mongol army fled in chaos, the citizens credited Marina with single-handedly defeating Genghis Khan's forces. Now that the Mongols were back, they wanted their heroine to inspire them.

Marina struggled to shake off the deep sleep she had been in.

"I can't do anything," she said.

"Just seeing you will inspire them," Rahim said. "Come on, you need to get moving. The Mongols have a battering ram headed for the gate. They're planning to overrun the city this time."

Marina quickly got dressed and made her way through crowds encouraging her to save the city from Khan's armies.

When she got to the top of the eastern wall, she looked over the vast Mongol army. It was even more ominous than the force of a few days earlier. Then she saw him.

"Jim! Oh, my gosh, it's Jim!"

About twenty yards to her right on the front line of the human shield was Jim.

What do I do? If war breaks out, he's a dead man.

Jim was standing between the heaviest armaments of the Mongols and those of the Nishapurans.

"I've got to get the others. Maybe between all of us, we can figure something out."

Marina made a mad dash down the wall and through the city to enlist the help of her friends.

"Hokolesqua, Jim's in trouble!" she shouted as she entered Rahim's house.

"Let's get Nemhsi and the others," Hokolesqua replied.

They sprinted for Farzin's home.

"It's Jim!" Marina yelled as she entered. "They're using him as a human shield. We've got to save him!"

The first thing that flashed into Tanner's mind was "Why would I want to help Jim?" But he quickly repented of the thought. It would be one thing if his nemesis needed help with homework or something, but his life was on the line, and Tanner wasn't about to sit idly by.

Tanner, Mick, Andrew, and Nemhsi followed Marina and Hokolesqua to the top of the eastern wall.

"See him? Over there?" Marina was frantically pointing to where Jim stood, perhaps moments from his death.

"What do we do?" she shouted. "It's all my fault."

"Don't worry. We'll figure it out," Andrew said. "Just give us a second to think."

The silence was heavy. The Brownsvillians were racking their brains trying to figure out a way to save Jim. The guards on the wall had hunkered down and were vigilantly awaiting instructions from their leaders.

"In honor of Toquchar!" The Mongol cry broke the silence of the still morning air. In an instant, it was all-out war.

Thousands of javelin-launching ballistae were being fired in an attempt to keep the Mongols at bay. A matching number was being deployed by the Mongols, who had also gathered hundreds of thousands of large stones to hurl at the walls with their catapults. Flaming projectiles were arcing over the walls and into the city.

"Noooooo!" Marina yelled through the fray. Jim had been pierced by an arrow and laid on the ground, struggling to remove it.

"Jim!" she yelled. It was pointless. The decibel level had risen so high it was hard to even hear the person next to you.

"I've got to go get him."

"You can't, Marina," Andrew said. "It would be suicide!"

The assault continued as wave after wave of projectiles battered the defenses of Nishapur.

"Isn't that Toquchar's wife?" someone shouted, pointing to a woman on a horse pacing back and forth among the troops

"I think so," came the reply. "They're here to avenge his death!"

"This is her fault!" someone yelled, pointing at Marina. "If she wouldn't have killed Toquchar, this wouldn't be happening."

As quickly as she'd become a heroine, Marina was being vilified.

"Yeah," another replied, and a mob began to form around Marina.

"We can't worry about that now," a man screamed as he made his way through the crowd, pushing the mob away from Marina. "Man your posts! We've got to keep the Mongols out. We can't worry about blame. We'll all be dead if we can't stop this assault."

Hour after hour the attack raged on. Sections of the wall near the War Gate were beginning to weaken from the onslaught.

Nearly twenty-four hours after the assault began, the Mongols breached the walls.

Mick watched in horror as Toquchar's wife rode into the city surrounded by a massive wave of warriors. "Kill them all!" she shouted. "I don't want a single living thing to remain. Kill the cats. Kill the dogs. Kill everything that moves." She motioned with her arms to the troops behind her with bird-like, swooping motions, and the warriors poured into the city.

"We can't chance that any of them will survive," she bellowed. "Behead them all. We'll make pyramids with their skulls!"

"How are we going to get out of this alive?" Mick asked.

"We've got to get beyond this wave of warriors!" Tanner replied. "I'm not the type to flee a fight, but this one's going to be a complete bloodbath."

"What about Jim?" Marina said. "What if he's still alive?"

"Marina, there's no way we can go out there! That's the point of entry for the Mongols. Best case, we'd be trampled to death."

Marina could hardly bear it.

"Follow me," Tanner said as he began to sprint along the edge for the southern wall with arrows flying every which way around him. "Stay low!" he yelled back to the others as they crouched so the waist-high ledge would protect them

Marina took one more longing look at Jim's body as it lay in front of the city before they turned and ran down the southern wall.

"We've got to get to the mine," Tanner said.

"What about Mayata and Livia?" Mick asked. "They must still be at Rahim's."

"Hopefully they're beyond this wave of fighters," Andrew said. "If our forces can slow down the first onslaught, we can get to them."

"We've got to try!" Tanner screamed emphatically. "We can't lose them again!"

CHAPTER 71

GO DOWN TRYING

(MARINA)

"I can't do it," Marina said after they rejoined Mayata and Livia and escaped through the southern gate. "I can't just leave Jim to die."

"You'll never survive if you try to get him," Andrew replied.

"Maybe not, but I'm going to go down trying."

And with that, Marina ran along the outer side of the wall toward the eastern gate, where the Mongols were pouring in.

As she sprinted along the wall, all she could think of was her own stupidity. Her anger and bitterness had created this life-threatening situation for Jim, her friends, and the entire city of Nishapur.

I've got to fix this. I'll never be able to forgive myself if I can't.

"Marina! Wait!"

She turned to see Andrew, Tanner, Mick, Hokolesqua, and Nemhsi sprinting to catch up.

"You can't do this alone," Andrew said when they finally reached her.

Arrows began to zing around them. A few Mongols had been positioned along the south side of the city. Mick and Marina began to load and fire back as they continued to run to where they had seen Jim on the ground.

"Give it to me," the young brave said as he grabbed the bow and arrows from Mick.

Marina, who was herself an expert with a bow, watched in awe as the Shawnee let arrow after arrow fly with extreme accuracy.

"We're almost there," Marina said.

Carefully they moved to the front corner of the city wall. The Mongols who had been shooting at them moved away toward the south gate, where the citizens of Nishapur were fleeing.

Marina peered around the corner of the wall and could see Mongols continuing to pour through the War Gate. She looked to where she had seen Jim. There was nothing there. No trace. The ground was completely barren.

"What happened?" she asked out loud. "He was right there. We're too late."

Marina buried her head in her hands. *I can't fix it. My stupidity has . . .* She couldn't even finish her thought.

"We've got to get out of here," Tanner said. "At least we didn't find him dead. Maybe he escaped."

Marina was shaking her head. She was distraught.

"We need to help people get out of the city," Tanner said. "Let's get moving."

He sprinted along the side wall with the others trailing.

"We've got to get everyone to the turquoise mine," Tanner said as they approached the southern gate, where people were scrambling in chaos to get out. "We might have to lead them into the underworld."

"You're kidding, right?" Mick said. "Are you really thinking about showing the whole city where the entrance is?"

"We've got to save them somehow," Tanner replied.

"I don't think that would end well," Mick said. "There's a reason those entrances are hidden. We can't."

"We could do it temporarily, then give them water from the River Lethe when we lead them back out after the coast is clear."

"How are you going to be sure they all drink the water?" Mick asked. "Do you have a couple hundred thousand paper cups hidden in your back pocket?"

"Very funny. Let's just get them to the mine."

"It's a death trap," Andrew replied. "If the Mongols know we've gone there, we'll all die."

"Plus, the mine is the home of the Manticore," Marina added.

"The what?" Andrew asked.

"The Manticore—a deadly lion with multiple rows of teeth and a scorpion-like stinger."

"Where'd you hear that?" Mick asked.

"One of the shopkeepers told us."

"Urban myth," Tanner said.

"We didn't see it when we came through the mine," Andrew said.

"From what we were told, it only attacks those who enter the forbidden passageway."

"Okay, we just won't go down that passage," Tanner said. "The mine is our only hope. We're about to see hundreds of thousands get slaughtered unless we can hide them somewhere."

"But what if the Mongols follow us into the underworld?" Mick asked. "Can you imagine Tohopka, Hades, and Genghis Khan teaming up?"

"I've got it!" Andrew said. "We'll lock the Mongols in."

"Huh?" Tanner asked.

"You saw how long it took to break through the front gate. If we can create enough of a gap between the Mongols and the Nishapurans, we can lock the Mongol army in the city."

"It will never hold," Mick said.

"There are too many of them," Tanner added.

"It just has to hold long enough for us to get everyone into the underworld," Andrew said. "Even if the Mongols know we went into the mine, if they aren't shown where the entrance is, they'll never find it. Plus, I don't think Demeter would let them through. She'll protect the entrance."

"You think she could stop the whole Mongol army?" Tanner asked.

"She *is* a goddess," Mick replied.

"Let's give it a try," Andrew said.

"Okay, guys," Tanner said, "how do we delay the army long enough to get everyone out and lock the gates?"

"The cauldron," Mick said. "The carpet-maker's shop was right in front of the bridge. If we can dump that boiling clay onto the bridge, we can stop the army on the other side. Until the clay cools down, the Mongols will have to stop."

"You think there's enough clay to stop them?"

"That cauldron was as big as a small elephant. It will be enough."

"Best plan I've heard yet," Tanner said.

"It's the only plan I've heard," Andrew replied.

"Like I said."

"Come on, let's go." Mick waved for the others to follow.

"We're right behind you."

When they arrived at the tapestry shop, Mick was shocked to see Farzin trying to set the building on fire.

"What are you doing?" Mick asked.

"We can't let it fall into Mongol hands," he replied.

"Wait," Tanner said. "You can't burn it down yet. We need your cauldron to stop the Mongols from crossing the bridge."

"Whaaat?" Farzin replied.

"We need to create some space between the Nishapurans and the Mongols," Mick replied. "The only thing we could think of was to dump the cauldron onto the bridge. Until that clay cools down, they won't be able to cross."

Farzin put his hand to his forehead. It looked like he was working out a big equation.

"I guess it could work," he said. "We'll need all of you to help push it over."

"We need to run farther into the city to let everyone know what we're doing," Andrew said. "We can hurry back and dump the cauldron before the Mongols get here."

"Good plan," Tanner replied.

Mick, Marina, and Andrew ran into the chaos, telling everyone to get over the bridge as quickly as they could, and then sprinted back to the shop.

"Everyone in place," Tanner said. "The Mongols are almost here."

Mick, Marina, Tanner, Hokolesqua, Nemhsi, and Farzin quenched the fire beneath the cauldron, and then enlisted the employees who were still in the shop to help. They wrapped their arms with carpet scraps and readied themselves to tip the cauldron toward the narrow street.

"Dump it!" Andrew yelled.

Exerting all the energy they had, the group tipped the massive cauldron over. Boiling clay and oil poured out the door and onto the bridge. The stone walls alongside the doorway created a perfect channel for the muck. Mick watched through the window as the Mongols' horses reared up on their hind legs, screeching wildly. The foot soldiers approached the line of scalding clay.

Unaware of the temperature, one of the warriors stepped into the quagmire.

"Eeeeyow!" he screamed in excruciating pain.

"Over there!" one of the warriors yelled, pointing to the shop window.

Vaulting over the small wall and into some bushes in front of the side window, several warriors began an assault on the shop.

"Shut the windows!" Farzin yelled. He closed the window in front of him and lowered a piece of wood to barricade it shut. Tanner did the same to the other window. The warriors began to pound on the wood.

"It's not going to hold," Tanner said as the sound of axes crashing against the windows grew. "We've got to figure a way out of here."

CHAPTER 72

Can I Trust You?

(Mick)

"Can I trust you?" Farzin asked Mick and the others, looking deep in their eyes.

"Of course," Mick said as an ax penetrated the wooden shutters.

"Then help me," he said as he grabbed a torch on a side wall. "Grab those." He pointed to torches around the shop. "We've got to burn the place down."

Everyone grabbed a torch.

"Not those!" Farzin barked as Andrew was about to set fire to a group of tapestries rolled up and tied along the back wall. "Burn everything else."

Mick looked over at the window. The Mongols had broken through, and the hole created by the pounding axes was large enough that she could see their angry faces. They were moments from breaking in.

"Jim?" Mick's heart sank after doing a double take and confirming it really was the angered face of her Brownsville friend alongside the Mongols trying to break into the shop.

Flames were now soaring. The open ceiling provided more oxygen than would be available in a typical building, and the fire was running rampant.

"Follow me," Farzin yelled, covering his nose and mouth with his elbow as he ran to the back of the store. "Father, forgive me if

I'm wrong, but I think it's time for a last resort." He began untying the tapestries along the back wall.

Mick stopped in her tracks as the tapestries began to levitate in front of her.

"Hop on," he said.

Mick looked at the roaring flames and angry Mongols. As illogical as what she was witnessing appeared, she had no choice but to follow the directions. She hopped onto one of the tapestries, unsure of what was going to happen. One by one the others did the same, each with puzzled expressions.

"Andrew! Get on," Tanner yelled as Andrew stood mesmerized by the small carpet hovering in front of him. He bent down to look under the rug.

"Right now!" Tanner yelled.

Crack!

Mick turned around to see that the window had completely broken open and Mongols were climbing through.

Andrew jumped on his carpet.

"Sit down and pull up on the front of your carpet!" Farzin yelled.

Mick and the others did as requested, and the carpets ascended above the flames and the Mongols, who began shooting arrows as the carpets continued to rise. The situation was still too precarious for any of them to fully appreciate what was going on.

Tanner was more aggressive with Farzin's instructions than the rest, causing his carpet to soar almost straight up. He was hanging on to the sides for dear life.

"A little more gently!" the young boy yelled to Tanner.

"Maintain your ascent," Farzin said as they cleared the side walls and the dangers below.

"You're quite the pilot." Andrew laughed as he came up parallel with Tanner. "I guess athleticism doesn't translate to carpet riding." He continued to chuckle.

Mick looked over the edge of her rug, and the reality that she was actually on a flying carpet high above the city with no idea how to control it sank in.

"You got any on-the-job training?" Tanner asked as he finally got his carpet back to a horizontal position.

"Just follow what I do," Farzin said as he leaned forward and to the left on the carpet. It moved left and slightly down. The group followed his lead and navigated above the hordes fleeing the city.

"You have to hurry!" Tanner yelled to the masses below. "The Mongols will be back on us soon."

"To the turquoise mine!" Andrew added. "We'll keep the Mongols at bay."

Parents nearly yanked the arms of their children out of the sockets as they tried to escape the onslaught of ferocious Mongol warriors. It was a dangerous stampede.

"We need weapons," Tanner said. "That way we can delay the Mongols at the bridge and buy more time."

"Follow me," Farzin said as he guided the posse of carpets to a small adobe warehouse full of bows and arrows.

Hokolesqua ran back and forth around the shop, gathering a small arsenal.

"Father would love this place," he said.

"Are these carpets battle worthy?" Tanner asked.

"Of course," Farzin replied. "Shapur used carpets when he defeated the Romans and captured the emperor Valerian."

"I don't remember reading anything about that," Mick replied. "And that's the kind of history I'm pretty sure I wouldn't forget."

"Well, Shapur didn't want anyone to know about his magic carpets, so his men flew under cover of night into the center of the Roman camp. The emperor himself may have been the only Roman who saw anything, and he wasn't about to tell anyone the Persians had technology that far surpassed his own."

"That's what I was afraid of," Tanner replied. "Unlike Shapur, we're not going to sneak up on anyone. We'll be flying in broad daylight with one of the most skilled armies of all time firing on us."

"We'll be fine," Farzin replied.

"We've got to get back," Mick yelled as she scampered around, adding to the weapons already under her arms. "That clay will cool down fast."

"Don't worry," Farzin replied. "The clay must be hotter than the seventh ring of hell to make flying carpets. It'll take a while to cool down."

After loading as much ammunition as they could onto their carpets, they flew back to the bridge.

"We need to harass the front line," Farzin said. "If we can keep the front few warriors from crossing, we can protect the entire population."

"Won't the others find an alternate route?"

"This is the only street that leads to the western gate. If we can keep them from getting to that gate and lock the others, I think the citizens will be able to get to the mine."

"Okay," Tanner said. "Let's harass some warriors."

Hokolesqua flew to the front and began firing arrows relentlessly. His success empowered the others, who fired far more clumsily as they flew back and forth around the bridge. The

Mongol warriors struggled to hit the speedy carpets with their arrows.

"It's working," Andrew said. "They're turning around."

"Don't celebrate yet," Mick reminded the boys. "Someone's got to make sure we get everyone out of town, and we've got to get the other gates locked.

"Farzin, take Mick and Andrew and get the gates locked," Tanner said. "Hokolesqua, Nemhsi, Marina, you stay here. I'll get everyone out of town. We'll meet at the turquoise mine later."

"Let's stay together," Mick replied. "Splitting up hasn't worked so well."

"We have to," Tanner said. "We'll be fine."

"Okay," Mick said hesitantly.

Before they went their separate ways, Farzin cautioned, "Whatever you do, no matter the cost, you cannot let one of these carpets fall into the hands of the Mongols."

CHAPTER 73

MAGIC?

(ANDREW)

"So, how long have you been making these carpets?" Andrew asked as he, Mick, and Farzin flew for one of the gates.

"Me?" Farzin asked. "All my life, but the tradition goes way back."

"Yeah?" Andrew replied.

"My ancestor Behnam discovered the secret of making flying carpets nearly a thousand years ago."

"A thousand years?" Andrew asked.

"That's right. Shapur was out hunting when he discovered a clay substance of exquisite color in a previously undiscovered spring. When he returned, he asked Behnam to use the clay as a dye for a carpet to adorn his palace."

"And I'm assuming he said yes?" Andrew said.

"Farzin smiled. "Let's get this first gate locked, and I'll tell you what happened."

The three hopped off their carpets and ran for the gate, which they pulled closed and locked.

"To the next gate!" Farzin said as he jumped on his carpet.

"We're right behind you," Mick said.

"So, you were telling us about Behnam," Andrew said as they flew toward the next gate.

"Right. Well, Benham struggled with the newly dyed fibers. It seemed as though they had a mind of their own and were trying to escape his grasp as he wove. After weeks of battling them, he finished and invited Shapur to come and collect his new treasure. When Behnam cut the rug free from its loom, it levitated as if actually alive, and a thousand-year tradition began."

The three hopped off at the next gate and locked it tight.

"It's magic," Mick said as Andrew examined his own rug.

"I guess," Farzin replied. "Science to one man is magic to another."

"Science?" Andrew asked. "This isn't science. It's just a carpet. How does it work?"

"Shapur gathered his greatest scientists, and they discovered that the combination of this clay and the Grecian oil created anti-magnetic properties in the fibers. The magnetic lines of the earth repel the force of the carpet, allowing it to glide as if by magic."

"It's like they're gliding on a railroad track," Andrew chimed in.

"Whatever that is," Farzin replied.

"Yeah, never mind."

"So Shapur, Behnam, and the scientists vowed to never divulge their great secret," Farzin said. "They knew this technology would be extremely dangerous in the wrong hands."

"Can you imagine if Nero had something like this?" Mick asked.

"I really don't want to," Andrew replied.

The three locked the remaining gates and made their way to the turquoise mine.

CHAPTER 74

Speaking Mongolian

(Tanner)

Tanner flew his carpet to the western gate, where the Nishapurans were escaping.

"You've got to move faster!" he shouted to the citizens, who looked in disbelief as he hovered above them. "We can't hold the Mongols back much longer."

Tanner had never seen such a mass of humanity.

"Here comes one!" someone shouted. "Look out!"

Tanner turned just in time to see a Mongol warrior ride along the outer wall just below him, bow drawn. He saw the arrow set sail. His reflexes weren't fast enough to get completely out of the way, and he watched as the arrow pierced his calf. He reached for the shaft and lost his balance, falling the ten feet from the carpet to the ground with a thud. The Mongol stood up on his horse and lunged for the carpet, securing the corner and tumbling to the ground himself.

"Get him!" Tanner yelled. He stood up to give chase and then collapsed again as the pain shot through his body like a bolt of lightning.

The man was back on his feet in a flash, and before anyone could reach him, was on his horse and galloping into the distance—carpet squirming under his arm.

What do I do? Tanner thought. *Farzin was adamant about not letting the Mongols get a carpet. If we ever get back to Brownsville, ten to one everyone will be speaking Mongolian.*

Tanner tried again to stand up and run for the man, who was quickly fading from sight. He collapsed onto the desert floor screaming in pain.

If Genghis Khan is as powerful as everyone says and I've just given his empire the secret of flying carpets, I've destroyed the fabric of the universe.

Tanner was brought back to the present as a surge of pain coursed through his entire body.

"Someone help me," he plead as Nishapurans dashed past in an attempt to rescue themselves from their own ominous fate.

"Please."

A man ran to Tanner and put his arm around his shoulder.

"I'll get this. Brace yourself. It's going to hurt."

"It doesn't exactly feel good right now, you know."

Tanner screamed in agony as the man yanked the arrow from his calf, then tore the shirt off his back and made an improvised bandage, wrapping it tightly around the wound.

"Can you stand?"

Tanner carefully pushed himself up. He was able to hobble, but only slowly.

"Put your arm around my neck. I'll help you to the mine."

CHAPTER 75

WHAT DO I DO?
(Marina)

"What do I do?" Marina asked Mick when she arrived at the mine.

"About what?" Mick replied.

"About Jim? I got him into this mess, and now he's a human shield for the Mongols. If he's even still alive."

"He's alive," Mick said.

"What makes you say that?"

"He was with the men trying to break down the windows of Farzin's shop."

"What?" Marina asked, stunned.

"He and I made eye contact just before we took off on the carpets. He's gone to the dark side."

"What does that mean?" Marina asked.

"He's joined up with the enemy."

"I don't believe it," Marina said.

"I do," Andrew said.

"He wouldn't do that."

"Marina, I saw him," Mick said. "He had an ax in his hand, just like the others."

"They probably threatened him," Marina replied.

"That's not what it looked like to me," Mick said.

"But I feel so bad about what I got him into."

"Look," Mick said. "We'll do what we can to save him, but it looks like he's made a choice."

"I'm not so sure," Marina replied.

"Right now we need to save as many Nishapurans as we can and get back to Rome to save your dad."

"Jim chose a different path," Andrew said. "But your dad—he didn't choose the fate he's headed for."

"No, you're right, but I don't know if I will ever be able to forgive myself."

"It will be harder to forgive yourself for betraying your dad than letting Jim choose his own way," Mick said. "He wasn't making the best choices back in Brownsville, either. Don't blame yourself. By the look on his face when he was trying to break in, I don't think he was being coerced."

CHAPTER 76

A DANGEROUS ALLIANCE

(TANNER)

After what seemed like forever, Tanner joined the others at the turquoise mine.

"We've got to get through the portal before the Mongols get here," Tanner said.

"I am not going back to the Inner World." Hokolesqua said.

"You have to. The Mongols are on their way, and it's the only way to get home," Mick said. "We need to get you back to your father."

"I would love to see my father again, but I'm not going back."

"Why?"

"It's too dangerous."

"What do you mean?"

"Methoataske is already dead, and Nemhsi and I were almost killed."

"By who?"

"Tohopka."

"Who?" Mayata asked.

"The king of Anatok," Hokolesqua said.

"No need to worry," Mick replied. "He's not a threat anymore."

"He's planning on taking over the world," Nemhsi said. "Inner and outer."

"He was overthrown by the followers of Spider Woman," Mick said. "We saw the whole thing."

"Tohopka escaped," Hokolesqua said.

"How do you know?"

"Tohopka and his guards captured Nemhsi and me," Hokolesqua replied. "He planned to use the visualizer on us to learn the location of the entrance to the Surface, but we escaped."

Tanner reached into his pocket and began to roll the visualizer nervously between his fingers.

"Tohopka has a large army," Nemhsi added. "His guards told us Tohopka was working on an alliance with another city before he was overthrown. Tohopka was headed there when we escaped."

"Well, we're about to bring hundreds of thousands of people to Inner Earth with us. I think we can handle whatever Tohopka can put together."

"Have you seen the weapons Tohopka's men have?" Nemhsi said. "If this group couldn't defeat the Mongols with their bows and arrows, I don't think they would have a chance against Tohopka's weapons."

Good point, Tanner thought.

"You'll be safe," Andrew said. "No need to worry."

"Why do you say that?" Hokolesqua asked.

"You're going back in time. Back to your time period. That was before Tohopka."

Relief swept across Hokolesqua's face.

"Hey, wasn't the passageway to the Cathedral over here?" Tanner asked.

"I think so," Andrew replied. "Yeah, that looks like it."

"Don't go down there!" came a voice from behind. "That's the forbidden passageway."

"What?" Tanner asked.

"It's forbidden. Those who enter never return."

Tanner nudged Andrew. "Get it?" he whispered. "Those who enter never return. They go to Inner Earth." Tanner chuckled.

"Seriously," a woman rushed to their side and pushed the two of them against the wall of the mine, away from the entrance to the passage. "It's the home of the Manticore."

"We'll be fine," Tanner replied, trying not to offend the woman, who was so sincere in trying to help them.

"Follow us," Tanner said. "He turned the flashlight from his phone on and shone it into the darkness as he stepped into the "forbidden" passageway.

Suddenly, massive bat-like wings flapped toward him and generated a rush of air that, combined with shock, nearly knocked a wounded Tanner off his feet. The beast raised its front paws into the air and spring-loaded itself. The most incredible set of fangs glistened in the blackness, and a deafening roar echoed through the mine.

Tanner turned and dove out of the way as the creature lunged for him and crashed into the mine wall where Tanner had just been. Tanner rolled over and looked up just in time to see the Manticore's scorpion-like tail wagging slightly until it was positioned above the beast's head and straight in font of Tanner. The beast snarled, and before Tanner knew what was going on, he watched hundreds of needles shoot from the Manticore's tail and pierce his shirt.

"Eyyyyyyow!" he cried out in pain

The Manticore's stinger struck at Tanner, who garnered just enough energy to slip to the side. He watched it strike the rock floor of the mine next to him. Fragments of rock sprayed everywhere, and the sharp point became lodged in the stone. The beast torqued its tail, trying to free the stinger as it growled fiercely and glared at Tanner.

Tanner heard a thump and a slight whimper from the beast, then another and another. Scanning the dimly lit mine, Tanner saw Hokolesqua firing arrow after arrow in rapid succession. The Manticore gave one last mighty heave, trying to free its tail, when another arrow finished it off and it fell to the ground with a thud.

Tanner was in a tremendous amount of pain, but there was no shortage of Nishapurans rushing to his aid. He screamed as each of the barbed needles was pulled out of his chest. If it weren't for the fact that Genghis Khan's army was in hot pursuit, Tanner would have lain motionless, but realizing that wasn't an option, he rose to his feet and nodded a heartfelt thank-you to Hokolesqua.

"You all right?" Mick said after she moved several Nishapurans away and rushed to Tanner's side.

"That was not there when we first came," he replied.

"Yeah, we would have noticed that," Andrew said.

"I think half the gods really are working against us," Tanner said as he cradled his abdomen and doubled over in pain.

"Demeter!" he cried weakly for the goddess.

CHAPTER 77

ANDREW'S BRILLIANT IDEA

(TANNER)

The mine was suddenly filled with light as Demeter appeared, clearing the rock away from the entrance to the Cathedral door.

"Right this way. Step right up." Tanner winced as he watched the crowds stream over the dead Manticore and into the Cathedral. "There's limited seating, so please move as quickly as you can to the back of the bus."

"Haven't lost your sense of humor at least," Mick said.

"We can't fit any more," Andrew yelled from inside the Cathedral to Tanner.

"Okay, everyone, this bus is full. Please wait patiently for the next to arrive." With Mick's help, Tanner hobbled down to the control room. "Let's get this party started. Mount Olympus, present day," he said as he watched Mick adjust the control-panel settings. "Perfect."

She pressed the pulsating green button and waited. No flashing lights. She pressed it again. Nothing.

"Andrew. It's not working," Mick yelled over to the platform.

"What do you mean?"

"I'm pushing the button, but nothing's happening."

"Maybe there's a weight limit," Andrew said in a puzzled tone.

"Clear half of them off and let's try it again," Tanner said.

Andrew struggled to clear half the Nishapurans off the platform. Everyone wanted to get away from the Mongols as quickly as possible, and no one wanted to be left behind. After a significant struggle and with Marina's help, he cleared half of them off.

"Try again."

"Nothing," Mick said after multiple attempts at pushing the button. "Come on," she said impatiently as she continued to press it. "Bad time for this thing to be broken."

"What do we do?" Tanner hollered at Andrew above the commotion.

"I'm thinking."

"Well, think faster."

"Everyone clear off," Andrew said. "Help me." He motioned to Marina. "We've got to get everyone off the platform."

After another struggle, the platform was fully cleared.

"Mick, on the platform," Andrew instructed. "Tanner, try again."

Once Mick made it over to the platform, he pushed the button, and the lights began to flash like usual. Then everything went dark, and when the lights came back on, Mick was gone.

"Wait a second. Where did she go?" Andrew said.

"To Mount Olympus. What did you expect?"

"Yeah, but usually the steps light up and we exit one of the doors, remember?"

"You're right," Tanner said. "I wonder what happened."

"Check the doors," Andrew yelled, soliciting help from the Nishapurans in the room.

"Locked."

"Locked."

The responses came back from all of the doors other than the one they'd entered.

"Why didn't the platform work for them?" Andrew's frustration level was escalating. "And why did Mick just disappear?"

"This can't be happening," Tanner said under his breath. "What's going on?" he yelled to Andrew.

"Wait, they haven't been judged," Andrew replied "They can't go to Olympus without being judged. Can you change the settings to someplace else?"

Tanner was trying to process the whole thing. *When we went back to Olympus from Rome, we didn't go through any judgment. But maybe once you've been found worthy, you can get back to Olympus without being judged again. That must be it.*

He tried to find a way to change the destination on the screen, but there was nothing that allowed him to do so.

"What do we do?" he yelled to Andrew. "Genghis Khan's men will arrive any minute. We've led the entire city to a literal dead end."

"I'm thinking."

"Andrew, you're not fast enough," Tanner said. "We've got to blow up the entrance to the cave. Mick always said you could make a bomb with a bobby pin and a piece of gum. Now's the time to prove it."

"We won't be able to survive in the mine," Andrew replied.

"It will buy us some time," Tanner said.

"Maybe there's some way the gods can do a mass judgment," Andrew said. "I don't know, but it's our only hope. Once we've sealed off the entrance, you and I have to join Mick and get to the Judgment Platform as quick as possible to plead with the gods."

"I like it. Good plan. Now get making a bomb. We don't have much time. Come on."

Andrew helped Tanner as he hobbled along. They pushed their way through the crowded passageways back to the entrance. When they arrived, they could see the Mongolian horses in the distance headed toward the mine.

"This is useless," Andrew said. "I can't make a bomb before they get here. We've only got a few minutes."

"All these lives are at stake, Andrew," Tanner said, motioning at the masses of Nishapurans in the cave. "The Mongols have probably already killed 10 percent of the population. We've led the other 90 percent into a death trap. We've got to figure this out. I don't want the deaths of an entire city on my conscience. It's bad enough feeling like I could have saved Anastasia—but a city? It would literally kill me."

"I've got it," Andrew said with a big grin. "It's a mine. There are probably already explosives here. We've just got to find someone who knows where they're kept."

"You're brilliant, Andrew. I owe you," Tanner said, but Andrew didn't hear perhaps the first sincere compliment Tanner had given him in a long time, because he'd made a mad dash around the cave, canvassing the Nishapurans in an attempt to find someone who might know where the explosives were kept.

Tanner waited at the entrance.

It wasn't long before Andrew returned, explosives in hand.

"They're almost here!" Tanner said as he looked out.

"That must be Genghis Khan himself," Andrew said, looking at a fantastically decorated man riding alongside the late Toquchar's wife, Genghis's daughter.

"No time to admire. We've got to get this thing sealed up."

Tanner busied himself moving everyone away from the entrance while Andrew created fuses from his shoe laces and arranged the explosives in an attempt to most effectively destroy the opening. "Light it!" Tanner yelled as the Mongols were close enough that he could start to distinguish facial features.

"Here goes," Andrew said as he lit the fuse and ran back. Just as they saw the first horse appear over the small crest in front of the mine entrance, the place exploded, sending Tanner and Andrew sprawling backward.

Tanner winced as he rolled over and looked at the cloud of dust, waiting anxiously for it to settle. The mine had become exceedingly dark. When the dust cleared, Tanner could see the entrance was completely sealed.

"You did it," he said, shoving Andrew.

"We haven't done anything but delay their deaths," Andrew replied. "Unless we can get the gods to agree to let them onto Olympus, they're all doomed."

"Let's get going, then."

The two traversed the crowds back to the door into the Cathedral. The place was still jammed with people. Tanner and Andrew made their way to the control room and in a flash were back on Mount Olympus.

Tanner felt better instantly. He looked at where the arrow had pierced his leg, and there was no trace it had ever occurred, and the same with the hundred small wounds from the Manticore's quills. Not even a mark.

"I'm beginning to like Olympus better and better all the time," Tanner said.

"What happened?" Mick asked as they emerged from the Cathedral.

"The Nishapurans haven't been judged," Andrew said. "But no time for the details right now. We've got to plead with the gods to let them pass through."

CHAPTER 78

ZEUS'S WRATH

(TANNER)

Tanner and his friends charged through the intricate gate of Mount Olympus and on to the Judgment Platform. Out of breath, Tanner began to form his first word to plead for the Nishapurans.

Zeus's voice thundered across the mountain as he pointed at Tanner with his scepter. "Do you realize what you've done?"

"No," Tanner replied sheepishly.

"You may have ignited a war between the gods. Hades is furious that his helmet is missing. King Tohopka and Cheveyo the bounty hunter approached him with escaped warriors from Anatok in an attempt to convince Hades to make war with the surface world, and do you know what Hades said?"

"No?"

"He said YES!"

Tanner gulped.

"In fact," Zeus continued, "his exact words were 'The Surfacers have already declared war on me by stealing my most valuable weapon.' Any idea what that might be, Tanner?"

"His helmet?"

"That's correct," Zeus roared. "So I guess you realize who would be responsible if a planetary war breaks out?"

"Me?" Tanner winced.

"Correct again." The booming voice rang so powerfully in his ears, Tanner thought Mount Olympus might actually break in two.

Mick gave him a little shove. "Told you stealing the helmet was a bad idea."

"But Tohopka approaching Hades," Mick asked meekly. "That wasn't on us, right?"

"Enough." Zeus dismissed Mick. "Now why have you approached my throne?"

Andrew was the only one who hadn't been rebuked by Zeus yet, so he explained the plight of the Nishapurans.

"I will allow a change to the Cathedral of Time in Nishapur," Zeus replied. "I know what Genghis Khan is capable of. If I let him run rampant, he'll kill them all. Also, I can't have someone like that finding the entrance to Inner Earth. The last thing we need is for him to join forces with Hades as well." Zeus snarled and looked glaringly at Tanner.

"Hermes, go to Demeter and tell her you need to add a setting for the forest of Delfi as a destination. Be quick. The Nishapurans still in the turquoise mine are in danger of being slaughtered. Help her to get them onto the platform and transported to the forest. As for you three, be gone," Zeus said, looking away in disgust. "Finish your mission, and please . . ." he paused, ". . . try to do so without wreaking any more havoc on the planet."

Leaving nothing but a streak of lightning behind, Hermes disappeared, and the three Surfacers walked somberly back to the Cathedral.

"That could have gone better," Tanner said as they trudged down the path.

"Could have gone worse, too," Andrew said.

"I guess," Tanner said.

"It could have gone a lot worse," Andrew continued. "Didn't you notice one enormous thing Zeus didn't mention?"

"What are you talking about?" Tanner asked.

"Decimus," Andrew replied. "Apparently he doesn't know we created an invincible man who knows how to get into Inner Earth and is only a few rungs down the ladder from becoming emperor of Rome."

"You're right," Tanner said in a hushed tone as the realization sunk in. "Could have gone a lot worse."

"Hopefully the fact we're about to save the entire population of Nishapur will offset some of your sins, Tanner," Mick said.

"Yeah," Tanner replied. "But it might take more than that to offset the idea that I might be responsible for the biggest war in the history of the planet."

"Actually, that meeting went even better than I was originally thinking," Andrew replied.

"What are you talking about?" Tanner said in complete disbelief. "Were you daydreaming about Marina or something when Zeus was yelling?"

"Shut it," Andrew replied, shoving Tanner. "Listen, I know Zeus sounded angry, but why did he tell us to continue our quest? And why didn't he ask for Hades's helmet back? If we weren't headed down the path we're supposed to be on, he had the opportunity to change it. He could have banned us from the Cathedral. From Inner Earth entirely. He didn't do any of that. In some weird, twisted way, I think we're actually doing what he wants us to do."

"You think?" Mick replied.

"I don't know where you come up with this stuff," Tanner said. "You seriously think Zeus would act like that if we were doing what he wanted?"

Andrew just shrugged his shoulders.

"We've got one other problem," Mick said.

"What's that?" Andrew asked.

"Jim."

"I don't think we can rescue him," Tanner replied.

"That's not what I'm talking about," Mick said. "Remember how I told you he was with the Mongols, trying to break into Farzin's shop?"

"Yeah?"

"He's obviously joined with them—and he knows all about the Cathedral of Time," Mick said. "With the Manticore dead, there's nothing guarding the entrance. Once the Mongols get into the mine there will be nothing to stop them from entering Inner Earth."

"And like Zeus said, the last thing we need is for Khan to join forces with . . ."

"Yeah, big problem," Andrew interrupted.

"But if the Nishapurans weren't able to use the Cathedral, surely the Mongols won't be able to," Tanner said.

"But Zeus had Demeter remove the block," Andrew said. "And unless he finds out the Mongols know about the Cathedral, they'll be free to enter as well."

"We should warn Zeus," Mick said.

"I'm not gonna be the one to break that news to him," Tanner said.

"Me neither," Andrew and Mick said in harmony.

"Let's just hope it doesn't happen," Tanner said.

"Guys," Andrew said, "we've got to move faster, or we're not going to even have the rescue of the Nishapurans to hang our hats on."

And with that, the Surfacers sprinted for the Cathedral.

CHAPTER 79

RETURN TO ROME

(TANNER)

Tanner, Mick, and Andrew watched in amazement as Demeter coordinated the movement of thousands and thousands of Nishapurans through the Cathedral of Time. After several hours, Livia spotted her friends.

"Musclosus!" she yelled as she ran through the crowd toward Tanner, Mayata following.

"Let's get back to Rome," Marina said with a sense of urgency as she grabbed Andrew by the hand. "I've got to see if I can save—"

Tanner, who was all set to razz Andrew, emphatically cut Marina off, realizing Livia didn't know her father had fallen into the hands of anti-Christian factions.

"We'll go back as soon as everyone is cleared out of here," Tanner said.

"Might as well make ourselves comfortable," Andrew said. "This is going to take a while."

When the last of the Nishapurans finally disappeared, Hokolesqua, Nemhsi, and Mayata approached Tanner and his friends.

"Can you send the three of us back to our place and time?" Hokolesqua asked.

"Yes, we can," Mick replied. "We'll miss you."

"I will never forget you." He hugged everyone.

"We couldn't have done this without you," Tanner said, picturing Hokolesqua's deadeye shots with a bow and arrow, while flying a carpet, and his taking down the Manticore.

"Thank you for reuniting my family," Mayata replied.

"I'll miss you, Grandmother," Livia said as she hugged Mayata's leg.

"Please come and visit," Nemhsi added.

"We'll definitely try," Mick quickly said. "Now, go stand on the platform, and you'll be home shortly."

Andrew set the timers and pushed the button. Lights flashed everywhere, and they were gone.

"Why is everyone disappearing from the platform now instead of needing to climb the stairs and go out one of the doors?" Andrew asked.

"We really should visit them sometime," Mick said.

"Agreed," Tanner added. "They're awesome."

"Did you say something, Andrew?" Mick asked.

"It doesn't matter," Andrew said.

"We need to get back to Rome and clean up the mess there," Mick said.

Tanner, Mick, Marina, and Livia climbed the metal stairs to the central platform. Andrew walked to the control room, adjusted the settings for Rome, pushed the button, and ran for the platform. The normal light show played, and when the lights came back on, the four of them were standing in the center of the platform with flashing lights directing them to the exit into the Mundus.

"I've got it," Andrew said with an expression that looked like he had just discovered the theory of relativity. "There must be more than one Cathedral of Time. I always thought when the light show was happening, the whole Cathedral was being transported to a different location. But when you watch someone else, they actually disappear from the platform. It must be they're being transported to another Cathedral."

"Did you say something?" Tanner said.

"Very funny," Andrew replied. "Seriously, though, don't you get it?" Andrew continued.

"As long as it gets us back to the Surface at least one more time, that's as much as I need to understand," Tanner said. "Don't clutter my mind with details."

When the five of them arrived in the Mundus, Tanner asked for Demeter's help to get past the guards, which she gave.

"Wish we would have thought to ask for her help a bunch of trips ago," Tanner said as they easily made their way past a couple of sleeping guards and went to headquarters.

CHAPTER 80

THE STATUETTE

(TANNER)

"Donald," Tanner said as he entered Lucius's carpentry shop. He ran over and gave the Praetorian a big hug. Every experience Tanner had with the man was helping to fill the void his own father had created when he'd split. Tanner's mind flashed back to the courtroom where he had seen his father for the first time in four years. It was such a brief moment, and Tanner hadn't really had a chance to stop and think about it since they'd left, but when he saw Donald, the emotions of seeing his father washed over him like a wave crashing down on a surfer. "It's so good to see you."

"It's good to see you too," Donald replied. "But we just saw each other earlier today."

"Ah, you're right," Tanner replied. "The whole time-travel thing. We've actually been gone for several days."

"You'll have to tell me all about it," Donald said. "But right now I'm headed over to the palace . . ." He paused. "What's *she* doing here?" He pointed to Marina.

"She's come to her senses. She wants to make things right."

"It might be too late," Donald replied coolly.

"It's never too late to repent," Tanner said angrily.

"No, but it might be too late to make things right," Donald said. "We've gotten word Nero's planning crucifixions later this week. Unless we can find Marcus soon, he's a dead man—that is if he hasn't already been killed."

Tanner looked over at Marina, thinking about how devastated she'd be if she couldn't repair things.

"I'm headed to the palace to see what I can find out about Nero's plans. I'm hoping I can find out something about where her father is."

"I don't think you should go." Mick inserted herself into the conversation. "Nero is so paranoid; at some point he's going to realize you're a mole, and you're going to end up dead."

"Don't worry. I know how to play my part."

"Nero is not someone to take risks with," Tanner added.

"You're right. But I must go. It's do-or-die for the empire right now, and, quite frankly, for us. I'll be careful."

"Hey, you still have the package I asked you to protect for me, right?" Tanner whispered as he thought about his conversation with Zeus regarding Hades's helmet.

"Of course," Donald replied. "You can trust me with your life."

Tanner exhaled.

Donald left for the palace knowing full well he might be making his way toward a very unpleasant death.

"Where should we put these?" Andrew whispered to Tanner, pointing at the flying carpets he and Mick had strapped on their backs.

"Hide them somewhere in the shop," Tanner said. "When Donald gets back, we'll have him hide them at his house, along with the helmet."

Andrew and Mick wandered around the shop until they found what they considered a suitable hiding place.

"Let's go look for my dad," Marina said.

"Good idea," Tanner replied.

The Edmonson Middle School trio and Marina went to the prison nearest Lucius's shop. It reminded Tanner of the walk from the on-deck circle to the batter's box with the game on the line—only this was life and death. He could see so many emotions parading across Marina's face. He attempted to buoy her up through conversation, but he could tell she wanted to be alone with her thoughts. When they got to the prison, the guards informed Marina they remembered her father but he was no longer there. They had no idea where he was. The four continued the search throughout the day and arrived back at Lucius's late in the evening, exhausted and without so much as a lead.

As they sat around talking about their search strategy, Donald returned in a somber mood.

"Any updates?" Tanner asked.

"Yes," he said dejectedly. "Before the week is over, the raving lunatic plans to burn down the rest of the city."

"You're joking, right?" Tanner said.

"I wish I were. But that's not the worst of it."

"How could it be worse than that?" Andrew asked.

"He's planning to let wild beasts loose in the streets and *then* set the city on fire," Donald replied. "That way the citizens will have to either choose to burn in their homes or flee the flames and face an angry lion, a pack of hungry wolves, a bear, or some other wild animal."

"What a monster," Andrew said. "We've got to stop him."

"I think he's been influenced by the evil spirits," Donald said.

"Evil spirits?" Andrew asked.

"You didn't hear?" Donald replied. "Someone broke into the Umbilicus during the blizzard and left the passage to the Mundus open. Evil spirits were pouring into the city for days before the breach was discovered. There have been so many horrible things happening all around the city."

Tanner, Andrew, and Mick looked back and forth at each other, eyes wide.

"We'll stop 'im." Lucius chimed in.

"We've got to count the money from the heist," Andrew said.

"Why?" Donald asked.

"Maybe we can bribe the Praetorian Guard to help us stop Nero. If there's enough gold, maybe you could coerce his guards to help with our cause."

"It's a little risky, but I think it's a great idea," Donald said. "The emperor has gone crazy enough that I don't think it would take much to tip the scales in our favor. With the whole guard on our side, it should be easy to overthrow Nero."

Everyone chipped in and began to count the money.

"We have enough to offer about ten thousand sesterces per man," Mick said after calculating everyone's totals.

"That is not enough," Donald replied.

"Promise them more," Andrew said. "Tell them we'll give them ten thousand now and twenty thousand more once Nero is removed from power."

"But we don't have that kind of money," Donald said.

"The incoming emperor will see that as a small price to have saved the city from complete destruction," Andrew said.

"You're brilliant, Andrew. I'll propose it. Hopefully by tomorrow night we'll have the entire Praetorian Guard on our side."

The mutineers in the room broke out in a chant. "Vindex is coming!" A double entendre indicating revenge was coming for all the evils done by the emperor and also referring to the name of the leader of a revolt that had broken out against Nero.

Tanner, Andrew, Mick, and Marina spent the next day searching for Marcus with no luck.

When Donald returned from the palace, he brought several guardsmen with him.

"The Praetorians have agreed to the deal. They're going to help us."

"That's fantastic!" The room was abuzz with the news.

"Hold on," Donald shouted, trying to get everyone to settle down. "There's some bad news as well. The Senate has strengthened their resolve to assist Nero. We've got to move immediately. He is so dangerous right now we have to finish him off."

Everyone agreed.

"I *was* able to secure the services of Spiculus, who, as you know, was once such a strong supporter of the emperor."

"The gladiator?" Tanner asked.

"Yes."

Tanner thought back to how 250,000 fans had unitedly chanted Spiculus's name over and over as he paraded through the Circus Maximus the day Tanner had fled for his life and hid in the crowd. He remembered how Spiculus's ripped body had glistened in the sunlight.

Good to have him on our side.

"Spiculus agreed to help us capture those protecting the emperor tonight. We'll need some of you to help. Any volunteers?"

Several Praetorians raised their hands.

"Once we have those closest to the emperor in chains, we'll have to lure Nero out of the palace somehow."

"What if we taunt him with 'Vindex is coming' chants?" Andrew suggested.

"It's perfect!" Donald replied. "Any of you willing to help taunt an emperor?"

There was no lack of volunteers.

"Perfect," Donald said. "We'll meet in the Cryptoporticus at sunset."

"The what?" Andrew asked.

"The Cryptoporticus. It's an underground passageway next to the palace."

"I'm surprised you didn't know that," Mick said with a grin.

"Come on, you didn't know that either," Andrew replied.

Mick had to confess she had never heard of the Cryptoporticus. While the two of them were bantering about their knowledge of history, Donald motioned to Tanner.

"Come with me," he said as he walked out the door. "I'm going to need your skills."

"But, what about . . ." Tanner started to reply, motioning toward Andrew and Mick.

"They'll be fine," Donald said.

Tanner was confident his friends, who were staying put, would be fine. He was, however, worried about following the fearless Donald Carlton and wanted to bring Andrew and Mick along.

"We've got to end this thing tonight," Donald said as the two of them walked through the forum.

"What's in the bag?"

Donald had a sack slung over his back.

"Just some things we might need tonight. Don't concern yourself with it."

The farther they went, the more convinced Tanner was that they were on their way to Nero's palace. It was one thing hearing Donald report about his traitorous activities inside the palace, but it was a whole different thing feeling like he was about to play a key role in them himself. Donald grabbed Tanner and pulled him behind as if to hide the boy. Tanner froze, wondering what Donald might have seen.

"I need you to sneak into Nero's office," Donald whispered, cocking his head in Tanner's direction.

"What?" Tanner said in shock.

"Shhh." Donald turned and covered Tanner's mouth.

"I want you to destroy something."

"I can't go into Nero's office," Tanner said quietly but with as much emphasis as he could muster. "You've got to be crazy."

"Tanner, we're all going to die tomorrow if we don't do something."

"Uh, no, you forget I could just go back to the Cathedral of Time and be on my way back to the good ol' US of A."

"Look, I'm more anxious to get back to Brownsville than you are. I've got my wife and kids, whom I haven't seen for years. But I'm not sure that's even an option anymore," Donald said. "The Umbilicus Urbis has been locked down tighter than the Brownsville Bank."

"Which wasn't locked down very well, if you remember," Tanner replied.

"That's true. Well, you know what I mean."

"Why has it been locked down tighter than usual?"

"Someone left it open, and evil spirits were allowed to pour into the city." The reminder that he was the one who had left the Mundus open made Tanner even more willing to help. If the evil-spirits thing really was true, he had been the cause of all the horrible things that had been happening in the city. He couldn't imagine anyone coming up with a plan to unleash wild beasts and burn down the rest of the city unless they were influenced by evil spirits. Tanner knew he had to try to help Donald with whatever he was up to.

"How am I going to break into Nero's office without getting caught?"

"I will create a distraction," Donald said. "It will give you enough time to get in and out safely."

"Are you sure we can pull this off?"

"I've seen you in action, Tanner. If anyone can do it, it's you."

Tanner wasn't sure that made him feel any better.

"What do you want me to destroy?"

"Nero keeps a small statuette of a girl on his desk," Donald explained. "He is incredibly superstitious about it. A commoner gave it to him and told him it would protect him against conspiracies. Immediately after, a conspiracy was discovered and thwarted. Ever since, Nero has worshipped the statuette as if it's a powerful goddess. If you can destroy that, along with everything else we're doing, I guarantee the emperor will abandon the throne on his own."

"Okay," Tanner said with some hesitation.

"I will enter Nero's private quarters," Donald said. "When you hear my sword drop, you will know I have distracted him and it is safe for you to enter. I can only assure you a short time, so you will have to get in and out quickly."

"All right," Tanner said.

Donald and Tanner moved carefully into the palace and through the corridor leading to the emperor's residence.

"Over there is his office," Donald said, pointing ahead and to his right. "I will be in the room just beyond that. Remember, wait until you hear my sword fall before you enter."

"Are you sure I can do this?" Tanner asked.

"You single-handedly pulled off the biggest heist in Roman history when you broke into the state treasury. This will be easy."

Yeah, right. Easy? Destroying something in Nero's actual office? I don't know about this.

Donald left, and Tanner began to panic.

I'm already a wanted man, and here I am, alone, with no weapons or anything. Is Donald turning on me? Did he do this just to hand-deliver me to the emperor? Is that why he wanted to split up? Doubts began to swell in his mind.

He thought about the statuette. *What if it really does have powers to prevent conspiracies? Then it has the power to stop me. I'm destined to fail.*

"You'll never amount to anything, Tanner." He was surprised to hear his father's voice ring in his head again. He thought he had moved past that with everything that had transpired.

Why did I agree to this?

Clang.

Tanner was so deep in thought he nearly missed it.

Oh, my gosh! That's my cue. He shook his head to snap himself out it.

Tanner slid along the wall, looking rapidly in every direction. He slipped through the slightly open doorway and found himself alone in Nero's office.

Lying on Nero's disheveled desk was a handwritten document. He knew he didn't have much time, but the temptation was too much. As he scanned the paper, he realized it was a prepared speech in which Nero was begging forgiveness from the citizens of Rome. There was a black robe draped across the chair. Apparently Nero planned to wear it as evidence he was mourning for his own wickedness.

I've got to smash that statue and get out of here.

He scanned the desk. No statuette.

Donald said it would be there. Have I been duped? Or is Nero on to us? Tanner thought.

He quickly looked around the room again to see if he was being watched.

He's hidden it.

Tanner dashed over to a small cabinet behind the desk. As he crouched down to look for the statue, he heard the door open behind him.

CHAPTER 81

LALAWETHIKA'S GIFT

(HOKOLESQUA)

Following the pyramid compass, Hokolesqua, Nemhsi, and their mother made their way through the underworld, into Mammoth Cave and back to their Shawnee village. The hardened warrior Lalawethika, upon seeing his family, ran for his wife, whom he'd presumed long dead. He embraced her, and his children joined the joyous occasion.

"I thought I would never see Mayata again," he said, looking deeply into her eyes.

"What about Methoataske?" he asked.

"Oh, Father," Hokolesqua said. "She died in a terrible fire."

Lalawethika solemnly bowed his head and held his family even tighter.

"You should have seen Hoko!" Nemhsi said. "He destroyed the most fearsome beast Nemhsi has ever seen."

Lalawethika put his arm around his son's neck and rubbed his hair.

"I knew Hokolesqua was a brave warrior."

"And he stopped the most terrible army ever. Worse than the armies of the white man. You should have seen him riding and shooting arrows." Nemhsi winked at Hokolesqua, who knew they could never divulge exactly what they'd been riding.

"That's my warrior son!"

"It's all because of him we were able to rescue Mother," Nemhsi concluded.

A smile larger than any Hokolesqua had ever seen on his father spread across the man's face.

"I have something for you, Hokolesqua. Follow me."

The four walked back to the wigwam, where their youngest sibling sat on the floor playing. Another series of embraces occurred as he welcomed them all home.

Hokolesqua's heart stood still as his father reached for the headband and feather Lalawethika had always worn so proudly.

"My brave son. You have proven yourself to be one of the greatest warriors this tribe has ever known."

Chills ran down Hokolesqua's spine as his father placed the headband on his head.

He was now truly a Shawnee warrior.

CHAPTER 82

PHAON'S VILLA

(TANNER)

"There must be other conspirators." Tanner heard the man in the doorway behind him say.

Lucky for Tanner, the man was talking to someone still in the corridor or he would have seen the teenager.

"Good thing you've protected the goddess all these years," he said.

"Yes. Bring her to me. I can't afford to let her out of my sight, not with everything that's going on." Shivers ran down Tanner's spine. It was Nero speaking.

Think fast.

Tanner quietly opened the cabinet, and, sure enough, there was the small statue.

Can't make any noise. Can't smash it now.

He stuffed the statuette into his tunic.

Now, how to get out of here...

Nero was still preoccupied in talking with the man. Tanner quietly snuck around the desk and behind the partially open door. He could see the emperor just feet away through the crack.

Don't breathe, he thought. *But where's Donald?*

Tanner's heart was racing.

The man pushed the door fully open and entered the room.

I can't stay in here, but I can't leave, either, Tanner thought. *Once he sees the statuette's gone, he'll lock the whole place down. But Nero's probably still in the corridor. Where do I go? Nero probably isn't as well armed. I've got to take my chances with him.*

Tanner waited until the man moved behind the desk and crouched down to open the cabinet, and then he slipped from behind the door and made his way into the corridor. Just as he suspected, Nero was still there, but he had his back to Tanner and was about to enter the room Donald had gone in.

They must have captured Donald. That's what the whole 'there must be other conspirators' thing was. I'm going to have to take over the whole operation, he thought.

Tanner ran for the exit.

"It's gone! The goddess has been stolen!" he heard Nero's henchman yell. Tanner was still in the corridor, but the door to the outside was in his sights.

"Lock the palace down!"

A fully armed guard stepped into the corridor, sword in hand. The man took a swing at Tanner, who hit the deck, sliding under the blade. *Just like stealing second base,* he thought. He sprang back to his feet. It was a footrace for the door. Adrenaline pumping, he blew past the man and was out the door and down the stairs.

Where did Donald say he was meeting Spiculus? Think. Come on. Some weird name. Where was it? Ah, yeah, the Cryptoporticus.

When Tanner arrived at the vaulted corridor near the palace, Spiculus and the others were there waiting.

"Change in plans," Tanner said, gasping for breath. "They've got Donald. May have killed him."

"Whoa, slow down," Spiculus said. "What's going on? Who's Donald?"

"Sorry, I meant Titus," Tanner said. "He asked me to destroy a statue in Nero's office while he created a distraction." Tanner pulled the small statuette out of his tunic. "While I was there, I overheard one of Nero's men talking about capturing a conspirator. We've got to move. Now. The element of surprise is gone, and the longer we wait, the harder this is going to be."

"I need the three of you to search for Titus," Tanner said, pointing to three of the Praetorians. "Spiculus, you and I will work on capturing anyone who might still be protecting the emperor."

"We're coming with you," came a voice from behind the Praetorians. Tanner was shocked when Andrew, Mick, and Marina stepped out from behind the guards.

"Let's go, then!" Tanner said.

The group ran for the palace.

"Follow my lead," Spiculus said.

It's no wonder he's considered the greatest gladiator ever, Tanner thought as he watched him make quick work of the two guards who had positioned themselves at the main entrance following Tanner's escape.

"Suit up!" Spiculus yelled to the teens, and they grabbed the swords, shields, and daggers of the fallen guards. The rebels worked their way through the palace and captured nearly everyone left. It happened with much less difficulty than they could have ever hoped for.

"Even his closest friends aren't willing to put up a fight anymore," Spiculus said.

Once they captured everyone except Phaon, the secretary of finance, whom Donald had already won to their cause through blackmail, Tanner snuck to the entrance of Nero's bedroom, where he could see the emperor looking nervously around while gathering some of his belongings. Tanner scanned the room, looking for any sign of Donald. Not seeing him, he signaled for the hecklers to begin their taunting.

From a passageway just outside the bedroom, they began yelling "Vindex is coming! Vindex is coming!"

Nero snapped his head in the direction of the voices. "Guards!" he yelled.

No reply.

He called for his closest friends. Again no reply.

"Spiculus!"

Spiculus remained silent.

"What is this? Have I neither friends nor enemies left?" the emperor's apprehensive voice shouted.

The chant resumed. "Vindex is coming! Vindex is coming!"

Tanner could see the terror on Nero's face and decided to play on the emperor's fears.

"Over here," Tanner said. The emperor looked over at him. Tanner panicked briefly when Nero's evil glare pierced him.

Gathering himself, Tanner flashed the statuette in front of the lunatic, making sure he got a good look at it.

"Catch," Tanner said as he threw it just out of Nero's reach and high enough he was sure it would break near the emperor when it landed.

Nero made a feeble attempt to reach for his treasured protector, then watched in horror as the 'goddess' shattered against the marble floor in front of him. The emperor dropped the items in his hands, then fled his room and ran down the corridor barefoot and wearing only a tunic. Tanner motioned for the others to follow as he, Spiculus, and Phaon trailed Nero out of the palace and into the darkness of the city. When they arrived at the

Tiber River, Tanner and the others hid in the shadows as Phaon approached the lunatic.

"Oh, Phaon, is it only you who is brave enough to support me in this hour of need?" Nero asked. He continued. "You shall be richly rewarded when I take my place among the other gods on Olympus."

Nero pulled himself up onto the wall of the bridge and looked out over the Tiber.

"Don't stop me, Phaon. I'm going to Olympus. Perhaps it's only there that my talents shall be appreciated."

Nero looked over at a young couple walking down the street holding hands.

"I can't jump," he said, gesturing at the couple. "The citizens of the empire need me. What will their desolate future be like without the divine Nero to lead them?"

A lot better, Tanner thought.

"Phaon, I need a place to gather my thoughts." Nero was talking excitedly. "Collect myself. Yes, that's it. I'm not thinking clearly."

"I have a villa about four miles from here," Phaon replied. "If we get some horses, we can go there. It will give you a place to think."

"Perfect," the emperor replied. "To the imperial stables."

Tanner, Andrew, Mick, and Marina followed discreetly behind. When they reached the stables, Nero grabbed a faded cloak and threw it over his shoulders.

"Help me get on this thing!" he yelled as he approached one of the horses.

Phaon struggled trying to help the gluttonous emperor onto the horse.

Nero spotted Andrew hiding in the shadows.

"You, over there! Help me." Andrew cringed and turned his head to avoid eye contact, then quickly moved to Phaon's side.

"Marina, Mick, help us," Andrew said as they struggled to get the emperor onto the horse.

Once Nero was situated, he placed a handkerchief over his face to hide his identity. They started for the villa.

"Get a horse and follow them," Tanner whispered to his friends.

Each one mounted a horse and carefully followed behind the emperor and his former ally, Phaon.

Crash!

A flash of lightning lit the night sky, and a nearly simultaneous clap of thunder shook the earth. Nero's horse reared back on its hind legs, and he whipped it to a frenzied gallop for the rest of the ride to the villa.

"Stand guard outside," Nero said, pointing at Andrew and the others as he dismounted in front of the villa. "Phaon, follow me."

As they were about to enter the villa, a man delivered a letter to Phaon.

"What does it say?" Nero said, sweat dripping off his forehead.

"Having been declared a public enemy by the Senate, Nero and his supporters will be punished in ancient style."

"Ancient style?" Nero demanded as he stood in the doorway of the villa. "What's ancient style?" he yelled. "Tell me!"

"It includes being stripped naked and flogged with sticks," Phaon replied.

"What *else* does it include?"

"I don't think you want to know."

"Ancient style is not an option for a god," Nero barked. "Besides, who would enforce such a decree?"

"Galba has been leading a rebellion. I'm sure he's the one behind the declaration."

"Spiculus," Nero said. "That's it. The great emperor killed by the greatest gladiator of all time. Yes, that would be a worthy way to die. Where *is* he?" Nero demanded. "He should be the one. I won't die at the hands of Galba's men!"

"We have no idea where he is!" Andrew replied.

"What's that noise?" Nero demanded as the sound of galloping hooves grew louder.

"It's Galba's men!" Nero shouted. "Dead! And so great an artist!"

"You," he said staring directly at Andrew, who cowered under the glare. "Find Spiculus. Now."

Nero and Phaon entered the villa.

A few minutes later, Phaon emerged from the same door.

"The emperor is dead!" he yelled as he ran out of the villa toward Tanner and his friends, who were waiting outside. "The reign of terror is over."

High-fives were being exchanged among Tanner and his friends.

"Grab them!" someone yelled in the darkness. Tanner, Mick, Marina, and Andrew nearly got whiplash as they tried to determine the source of the voice. It was Galba's men who were quickly closing in on the teens.

"They're supporters of Nero!" one of the men angrily growled.

CHAPTER 83

FRIEND OR FOE?

"Get on the horses!" Mick yelled. In a blur they were on and fleeing for their lives. After following them for a few hundred yards, one of their pursuers shouted to the others.

"Let them go. Shortly they'll have no one *to* support."

The four rode as quickly as they could from Phaon's villa to Lucius's shop.

"Nero's dead!" Tanner shouted as he entered the shop. A large gathering was taking place.

Cheers erupted from every corner. Hats and helmets were tossed into the air. Tanner had never experienced anything like this transformation from oppression and fear to freedom and hope. It was exhilarating. Tanner, Andrew, and Mick were swarmed by mutineers asking questions and confirming the veracity of it all. Once the excitement finally died down, the atmosphere suddenly changed.

"Were any of you able to find Titus?" Tanner asked, worried about what might have become of his friend and mentor."

"No sign of him," one of the guardsmen replied.

"By the way, when will we be getting the money Titus promised us?" one of Donald's fellow Praetorian guards shouted angrily.

"Galba will honor Titus's promise. Don't worry," Cornelius replied.

"That's easy for you to say," another guardsman said. "You have no family to provide for. Most of us have hungry mouths to feed.

We need that money." It wasn't long before Cornelius was surrounded by Praetorians demanding he find out when they would be paid what Donald had promised for helping overthrow Nero.

"We risked our lives to help you," one of the Praetorians snarled. "We better get the rest of the money."

"He'll pay you!" Cornelius shouted back. "You must give him some time. Galba hasn't even been officially made emperor!"

"One week! That's what we'll give you, and if Titus doesn't have the money, there's a collection of nice crosses near Nero's circus that should be available by then!" one of the Praetorians said as they stormed out of the shop.

Tanner and his friends built a small fire and discussed the current state of affairs with Cornelius, Lucius, and his son before they finally fell asleep from exhaustion. They had been up almost the entire night.

Tanner was awakened by a relentless knocking at the door.

"Who could that be?" Tanner said, trying to shake off the grogginess he felt.

"Maybe it's Donald," Andrew mumbled.

Tanner walked over and stood on his tiptoes to look through the metal bars in the small opening in the door.

He excitedly opened the door upon seeing the man who had come to the rescue and helped in the heist. "Aquila. How are you?" he asked, the two clasping forearms.

"Bad news. I've got bad news," Aquila said. He was completely out of breath and puffing and wheezing as he tried to get the words out.

"I'm not sure if you remember Erastus. Longtime friend, brother-in-law of mine. Chamberlain of the city. Worked with Phaon, Nero's secretary of finance."

Aquila was talking in quick, fragmented sentences, and Tanner could barely follow along.

"Slow down. Take a breath," Tanner said. "Yes, I remember Erastus. He helped carry the litter so I could get into the tunnels."

"The very one," Aquila replied. "Since you didn't realize he worked with Nero's secretary of finance, you made the mistake of asking us to help you with the heist of the state treasury. When Erastus figured out what you'd done, he wanted to help his fellow Christians, but being responsible for the city's finances, he had an obligation to Phaon and the emperor. After helping you get into the tunnels, he decided to just stay out of the way and let things just play out."

"So what's the bad news?" Tanner asked.

"When he got word that Nero died, Erastus knew he'd be out of a job unless he could quickly gain favor with the new emperor. He decided to rat us all out. Galba's men will be here anytime now."

"Are you sure?" Tanner asked. "Who told you this?"

"My sister. He told her he had no choice but to turn us in to secure employment for himself. If he finds out she warned us, he's going to be furious, but I guess she values her brother's life more than her husband's employment."

"Grab whatever you can, and let's get out of here," Tanner exclaimed.

CHAPTER 84

NO PLACE LIKE WIGWAM

(HOKOLESQUA)

Hokolesqua carefully removed the headband and gazed proudly at the feather. He placed it near his bed. It was time for a well-deserved night's rest.

He lay down, reached over for the small bag on the floor next to him, and caressed the pyramid inside. It had guided him from the moment he'd received it on his vision quest until now. He mentally celebrated the adventure he had just lived through. Images of Tecumseh, Anatok, the escape from Tohopka, the rescue of his mother, and the battles with the Mongols and the Manticore stampeded across the stage of his mind. He was finally a Shawnee warrior.

It was in this victorious state that he fell asleep.

"Hoko," the young brave heard a voice say as he felt someone softly shake his arm, trying to wake him. As hard as he tried, he couldn't wake himself and dropped off into a deeper slumber. He was soaking wet and lying exhausted on the back of the mighty panther from his vision quest. He slowly raised up and smiled as he thought about what he had accomplished. He threw his shoulders back in pride as he looked around at the peaceful woods surrounding them. In an instant, beasts emerged from all corners and began to circle the two of them. Confused and alarmed, Hokolesqua watched and listened to the sounds of the creatures he had originally seen in his vision quest. He felt a sharp object tap his shoulder and turned to see what it was. It was the creature who had slashed his chest. The beast pulled back its paw, extended its claws, and started to swing its arm toward Hokolesqua's face.

"Hoko! Wake up!"

The young brave opened his eyes and saw Nemhsi standing in front of him with a big smile.

CHAPTER 85

DESPONDENT

(TANNER)

Andrew and Mick removed the carpets from their hiding places and quickly fled Lucius's shop. The city was in jubilant chaos.

"Maybe someone will finally tell us what's happened to my father," Marina said, "now that Nero's no longer a threat."

"Yeah, where is Dad?" Livia asked.

"I'm sure he's around. We just have to find him," Marina replied. Tanner had been watching Marina over the past few days and could see her fear that her father had been executed was growing with each passing day.

Andrew pulled Tanner aside. "I don't know why I didn't think about this before, but we need to work from worst to best."

"What do you mean?" Tanner asked.

"We have to look in the worst possible places Marcus could be. Once we rule those out, we start moving to less-threatening places."

"So where do you want to start?"

"I'm afraid to say it, but you heard the Praetorians threatening Cornelius, didn't you?"

"Yeah."

"The one guard said something about how the crosses near Nero's circus would be available in a week?"

"Yeah, you're not thinking..."

"We've got to check—and the sooner the better. We know they've been executing Christians over there. Remember how Decimus acted so callous about the crucifixions on the hill over there when we first met him?"

"I think you're right," Tanner said. "But you can't let Marina know why you're going there. She's a wreck. No telling what would happen if you told her why you wanted to search by the circus."

"I've got to look for Donald," Tanner continued. "You take Marina. I'll take Mick and Livia."

"Let's meet up at the Regia tonight," Andrew said.

"Which building's the Regia again?"

"Remember the small little building near the Temple of Vesta? The one where they keep Mars's shield and lances?"

"Oh yeah, Marina showed us that place when we came to Rome last time."

"Yeah, that's the place. See you tonight."

With that, Andrew and Marina left, and Tanner, Mick, and Livia worked their way through the jubilant citizenry toward the Imperial Palace.

"Are we going to be able to get into the palace, or do you think Galba's men have already taken over?" Mick asked.

"Good question," Tanner replied. "Hades's helmet would come in handy about now, but I have no idea where Donald lives."

"I hope it's safe," Mick replied. "What if we never find Donald?"

"Ugh," Tanner said. "I never thought about that."

"The helmet may be lost to history," Mick said.

"I'd be less concerned about it getting lost to history than getting found. Man, I've really messed things up. I created Decimus, and now I may have lost one of the most valuable objects on the planet." Despondent, Tanner ran his fingers through his hair with both hands. "Zeus will have my head," he added.

"Let's hope it never comes to that," Mick said. "Let's just find Donald."

Tanner was already distraught over the possibility of losing his mentor, friend, and father figure; but adding the weight of personally-caused planetary instability was almost more than he could bear. He wanted to fall down and curl into fetal position right there in the middle of the street, but he had to press on.

They walked through the Cryptoporticus and up to the entrance of the palace.

Tanner cautiously approached the doors.

"This is too much pressure for someone my age."

"No one else is going to do it, so it has to be us," Mick replied.

Tanner gave a push on the door, and it opened. Bracing himself for an attack by a guard, he slowly stepped into the corridor.

CHAPTER 86

DON'T MENTION THIS

(ANDREW)

Andrew approached Marina. "We haven't really looked on the other side of the Tiber River for your dad. Why don't we try over there today?"

"Yes, let's do," Marina said.

The two crossed the river and made their way to the other side of the city where Nero had built his circus. As they arrived at the site and rounded the corner of the gigantic arena, Marina saw the crosses in the distance on the hill and realized what was going on.

"You don't think . . ." She couldn't finish.

She ran toward the crosses. Andrew could tell she was terrified of what she might find.

"Wait!" he yelled as he ran to catch up.

"Halt!" a muscular Roman guard barked when they got close to the site.

Andrew watched Marina scan the crosses for her father.

Suddenly she bolted for one. Two guards grabbed her. In an amazing display of courage, Marina struggled to free herself but was unable to get past the guards.

"You can't go any closer," the man growled.

"Father!" she yelled. Andrew looked and saw Marcus's head lift.

It's him, Andrew thought, unable to imagine what Marina must be going through. He was horrified to actually witness someone he knew being crucified.

"But Nero's reign is over," Marina said. "Free them."

"Doesn't matter," the larger of the guards said. "They still burned down the city."

Marina lowered her head and ran straight for the gut of one of the guards. "The Christians didn't do it," she yelled. "Nero started that fire," she continued as she again wrestled to get past the guard. "He killed my mother in that fire." By this time, the two guards working in concert had taken her down to the ground and had her pinned.

"We have orders to keep everyone away. You're not getting any closer. Do you understand?"

Andrew saw his chance. The guards were completely focused on restraining Marina, and there it was–the handle of one of their swords showing itself to him as if to say "Steal me." Surprising even himself, he pounced, and before he knew what happened he had the sword in hand and was fleeing from the guard. He ran for the circus, his only hope the small head start he had. Two at a time he climbed the stairs until he reached the upper balcony. He was trapped. An open archway looked out over the crucifixion scene behind him, and a large legionnaire in front of him blocked the stairway back down.

"I'll run you through if you take another step," Andrew said, sword in his right hand pointing directly at the man, sure that he didn't have the courage to actually do it.

"That sword will do nothing to this armor," the man replied.

"I was talking about your head," Andrew said, trying to sound as fierce as he could.

Andrew reached over his shoulder with his left hand and untied the straps of the bundle he had slung over his back while he kept the guard talking.

"We're going to get closer to those crosses, and you can't stop us," Andrew said. In a blur, the bundle on his back fell to the ground, and Andrew turned around and grabbed hold of the carpet and flew through the open archway toward the crosses.

"Forgive me," Andrew said to the gods as he swooped toward the crosses. "Probably not supposed to use this out in the open like this."

He flew for Marcus's cross and cut the ropes binding the man's wrists and ankles. Marcus tumbled off the cross and onto the ground. Out of breath, Marcus ran toward the single remaining guard who was still struggling with a valiant Marina.

Andrew flew to the other crosses, cutting their ropes and adding fuel to their small uprising.

Then he flew to where Marina and Marcus were and landed his carpet.

Marina was hugging her father so tightly Andrew thought she might break his ribs. "I thought I'd never see you again," Marina said. "I'm so sorry for everything I did. Can you ever forgive me?"

Marcus pushed her slightly back and looked directly into her eyes.

"Yes, Marina. I forgive you. Nothing you can do will ever stop my love for you."

He hugged her tightly again.

"Where did you . . ." Marcus started, pointing at Andrew's carpet.

"Probably best if you don't mention this," Andrew said in an authoritative voice as he kneeled down and rolled up his carpet.

Marcus nodded, and when Andrew stood back up, arms wrapped tightly around his carpet, Marcus hugged Andrew from the side.

"I don't know how you did it, but that was fantastic," Marcus said.

An ecstatic Marina wrapped her arms around the carpet and Andrew. "You were amazing!"

They went back to Nero's circus, and Andrew grabbed the straps and bundled his carpet back up.

"Let's get back to the others," Andrew said.

They crossed the Tiber and made their way over to the Regia, hopeful that Tanner and Mick would meet them there with Donald.

CHAPTER 87

YOU DID WHAT?

(TANNER)

Tanner looked around the corridor and, seeing nothing, began to walk to where he had last seen Donald.

Clank!

Tanner whirled around to see what had made the noise.

As if out of nowhere, a Praetorian guard stood there. Tanner swung his sword as quickly as he could, clanking it against the beautiful golden breastplate.

"What are you doing?"

Tanner looked at the face of the guard. It was Donald.

Tanner dropped his sword and started shoving the Praetorian.

"You scared me to death," Tanner said. "I thought they captured you."

"They almost did," Donald replied.

"So what happened?" Tanner asked.

"Well, I was ratted out. When I walked into Nero's private quarters, I expected to do so on my own terms. But the legionnaire who nearly killed me on the streets was standing next to the emperor with a sickening grin on his face."

"Decimus," Tanner replied.

"I was bound and gagged by Decimus and another legionnaire who attacked me from behind. They took my bag and weapons. I knew you were waiting for my signal—the sound of my sword dropping on the marble floor, but I no longer even had the sword."

"But I swear I heard the sword fall," Tanner replied.

"That's because I realized you needed to get started, so I kicked my sword out of the hand of the legionnaire who had stolen it."

"Wow! That may have saved my life," Tanner replied.

"The two legionnaires restrained me and shackled my legs. Then something surprising happened."

"What?" Tanner asked anxiously.

"Decimus warned Nero that since a conspiracy was underway, he should go with the other legionnaire to protect the statuette. Decimus said he'd keep an eye on me."

"That's not surprising. You said the statuette had always protected the emperor from being overthrown."

"That's not the surprising part."

"Okay."

"When Nero left the room, Decimus grabbed my sword from the ground and ran for the emperor. He was just about to run him through when the other legionnaire turned around and began talking with Nero. Decimus hid the sword and returned to the room with me."

"Actually, that makes more sense to me," Tanner said. "What is surprising to me is that Decimus seemed to be trying to help the emperor."

"Why do you say that?"

"I first met Decimus the night Nero stabbed him, threw him into the Tiber, and left him for dead. So it makes more sense that he would rather try to kill the emperor than try to work with him."

"Anyway, Decimus grabbed my bag, and, to my horror, he looked inside."

"Why? What was in there?"

There was a long pause.

"Tanner, I made a big mistake." Donald sheepishly continued. "I placed the object you asked me to protect in the bag."

"You did what?"

"The object you asked me to protect. I brought it with me to the palace."

"Donald, what were you thinking?" Tanner asked. He was terrified. "Why would you do that?"

"My curiosity got the best of me. One day I looked in the bag, and not being able to see it well, I pulled the helmet out to get a better look. When I saw my hand disappear and realized the magical properties of the helmet, I knew it might come in handy when we tried to overthrow the emperor."

"Okay, okay. But are you telling me Decimus has the helmet now?"

"Yes," Donald replied.

Tanner put his head in his hands.

"When Decimus heard the legionnaire yell that the statuette was missing, he put the helmet on and disappeared. Literally."

"Do you realize what you've done?" Tanner asked.

"Yes," Donald replied.

"No, I don't think you do. You allowed an invincible man to capture one of the most powerful objects on the planet. That was Hades's helmet. When Zeus finds out, he's going to destroy the entire zip code I'm in."

CHAPTER 88

LET'S GET HOME
(TANNER)

"You ready to head home?" Andrew asked Tanner when he arrived at the Regia with Marina and Marcus. "Looks like you found Donald and we rescued Marcus. We've done everything we came to do,"

"Slight change in plans," Tanner replied.

"What do you mean?"

"It seems Decimus has Hades's helmet."

"You're joking, right?" Andrew replied.

"I wish I were," Tanner said. "But I'm not crying wolf this time."

"What are we going to do?" Andrew asked. "That makes him one of the most dangerous men on the planet. More powerful than Hades himself."

"We've got to find him and get it back."

"Pretty hard to do if he's invisible," Andrew retorted.

"And invincible," Mick added.

"Donald, where do you think he went after he put the helmet on?"

"He could have gone anywhere," Donald said. "I don't know. Maybe he went back to his legion to march on Rome."

"That makes sense. With Nero's demise, there would be a window of opportunity for him to seize control of the city before Galba establishes himself as emperor."

"We've got to lure him into the underworld," Andrew said.

"How will that help?"

"Before our original trip into the underworld, had any of you ever heard of Decimus?"

"I hadn't," Tanner replied.

"I figured that," Andrew replied, chuckling. "You probably hadn't even heard of Nero."

Tanner stuck his tongue out and wagged his head back and forth while rolling his eyes.

"How about you, Mick?"

"No."

"Then we can't let him gain control of the city. This is one of those moments that could drastically alter the history of the world. If one of the most powerful men on the planet, rivaled only by Zeus himself, takes control of Rome, who knows what will happen. We might never be born."

"We've messed up history," Mick added. "We've got to make this right."

"How do you propose we get him to the underworld?" Tanner asked.

"We'll use Mick as bait," Andrew said. "Remember how he tried to kill her that night? He's got something against her."

"Um, what's your plan B?" Mick said. "I don't like plan A."

"Andrew, come on, think about it," Tanner said. "He tried to kill her. If given another chance, he's going to succeed."

"I'll do it," Donald chimed in.

"He almost killed you, too," Tanner replied. "It can't be just one of us. We need to all work together. Each of us uses our strengths. I know he's invincible, but that doesn't make him fast. I know I can outrun him. And he doesn't know past, present, and future like we do. Mick, you know the most about history, there has to be something you know that can give us an advantage. Donald, you know the most about Decimus's position as provincial governor. Maybe there's a way we can use his position against him. Andrew . . ." Tanner paused. "If you had any strengths, we'd use them too, but . . ."

"Give it a rest, would you?" Andrew replied.

"Donald, what legion did you say Decimus was given authority over?" Mick asked.

"The ninth."

"Then I think I *can* help," Mick replied.

"We're all ears," Tanner said.

"The ninth legion disappeared from history," she said. "I watched a show about it. No one knows what happened to them. I bet we're supposed to . . ."

". . . lead them into the underworld," Andrew said.

"I underestimated you," Tanner said. "You are good at something–finishing Mick's sentences."

Andrew just shook his head.

"Okay, makes sense to me," Tanner continued. "But how are we going to lead an entire legion into the underworld?"

"The Roman Standards," Donald said. "The Eagle or Aquila."

"Pretend for a minute that I don't know much about Roman history and please explain," Tanner said.

"No need to pretend," Andrew added.

"Well, the Aquila is a golden eagle on a pole that someone carries in front of the legion. This person, known as the Aquilifer, directs the troops using this 'standard.' The Cornicen blows a horn, and that means everyone is supposed to look to the Aquila for direction. If the man holding it moves it left, the troops move left. There are different movements that mean different things."

"So you're thinking if we steal this Aquila thing, everyone will follow us?" Tanner asked. "Come on, Donald, you can do better than that. Roman troops aren't that dumb."

"Stay with me, Tanner. I'm not done."

"Sorry."

"The Aquila is also a powerful symbol to the troops," Donald continued. "It is designed to inspire them, remind them what they are fighting for. There have been times when the Aquila was stolen and the Romans actually went to war in order to get it back. The Aquila is one of the most important symbols we have in Rome. If we steal the ninth legion's standard, they'll follow us anywhere to get it back."

"So we take the Aquila into the underworld," Andrew said, "and then use your trick."

"What trick?" Donald asked.

"You know, how you led the bank robbers far enough into the underworld they were forced to eat, and because of the rule of the Fates, they had to live in Inner Earth forever."

"It's brilliant," Tanner added. "Let's go steal a standard."

"The timing is perfect," Donald said. "The ninth legion was stationed not far from the city. I won't be surprised if they arrive in Rome sometime today. It would be a great time to catch them off guard and steal the Aquila."

"Where do you think they'll camp?" Tanner asked.

"Probably in the Campus Martius, just north of the Forum. That area has been used for military purposes for centuries. It was dedicated to Mars, the god of war."

"Let's go scout it out," Andrew said.

Tanner and the others made their way to the Campus Martius, where they spotted Decimus and his legion setting up camp.

"I wonder where the helmet is," Tanner said.

"There's the Aquila," Donald said, pointing in the direction of a large leather tent in the center of camp.

"You really think you can get into the middle of their camp, steal that thing, and get back out without getting killed?" Mick asked Tanner.

There was a pause.

"I have a better idea," Andrew said. "We use one of the carpets."

Donald looked at Andrew as if he were alien.

"That's a great idea," Mick replied.

"I don't know," Tanner said. "I'm not sure they'd chase me. If I fly into the middle of camp, grab the Aquila, and fly off, they'll be so overwhelmed they might not follow. I mean, think about it. If a UFO flew into Brownsville and robbed the bank, the police would probably just stand there speechless as they flew away."

"What are you talking about?" Donald asked.

"Long story," Tanner said.

"I guess you're right," Andrew said. "But it would be a lot safer."

"Let's just use them in case of an emergency," Mick said. "As a backup."

"Okay," Andrew replied.

"I wish I knew what was going on," Donald said.

"Hey, wait a minute. Is that Greek God Boy over there?" Tanner asked.

Sure enough, Appius was about ten yards away and appeared to be spying on the ninth legion as well.

"Psst. Over here," Mick said.

Appius looked over and spotted the Brownsvillians. He cautiously made his way to where they were.

"What are you guys doing?" he asked as he lay down on the small ridge that overlooked the camp.

"It's an incredibly long story," Mick said. "What about you?"

"Your friend Aquila and the others sent me to spy on the ninth legion. Someone got wind that their new leader was anti-Christian, and they wanted me to see what I could find out about them. Then to my surprise–"

"Look out!" Donald yelled.

Appius rolled over and looked up just in time to see a Roman soldier thrust his sword into the ground where he had been.

Donald leapt to his feet, and in a flash of shiny steel, the two were locked in a wrestle. After a difficult battle, Donald was able to subdue the soldier, and they tied him up.

"Are you okay?" Mick rushed to Appius's side.

"Are you okay? Are you okay?" Tanner rolled his eyes and whispered sarcastically to Andrew.

"Looks like you're not going to need *my* armor after all," Donald said as he began removing the man's armor and dressing Tanner.

The sun was setting as Donald finished getting Tanner fully outfitted. Tanner felt empowered by the armor he now wore.

"We need to wait until it's completely dark," Donald said. "You sneak in, steal the Aquila, and then, at dawn, we'll lure them after you."

"How do we alert the legion that we have it without being too close?" Tanner said.

"Steal that one thing, too," Andrew said. "The horn."

"You mean the cornu?" Donald asked.

"Yeah," Andrew replied. "Didn't you say that when the troops hear that, they look for the standards and follow them? If one of us plays the cornu, they'll spot us on the ridge with the Aquila and the chase will be on."

"Good thinking, Andrew," Donald said.

"So I'm stealing the Aquila and cornu, then, right?" Tanner asked. "What does this horn thing look like?"

"It's a long small tube in the shape of a circle and about two thirds as tall as you are. Should be easy to spot," Donald replied. "It usually has a spike on the bottom so they can stick it upright in the ground."

"Got it," Tanner said.

"It's getting pretty dark," Donald said. "Let's wait a couple more hours so everyone's asleep, and then you can make your move."

Tanner spent the next couple hours envisioning the heist and escape in his mind. Recognizing everything that could go wrong, he leaned over to Andrew and whispered, "You were right. I'm using your carpet."

"Looks like all the torches have been extinguished," Donald said. "Do your thing, Tanner."

Andrew removed the carpet from his back, undid the straps, and Tanner hopped on. He flew down into the camp, and fifteen minutes later he returned with the Aquila and cornu.

"You're amazing," Donald said as he approached. He and Appius reached for the carpet, obviously befuddled by the magical object. Andrew yanked it away and said, "I'll take that." He rolled it up and slung it over his shoulder while Donald and Appius continued to gawk.

"Let's get some sleep," Tanner said. "We've got the race of our lives ahead of us."

Tanner slept well. If there was one thing he was confident in, it was his ability to outrun most anyone.

✧ ✧ ✧

"Get up."

Tanner awoke to Donald shaking him.

Andrew was standing next to him. "Let's get this show on the road."

"All right," Tanner said. "Who's going to play the horn?"

Appius volunteered.

"How fast are you?" Tanner asked. "We're going to have to outrun the entire legion from here to the Umbilicus Urbis."

"I'm pretty fast," Appius replied. "I think I can do it."

"All right," Tanner said. "The rest of you need to get over to the Umbilicus. Andrew, you've got to pick the lock."

"Decided you needed my skills after all, eh?"

"We'll pull up the rear and make sure they follow you into the Umbilicus," Donald said, pointing to himself, Marcus, and Livia.

Andrew and the others left, and just Tanner and Appius remained.

"Here we go," Tanner said. "Let's see what you've got."

Appius blew the horn mightily.

The two boys watched as the legionnaires began to emerge from their tents.

Appius blew the horn again.

A lot of shouting ensued as they spotted Tanner moving the Aquila from side to side up on the ridge—and the chase was on.

Tanner was shocked when Appius easily outdistanced him.

Am I losing my touch?

He looked behind him. He still had a sizeable lead on the closest soldier. But he continued to eat Appius's dust all the way to the Umbilicus. Tanner watched as Mick helped Appius onto the ladder and down into the Mundus.

Some thanks I get, Tanner thought as he climbed down by himself.

"How did you guys get the Umbilicus open?" Appius asked. "They've been keeping the place tightly locked lately, especially after the whole incident with the blizzard."

"It was actually unlocked, and the door was partially open," Mick said.

"Very odd," Appius replied.

"Pull the stone closed," Andrew said once Tanner climbed into the Mundus.

"But we need the legionnaires to follow us," Tanner replied.

"We need Demeter to clear away the opening to the Cathedral, though," Andrew said.

"Good thinking," Tanner said as he slid the stone back into position.

The Mundus filled with light, and Demeter began to clear away the boulders in front of the Cathedral door.

"Hey, Demeter," Tanner said as he climbed down into the space. "We need you to leave the Cathedral door accessible."

"Why? That's against normal procedure," she replied.

"Maybe so, but we're trying to lure an invincible man and the ninth legion off the Surface."

"An invincible man?"

"Yeah," Tanner said, head slightly down.

"Brilliant over there created an invincible man by pouring water from the River Acheron on him," Andrew said. "We've changed history, and unless we can lead him into the underworld, the future of the Surface is going to take an alternate course."

"I guess under the circumstances I can do it. But does Zeus know about this?"

"No, and whatever you do, don't tell him." Tanner said.

"Probably a good idea," Demeter replied, and she was gone.

Tanner and Andrew slid the stone covering of the Mundus out of the way so the legionnaires would follow them to the Cathedral of Time.

"They're coming!" Tanner said in a panic as he saw legionnaires climbing down the ladder toward the Mundus.

"Everyone into the Cathedral. Quickly."

The Brownsvillians and Appius went into the Cathedral.

"Wow! What is this place?" Appius asked.

"No time to explain," Andrew said. "We've got to get onto the platform and out of here."

"But won't they just follow us?" Appius said not waiting for an answer as he began to wander aimlessly around the Cathedral.

"They won't be transported anywhere since they haven't been judged," Andrew replied.

"But Decimus must have been," Mick said. "Don't you remember? He followed my journal and made it all the way to Brownsville."

"True," Tanner said. "But the Nishapurans couldn't get through."

"Maybe the gods wanted Decimus to follow us?" Andrew said.

"Why would they want that?" Tanner asked.

"It's like we were talking about before. If half of them are working to help us, the other half is probably working to stop us."

Tanner went into deep thought. Andrew was right. The fact that Decimus was able to pursue them without being judged might have been the most compelling evidence yet that it was more than just Hades who wanted to thwart them.

"We'll just approach the gods and let them know we accidently created an invincible man and need to make sure we don't leave him on the Surface," Mick said. "I'm sure they wouldn't want Decimus roaming around the Surface either."

"Oh, sure, and let's tell him this invincible man just happens to have Hades's helmet. This is going to go over really well." Tanner paused. "Have you been drinking from the River Lethe again? You really don't remember how our last visit with Zeus went?"

"Yeah, that's true," Mick replied.

"Let's go to Mars, the god of war," Andrew said. "He'll recognize the danger of leaving Decimus on the Surface."

"I was wrong about you," Tanner said. "If you can save me from a face-to-face with Zeus, you might be the most valuable contributor to this plan."

"What river have *you* been drinking from?" Andrew asked, unaccustomed to compliments from Tanner.

"I'm not feeling right about talking with Mars," Mick said.

"But it makes perfect sense," Andrew replied. "Give me one good reason why we shouldn't talk to him."

"I really can't, other than I'm just feeling uncomfortable about it."

"Come on, Mick. Look at what he did for the Romans over the years," Andrew said.

"What are you talking about?" she asked.

"Oh yeah, you weren't there when Marina told Tanner and me how Mars dropped his shield into Rome and promised that as long as they kept it safe they'd be the mistress of the world—and he really did protect them for centuries."

Tanner grabbed Andrew by the face and examined him closely.

"What have you done with my logical friend?" he asked.

"Ha, ha," Andrew replied.

"Everyone up on the platform," Mick said. "We'll just make it up as we go."

Tanner looked up, shaking his head. "What is happening to my friends?" He looked over at Mick. "Make it up as we go? What happened? Did you run out of index cards?"

"You're really on one today, aren't you?" Mick replied.

Andrew ran to the control room and started changing the settings to send them to Olympus.

"Appius!" Mick yelled in a panic looking across the Cathedral. "Get over here on the platform."

"Here comes the legion," Tanner yelled, pointing to one of the stairways, where a group of soldiers was descending. "Get over here."

Andrew touched the green pulsating circle on the screen and ran for the platform. Moments later they were exiting onto the lush Olympus landscape.

"Why don't the two of you go speak with the gods?" Tanner suggested, pointing to Andrew and Mick. "I don't have the same kind of relationship you do."

"Okay," Mick said. "You don't have to come."

"Perfect," Tanner replied.

"Let's go, then," Mick said, looking at Andrew.

"What he said," Andrew replied, pointing at Tanner.

"Fine," Mick replied, turning back as she quickly walked away. "I'll go by myself."

"I'll go," Appius said as he jogged to catch up with her.

"But..." Tanner said, reaching slightly forward with his hand. The last thing he wanted was for Mick to be wandering around alone with Greek God Boy. Actually, it was the second-to-last thing he wanted.

Better to let them go than to have another encounter with Zeus.

"A little jealous?" Andrew said with a big grin.

"Of that?" Tanner said as he watched Mick grab Appius by the arm, his ripped, bronze physique glistening in the Olympus afternoon. Tanner thrust his shoulders slightly back and tried to stand a little taller.

CHAPTER 89

MICK AND THE GODS

(MICK)

Mick and Appius approached the Judgment Platform of the gods. Eleven of the twelve members were assembled there. Everyone except Mars.

Perfect, Mick thought.

"Excuse me," Mick said loudly as they stepped into the middle of the twelve thrones.

A hush fell over the platform, and Mick gulped. Appius grabbed her hand, and she looked down in pleasant surprise.

"We have a small problem," Mick said.

Zeus's wife, Hera, responded. "What is it?"

"Well, you see, we think my friend Tanner accidentally created an invincible man when he tried to heal a knife wound with water from the River Acheron."

"WHAT!" Zeus's disbelief shook the platform like a massive earthquake. "Did you actually just say Tanner created an invincible man?"

"Uh, yeah. We think he might have," Mick replied.

"We have to get rid of the boy," Zeus replied as he leapt down from his throne and began pacing back and forth across the granite floor. "He's too impulsive. He doesn't think straight. He's completely incapable of the task before him."

"He was only trying to save the man's life," Hera chimed in.

"By jeopardizing the entire planet?" Zeus barked. "Where is he?"

Mick stayed silent.

"Where is he?" Zeus yelled.

"Um, he's over by the Cathedral of Time. He and the others are trying to make sure the man I was referring to, and the entire ninth legion, followed us into the underworld but don't come to Olympus and start roaming around arbitrarily."

"Well, that's awfully big of him," Zeus said sarcastically. "Demeter, switch the polarity of the dome." Zeus pointed toward the Cathedral. "We've got to protect Olympus."

Demeter dropped the flowers she had been gathering and fled to the platform.

"Now," he continued. "What to do about the boy."

Hera grabbed Zeus's arm and began whispering to him. He continued to shake his head in angry disagreement with her. Mick and Appius stood nervously on the platform. She could see things weren't going well. Finally, he rolled his eyes toward the sky as if in thought. After what seemed like forever, he spoke.

"All right, I won't banish him, but *he* created this problem. He needs to fix it. That's the only way he'll learn anything."

"But, Zeus—" Hera tried to interject.

"My decision is final. I've protected Olympus from the threat. This 'invincible man' is now Tanner's problem."

Zeus stormed off the platform, and the others followed until only Hera, Mick, and Appius remained.

"Mick," Hera said. "You must keep a close eye on your friend Tanner and prevent him from further disrupting the delicate balance that exists on this planet. Without my intervention, Zeus would have banished Tanner to an underground pit in Tartarus, as he did with Kronos. Next time he might not be so generous."

"I won't let Tanner out of my sight, ma'am," Mick replied.

"It will probably take more than that," Hera said.

"Good point."

Hera hugged Mick, an overwhelming sense of love enveloping her—like nothing she had ever felt before.

"Good luck," the goddess whispered into Mick's ear. "I know you can do it."

Mick pulled back just enough to look Hera in the eye as she tried to communicate her question of exactly what "it" was.

Hera just smiled.

"Now, you must be on your way," Hera said. "There's still a lot to do."

Hera's hug dissolved, and slowly she let go of Mick's hand, like a parent whose child was leaving the nest for the first time.

As Mick and Appius made their way toward the Cathedral, she heard a voice from behind.

"Makayla, wait." She turned, and, to her surprise, Mars was striding purposefully down the path toward her, dressed in full armor and looking ready for battle.

"I apologize I wasn't able to make it to the meeting. Is everything all right?"

"Everything's fine," Mick replied.

"What's going on?"

Mick hesitated. "Nothing."

"Come on, I'm sure I'll get a full briefing anyway. What is it? How can I help?" Mars pressed.

"Well, Tanner created an invincible man. We're trying to make sure he doesn't wreak havoc on the planet."

"Look," Mars said. "I know you've got your hands full with Tanner as a partner."

"Partner?"

"Partner, companion, teammate—whatever you want to call it. The bottom line is you share the same mission."

Mick paused as she thought about this mysterious "mission" all the gods were referring to.

"Yeah, I guess I do have my hands full."

"I'm prepared to help you with this 'invincible man' problem."

"But Zeus said Tanner needs to be the one to fix it," Mick said, feeling even more uncomfortable.

"He's being completely unreasonable. Tanner can't solve the problem of an invincible man and an entire legion alone. It's ridiculous. Zeus knows that. He's setting him up to fail."

"But Zeus wouldn't ask us to do something we couldn't do," Mick said, her voice full of doubt.

"Listen. I've got this," Mars replied. "You don't have to worry about a thing. I'll just have Anatolia send them all to the forest of Delfi—present day. The Delfians are best suited to deal with them."

"Wow," Mick replied. "And you really think Zeus will be okay with that?"

"Of course," Mars replied.

"Thank you. Thank you so much." Mick was appreciative though still a bit uneasy.

"Not to worry," Mars said as they parted ways.

CHAPTER 90

BACK TO THE SURFACE
(TANNER)

"How'd it go?" Tanner asked.

"It turned out okay—I guess," Mick replied. "A little sketchy at first, but all's well that ends well."

Mick explained what had happened on the platform and about her conversation with Mars.

"What a lucky break," Tanner said. He shuttered as a feeling of immense relief swept over him.

I didn't realize how much the whole Decimus thing must have been weighing me down, he thought. *But I guess if Mars has it covered, I'm off the hook.*

"I hope it's all right that Mars is handling this whole thing. Zeus was pretty clear that you needed to be the one to fix it."

"He's probably right. I could have resolved it better myself," Tanner said, "but Mars—I'm sure he'll do fine."

"Puh-lease," Mick replied.

"Do you think Donald's okay?" Tanner asked.

"Sure," Mick replied. "He was just going to stay behind and make sure the whole ninth legion made it into the Umbilicus."

"Well, let's get back to the Surface," Andrew said excitedly.

"Shouldn't we say goodbye to Donald?" Tanner said. "We might never see him again."

"I'd love to," Mick replied, "but we've got the entire ninth legion between us and him. They know we stole the Aquila. There's no way it will end well if we try to get past them."

Tanner knew Mick was right. He hung his head dejectedly, knowing he had probably seen his friend and mentor for the last time.

"We really need to just get back home," Andrew said. "You've got some catching up to do with your dad."

"You're right," Tanner replied anxiously, a deluge of emotions sweeping over him. He wanted so badly to reconnect with his dad, but his father had never been very pleasant to be around. It might just be a dream that things would be different now, but he wanted a good relationship so desperately he was excited to give it a shot.

"We can't get back the usual way," Andrew said.

"Why not?" Tanner asked.

"T, we can't go near the kingdom of Hades. I'm sure he knows it was us who stole his helmet."

"Good point," Mick replied.

"But that's the only way," Tanner said. "The only place in the underworld we can access from Mount Olympus is the kingdom of Hades. It's the only place Golden Orb Airlines flies."

"We've got to find a different route. Remember how Hades banned Persephone to Tartarus and it snowed for days in Rome after we stole the helmet?" Andrew asked. "Hades is not happy."

"But there is no other way," Mick said.

"Well, I want to get back to the Surface," Tanner said. "Last time we flew in the golden orb, you were able to steer it away from the Judgment Platform, Andrew. Remember? When we fly to the kingdom of Hades, you can just steer it as far away from his palace and the Great Hall as possible."

"True, but remember how Hades batted us around like a ping-pong ball until we final entered the realm of Olympus."

"Maybe that was just an unlucky weather pattern."

"Funny."

"We've got to try. I'm not staying here forever. If I were planning on that, I would have just ignored the Rule of the Fates and eaten some of the amazing food around here." Tanner reached for what looked like a blackberry the size of a small football and stroked it longingly.

"I guess we have to try," Andrew replied.

"Let's go see if the orb is on the platform."

"Do you mind if I come with you?" Appius asked. "I really don't have a place I can call home back in Rome."

"We'd love to have you come with us," Mick replied, starry-eyed.

Tanner looked at Andrew with an "I want to barf" expression.

"I guess I'm coming along too," Marina said, giving Andrew a big hug. "Since we can't get past the ninth legion and back to Rome."

For once, Tanner trailed behind, knowing that if Zeus spotted him, he might end up in Tartarus. He watched his "smitten" friends walking along in front of him with a different spring in their step.

As they approached the platform, Tanner tried to remain hidden while looking for the orb. He could see something on the platform, but it definitely wasn't the transportation device they had used before.

"Hades must have upgraded," Andrew said.

When Tanner could see the gods weren't present, he took a closer look and saw there was definitely a golden object in the center of the platform, but it wasn't the sun-shaped golden orb he expected to see. This golden object was flying-saucer shaped but with decorative golden wings extending up and angled slightly back from the center of the craft. It was covered with elaborate carvings and was weathered and dirty, with the gold darkened and grungy in all the nooks and crannies.

"Maybe Hades has more than one aircraft," Mick replied. "There must be times when more than one person needs to get from his kingdom to Olympus."

"Makes sense," Tanner said. "Let's hurry and board before someone shows up."

They began to scamper up the open ramp and onto the craft.

"Here comes someone. Hop in! Quick!" Tanner said to Marina as he reached down to help pull her into the saucer.

"Close the hatch," Tanner said to Mick, who pushed a button near the ramp. Tanner could hear a creaking noise along the long hinge that fastened the ramp to the vehicle.

He could discern a man with a long beard and flowing golden hair quickly approaching the Judgment Platform on a large stallion.

"Start this thing up, Andrew. Let's get out of here!" Tanner said.

The ramp was not closing fast enough for Tanner, who could see the man more clearly now. He was carrying a large spear and wore a helmet with wings protruding from it, similar to those on the golden saucer they were in. An elaborate bronze patch covered his left eye. Tanner noticed around forty women in exquisite armor emerge over the ridge on horseback behind the man.

This can't be good, he thought. "Get this thing airborne!" he yelled at Andrew. Just then he felt a quick jerking motion that nearly knocked him over, and the opening into the craft quickly slammed shut.

"I can't see anything," Tanner said, glancing rapidly around the saucer. He hadn't noticed before that there were no windows in the vehicle. "How are you supposed to know what's going on around you?" He wanted to see the reaction of the warrior women and their leader. "Stupid thing," he said and he pounded his fist on one of the side walls of the craft. Immediately, the spot where his fist made contact became transparent. "What the . . ."

He put his full hand against the spot, and to his surprise there was still substance there, but the whole area his hand had touched became invisible. He began moving has hand back and forth along the wall, like when he wiped the condensation from the windows of his mother's old station wagon, creating a larger and larger viewing area for himself. He could see the warriors and their leader circling their horses anxiously on the platform and looking up at the craft as it soared into the Olympian sky.

"Looks like we made it out just in time," Tanner said as he continued to watch while the warriors slowly disbanded.

"Who do you think they were?" Andrew asked.

"No idea," Mick replied. "Might have been someone Zeus sent to escort Tanner to the depths of Tartarus, for all I know. I wasn't about to wait around and see."

"I think we're pretty much done coming to Inner Earth," Andrew said.

"Why do you say that?" Mick asked.

"Well, let's see," Tanner replied. "Tohopka and his followers are after us, the ninth legion are giving chase, as is Zeus himself."

"You didn't mention Hades," Mick added. "And he doesn't have the personality traits that would lend themselves to mercy."

"Well, the good thing is," Tanner said, "I don't think there's really a *need* for us to come back. We can spend the rest of our lives just living peacefully on the Surface."

"And hoping none of them pays us a visit?" Andrew asked. "Remember, Hades came to the Surface to steal Persephone."

"Hadn't thought about that," Tanner said, concern running rampant across his face.

"So, I guess you were right, Mick," Andrew said. "We'll never have a normal life again."

"Well, I'd still rather be on my home turf if any of them do come after me," Tanner replied. "Nothing like home-court advantage. Let's get to the River Styx and sail home!"

"Where *is* home?" Andrew asked.

Tanner thought about his friend's statement for a second. "Unfortunately, that's a good question. But you know what? I'm figuring out a way to see my dad again. I don't care what they're planning to do to me if I go back to Brownsville."

"So, how do you steer this thing?" Andrew walked to the center of the craft and began to scrutinize the controls. Tanner watched the same expressions he had seen many times in science lab cross Andrew's face as his friend touched and dragged the various objects on the control panel. When he looked up to see the effects of Andrew's "navigating," he noticed the small section of the craft he'd wiped clean had returned to its normal dingy gold color.

As he ran for an exterior wall, a voice announced. "Please prepare yourselves for landing as we begin our descent."

Tanner quickly began wiping the wall clear again. He could see an entire city that looked similar to the craft they were in. Stylized buildings of grungy, but beautiful, weathered gold soared into a purple-and-orange sky. Decorative gems adorning the structures gave spectacular color to the otherwise monochromatic city.

"Check this out." He beckoned for Mick to come to the wall. "Either Hades did some massive remodeling while we were away, or we took a wrong turn somewhere."

There was a slight jolt, and the craft was on the ground.

Mick pushed the button adjacent to the doorway where they had boarded the ship, and the ramp opened, allowing them to descend.

"Where are we?" Marina asked as she stepped onto the ramp and got her first unobstructed view of the city before her. "What is this place?" No sooner had she spoken than a voice coming from within the craft announced, "Welcome to Asgard."

"Asgard?" Tanner said excitedly. This is so cool. Home of the Norse gods? Now we're talking."

Thor had been Tanner's favorite superhero for years. Sandwiched between the sports posters that adorned the walls of his bedroom was a poster of Thor that had been there as long as he could remember.

A thundering voice from behind startled Tanner. He turned to see about a dozen Asgardian warriors approaching on his left.

"They're spies," a woman with flowing black hair and golden armor barked.

"We're not spies," Tanner said. "You've got the wrong people."

"Silence!" a bearded warrior with a golden ax glared.

"Seize them."

THE ADVENTURE CONTINUES WITH BOOK THREE...

VISIT WWW.THEWORLDOFAGARTHA.COM

...AND THE UPCOMING VIDEO GAME...

REVENGE OF THE PRAETORIAN

VISIT WWW.REVENGEOFTHEPRAETORIAN.COM